JOE COFFIN

SEASON FOUR

KEN PRESTON

Joe Coffin
Season Four
Content copyright © Ken Preston, 2018. All rights reserved

Cover Design: Xavier Comas

✸ Created with Vellum

EPISODE THIRTEEN

SCORES TO SETTLE

Mary clutched the handles of the shopping bags crowded around her feet. She was sitting about halfway down the length of the empty bus, looking out of the window as the bus crawled around the sharp bend in the road. Low cloud covered the mountain tops, the grey rock merging with the grey cloud forming an oppressive roof over the valley. The weather never changed here, always cloud and rain and then more rain.

The bus began picking up speed as the driver finished navigating the steep bend. To Mary's right, there was a drop of several hundred feet down to fields dotted with sheep, a river cutting through the landscape before the hills rose behind it. To her left, the bus windows were filled with slate grey rock, piled on one another and rising up and up

Mary clutched the plastic handles tight, her fingernails digging into her palms. Bloody stupid, bringing all this shopping with her. It had slowed her down getting to the bus stop and it would slow her down again when she got off the bus and made her way down to the cottage. She could have travelled faster if she had left the shopping behind, just dropped it where she stood and left it there for some lucky bastard to find and take home. But she couldn't do that. Her mother, that's what that was, teaching her frugality and responsibility from the earliest age.

Shopping or no shopping, the bus wouldn't go any faster than it was now. Maybe when she arrived, when she clambered off the bus, she would leave the shopping at the top of the lane. She would be free to run down to the farmhouse. And then she could come back, once she knew he was all right, she could come back and pick up the shopping. It would still be there.

Out here, out of town and in the arse end of nowhere, there was nobody to steal it, anyway.

Mary running. Well, that would be something to see, wouldn't it? Mary doubted she had run anywhere in the last ten years or more. And it showed in her shape and size. Mary wasn't built for running, wasn't built for anything but going getting the shopping, cleaning the farmhouse, cooking the meals. She wasn't made for anything else.

The note of the engine changed as the driver shifted down a gear and the bus began crawling up the incline as it grew even steeper. Apart from Mary and a couple of Japanese tourists sat in the back seats, giggling and talking rapidly in Japanese, the bus was empty. And yet still the engine would groan and rumble as it pulled them ever higher.

Mary unclenched her hands from around the shopping bag handles and wiped her clammy palms on her trouser legs. She had to hold back from screaming at the driver to get a move on, to force this old bus to go faster. There was no point, he probably had his foot to the floor, anyway. What gear would they be in? Second? First even?

Mary closed her hands around the plastic shopping bag handles once more, gripping them hard.

It had been Niall who had told her they were coming. Niall with his white, greasy skin and the permanent shakes. Said he'd heard it on the 'radio', which for Niall meant whatever means of communication he had that were underground, on the sly. Said they were coming today, maybe they were here already.

You stupid bastard, Mary had said. *Didn't you think to let us know sooner?*

Niall had shrugged, said, *I only just found out mesel', told you right away is what I did*, but the smirk on his face told Mary otherwise. Niall had always hated Mary, ever since they were children. She never knew why, could never fathom it. And she had always just ignored him, ignored his veiled insults and his attitude. He was a watcher, a listener, not a doer. He lived on the sidelines of life, too scared to actually commit to a decision of any kind.

But today he had found a way of sticking the knife in without actually having to do anything. Mary knew he would have had that information for a day or two, at least. But by withholding it until today, until the last moment when it might be too late, and to be there and see her face when he told her the news. That was something Niall would have enjoyed.

The bus driver shifted down again, crunching the gears. The bus shuddered for a moment as it fought to keep its upward momentum.

Now they were in first gear.

The Japanese pair giggled some more. A boy and a girl, obviously in love from what Mary had seen. Couldn't keep their hands off each other. What on earth had brought them out here, to the outer edges of the British Isles, Mary had no idea. Surely there were better places to go on holiday? Yes, the hills and the valleys were beautiful in their own, rugged way, but couldn't they have found somewhere dry and warm where the sun occasionally shone, rather than here where it was damp and cold and if the sun did manage to show its face everyone scurried inside for fear of getting sunburnt?

But then, none of that was her business. And Mary prided herself on keeping her own business and not minding others'.

If only Niall had felt the same way.

Slowly, laboriously, the bus crawled to the brow of the hill where, just a few hundred yards further, was Mary's bus stop. She reached up and pushed the button for the bell. Not that she needed to have bothered. Lachlann Stewart had been driving this bus route for the last twenty years or more and knew exactly where Mary got off. But she rang the bell, anyway.

The bus slowed to a halt, and Lachlann opened the doors. Mary got to her feet and picked up her shopping bags. She walked down the aisle, past all the empty seats.

'Thank you, Lachlann,' she said, and took the steps carefully down onto the tarmac surface of the road.

The doors hissed shut, and the bus juddered into motion and drove away.

There, in front of Mary, on the other side of the road, was the lane, wide enough for one vehicle, leading down to their cottage. The twin tracks, deep grooves in the ground separated by a mound of dirt with grass sprouting from it, revealed how often the lane was used by their jeep. If only the jeep hadn't been out of action, then Mary would have used that to do the shopping and could have returned home that much quicker. If only the mobile signal wasn't so weak around these parts, she could have phoned ahead and warned Brianan.

But no, this was the life they had chosen. One of seclusion, of being cut off from the rest of the world, as much as was possible these days, anyway.

Mary looked at their cottage, down in the valley at the end of the track. Wisps of white smoke trailed from the stone chimney. There was no sign of any other vehicles down there.

All looked quiet, as it should be.

Mary hefted the shopping bags, forgetting that she had intended leaving them by the roadside until she was sure all was safe, and began making her way down towards the family cottage.

The shopping bags banged against her legs as she walked. Tomorrow, they would be covered in bruises.

If I'm still alive tomorrow, she thought.

When she reached the bottom of the lane, she hurried across the yard, past the jeep with its bonnet open and its engine exposed to the elements, and up to their front door.

'Brianan!' she shouted, dropping one of the bags and opening the door. It hadn't been locked, was that a good sign or a bad one?

She picked up the shopping bag and went inside the house. 'Brianan!'

A large mountain of a man appeared in the tiny doorway leading to the kitchen.

'What's all the shouting about now?'

'He found you. He's on his way here now.'

Brianan's eyes narrowed. 'Then we'll be ready for him, won't we?'

'Ma? What's happening?'

Brianan moved to one side, revealing a boy standing in the shadows. He was in pyjamas and clutching a teddy bear.

'Nothing, love,' Mary said, pushing her way past Brianan and into the kitchen. 'Come on, let's get you back upstairs and in bed.'

Placing her hands on the boy's shoulders, she turned him to face the stairs and started ushering him on. She glanced back at Brianan, his mouth set in a grim line.

'Don't you worry,' he said. 'He's come for *me*, not you and the boy.'

'I don't want to lose you,' Mary said.

'Don't worry, you won't,' Brianan said. 'That bastard's getting nowhere near me.'

HE HANDED the binoculars over and, pointing, said, 'Over there on the rocks, there's a sandpiper.'

'A what?' he said, raising the glasses to his eyes, unfamiliar with their use.

'A sandpiper, it's a bird.'

He fiddled with the controls, the image blurred and wobbly through the binoculars. Caught a flash of grey water amongst the green grass and grey sky. Couldn't focus on anything, it was all too close, too large. He couldn't get the bigger picture.

'Can you see it?'

'No.' He handed the binoculars back. 'Never figured you for a bird watcher.'

'Used to be, when I was a lad.' He had the binoculars up, scanning the lake of cold, grey water at the foot of the mountainside.

'Not anymore, not for years now. But then I saw we had these, and I thought, while we were here, I might as well have a look.'

Joe Coffin turned his back on the lake. What had Gilligan told him it was called? Loch Muick. Stupid bloody name.

Coffin watched the Stig struggling to keep the pages of the road atlas laid flat on the bonnet of the black Range Rover. A cold breeze was picking up.

Shaw was sitting in the back of the Range Rover. He'd refused to get out, said he didn't want to stand around in the cold wind while the Stig tried to work out where the hell they were.

'You know where we went wrong yet?' Coffin said.

'We should have stayed on the A93, just like I told you,' the Stig said. 'It's that fucking Gilligan, took us down a dead end.'

'Fuck you, Stig,' Gilligan said, not bothering to lower the binoculars and turn to face the others. 'If you didn't drive like a fucking maniac all the time, I'd have been able to pay more attention to the map book.'

'Cut the crap, you two,' Coffin said. 'Do you know where we're going now?'

The Stig massaged his beard thoughtfully while he peered at the markings on the page. 'Yeah, we just need to turn round and go back about a mile.' He closed the road atlas and looked up at the grey cloud hanging above them. 'Bloody hell, it's a good job we brought the map book. It's murder trying to get a signal up here.'

Coffin pulled his mobile from his back pocket. No bars. Felt like they were cut off from the rest of the world, and he didn't like it. It was bad enough being out of Birmingham, but to come up here, in the middle of Scottish Fucking Nowhere? Coffin slipped the mobile phone back in his pocket.

'Let's get going,' he said.

Coffin climbed into the car, the front passenger seat. He'd ratcheted the seat all the way back. There was plenty of room inside, and the elevated position was good. But he still felt hemmed in, trapped and uncomfortable. He had no room to move his legs, and his head was constantly brushing the roof. It had been a hell of a long journey and once they had crossed the border, Coffin had done his best to stay out of sight inside the Range Rover, behind the tinted glass.

The Stig climbed in the driver's seat and Gilligan sat in the back, still holding onto the binoculars.

Coffin gazed out of the windscreen at the lake, at the cold grey water, at the ripples across its surface from the stiff breeze. A good place to hide a body in there. A suitable grave for those that deserved it.

The Stig swung the car round in reverse, the wheels skidding on the ground's loose surface. He shoved the gears into first and gunned the engine. The wheels skidded again before they shot forward and they were back on the tarmac road, winding through the hills.

'Can't you just drive normal?' Gilligan said. 'Do you always have to act like you're on timed laps on a fucking racetrack?'

The Stig had his sunglasses on again, but Coffin was pretty sure he saw him looking in the rear-view mirror, probably holding Gilligan's gaze in a stupid, pissy staring contest, when Gilligan couldn't see his eyes, anyway. Coffin just wished he would concentrate on the driving.

'Why don't you leave the driving to me?' the Stig said. 'And you concentrate on what you're good at, although I've yet to see any evidence that you're good at anything apart from whingeing.'

'Hey, didn't I tell you two to cut it out?' Coffin said. 'I feel like I'm your fucking mother. Now just shut the fuck up before you give me a headache.'

The Stig spun the steering wheel as he took the curves in the road too fast. Rocky ground rose beside them on their right, making it difficult to see what might be around the next bend. On their left, the ground dropped away and sometimes Coffin could see the road cutting its way through the valley. It appeared they were the only vehicle out today, the road deserted apart from a bus in the distance, making its way towards them.

'I'm hungry,' Shaw said from the back. 'You think they've got a McDonald's around here?'

The Stig laughed. 'Are you kidding? They probably haven't even heard of fast food in these parts. Besides, you're in the Highlands now. You can eat haggis like the rest of them.'

'I'm not eating any of that shit, now I'm not,' Gilligan said, before Shaw had a chance to reply. 'I saw something on TV once about what they put in there, sheep's heart and brains and shit like that. Sounds to me like the sweepings off the abattoir floor after they've finished carving off all the good parts for the butcher. And you know it's all shoved inside a sheep's intestine, don't you? Fucking barbarians, that's what they are round here.'

'The trouble with you, Gilligan, is you've got no sense of adventure,' the Stig said. 'But then I suppose that's what'll happen to a man when you grow up eating nothing but potatoes.'

'When we're done here today, Mr Stig, I'm going to give you an education in Irish history, that I am,' Gilligan said.

Shaw laughed and looked out of his window.

The bus passed them, going in the opposite direction. It looked empty, although Coffin thought he might have seen a couple sat in the back.

'Keep your eyes peeled,' Coffin said. 'We don't want to miss the turn off again.'

The Stig took another bend in the road and then slowed as they came to the brow of the hill. He parked up on the side of the road.

'I think this might be what we're looking for,' he said.

They all looked at the farm track leading downhill. At the end of the lane, they could see a cottage, wisps of smoke curling from the chimney.

Coffin heard the electric window sliding down in the back. He twisted in his seat, saw Gilligan peering through the binoculars.

'See anything?' Coffin said.

'Apart from fucking sandpipers,' the Stig said.

'Nothing, it all looks quiet down there,' Gilligan said.

Coffin pressed the button on the car door and his window slid down with an electronic hum.

'Hand them over, let me see.'

Gilligan passed him the black binoculars. Again, he struggled to focus the view through the lenses. They felt too small in his large hands, too delicate. He turned the focusing wheel one way and then the other, trying to hold the binoculars steady enough that he could keep the image from bouncing around.

'Prop your elbows on the edge of the door,' Gilligan said.

Coffin tried it, and immediately the image settled down. He twisted the focusing knob again and this time the view came into startling, vivid focus. He was looking into the branches of a tree, so close he felt he could reach out and pluck the leaves from it. Slowly, so as not to disturb the view too much, he tracked the binoculars right and then left.

The cottage suddenly came into view. A thin wisp of smoke still curling from the stone chimney. The windows dark against the grey stone of the cottage walls. No vehicles visible in the front yard. No sign of life.

Except that trail of smoke from the chimney. As though someone had just extinguished a fire?

'What do you think? Is that the place?' Gilligan said.

Coffin lowered the binoculars. 'Let's find out.'

They climbed out of the Range Rover. Coffin gave the binoculars to Gilligan, who tossed them onto the back seat and then shut the door. Coffin walked around the car to the back where Gilligan and the Stig joined him. He unlatched the rear door and lifted it up.

The boot was full of large, green jerry cans. Coffin and Shaw lifted them out one by one and placed them on the road. Once the boot was empty, Coffin dug his fingers down between the bottom of the boot and edge of the car. He pulled and lifted the false bottom, propping it up.

'Take your pick,' he said.

Inside the cavity below the boot floor space were four identical shotguns. After a quick glance in both directions to check for oncoming traffic, Gilligan picked up first. He snapped the gun open and pulled a box of shells out of the car's hiding space.

Shaw reached inside the boot and did the same. While he slipped the shells into the chamber, the Stig pulled a shotgun out and examined it.

'You ever fire one of these?' Coffin said.

The Stig still had on his sunglasses and Coffin couldn't read his expression. But he thought he caught the hint of a smile on his lips.

'Once or twice, maybe,' he said. 'Don't you worry about me.'

Coffin picked up the last shotgun and broke it open.

'Load up and put spare ammo in your pockets. You're going to need it.'

'Aren't you being a bit over the top, Joe?' the Stig said. 'After all, there's four of us and only one of him.'

'That we know of,' Coffin said. 'And besides, this is Shocker Stronach we're dealing with. He's a dangerous man.'

'Aye, and a man I've been looking forward to meeting for a while now,' Gilligan said. 'I know what he did to you, Joe, that I do. But this here bastard murdered my good friend Brendan. So, we've both got scores to settle today.'

'Let's go,' Coffin said.

THE GOLDFISH

They put the jerry cans back in the Rover's boot and replaced the false bottom.

They split up. Coffin and Gilligan walked further down the road, Shaw and the Stig walked up. Coffin left the road when he was hidden from the cottage. He stepped from tarmac and onto the wet grass. His boots slipped on the ground, but he kept his footing. He swore quietly.

Gilligan took a different route. The plan was they would all approach the building from different directions.

The rolling landscape was littered with huge, dark rocks. As though God had simply thrown them from the heavens, scattering them across the landscape for people to puzzle over. Coffin moved up to one of the rocks and peered at the cottage from behind it. There was no more smoke trailing from the chimney. The house really did look empty now.

Except, from this new angle, Coffin could see a jeep parked behind the cottage. The jeep was squashed between the cottage and a small outhouse. Not an ideal parking space when there was so much more room at the front. As though someone had tried to hide it there.

Coffin saw movement further out.

The Stig, closing in. He was heading for the outhouse, getting in close. Between the outhouse and the Stig was a broad, open expanse of long grass. The Stig was running up the slope, clutching the shotgun to his chest.

Just as he reached the outhouse, there was a rapid burst of gunfire from the cottage. The windows in the jeep shattered, shards of brick and mortar exploded from the outhouse wall.

Coffin ducked behind the boulder.

The gunfire stopped. Sounded like a semi-automatic assault rifle.

Apparently, there was somebody home after all.

Coffin risked a look around the boulder, couldn't see the Stig anywhere.

The explosion of a shotgun echoed around the hills, followed by more rapid, stuttering gunfire. The Stig was still out there, pinned down behind the outhouse. Assuming Stronach was living on his own there and didn't have a house full of his ex-SAS mates then now was the time to get up close to the farmhouse whilst Stronach was distracted.

Coffin left the protection of the boulder and ran for the cottage's front.

A tinkling of glass, the high-pitched whine of a bullet passing close by Coffin's left ear.

Two people in the house. Stronach on the rear with an assault rifle. One in the front with a handgun.

Coffin kept running.

He slammed into the front door and it shuddered in its frame. The walls of the stone cottage were thick and the front door recessed so that Coffin had some slight protection from the shooter at the window.

A shout from inside. 'Bastard!'

A woman.

Coffin stepped out of the recess and to one side. The door thudded and splintered with the impact of bullets fired from the handgun. Coffin lifted the shotgun and discharged one barrel at the door's lock. The wooden panels exploded, and the door swung inward.

Coffin stepped inside, using this moment while the shooter was confused and disoriented from the noise and the smoke.

A small entrance hall, empty. The woman was gone already.

To his left, through an open door, Coffin saw a kitchen. To his right, through another open door, a lounge area. A couple of steps led down to it. Flag stoned floor, coffee table, sofas, a television. At the opposite end of the lounge was an open staircase. Coffin saw feet running, disappearing up through the space in the ceiling.

He cracked open the shotgun as he stepped down into the lounge and replaced the discharged shell.

More rapid gunfire from upstairs.

Where the hell were the others?

Coffin approached the stairs cautiously, careful not to step in an attacker's line of sight from the first floor. Cast his eyes around the lounge once more. Saw a sideboard of dark, polished wood. A vase of yellow flowers sitting on top.

The interior of the cottage looked nice, well-kept, and looked after. Someone was a homemaker.

Coffin doubted it was Stronach.

The shooter upstairs had stopped. The silence after the gunfire was heavy, startling almost, and broken only by the sound of muffled sobs. A woman.

'Hey, Joe!' came an urgent hiss.

Coffin spun round, raising the shotgun.

Gilligan, entering the lounge. Hands up, palms out.

Shaw followed him.

Coffin turned back to the stairs.

'Stronach! Are you up there?' he shouted.

'Aye,' came the reply.

'Are you coming down?'

'What do you think, Coffin?'

'I think you're a fucking dead man!' Gilligan shouted.

Coffin motioned for him to be quiet.

'Who's up there with you?' Coffin said.

Silence, apart from the muffled sobs.

'My wife, Mary,' came a reply, eventually.

'I've got no argument with her,' Coffin said. 'You know that. But if you insist on keep firing that gun at us, I'm not going to be selective about who I shoot and whether or not anybody's getting in my way. You understand what I'm telling you?'

In answer, the ceiling erupted under more automatic gunfire. Shards of plaster and dust exploded over Coffin and Gilligan as a hail of bullets smacked into the sofas and the flag stoned floor.

Coffin hit the ground hard and crawled behind a sofa. He had no idea where Gilligan or Shaw had gone.

The vase with the yellow flowers exploded, showering Coffin in ceramic fragments and yellow petals. A window smashed, a photograph fell from the wall, and the bullets made hard thudding noises as they hit the stone walls.

Coffin kept his head down and waited. Stronach had to run out of bullets soon and Coffin wasn't worried about the sobbing woman, she was too scared to come down with her handgun whilst her husband distracted them with his hailstorm of bullets. And Coffin was sure there was nobody else in the house.

The sound of gunfire suddenly stopped.

Coffin climbed to his feet and ran for the stairs. The wooden risers shook under his boots as he pounded up the steps.

Stronach was there, right in front of him, with the assault rifle. He didn't even look at Coffin as he shoved a fresh magazine into the gun.

Coffin raised the shotgun and fired both barrels.

Stronach did a backflip, spraying scarlet blood over the walls as he smacked into the bedroom door behind. The door rattled in its frame as he hit it. Stronach crumpled to the floor, leaving behind a smear of red on the bedroom door.

Gilligan and Shaw arrived at the top of the stairs.

Coffin opened the shotgun and replaced the shells.

He snapped the chamber closed and walked over to Stronach, who was lying on his back in an expanding pool of blood, his arms and legs twisted out of shape, his head propped up against the door.

He was taking fitful, halting breaths, his eyelids fluttering as he struggled to look up at Coffin.

Coffin placed the muzzle of the shotgun barrel against Stronach's knee.

'Where's your friend, Stronach?' Coffin said.

'Fuck you, Coffin,' Stronach gasped.

Coffin nudged his knee with the shotgun. 'Now come on, Stronach, we both know you're going to die, right? Why make it any more protracted and painful than it has to be?'

Stronach ground his teeth together, and for a brief moment, his eyes rolled back, disappearing beneath his eyelids.

Coffin glanced back at Gilligan standing at the top of the stairs. Gilligan walked over and picked up the assault rifle, weighed it in his hands.

'This the bastard who murdered Brendan, is it?' he said, pointing the rifle at Stronach.

'One of them,' Coffin said. He nudged Stronach's knee with the shotgun again. 'Tell me where your friend is. Shanks Longworth.'

Stronach shook his head jerkily, baring his teeth.

Coffin pulled the trigger.

Stronach screamed as his leg kicked out and his knee disappeared in a cloud of blood and bone.

Stronach passed out.

'Go find a bowl or a pan and fill it with cold water,' Coffin said, not taking his eyes off Stronach.

Gilligan passed the Stig as he hurried downstairs.

'You've made a lovely mess up here, Joe,' he said. 'Is he dead?'

'No, passed out.'

'You going to kill him?'

'In a minute.'

'Anyone else in the house?'

Coffin gestured to the door that Stronach's head was propped against. 'His wife's in there. Might be a good idea if you go in and check it out.'

'Yeah, be careful, I think she's armed,' Shaw said. He was

standing well out of the way. He looked a little pale, like maybe this was getting too much for him.

The Stig ambled over to the door and stood beside Stronach, doing his best to keep his feet out of the blood soaked patch of carpet. He turned the door handle and pushed the door open. Stronach's head hit the carpet with a soft thump.

'I'm coming in and I'm armed,' the Stig said. 'I don't want any trouble now.'

Holding his shotgun out, the Stig stepped over Stronach's head and into the bedroom. Coffin watched from the doorway as the Stig searched the bedroom.

'No one in here,' he said.

Gilligan arrived clutching a big glass bowl full of water and greenery to his chest. A goldfish darted around and around inside the bowl.

Coffin looked at the fishbowl and then at Gilligan. 'Really?'

'There's a fucking ton of water in here, Joe,' Gilligan said. 'Almost went arse over tits carrying this bastard up here.'

'Pour some of it on his head, over his face,' Coffin said. 'But not all of it.'

Gilligan shuffled up to Stronach. His feet slipped on the blood soaked carpet.

'Oh, shit!' Gilligan said, as he struggled to stay on his feet.

Some water slopped over the edge of the bowl, and the goldfish swam round and round in frantic circles.

Shaw, watching Gilligan, giggled.

Gilligan stayed upright.

He bent at the waist, tilting the bowl until a stream of water began pouring over the lip. Stronach coughed and spluttered as the water splashed over his face.

'Fuck!' he gasped.

Gilligan leaned back. The stream of water stopped.

'Yeah, we're still here,' Coffin said, nudging Stronach's other knee with the shotgun. 'Sorry about that.'

Stronach blinked water out of his eyes. His breathing sounded harsh and jagged.

'Fuck you, Coffin. Fuck you, I'm not fucking telling you anything.'

Coffin discharged the second barrel. Blood splattered across the wall as Stronach's other kneecap disintegrated. Stronach screamed, but this time he stayed conscious. The scream turned into a wail.

Coffin cracked the shotgun open. 'It will be your hands next and then maybe your elbows, your feet, your shoulders. We can go on like this for a long time yet, Stronach.'

'Can I pour more water over him?' Gilligan said. 'Maybe drop the goldfish in his mouth, now that would be something to see.'

The Stig was standing in the bedroom doorway, watching everything. Coffin happened to glance at him, saw his eyes grow wide, his mouth drop open. Before he uttered a noise, the fishbowl shattered, showering Coffin in glass and water. Gilligan fell down on his back.

Coffin turned to see a woman charging at him from another bedroom doorway. She was holding a handgun.

Coffin snapped the shotgun closed, pointed it at the charging woman and pulled the trigger. The hammer clicked on the empty shells.

The woman was pulling the trigger on her gun, over and over. Coffin hit her in the face with the stock of the shotgun and she went down, hard.

Gilligan got up on his hands and knees, wiping water off his face. The Stig was pointing at him and laughing. Shaw was laughing too.

'You've got fucking seaweed in your hair!'

Gilligan pulled at the green stuff, stuck to his head, and started laughing hysterically.

'Shut up, both of you,' Coffin said.

The woman, lying on the floor, wailed.

Stronach was silent. He was dead.

'Let's get out of here,' Coffin said.

'What are we going to do about her?' the Stig said. 'She's seen us. She's seen you. And you're on the fucking TV all the time now. She's got to know who you are.'

Coffin looked at the woman lying crumpled on the carpet,

drenched with water and blood. She lifted a shaking hand to her face as though to cover her eyes. As though to blot out the sight before her.

Gilligan stood up, picked up the assault rifle and shot a single bullet through Mary's head.

'There, problem solved,' he said.

Movement, behind them.

All four men turned as one, swinging around, guns raised. Gilligan strafed the area with a firestorm of bullets, punching holes in the walls. A body flipped back beneath the force of the bullets, hit the floor.

Gilligan stopped firing.

Coffin walked over to the body.

A young boy in pyjamas lay on the floor, eyes closed, his body ripped apart and bloody.

'Oh shit,' Shaw said, standing beside Coffin. 'You killed a little kid, Gilligan. You fucking killed a little kid.'

THE STIG WALKED BACK up the lane to the car and drove it down to the cottage. The four men pulled the jerry cans out of the boot and doused the bodies inside the cottage in diesel. They poured more diesel over the carpets and the beds and the sofas. They emptied all the jerry cans and tossed them to one side.

Gilligan lit a match and dropped it onto the fuel soaked carpet. With a soft *WHOOMPH!* the diesel ignited, dirty yellow flames springing into life and running rapidly across the carpet.

They got out of the house and into the car.

They drove up the lane and onto the road. As the Stig drove back down the road, navigating the twists and turns with practised ease, Coffin gazed out of his window at the cottage, at the black smoke pouring from its shattered windows.

The men in the car were silent.

The next morning, they were back in Birmingham.

NAUGHTY GIRL

Her name was Chitrita.

It had taken her a long time to remember that, for her name to come back to her. No one else here knew her name. She'd had to remember it, to fight to recover it on her own.

But she knew it now.

She knew other things, too. She knew that she was growing stronger with each passing day, and with each fresh mouthful of blood. And she knew that she had been waiting, gathering her strength, biding her time until she could make her escape.

She pressed the flat of her hands against the cold wire cage of her prison.

She knew that she had once been in love with a vampire named Merek Guttman. She knew she had been asleep for a long, long time. Over a hundred years. The sleep of rejuvenation, buried in a coffin filled with the blood of virgin girls. She knew she had been asleep for too long.

Were the other vampires still asleep, waiting to be pulled from the ground and restored to their former selves?

The ones who had dug her up, they hadn't told her that. They hadn't told her much at all.

They had pulled her from her coffin of blood and brought her here. Put her in this prison.

Prisons couldn't hold her. They didn't know that, but they would find out soon enough.

Today?

Yes. Today.

She was strong enough.

She would escape today and join the others.

Her brow furrowed as she thought about this.

The others. Were there still any others?

Guttman. Guttman was dead. Murdered by the man they called Joe Coffin. They had told her that much, her captors.

How wonderful, that name. She would be the one to put him in a coffin. Bury him deep underground, maybe while he was still alive. Wouldn't that be fun? Joe Coffin in a coffin.

A Coffin in a coffin in the ground.

Alive.

Just.

Holding her hands up before her face, Chitrita balled them into fists and began squeezing, squeezing. Her long fingernails cut into the soft flesh of her palms, drawing blood. The blood ran down her arms and dripped off her elbows and onto the bottom of the cage and through onto the floor. Chitrita opened a hand and licked at her palm.

The blood tasted sweet.

Her tongue was rough against the skin of her palm.

Her senses twitched at the sound of a door shutting high above. Footsteps, two pairs of them, descending the steps.

Them. Back again.

With more blood?

Yes, more blood. She could smell it on them.

Good. She would drink the blood first and then she would escape. Or maybe she would kill them first. Their blood would be warm, fresh. It would spurt into her mouth, not like the sterile, cold blood that she had to suck from the bags.

'Is that them, the bastards? They're coming back, aren't they?'

Chitrita crouched in the cage, both hands clenched once more, and ignored the man in the other cage. The cage on wheels. They wheeled him around, up and down the corridors sometimes, laughing and banging on his cage with metal pipes.

They never did that to her.

Was her cage on wheels? She thought so. But they never wheeled her around or banged on her cage, or did anything but feed her blood or sit on that tattered sofa and watch her whilst they held hands.

They had brought the man down here only a couple of days ago, his face purple and swollen with bruising. His shirt was ripped and stained with patches of blood. At first he hadn't said much, but then he had started getting angry, banging his fists against his cage, spitting out curses on his captors.

They had just ignored him.

The man had tried talking to Chitrita, but she had ignored him too.

There had been another man before him, in another cage, but he had died. They had wheeled his corpse out and a few days later had returned with this man.

This man talked too much.

'Bastards,' he muttered. 'Fucking bastards.'

Chitrita waited.

They arrived.

When they saw her, they paused for a moment, as though sensing that something had changed within her. That maybe something was different. The tall, skeletal one called Corpse was holding the carrier bags, both of them bulging with packets of blood. Stump was next to him, her eyes hidden as always by the dark, wraparound sunglasses.

'The toothy biter is unsleepered, Mrs Stump,' Corpse said.

'Indeed, Mr Corpse,' Stump said.

Chitrita wished she could see Stump's eyes. The vampire sensed a sharp intelligence at work in that woman, but the glasses, they hid her from view.

'Hey, fat bitch, when are you going to let me out of this fucking cage?' the man said.

Stump rotated her head in the man's direction. She was wearing what she always wore, long black leather coat, black leather trousers and boots. Her black hair was tied severely back. All her clothes strained against the weight of her rolls of fat.

'Never, Mr Morel, but you already know that.'

'Yeah, that's what you said yesterday,' Morel said. 'Fuckers. You're both fucking dead meat, you know that, don't you? Fucking dead meat is what you are.'

Morel's body sagged against the back of the cage, as though his outburst had drained him of all energy.

Stump and Corpse approached Chitrita, slowly, cautiously. The bags rustled against the stiff, stained fabric of Corpse's trousers as he walked.

Chitrita backed up against the wire meshing of the tall, narrow cage. She was still wearing the white ball gown she had been buried in all those years ago. The fabric was stained with dried blood and dirt, and it was ripped in places. Neither Stump nor Corpse had expressed any desire to offer her a change of clothes. The only times they approached her were when they were pushing the packets of cold blood into her cage.

Stump and Corpse stopped again, just out of reach, perhaps fearing that somehow she might be able to reach through the wire meshing and grab at them if they drew too close. At the beginning, when they first put her in here, when her arms were nothing more than sticks of dried flesh and bone, they knew she was helpless, like a newborn kitten. But not anymore. Now her arms had fleshed out, the skin grown young and soft again. Her hair had grown back, luxurious and soft, and her eyes were clear once more.

And she was stronger.

'Give her the blood, Mr Corpse,' Stump said. 'I will be in the kitchen, making us a nice pot of Darjeeling tea.'

'Ooh, smashioning,' Corpse said.

Corpse dropped the two bags on the floor as Stump left the room. He pulled out one of the clear plastic packets of blood. They had started off by cutting the bags open with scissors before care-fully handing them into the cage. Now they knew that Chitrita liked to rip the bags open with her teeth and suck the blood out.

Corpse reached out, his arm outstretched, trying his best to keep as far away as he could from the vampire inside the cage. The top of the cage could be flipped open on hinges, but Stump and Corpse had secured it with chains, leaving just enough give in them that the top could be opened enough to slip the bag of blood inside. Corpse pushed the bag through the gap and let go. The bag dropped to the cage floor.

Chitrita ignored it, despite her senses screaming at her to scoop it up and rip it open, and pour the blood out over her open mouth.

Corpse tilted his head to one side and looked quizzically at the vampire.

'You shoulded be ingurgitating the sanguinous,' he said.

Chitrita turned away, letting her long hair hang down over her face so that Corpse could no longer see it. She squeezed her hands into fists once more, her blood dripping from between her fingers. Each drop made a tiny *PLIP!* as it hit the floor.

Chitrita sensed Corpse drawing a little closer. Had he noticed the blood pooling on the floor? Chitrita squeezed her hands together tighter, pushing out more blood.

Plip! Plip! Plip!

Corpse saw the blood now and his eyes grew round and wide.

Chitrita remained silent. In all these months, the power of speech had slowly come back to her, but not once had she spoken to her captors.

She tensed, ignoring the primal scream for the need to grab the bag of fresh blood lying on the bottom of her cage and rip it open with her teeth. There was a much tastier bag of warm blood just outside the cage, making its way slowly to her.

Patience, Chitrita. Patience.

Corpse was up against the cage now, peering at her through the mesh work of metal. She had angled herself so that he couldn't see where the blood was dripping from. Still, she refused to turn her head and look at him.

What would he do? Would he go and find Stump? Get her to come and take a look at Chitrita, her pet, as she liked to talk about the vampire? If he did, if Corpse brought Stump to take a look, then Chitrita's escape attempt would be over for the moment. Stump was cleverer than Corpse, more cunning. Chitrita sensed that Stump was beginning to wonder what they should do with her, that perhaps it had been a mistake letting her grow this strong and youthful once more.

Chitrita could sense Corpse staring at her. He was attracted to her, she knew that much. He had been fascinated by her slow transformation from ancient wizened crone into youthful beauty. The process had taken longer than it should have done because of the sterile, cold blood they fed her with. But it had still worked.

Chitrita made a tiny whimpering sound.

Corpse began unlocking her prison, the padlock rattling against the cage as he fiddled with it.

When the door swung open, Chitrita turned and pounced.

'Kill the skinny bastard!' Morel shouted, banging his fists against the cage. 'Rip his fucking head off!'

Corpse fell back with a cry as Chitrita enveloped him in her embrace. The dirty, tattered ball gown hindered her movements and Corpse managed to struggle free as he kicked and screamed. She swiped a bloody hand at him, fingers like claws. Corpse skittered away on his back, eyes wide as saucers, until he bumped into the battered old sofa they kept down here. So many times Chitrita had wished to open up their throats and drink their blood whilst Stump and Corpse had sat on that sofa, watching Chitrita inside her cage.

She had wanted to rip them apart and slaughter them for so very long now.

'You're overflowing out with badliness,' Corpse said. 'You were acting up a storywise to be drip-drip-dripping sanguinous.'

Chitrita bared her teeth and snapped them together. Corpse flinched and clambered backwards up onto the sofa, never taking his eyes off the vampire.

Chitrita licked the blood from her palms and her arms, all the while gazing at Corpse. Leaping at Corpse had drained her of energy. She was still much weaker than she had realised.

She saw Stump enter the room.

'Aww, fucking hell,' Morel said. 'Why didn't you kill him?'

Stump looked disappointed, more than shocked or frightened. Almost as though she had been expecting this moment.

'Oh dear, Mr Corpse, what have you done?' she said.

Corpse whimpered slightly. 'But it wasn't my gremlin, the toothy biter contrifuged me with her chicanerinous.'

Chitrita ached to rip them apart right now, to shower this place in their blood and to rub it into her face and over her body even as she was drinking it.

She crouched, the blood from her hands smeared across the concrete floor.

'Well, this is a problem, isn't it?' Stump said. 'And here I was looking forward to a nice cup of tea.'

'Fucking fat slag,' Morel said.

Stump began stroking her mannequin hand, fingers sliding up and down the shiny, yellowed plastic.

'Watch out,' Morel said. 'I've heard she's got a fucking blade inside there, slice and dice you before you know what's happened.'

Chitrita regarded the plastic hand. Was she as strong as she thought? Was she as fast? At the height of her powers, she could be near indestructible, but right now? No, she was too tired, too weak. She still needed to feed, needed fresh warm blood straight from an open wound.

She needed to be back outside where she could hunt down the human cattle and gorge herself. Even though she was inside, deep underground, Morel had said, Chitrita could still sense the night outside. Her time. Feeding time.

She needed to get outside. And feed.

Chitrita opened her mouth and for the first time in over a hundred years, she spoke.

'Let me out,' she said. The words came out clumsily, slurred.

Stump and Corpse glanced at each other.

'The toothy biter can speechify, Mrs Stump,' Corpse said.

'Indeed, Mr Corpse,' replied Stump.

'Hey, lady, take me with you,' Morel said, rattling the metal cage.

Chitrita ignored him. Held Stump in her gaze. Stump gazed back, the dark sunglasses hiding her eyes.

'Let's do as she asks, shall we?' Stump said. 'Mr Corpse, would you be so good as to escort her to the front door?'

'By me and my particulars?' Corpse said.

'Oh yes, I think so,' Stump said. 'I'd quite like to play with Mr Morel here for a few minutes.'

Corpse climbed off the sofa and stood up. He motioned to Chitrita.

Chitrita rose slowly from her crouch and followed Corpse as he walked away.

He led her through several connecting corridors and to a set of concrete steps. He kept his eyes on her at all times. He motioned at her to follow him up the steps. Their path was illuminated by bare bulbs set into metal grilles. At the top was a short corridor leading to a metal door.

Corpse, head twisted around to look at Chitrita all the time, unlocked the door and pushed it open.

The sound of Morel screaming echoed faintly up the stairwell.

Chitrita stepped outside, the cool, damp air like a balm on her flesh. On the ground were train tracks. Brickwork arched overhead. Her nose twitched and her tongue flooded with saliva at the smells she could pick out.

The door clanged shut behind her.

She was on her own.

She was free.

WASTE MY TIME ON FACEBOOK

The torchlight illuminated the towpath, picking out the bank on his right where the ground fell away and the water began, and the grassy verge on his left. Coffin could hear the city centre, its life, its heartbeat, the drone of traffic. This early in the morning and the city was coming alive already. But here by the canal, all was quiet. Overhead there was the soft whisper of leaves in the wind, and below him the soft splash of water as something disturbed the canal's surface.

Coffin hated it out here.

The city centre was where he belonged.

Coffin ran his torchlight over the boarding on his left. He knew what was on the other side, even if it was no longer there. Number Ninety-Nine had been demolished, and the rubble taken away by order of the Birmingham council. Now only the ground was left, the scar, the reminder of the horrors that were perpetrated there, waiting to be redeveloped and landscaped. There would be a pathway through the gardens down to the canal and a piece of artwork in tribute to Peter Marsden, who had been kept inside that house and turned into a vampire.

Peter's mother, Brenda, had made a tearful tribute to her son on the local news and there was a lot of sympathy for her.

Coffin had no sympathy. For her son, maybe, the poor little bastard. But not Brenda. From what Coffin knew of her, she had never been much of a mother.

Besides, Coffin had his own bad memories of number Ninety-Nine.

Abel Mortenson and Steffanie.

Coffin had battled Mortenson twice, once inside the house down in the cellar and the second time out here on the canal. And when he had finally killed Mortenson, Coffin had carved his body up into pieces and tossed them into that pit in the cellar where Guttman had been buried and set the pieces alight.

Coffin had thought that might be the end of his association with the house, but then he had fought Guttman in the very same place, down in that cellar once more where Jacob had been held prisoner.

Coffin had made sure Guttman wasn't coming back either.

And now the cellar was filled in and the house of horrors flattened to make way for a park.

Coffin swung his torchlight up and down the towpath. Thought he caught the flutter of wings in the darkness. A bat maybe.

He carried on walking, swinging his torch back and forth. The surface of the canal water looked pitch black, even in the light of the torch.

The beam of light caught movement up ahead, a figure emerging from the shadows.

Coffin's free hand instinctively moved towards the sharp wooden stakes he kept on his belt, beneath his jacket. Guns didn't kill vampires, but a stake through the heart did the job. At least for a while, anyway.

The figure drew closer. Threw a hand across its face to shield its eyes from the glare of the torch.

'Bloody hell, Coffin, couldn't we have met at Starbucks or something?' Nick Archer said. 'I can't see a bloody thing out here. And what the hell do you call this time of the morning? Never took you for an early riser.'

'How's the leg, Detective?' Coffin said, lowering the torch.

'Yeah, it's fine, what the hell do you care?' Archer replied.

'Just making conversation,' Coffin said.

'Really? That'll be a first.' Archer looked up and down the canal. 'So come on, tell me, why the hell did we have to meet here? This spot got some special memories for you or something?'

Coffin grinned. 'Sure it has. Like that night I slapped your own cuffs on you and left you to keep my son company on that narrowboat, remember?'

'Like I'm ever going to forget.' Coffin noticed Archer's hand unconsciously move to his thigh and massage it. 'You done gloating now, or can we get on with business?'

A bat darted past, its dark shape a blur in the gloom. Archer ducked.

Straightened up, staring at Coffin.

'Are those knives you've got strapped to your waist?' he said.

'No, stakes,' Coffin said, pulling one out of its strap and holding it up for Archer to see.

'Bloody hell, I feel like I'm stuck in a Christopher Lee film,' Archer said. 'Bats and stakes, and...'

Vampires, Coffin thought.

'You come across any of the bastards recently?' Archer said.

Coffin shook his head. 'No. You?'

'Still got a mortuary full of them. They were meant to be moving out last month but there's been a holdup, don't know what, probably somebody lost the bloody paperwork or something.'

'Where are they going?'

'Some research lab down in London I think, nobody really knows for sure.' Archer looked at the black surface of the canal water. 'You think there are any more out there? Besides...'

'Steffanie and Michael,' Coffin finished for him. 'I don't know.'

'You missed one out,' Archer said.

Coffin waited.

'Julie Carter, teenager, she was on the narrowboat with Emma, had her throat ripped open by that bastard you chopped into pieces and barbequed.'

'Wasn't me, officer,' Coffin said. 'I was found not guilty by a jury in a court of law, remember?'

'Yeah, a jury that had been paid off by that pathetic excuse for a solicitor of yours,' Archer said.

'So there are three of them out there,' Coffin said. 'Not that I've noticed, though. Have you?'

'No, it's been quiet lately, hasn't it? Sometimes I get to thinking that maybe it was all a delusion of some kind, like a dream. I have trouble remembering that it all really happened. And then I go down to the mortuary and sit in the viewing gallery and stare at all the blood smeared across the glass and the shapes behind it and I soon get to remembering again.'

'I've been doing some remembering of my own recently, Detective,' Coffin said.

Archer looked at him. 'Yeah?'

'Yeah. That night when I cuffed you up and left you inside the narrowboat cabin with Michael.'

Archer said nothing.

'And then I got back, and you were outside, bleeding from that wound in your thigh.'

'Well, as you can see, I'm back to full health, although I'm never going to be able to compete in the one hundred metre sprint again.'

'Shut up, Archer, you know where I'm going with this. You should have been dead that night. Once Michael got free, he should have ripped you apart, but he didn't. Why not?'

Archer said nothing, turned his head and stared at the canal water again.

'What happened, Detective?'

'What the fuck do you care, Coffin? He's out there somewhere, isn't he? Him and his mother, and they're monsters, both of them.'

'What happened?'

'You're right, the kid should have ripped me to shreds and bled me dry.' Archer took a deep, ragged breath. 'He was all over me, I thought I was dead meat. It was that bloody sword you brought with you. Fuck knows where you found that, but you left it on the barge.'

Coffin waited whilst Archer paused, maybe thinking about what he was going to say next. Coffin had a good idea what it might be.

'I had to defend myself with something.' Archer stared at Coffin, suddenly defiant. 'He was like a wild animal, hell he was worse than a wild animal. He would have killed me.'

'What did he do when you attacked him? Run?'

'No. He wouldn't let up. I had to defend myself, you understand that, don't you?'

'And?'

'And I kept on hacking at him with the sword until he stopped attacking me. Bloody hell, Coffin, what do you want from me? I thought I'd killed a little kid, your kid.'

'But he wasn't there when I got back to you.'

'No. I shoved his body over the edge of the boat, into the water. I didn't know what to do, how could I tell anyone what I'd just done?'

'*Did* you tell anyone?'

'No, just Emma.'

Coffin ground his teeth together at the mention of Emma. Another betrayal from her. Maybe he needed to have a chat with her, find out what else she had been keeping from him.

'So, that's it,' Archer said. 'What now? Are you going to go all mental on me and bash my head in? Maybe shove one of those stakes through my chest?'

'No,' Coffin said. 'Once maybe, but not today. Things have changed. When I find Michael I'm going to kill him myself.'

Coffin heard Archer suck in his breath. 'Your own kid?'

'He's not my son anymore.'

'I guess not. Is that it then? Are we done?'

'No, not quite. This is the last time we meet, Detective. I'm done being your lackey.'

'Is that right?'

'Yeah, that's right. We're done.'

'Your fan club's going to be disappointed.'

'Yeah, well, my fan club will get over it.'

'I thought you'd enjoy being a celebrity, Coffin. Big vampire killer, the hero for once instead of the villain. Did you know you've got Facebook groups dedicated to you?'

'Do I look like I waste my time on Facebook?'

'I suppose not,' Archer said. 'Seems a shame though, especially when we've still got a vampire problem.'

'Yeah, well, I'll deal with them in my own way.'

Coffin turned to move off, but Archer stopped him.

'What's going on? The celebrity life cramping your style? I heard Piers Morgan wanted an interview.'

'I had my agent turn him down,' Coffin said.

'You got an agent now?' Archer said.

Coffin sighed. 'No.'

'Oh right, it was a joke.' Archer chuckled. 'Well, I can see how your association with the police and your profile as vampire slaying hero of the day might make your main career choice a little more difficult to carry out. Put you on the front page of the Sun and the Mirror and you're the working man's hero, right? The Daily Mail loves to follow your love life whilst starting petitions to close down Angels, and the Guardian and the Times are in a race to write the definitive history of the Slaughterhouse Mob. That one's pissing Emma off, as that was her baby. But your problem?' Archer paused, eyeing Coffin uneasily. 'Your problem is the publicity itself, am I right?'

Coffin said nothing, waited to see where Archer was going with this.

'You agreed to help us with the vampires and we agreed to maybe turn a blind eye to some of your less legitimate dealings. Problem is, neither of us predicted how much of a public figure you would become. Everyone loves you, Coffin. Except those that don't, and they hate you. Problem is, whether they love you or hate you, everybody's watching you.'

'Goodbye, Archer,' Coffin said, and moved to turn away.

'Hey, Coffin, talking about people watching you, you been on holiday recently?'

'What are you talking about, Detective?'

'Oh, just making small talk, that's all. Somebody said to me, said they thought they might have seen you up in Scotland, the high-lands. You been to Scotland recently, Coffin? Like maybe yesterday? You're looking a little tired to me, like you just got back from several hours sitting in a car on the M6.'

'What do you think, Archer? After all, you're the detective.'

'Yeah, that's right, and you're a cold-blooded killer.'

Coffin turned his back on Archer once more and began walking away.

'Not according to the law, I'm not,' he said.

'Don't forget, Coffin, you're a celebrity now, everybody's watching you,' Archer shouted.

Coffin walked back down the canal towpath, the torch picking out his way in the darkness. Archer was lying, the only people who had seen Coffin in Scotland were dead. So what was he doing, fishing for information like that?

Coffin saw the kid, Stronach's boy, lying on the floor, his body ripped apart by bullets. Dismissed the thought, pushed it away.

A bat darted by, its wings almost brushing Coffin's head.

Movement up ahead in the darkness.

Coffin lifted his torch as a figure appeared from the darkness.

'Hey,' Leola said, 'put that torch down, will you?'

Coffin lowered the torch.

More fluttering of wings, a dark shape shooting past.

Leola approached Coffin slowly. Despite the chill of the evening, she was wearing nothing more than a thin, short summer dress. Coffin played the torchlight across her body, the beam illuminating the spidery tattoos crawling across her dark skin, over her shoulders and arms, down the top of her breasts before they disappeared beneath the fabric of her dress.

Coffin had seen those tattoos, examined them closely many times now. Most of them were indescribable patterns repeated across her flesh but some, when stared at intently, metamorphosed into words. Not words he understood, but that hadn't stopped him once trying to speak them out loud, to feel the shape of them in his mouth, to hear them said.

Leola had placed her hand over his mouth and told him to

shush. *These words have a terrible power*, she had said. *They must never be spoken aloud*.

'What are you doing out here?' Coffin said. He had to duck as another bat darted by, alarmingly close to his head.

'Looking for you,' Leola said.

Coffin grunted. 'Well, you found me.'

A small, dark shadow twisted and turned over Leola's head.

'Watch out,' Coffin said. 'You've got a bat hovering over your head.'

Leola smiled.

The bat landed on her naked shoulder as a second one deposited itself in her hair.

A moment later and they both took off, disappearing into the dark sky and the shadows by the canal.

Coffin watched wordlessly as more bats fluttered out of the shadows and landed on Leola before taking off again. Some of them flittered around over head as though they were confused.

Leola lifted her face to the sky and watched the bats. There were more of them on the opposite side of the canal, hovering in a dark cloud over the stunted trees and bushes.

'What's going on?' Coffin said. 'Are they friends of yours?'

'I don't know,' Leola said, her face still upturned.

'Can't you ask them or something?' Coffin said.

'You've watched too many stupid vampire movies,' Leola said.

Coffin grunted. 'I suppose that's a no, then.'

'Not quite,' Leola said.

'What's that supposed to mean? You can either talk with them or you can't, right?'

'It's complicated.'

'That's your answer to every question I ask,' Coffin said. 'It's like you think I have trouble understanding anything.'

Leola looked up at the morning sky, still dark but showing faint signs of the dawn. The bats darted to and fro, seemingly in random directions but never going far from Leola.

'You said you were looking for me,' Coffin said.

'I was bored,' Leola said, lowering her gaze to look at Coffin once more. 'I wondered where you were, thought you might like some company.'

Coffin grunted. 'Company,' he said. 'Right.'

'I thought we could go hunting,' Leola said.

'Yeah?'

'Yeah,' Leola said, mimicking Coffin. 'We've still got two more vampires to dig up, remember? Maybe we could go visit Emma, get the addresses off her.'

Coffin had to duck again as a bat dive bombed him. 'Are these things dangerous?'

Leola laughed. 'No, they're just playing with you. Come on, what do you say, about digging up the vampires? That'll be all of them gone then.'

'Apart from Steffanie and Michael.'

'We'll find them too.'

Coffin scrubbed at his face. 'No, I'm tired. I'm going back to the club, get some sleep.'

'Maybe I'll go visit Emma, get the addresses myself.'

'No,' Coffin said. 'You stay away from her. I'm having nothing to do with that woman.'

'Joe, you've got to—'

Leola yelped and smacked something off her shoulder.

'What?' Coffin said, stepping up closer to Leola.

'The bat, it bit me,' she said.

There were two tiny wounds on Leola's shoulder, two puncture marks filling with blood.

'You ever known a bat to do that before?'

Leola looked up at Coffin, her eyes round and questioning.

'No,' she said. 'Never.'

WHERE'S LOVER BOY?

Was she crying?

Emma held her breath, listening. The house was silent.

No, she was asleep still.

Emma kept listening. She could hear him breathing beside her in the bed, that slight noise in his throat that was almost a snore, but not quite. Apart from that, the house was silent.

Maybe too silent.

Emma scolded herself. She knew the thought that came next.

Her baby was dead.

Emma knew that wasn't true. She knew there was no need for her to get out of bed and go check on her baby. And she knew that if she did, she would find Louisa May sleeping in her cot.

Emma knew all these things, but she pulled the duvet back and climbed out of bed, anyway.

A muffled snort, a grunt and movement beneath the duvet.

'Wha… what's happening?'

'Shush,' Emma whispered, placing her hand softly on his shoulder. 'Go back to sleep, it's fine.'

Emma padded barefoot out of the bedroom and across the

landing, into the nursery. As she stepped through the door, she reached behind her and switched the landing light on, to give her a little light in the bedroom. She stood beside the cot.

Louisa May lay on her front, head turned to one side, sleeping peacefully. Emma leaned over the cot and caressed her baby's cheek with her fingertips. Louisa May's cheek was soft, almost downy to the touch. Except that one tiny patch of rough skin, that last remaining bit of eczema that stubbornly refused to disappear no matter how often Emma used the cream on it.

Maybe she should take her back to see the doctor again. But it seemed so silly for such a tiny patch of rough skin.

Emma leaned into the cot and gently kissed Louisa May on the cheek.

She walked softly back into her bedroom, turning the landing light off as she went.

As she got back into bed, Mitch rolled over to face her.

'Everything all right?' he said.

'Fine,' Emma said, snuggling down beside him. 'I'm just being an old mother hen, worrying over nothing. I swear I'm turning into my mother.'

'What's the time?'

Emma twisted around to look at her bedside clock. 'Ten past six.'

'Thank God for that,' Mitch said. 'That means it'll be light soon.'

Emma sat up when she heard the knocking at her front door.

Mitch scrubbed his face with his hands. 'Who the hell is that?'

Emma climbed out of bed again and pulled on a dressing gown. 'I'll go find out, I don't want whoever it is waking up Lou.'

Emma padded quickly down the stairs, hoping to get to the front door before the caller knocked on the door again. At least whoever it was hadn't used the doorbell.

She unlocked the door and pulled it open a crack.

'Good morning,' Archer said. 'May I come in or do I have to show you my warrant card?'

'Fuck!' Emma hissed. 'What the hell are you doing here at this time of the morning?'

'And it's nice to see you too, Emma,' Archer said. 'And may I just remind you that I still have a key and could have simply let myself in?'

Emma swung the door open. 'All right, come in, but be quiet, Lou's sleeping.'

Archer stepped inside and took a deep breath in. 'Ah, the sweet smell of home, just a pity it's not my home anymore.'

'If you just came round to make snide comments, you might as well leave again,' Emma said.

Archer headed for the kitchen. 'You want coffee?'

Emma bit back a smart reply. She didn't want to get into an argument, especially with Mitch around.

'Yeah, why not? I'm up now, I might as well stay up.'

Emma joined Archer in the kitchen, at the coffee machine.

'Where's lover boy?' Archer said. 'Is he here?'

'Oh well done, Nick Archer,' Emma snapped. 'Forget your daughter, the first person you ask after is Mitch. How very mature of you.'

Archer didn't miss a beat as he prepared the coffee machine. 'It's because I'm thinking of Louisa May that I'm asking if lover boy is here. You know what I said, I don't want him anywhere near my daughter. I'd rather he wasn't anywhere near you either, but it seems I don't get much say in that.'

'Too right you don't, I'll see who the hell I want and when I want.'

The coffee machine began hissing and spitting. Archer turned to face Emma.

'You still haven't answered my question. Is lover boy here?'

'No,' Emma said. 'Happy now?'

Archer folded his arms and stared at Emma. 'Not particularly, no. You're probably lying, but I'll leave that for now, I can always have a look around before I leave.'

'The fuck you will!' Emma said.

'Don't forget, I still own this house as much as you do. I only agreed to move out for Louisa's sake. I can't have my own daughter being homeless.'

'Don't worry about us, Detective, I can always move us in with my mother.'

Archer snorted. 'Right, sure, I can see that happening.'

Emma's mouth twitched into a reluctant smile. 'I suppose.'

'Is Lou awake?'

'No, she's still asleep. She's been having a few bad nights with this eczema, so I want to let her sleep in this morning.'

'Don't worry, I wasn't suggesting we go upstairs and wake her up.'

'Yeah, I know.'

'Is the eczema getting better?'

'Mostly cleared up, just one stubborn patch left. Is this coffee ready yet?'

Archer turned back to the coffee machine. 'Yeah, you go sit down and I'll bring it over.'

Emma sat down at the kitchen table. She propped her elbows on the table top and put her chin in her hands. All of a sudden, she felt exhausted. It was as though she hadn't had a sleep in days.

Archer put the coffee mugs on the table and sat down opposite Emma.

'What the hell are you doing here so early, anyway?' she said.

'I had to meet up with your friend and mine Joe Coffin, and for some reason he wanted to meet at some ungodly hour on the canal, all so he could tell me our special relationship is now over. Why he couldn't have broken up with me over the phone like all my other girlfriends, I don't know.'

'And so you thought you would come round here and wake us up?'

'Us?'

'Me and Louisa.'

'You sure that's who you meant?'

'Oh for fuck's sake, will you just leave it alone?'

'You're like a little child, Emma, I know you're lying.'

Emma took a sip of her coffee. It was hot.

'Anyway, afterwards I followed him along the towpath and saw him meet up with that weird girlfriend of his.'

'Leola?'

'That's the one. You know much about her?'

Emma shrugged. 'Not really. I met her a couple of times. You know she's a vampire, don't you?'

'Yeah.' Archer drank some coffee, put the mug back down. 'But she's in control of her blood sucking impulses, right? Remind me how that works again.'

'I don't really know. She's big on religion, seems to think she can control herself through the power of Jesus Christ. And she's covered in tattoos, which I think have something to do with it too. Whatever it is, it works because I've seen her wandering around in broad daylight and it has no effect on her at all.'

'Maybe your mother's right after all and we should all go back to church and repent of our sins.'

'No, I think I'd rather not.'

'Thing is, we've been doing some checking up on her and found out she runs some kind of business in the USA organising sex parties. Can you believe it?'

'There's not much at all that would surprise me about that woman,' Emma said.

'Anyway, she's been over here in the UK long enough that she is now considered an illegal immigrant and we should be deporting her.'

'But you're not?'

'Not yet, no. I think I'd like to talk to her first, find out more about the vampires. But now that Coffin's flounced off in a huff for some reason, I don't know how we can get to her.'

Emma took another sip of her coffee. Still too hot for her liking. 'I should imagine she's living at Angellicit with Joe.' The small pang of jealousy she felt inside her stomach at saying those words took Emma by surprise. She took another sip of her coffee, even though it was still too hot.

'I know, but there's no way Coffin's letting me in there,' Archer said. 'I don't suppose there's any way you could get in there and talk to her, is there, maybe arrange a meet?'

'No, afraid not,' Emma said. 'Joe's cut off all contact with me, I haven't seen him since that morning at Angellicit.'

Archer grimaced. 'Thing is, we still know fuck all about these monsters. Some people from the CIDE tried taking one of the vampires we've still got in the mortuary, but nobody could figure out how to get in there and back out again without losing a couple of pints of blood.'

'What's CIDE?'

'The Centre for Infectious Diseases and fuck knows what the E stands for. A bunch of these professor types came up from London to take a look.' Archer rubbed his hand through his tousled hair and Emma couldn't help but wonder if he was looking after himself. 'I swear to God one of them looked no older than twelve.'

'That's you, that is, growing old.'

'Tell me about it.'

'You look tired, are you getting enough sleep?'

'Yeah, yeah. I'll look a lot better once I've had another of these,' he said, and held the coffee mug up.

'I'll make another one,' Emma said, getting up. 'Where are you staying at the moment?'

'With Amrit and his family,' Archer said. 'They've got a granny annexe at the back of the house, fully self-contained, bathroom, kitchen, everything except the granny.'

'You could always come back here, you know,' Emma said.

Archer twisted in his chair to face Emma at the kitchen counter, pouring ground coffee into the machine. 'Seriously?'

'No, I meant… I meant I could move out and you could have the house back.'

Archer turned to face the table again. 'No, I hate the thought of Lou homeless.'

'She wouldn't be homeless, I'd find somewhere.'

'You know what I mean,' Archer said. 'It doesn't sit right with me that she be anywhere else but here. This is her home.'

'Okay,' Emma said, switching the machine on.

'The thing is,' Archer said. 'The thing is, I don't see why I can't move back in anyway. Doesn't mean to say that we're getting back together again, but can't we share the same house for a while at least? It's big enough.'

Emma stood behind Archer and placed her hands on his shoulders. 'No, it's not big enough. Not for us two. You move back in here and we'd be at each other's throats before the day was out.'

Archer was twisting his empty coffee mug around and around in his hands. 'Yeah, I suppose you're right.'

'Hey, did you find out who was—'

Emma felt Archer's shoulders stiffen at the sound of Mitch's voice.

'Oh, fuck,' she said, and closed her eyes.

Mitch had entered the kitchen wearing nothing but his boxer shorts and showing off his lean physique. He had a tattoo on his right bicep, his unit number and logo inked in black.

Archer stood up suddenly, knocking the back of the chair into Emma's midriff.

'Bloody hell, Emma, I'd started believing you when you said "Dum Dum" Dugan wasn't here.'

'Hey, did he just call me dumb?' Mitch said.

'Ignore him,' Emma said, rubbing at her stomach where the chair had hit her. 'He's just trying to be funny.'

'Funny?' Archer shouted, wheeling on Emma. 'You think this is funny? All this time we've been sat down here and you've been lying to me, you think I find this funny?'

'God, no, of course not,' Emma said. 'I wish I hadn't lied to you, I don't know what came over me, the lie just sort of popped out and then I couldn't take it back.'

'Is he in our bed?' Archer screamed, pointing at Mitch. 'Is he?'

'Look, why don't we all just calm down?' Mitch said.

'I'll calm down when you've put some fucking clothes on and pissed off out of my house,' Archer said.

Emma saw Mitch's muscles tensing, saw him take a step forward, his hands curling into fists by his side.

'Go back upstairs, get dressed,' she said.

'Are you being serious?' Mitch said and pointed at Archer. 'You're taking his side over mine?'

Emma rolled her eyes. 'Oh God, I'm not taking anybody's side. But dealing with one sulky little boy at a time is about my limit, so why don't you go upstairs and get dressed and I'll talk to you later? Okay?'

Mitch and Archer eyeballed each other for a few seconds longer. Mitch broke eye contact first and turned and left the room.

'Dickhead,' Archer muttered.

'For fuck's sake Nick, will you just grow up please?' Emma said.

'I don't want him in this house,' Archer said.

'All right, all right, I won't have him around again, I promise,' Emma said. 'As soon as he's gone today, that's it. But Nick, you can't stop me seeing him, okay?'

'How long have you known him, Emma?' Archer said. 'Did the two of you have something going on before?'

Emma let her head fall back and said, 'Oh God! Of course not. Don't be such an idiot.'

The coffee machine hissed as it finished spitting coffee into the mugs.

'It's just, you got together with him pretty quick after we split, you've got to admit that,' Archer said.

'I know, I know,' Emma said. 'We were encouraged by our counsellors to meet up and talk through what happened at Angellicit. It just kind of happened from there, really.'

Archer sighed, rubbed his hands through his hair. 'Bloody hell, Emma, what a fucking mess.'

'You, me, or the situation in general?' Emma said, trying for a smile to lighten the atmosphere a little.

'You know what I mean,' Archer said, turning away and heading for the door. 'Make sure lover boy is out of here this morning.'

'Yes Sir, Detective Inspector Archer,' Emma muttered as he slammed the door shut on his way out.

THERE IS NO KEY

Chitrita had spent the day watching television. The little girl, Tilly was her name, had switched the television on for her and showed her how to operate the remote to change the channels. At first, when the huge, dark, glassy window on the wall had bloomed into bright, noisy life, Chitrita had cowered against the opposite side of the room, hissing and spitting. She had almost leapt on the girl right then and ripped her apart, believing that this was a trick. But Chitrita soon calmed down as she realised the television was a window into other worlds and nothing more.

The window calmed the little girl down, especially the noisy, colourful drawings that moved and spoke. She had been crying, her skinny little chest hitching up and down with loud sobs. The window on the wall seemed to hypnotise her.

Chitrita soon grew bored with the cartoons and flicked through the channels. There was so much to see and hear, so much noise and sex and violence on the other side of this window. Was this what the world had become now?

Chitrita thought it was wonderful.

She lay on the sofa and laughed at the news reports of death and destruction, and then she switched channels and masturbated whilst watching music videos.

She watched TV all day, mimicking what she heard, learning to talk again.

Chitrita kept the curtains closed. Not just to block out the daylight, but to stay hidden too. Tilly's parents lay on the living room floor leaking blood into the carpet. Sometimes Chitrita got down on the floor beside them and licked some more blood off them, but really, their blood was growing sticky and tasteless now. She'd had her fill earlier, drinking until she thought she might throw up. But as the day drifted into evening, she grew hungrier again.

Chitrita had taken off her ruined and ancient wedding dress and explored the house. She found the bathroom and showered. Afterwards, she moved into the bedroom and sat naked on the bed whilst she explored the perfumes and makeup and nail varnishes. She put on lipstick and eyeshadow and puffed clouds of talcum powder over her face and chest, giggling at the feel of it.

She rifled through the dresses in the walk-in wardrobe, throwing them aside until she found one that she liked. She slipped it over her head and smoothed it down against her flesh. The ivory dress hugged her figure, the neckline plunging to reveal the space between her breasts. Her arms were bare, and the dress revealed her legs and thighs.

It was perfect.

Downstairs, Chitrita found Tilly lying on the floor with her mother. The woman had been dead for some hours now. Tilly was stroking her hair and crying softly.

Chitrita knelt down and opened up Tilly's throat with one smooth swipe of her fingernails.

She leaned closer and caught the pulsing stream of arterial blood in her mouth. It ran down her chin and neck and over her new dress.

When she had finished feeding, she stood and stretched and ran her fingers through her hair.

It was night time once more.

Chitrita heard a scratching at the windows. Dark shapes hovered outside, bumping up against the glass window pane.

Bats.

Chitrita had seen them early that morning, while it was still dark enough for her to be outside. She had seen them hovering over that silly little girl, Leola, as she talked to that man.

Joe Coffin.

It had amused Chitrita to see the bats attack Leola. Chitrita hadn't even wished for it, and yet the bats seemed to know what she wanted.

And now they were here again. Waiting for her.

The others, the other vampires, they were waiting for her too. Calling to her. She could hear them as though they were in the room with her.

And because of the window in the wall, she knew exactly where they were.

DS AMRIT CHOUDHRY wasn't a happy man.

There were several reasons for this. And most of them seemed to be related to Nick Archer.

Choudhry had known it would be a bad idea to offer Archer the granny flat while he got himself sorted out with new accommodation. Either that or got back together with Emma. But he had offered it to him anyway, and now he was finding out what a bad idea it really had been.

It wasn't just that Choudhry was now the butt of jokes from his colleagues, or that Archer was on at him even more than before about work and progress on shifting the vampires out of the mortuary and off their hands.

No, the worst part of it all was how his wife, Parvin, was dealing with having Archer living with them.

She hated the man.

Hated him with a passion.

But then Parvin was a passionate woman, and it didn't take

much to provoke her. Choudhry was often at the wrong end of her sharp tongue and most of the time he had no idea what he had done, or not done, to deserve the verbal whipping. But then most of the time her anger faded away quickly and the slight, whatever it might have been, was forgotten.

Not with Archer, though.

Whatever he had done or said, or not done or not said, Parvin was now holding a grudge.

Which would have been all right if Parvin was directing all her anger and righteous fury at Archer. He was a grown man, he could look after himself. But no, with Archer, Parvin was sweetness and light. She fawned over him like a long-lost relative, a member of royalty even. And then as soon as he was out of the room her mask slipped and she began hissing and spitting curses at Choudhry for bringing that man into their house and family, and when was that mouse of a husband of hers going to man up and tell Archer to pack up and leave?

Choudhry stretched, wincing at a crack in his spine. Seemed his aches and pains were growing more frequent with every passing day. Was that simply because he was getting older? Maybe he should buy himself a gym membership. All this sitting down at a desk wasn't doing him any good. That's what police work mostly seemed to involve these days, sitting in front of a computer and exercising nothing but his fingers.

Choudhry nudged the mouse and woke up the monitor.

The new health and safety policy he was supposed to be reviewing reappeared on the screen. Pages and pages of turgid information. No wonder he had drifted off.

'Hey, what was that?' Lewis said from the pod next to him.

'What was what?' Choudhry said. He hated working within the confines of these three panels, even if looking out of them meant all he had to do was stand up.

'That,' Lewis said, as something brushed past Choudhry's head.

Choudhry looked up, instinctively swiping at his head as though getting rid of a spider. He dropped his hand by his side as he looked up, not quite able to believe what he was seeing.

'Is that a bat?' he said.

Another bat joined the one already fluttering just beneath the ceiling. They dived and swerved around each other, almost as though they were putting on a display.

'How the hell did they get in here?' someone said, as more officers drew near to look at the unexpected addition of wildlife to the station.

'Oh shit!' Lewis shouted.

Choudhry stood up, forgetting the bats, forgetting the health and safety policy and his aches and pains.

Forgetting Parvin and her irrational hatred of Nick Archer.

A woman in a tight, figure hugging white dress was striding through the operations room. Her hair was wild and her face a mask of white, apart from dark shadows around her eyes, her scarlet lips, and the red blood splattered down her chin and neck and over the dress. Police officers were scattering before her advance, whilst others followed her at a distance.

'She's one of them!' someone shouted, Choudhry wasn't sure who.

'Somebody call the Armed Response Vehicle!' Choudhry yelled.

The woman, the vampire, passed the cubicles and the desks, staring straight ahead as more bats flooded into the police station behind her.

It seemed as though she knew exactly where she was going.

And Choudhry thought he knew too.

'She's going for the others,' he muttered. And then, louder, 'She's going to set the other vampires free!'

Hamilton stepped in her way, shirt sleeves rolled up as though he was about to engage in a round of old fashioned fisticuffs. He hadn't been downstairs, where they kept the vampires. He hadn't seen them, seen what they were like.

Hadn't seen how utterly vicious and wild they could be.

'Hamilton, out of the way!' Choudhry yelled.

The vampire lashed out at Hamilton. He lifted his hands in defence and the vampire gouged a series of jagged lines in his bare forearms.

Hamilton cried out in pain as the blood began welling from the ragged slashes and dripping on the floor. He staggered, instinctively pulled his arms out of harm's way, and opened himself up for another attack.

The vampire swiped at him with her claws and ripped the left side of his face away. Hamilton screamed and collapsed.

The vampire stepped over him and continued on her way.

Choudhry followed at a safe distance. He wasn't sure why, or what he intended to do. They needed to wait for the Armed Response Vehicle to arrive, but even then, Choudhry wasn't sure they would be of much use. The vampires in the mortuary had been tazered and tranquilised, with no effect at all. Choudhry doubted guns would make much difference either.

The vampire hissed at a female officer approaching her.

'Kirstin, stay back,' Choudhry said. 'You saw what happened to Hamilton.'

Kirstin glanced at Choudhry and back at the vampire. She was new, transferred from Stafford a couple of weeks ago. Still trying to find her place in the male-dominated hierarchy of the Birmingham station. Hair scraped back in a bun, severe, angular face, obviously kept in shape and took no shit off anybody.

'We can't let her set the others free,' she said.

'Do you want your face taking off too?' Choudhry said.

A small group had gathered around Hamilton. Choudhry wondered if they were trying to put his face back on. He had seen the long flap of skin hanging from Hamilton's skull, exposing the red, glistening flesh beneath. He pushed the thought away.

'The mortuary's locked up,' Choudhry said. 'There's no way she can get in there.'

The vampire was moving on, twisting and turning, teeth bared at anyone who drew too close.

She started down the steps toward the mortuary, head twisted around, keeping her attention focused on the threat behind her.

Choudhry didn't think they were much of a threat at all.

'We need help,' Kirstin said, walking beside Choudhry as they followed the vampire at a respectable distance.

'The ARV is on its way,' Choudhry said. 'Not that I think they will do much good.'

The vampire was at the bottom of the steps now, glancing in both directions as if unsure which way to go. She turned right, headed down the brightly lit corridor. A dark cloud of bats followed her.

Choudhry and Kirstin walked down the steps, taking each one slowly and deliberately. Behind them was a crowd of uniformed officers and admin staff. Seemed like the entire station was following them.

'You really believe in this vampire stuff?' Kirstin said.

'You haven't been down to the mortuary yet, have you?' Choudhry said.

They had reached the bottom of the stairs now. The vampire was almost at the other end of the corridor. One more corner and she would be facing the mortuary door.

'Haven't been allowed,' Kirstin whispered.

'That's a shame, you'd believe in vampires all right if you had been.'

The vampire disappeared around the corner.

'I thought they couldn't come out in the light?' Kirstin whispered as they began slowly walking down the corridor.

'That's sunlight, not indoor lighting,' Choudhry said. 'And in case you hadn't noticed, it's dark outside now.'

They both slowed as they reached the turning in the corridor. Choudhry looked back at the others following.

'Give us space!' he hissed. 'If we need to run, I don't want you lot in my way.'

'What are you going to do?' Peterson said. He was a constable, tall and gangly, with a bad case of acne scarring on his cheeks.

'You got some cuffs on you?' Choudhry said.

'Yeah.' Peterson handed his handcuffs over. 'You going to try and cuff her?'

'Maybe,' Choudhry said.

'She'll shred you to pieces,' Kirstin said.

'Yeah, thanks for that piece of advice,' Choudhry said.

They had both reached the turning in the corridor. They hung back, reluctant to make themselves visible. Choudhry heard a soft moaning and a knocking.

'What's she doing?' Kirstin whispered.

'How the hell should I know?' Choudhry said. 'Why don't you go down there and ask her yourself?'

Kirstin glared at Choudhry and then quickly stepped out from behind the wall. She stared down the corridor for a moment and then beckoned to Choudhry to join her. Taking a deep breath, he stepped up beside her.

The vampire had her back to them. She was pressed up against the door to the mortuary, the palms of her hands flat against it. She was smearing blood over the gunship grey metal in red streaks. Just beside her on the wall was the keypad that unlocked the door.

'Is she bleeding?' Kirstin whispered.

Choudhry shook his head. 'I don't know.'

There was more knocking, becoming frantic and louder. Choudhry realised it was from the other side of the door. The vampires in the mortuary were gathering, trying to get out. As if they knew one of their own was here to set them free.

Choudhry looked at the cuffs he had taken from Peterson. Now was the moment to use them, while the vampire was distracted, her back to them. But he had seen the other vampires in the mortuary, seen what they did to Johnson when that girl Julie Carter escaped. A wave of cold flushed through his chest and stomach.

Maybe it would be better to concentrate on evacuating the building, getting everyone safe and then waiting for the ARV to turn up. Let them deal with it.

The vampire twisted around to face them, her face contorted in a snarl. Choudhry heard movement behind him as everyone moved back a step.

'The key,' the vampire said. 'Where is the key?'

To Choudhry, her voice sounded like stones being rattled around in a clay pot.

'Everyone back up,' he said. 'But do it slowly, keep your eyes on her.'

They had been stupid, all of them. They should have got out. Instead, they had followed the vampire like a bunch of children following Mickey Mouse at Disneyland.

'Open the door,' the vampire said, advancing upon them.

Choudhry heard gasps and movement. People were getting out of the way, running back up the stairs. He didn't blame them. Kirstin stayed by his side.

'We can't let you do that,' Choudhry said.

'You will do as I tell you,' the vampire replied.

Now she was a little closer, Choudhry could see her face was covered in talcum powder, and heavy, clumsily applied makeup. Her tongue flicked out, and she licked her rouged lips. Choudhry caught a flash of teeth, the incisors pointed and unnaturally long.

She walked closer, her eyes flitting from Choudhry to Kirstin and back again.

'Let's back up,' Choudhry said quietly. 'But keep your eyes on her.'

Choudhry had barely finished his sentence before the vampire leapt at them. She seemed to fly down the corridor, her mouth twisted in a snarl. As Choudhry and Kirstin both turned to run, they smacked into each other, their legs getting entangled, and they both fell over.

The vampire was on top of them before they could move.

Kirstin kicked out, screaming in the vampire's face.

The moaning and the cries from behind the mortuary door grew in volume, along with the insistent pounding on the door.

The vampire picked Kirstin up and threw her away as though she weighed nothing. Choudhry was vaguely aware of hearing her cry out as she tumbled along the floor and smacked into a wall. The vampire was on top of him, her twisted face close to his. He could smell blood and death on her, could see flecks of flesh in the gaps in her teeth. Her pink, pointed tongue flicked out and caressed his cheek.

'The key,' she whispered.

Choudhry twisted his face away. Where the hell was that ARV?

'There is no key,' he said through gritted teeth.

The vampire leaned closer. Her teeth brushed his throat, the incisors nicking the flesh.

The mortuary door crashed open. The vampire snapped her head up and Choudhry saw, through a cloud of fluttering wings and dark bodies, the other vampires flooding from the mortuary. He caught a glimpse of his colleague Malcolm Crouch, his emaciated frame barely covered in tattered, ripped clothing.

Choudhry snapped his eyes shut and for the first time in many years, he prayed to Allah for help. Feet kicked and pounded him as the vampires ran over him. A wave of cold swept across him along with the stink of their flesh.

Choudhry thought he might die, but within a few seconds it was over and he could hear the vampires scrambling up the stairs, could hear the screams of his colleagues and the scattered shouts of warnings to get out of the vampires' way.

Eyes still screwed tight closed, Choudhry screamed when he felt hands gripping and pulling at him.

'It's me, it's me Kirstin!'

Choudhry snapped his eyes open. Kirstin looked like she had been slapped across the left side of her face where an angry bruise had blossomed, the swelling closing her eye.

The vampires had gone. So had the bats.

'Oh shit,' he gasped. 'I thought I was dead.'

Kirstin sank to the floor, her back against a wall. She was shaking.

'What happened?' Choudhry said. 'How the hell did they get out?'

'It was me,' Kirstin said. 'I let them out.'

'You did what?'

'She was going to kill you. I had to do something.'

Choudhry closed his eyes again.

'I did the right thing, didn't I?' Kirstin said. 'What else could I have done? She was going to rip you apart. But when I saw them, when they came out…'

'I know, I know,' Choudhry said.

'I never realised.'

Shouts from upstairs.

The ARV had arrived.

'It's all right,' Choudhry said. 'It's over now.'

'But it isn't,' Kirstin said. 'It isn't over at all. It's just starting again.'

A COOL TWO MILLION

A man dressed up as a woman tottered across the stage on high heeled, thigh length boots. Tight leather mini skirt, gold lame crop top revealing a defiantly masculine, hairy stomach, blond fright wig and the most appalling makeup Gilligan had ever seen. He/she looked more like something out of a zombie movie than a nightclub act.

Gilligan and Shaw were sitting at the back of the club. They watched Duchess Swallows totter off the stage to some half-hearted applause and boos.

'What the hell was that?' Gilligan said.

'Fuck knows,' Shaw said.

Gilligan took a pull on his pint of Guinness and grimaced. 'Bloody hell, but this is shite, this is.'

'I suppose you're going to start banging on about how Guinness is better in Ireland now, aren't you?' Shaw said.

'Aye, I might do that and all,' Gilligan said. 'And it's the truth, it surely is, that the transportation over here doesn't do it any good. But this here pint in my hand, it surely has to be the most shocking pint of Guinness I've had in my entire life.'

'Not sure I believe it myself,' Shaw said.

Gilligan leaned in closer to Shaw. 'The thing is, this pint has probably been sat in the tap all day. You go to Ireland and the black stuff never stops flowing, it doesn't, so you're always guaranteed a fresh pint, that you are.'

Shaw laughed. 'Bloody hell, Gerry, you're sounding more Oirish by the minute.'

'Well, you can just fuck off now, can't you? Here I am trying to educate you in the truth of the matter, and all you want to do is make fun of my Irishness. You do know, don't you, that you're being politically incorrect, which is another way of saying you're a racist twat.'

Shaw laughed. 'As if you give a shit.'

'Now then, Shaw, we could have a little chat about that later if you like,' Gilligan said.

'Seriously?'

Gilligan placed his pint carefully on the table and gazed at Shaw. 'That's right, we could and all. Along with why you and your girlfriends decided to back out of our deal.'

Shaw picked up his pint, a cheap lager, and watched the bubbles clinging to the inside of the glass. Occasionally, one would detach and rise to the top. 'Fuck you, Gilligan. You know what happened. You know we didn't back out. Things changed, that's all.'

'Aye, well, shit happens, as they say. But it's been six months since Joe took over, and what the fuck has he done since then? We've got the protection rackets going on, and the clubs and the gambling and fuck knows what else. But we're losing out on the big money, that we are. Mort's gone, but seriously, what the fuck else has changed since we agreed to take both Mort and Coffin down?'

Shaw leaned forward to speak, but Gilligan cut him off. 'On top of that, Joe's even cosying up to the filth,' he hissed. 'Fucking Mort's got to be turning in his grave!'

'Nobody would argue with you there, but there's more going on that you don't know about.'

Gilligan sat back in his chair, silent for a moment. 'Is that right? More going on, is there? You want to tell me about that, then?'

Shaw glanced at the stage. It was still empty. Customers milling around, chatting, going to the bar to get drinks.

Shaw lowered his voice. 'Coffin had Robbie in a couple of weeks back to—'

'Who the fuck's Robbie?' Gilligan said, picking up his pint of Guinness.

'If you'd just shut up and listen, I'll tell you,' Shaw hissed. 'Robbie's the Mob accountant. He came in for a meet with Joe. Joe says that Mort left a shitload of debt behind him. He's been borrowing money left, right and centre to keep the Mob afloat, and it's looking like now's the time to pay up.'

'Are you serious?' Gilligan said, putting his pint glass back down. He hadn't taken a drink from it.

'Of course I'm serious,' Shaw said. 'The Slaughterhouse Mob is up to its eyeballs in debt and if we take Coffin out, then we're fucking responsible for paying it back.'

'What a shitting mess,' Gilligan said. 'And you didn't think to tell me about this before now?'

Shaw put his pint down on the wet beer mat. Turned it round and round on the spot. 'I thought about it, yeah, but me and the others, we've been talking—'

'Without me, is that right?'

Shaw stopped twisting the pint glass around. 'Yeah, without you. The Stig, he thinks you're a loose cannon, that you're dangerous. And Stut agrees with him.'

'Ah, they do now, do they? And what about you, Shaw? What do you think?'

Shaw started twisting the pint glass around and around again. 'Fucking hell, Gerry. That kid, Shocker's lad, I can't stop thinking about him, I can't get his face out of my head. But you, I don't know, you're a cold bastard sometimes. Seems to me you shot that poor kid and whether or not you meant to, whether or not it was an accident or you would have shot him anyway, seems to me you're not bothered. Like you don't really give a shit.'

'You've killed before, Shaw, and there's no doubt you'll do it again. What's different about this one?'

Shaw leaned forward, in Gilligan's face. 'Fucking hell, Gerry, he was fucking ten years old! I've got a lad of my own his age. Doesn't that get to you at all? Not one fucking bit?'

'We live, we die, it's all the same really,' Gilligan said.

Shaw leaned back again. 'It's not the same, Gerry. The big bastard had it coming, yeah, but that kid? Fuck.'

'All right, so I shouldn't have shot the kid, but it was an accident,' Gilligan said. 'We were all running on adrenaline and when that lad walked out of the bedroom, we all turned around and any one of us could have shot him. But it was me, I was the first one to pull the trigger. The thing is, I don't see what the fuck that has got to do with Coffin. The big bastard hasn't got a clue, and he's slowly grinding the Mob down. We need to go back to the plan we had originally, and take Coffin out.'

The crowd began whooping and cheering and clapping.

'Looks like he's coming on at last,' Shaw said.

'About fucking time,' Gilligan said. 'But this conversation isn't finished, my friend. Not by a long way.'

Jim Gosling ambled on to the stage and slowly approached the microphone. His forehead and upper lip were already shiny with sweat. His eyes darted around the room, scanning his audience. He took hold of his trousers and hitched them up under his massive belly. Gilligan had seen some fat people in his time, but this man was massive.

'Sorry about that,' Gosling said, 'but I've just been and pebble dashed the porcelain, like.'

A ripple of laughter from the audience.

'Did you know, we have more slang for going to the toilet than anything else? Laying a brownie, choking a darkie, cutting a monkey tail, working the turd saw.' He sighed. 'Fucking hell, who thinks all these things up? Haven't they got anything better to do with their lives? Faxing a shit, there's another one.'

More laughter.

'We've got slang for everything, haven't we?' Gosling said. 'Punching the munchkin, what do you think that one's about?'

'Having a wank!' someone shouted.

Gosling grinned and pointed into the audience. 'Look at you, eh? You're obviously an expert on wanking, aren't you? A right wanker, that's what you are.'

Shaw leaned in close to Gilligan. 'Where's Joe? He's going to miss the act.'

'He's not going to miss much, is he?' Gilligan said.

Gosling wiped his face with a small towel. 'You've got to laugh, haven't you? Take my dad, for example. I was dead proud of my dad, I was. Medical man, he was, the only one in the family to really make something of himself. That is, until he got struck off the medical register for having sex with his patients.'

Quiet, scattered laughter and applause. *They all know that wasn't the punchline*, Shaw thought.

'It's a shame, because he were a fucking good vet.'

The club erupted, people laughing and clapping, looking at each other like they'd just heard the funniest joke in the world.

Shaw glanced around the club. 'Bloody hell, Gerry, I think every hard man of Birmingham is in this club right now.'

'You think there's something else happening here, do you?'

'I dunno,' Shaw muttered.

'They're all laughing very hard at Gosling's jokes,' Gilligan said.

Except now they weren't. Silence had fallen over the club.

'Am I boring you two gentlemen?' Gosling said, his amplified voice accompanied by a slight feedback.

'Oh, shit,' Shaw muttered.

Gosling was standing there on stage, a pint in one hand, the microphone in the other. He had moved away from the mic stand, walked across the stage so that he was a little closer to the two men.

'Now, Shaw, I recognise you, you're one of the Slaughterhouse Mob, aren't you? And I hear Joe Coffin's in charge, now that your beloved leader Mortimer Craggs has slipped off this mortal coil.'

'Yeah, that's right,' Shaw said. One of the spotlights trained on the stage had been turned around and angled on Shaw and Gilligan. Shaw felt exposed, like all his clothes had been stripped off him and he was being examined.

'But your friend now, no, I don't know him,' Gosling said.

'Gerry Gilligan,' said Gilligan.

Gosling chuckled. 'Ah, we have an Oirishman in the Punchline tonight, ladies and gentlemen.' Gosling took a deep pull on his pint while he let his audience think about that for a moment. He wiped his mouth with the back of his hand and said, 'Did you hear about the Irish attempt on Mount Everest? They ran out of scaffolding.'

Scattered laughter, faces turned towards Gilligan and Shaw.

'Paddy got arrested in B&Q for punching an African woman in the face. Says it wasn't his fault as his father had told him to go and get a Black and Decker.'

More laughter at this joke and some applause. Gosling looked like he was enjoying himself. He took another swallow of his beer.

'You've got to laugh, haven't you?' he said. 'Paddy was in the delivery room when the midwife hands him a black baby. "Is this yours?" she says. "Probably," says Paddy, "she burns everything else!"'

Shaw glanced at Gilligan. He was staring at Gosling, his mouth clamped shut. There was a muscle twitching along the side of his jaw.

Lots more laughter, the men at the surrounding tables straining to look at Shaw and Gilligan. Teeth bared in grins, eyes alive with mischief.

Shaw had a flashback, like he was back in Angellicit and surrounded by vampires. Harry Frazer and the Noonan twins, Danny 'The Butcher' Hanrahan, and the others, their faces falling apart, teeth grown long and sharp. All of them grinning at him, licking their lips, waiting to pounce.

Shaw had to concentrate on not standing up and dashing for the exit.

He had to work at not letting out that scream building inside his chest.

———

THE MAN on the door was big, but not as big as Coffin. He waved Coffin through, looking like he was trying to appear nonchalant, as though he didn't give a shit that Joe Coffin had just turned up. Behind Coffin, through the doorway and outside, in the amphitheatre style shopping and leisure complex, a crowd had gathered.

'You bring your fan club with you?' the man on the door said.

Coffin turned and looked at the faces turned up to him. They all shifted back a little.

'Looks like it,' Coffin said.

'What's it like, being a celebrity?'

'It's a bloody nightmare,' Coffin said. 'Can't go anywhere without being stared at. Even got asked for my autograph the other day.'

'What did you say?'

'I told him to get lost.'

'Did he?'

'Yeah, he went running back to his mates, big stupid grin on his face like me telling him to get lost was the best thing ever happened to him.' Coffin looked up the stairs leading into the club. The walls were painted purple. Posters were stuck to the walls, all showing off Jim Gosling and advertising future dates.

'Nobody else play here except that fat bastard?' Coffin said.

The bouncer hesitated a moment, as though unsure how to answer. 'I dunno man, I just work the door.'

'How's business?' Coffin said.

'S'all right,' the bouncer said. 'Got just the one type that comes here, though, y'know.'

'No, I don't know. Tell me.'

The man shifted slightly, looking uncomfortable, like he wished he hadn't said anything.

'You can talk to me,' Coffin said. 'I won't say anything.'

'It's just like, hard men, y'know? Hard men and their wives, or their girlfriends. I've worked the door in loads of places and everywhere has its own type of people who come to it, but still there's, like, a bit of variety in them, you know what I'm saying? But here it's just the one type and nobody else.'

'Hard men,' Coffin said.

'Yeah, and their girlfriends.'

'You ever hear of him before, Jim Gosling?'

'Nah, he's a new one to me. One of the lads said he was down London before this, working the clubs down there, but I never heard of him.'

Coffin looked at the posters again. 'Seems a strange type of club that just employs the one act over and over.'

'You coming in or what, girl?' the bouncer said.

Coffin turned to see a young woman standing behind him. Petite little thing, dwarfed by the two men. She was holding a mobile phone.

'You're Joe Coffin, aren't you?' she said, looking up at Coffin and biting her bottom lip shyly.

Coffin grunted.

'Can I have my picture taken with you?' she said, eyes wide and round like a baby deer's.

'No,' Coffin said, and turned his back on her.

He took the stairs two at a time. Turned left at the top, through a set of double doors and down a short corridor. No posters on the walls here. He could hear laughter now. Through another set of double doors and he was into the club. The lights were low apart from the stage, which was illuminated, and one table which had a spotlight trained upon it. Jim Gosling was standing on the stage, holding a microphone in one hand and a half-finished pint of beer in the other.

The laughter died as everyone turned in their seats to see what Gosling was staring at.

'Bloody hell, it's Joe Coffin,' Gosling said.

Coffin hesitated. This wasn't what he had expected, to be the centre of attention.

Gosling lifted his pint glass to his lips and drained it of the remaining beer. He held the empty glass out and a small person hurried onto the stage and took it from him. Coffin thought it was a child at first. But no, it was a man, a dwarf.

The dwarf hurried off, disappearing to the side of the stage.

Gosling wiped his mouth with the back of his hand.

'We're going to take a little interlude, folks,' Gosling said. 'Me and Joe have got a few things to talk about. Go and get yourself a drink at the bar, the first one's on the house.'

Like a herd of sheep, much of the audience obeyed, climbing to their feet and heading for the bar. Coffin stepped out of the way as they filed past, casting hostile glances at him.

Gilligan and Shaw remained seated at their table as Gosling climbed down off the stage. The fat man walked over to their table.

'Come and join us, Joe,' he said.

'What the hell's going on?' Coffin said.

'Come and sit down, Joe, and we can talk about that,' Gosling said.

Coffin walked over to the table and sat down. Looked at Shaw and Gilligan. They looked just as puzzled as Coffin felt.

Gosling sat down, the chair creaking under his weight.

'I wondered if you might come on over and check me out tonight,' Gosling said. 'Especially when I saw Shaw and his Oirish friend sitting here.'

'I didn't appreciate your comedy tonight,' Gilligan said. 'A little old fashioned, and well past its sell by date.'

'What can I tell you? I like the old jokes the best,' Gosling said.

The dwarf approached the table carrying a tray of drinks. Beers for everyone except Coffin. The dwarf handed him a whisky.

Sitting down, Coffin was still a couple of inches taller than the dwarf, who was dressed in a black suit and bow tie, and a white shirt.

'This is Stilts,' Gosling said.

'Stilts?' Coffin said, looking at Gosling.

'Yeah, that's his nickname on account of how tall he is,' Gosling said, and wheezed with laughter.

Stilts placed the rest of the drinks on the table and turned and walked away.

'He doesn't say much,' Gosling said. 'In fact, he doesn't say anything at all. He's a mute.'

Coffin watched Stilts as he walked to the bar, pushing his way through the crowd of punters, and then disappeared behind it. A moment later, he reappeared at the top of the bar and started collecting empty glasses. Coffin guessed he had to be standing on a chair or a foot stool. A young woman in a pair of blue denim dungarees was pulling pints for the customers.

'He's got everything he needs to talk with,' Gosling was saying. 'He just chooses not to speak. That's what the doctors say, anyway. They've got a name for it…'

'Elective mute,' Shaw said.

'That's right,' Gosling said. 'Elective mute. Fucking hell, they've got a name for everything nowadays, haven't they? Next thing you know, they'll be saying laziness is a disease and giving it some fancy arsed name.'

'I had a cousin who was an elective mute, until she was about six or seven,' Shaw said. 'Nobody ever found out why she wouldn't speak until then.'

Coffin picked up his glass, took a sip of the whisky. It was good. Smooth.

'How did you know what I drink?' he said.

'You just look like a whisky man to me, Joe,' Gosling said. 'It's a party trick of mine, my superhero power. I can look at a person and I can tell you what their favourite alcoholic beverage is, just by looking at them.'

Shaw held up his lager, condensation running down the side of the glass. 'He got mine right.'

Gilligan looked at his Guinness, still sitting on the table. 'The Guinness in this place is fucking awful. Fucking rancid.'

'Now that's a shame, that is,' Gosling said quietly.

Coffin shot a look at Gilligan and said, 'Cut the crap, will you? We didn't come here to argue about the Guinness.'

'What did you come here for, Joe?' Gosling said. 'To check me out, right?'

Coffin took another pull on the whisky. 'You open up a comedy club, but you're the only act. No one's ever heard of you before, but everyone knows you're a hard man and your nightly audience is thugs and enforcers and their girlfriends. Of course I'm going to check you out.'

Coffin glanced over at the bar. It was thick with customers.

'Think I'm moving in on your turf, is that right?' Gosling said. 'The Slaughterhouse Mob is the only outfit in town these days, and yet I hear you're in with the coppers right now. That's a strange situation isn't it?'

'You've seen the news, you know what's been going on.'

Gosling switched his attention to Shaw and said, 'How can you tell if a vampire has a cold?'

'I don't know,' Shaw said.

'He starts coffin!' Gosling laughed. 'Get it? Coffin?'

Shaw looked like he hadn't got a clue what was going on.

A high pitched voice cut across the empty club. 'I ay got a thing to weer, I ay!'

Coffin stood up, scraping the chair back along the floor, as he stared at the bizarre creature staggering onto the stage. Big hair, like nineteen-eighties era Dolly Parton, a huge, shocking yellow dress revealing hairy arms and legs, and feet in extremely high heeled stiletto shoes.

'Well fuck me sideways, weer the fucken hell is everyone?' His voice had dropped a couple of octaves now. He looked up from the half empty tables and at the crowded bar.

'We're having a break tonight, Duchess,' Gosling said. 'Come and join us, we've got company.'

Coffin watched as Duchess carefully navigated the steps leading down from the stage. The shoes looked impossible to walk on.

'Ooh, is tha' Joe Coffin I c'n see over theer?' The high falsetto was back.

'Sit down, Joe,' Gosling said. 'Relax, have your drink.'

Coffin sat down. Picked up his whisky glass.

'I cor wait ter say hallo ter Joe Coffin.' Duchess said, tottering towards them. The few customers still left sitting at the tables watched him, delighted grins on their faces.

Coffin drained the whisky glass. Thought about leaving.

He was aware of Duchess making a line straight for him at the last moment, just when it was too late. Duchess wrapped his arms around Coffin, enveloping him in the folds of the yellow dress, his big hair brushing over Coffin's face, and planted a big kiss on his cheek.

Coffin shot to his feet, shoving Duchess away. The chair toppled over and fell on its back with a sharp crack against the floor.

Duchess tottered on his high heels, arms pinwheeling, and let out a high-pitched shriek as he fell over.

'What the hell do you think you're doing?' Coffin snarled.

The crowd at the bar was laughing, enjoying the spectacle. Duchess lay on his back on the floor, knees bent and legs splayed, his wig sitting at an angle on his head. He was laughing too, his bright red lipstick smeared across his lips and cheek.

'Oh, I just cor 'elp meself. I 'ad ter gi' yer a smacker I did, yow lookin' soo 'andsome an' all,' Duchess said.

Shaw and Gilligan were both laughing, too.

'You've got lipstick on your cheek,' Gilligan said, pointing.

Coffin wiped at his cheek. His fingertips came away smeared with red. Made him think of blood. Of vampires.

He pointed at Duchess. 'Keep away from me.'

'Calm down, Joe,' Gosling said, still chuckling. 'Duchess doesn't mean anything by it.'

Coffin stayed on his feet. Watched Duchess as he stood up and adjusted his wig.

'What the hell are you up to, Gosling?' Coffin said.

Gosling held his hands out, palms up. 'Nothing, Joe. You're the one who came to check me out, remember? You're the one who sent your two goons here to take a look.'

Coffin kept his eyes on Duchess as he talked. 'Yeah, and you're the one who put a stop to the evening's entertainment as soon as I walked through the door.'

'True, I suppose. I thought you might want a little chat, that's all. It must be difficult for you to get 'me time' when you're a celebrity. Is that right, Joe? Is it difficult?'

Duchess was fixing his false eyelashes. Coffin couldn't take his eyes off him.

'Don't fuck with me,' Coffin said. 'All this crap about you

opening a comedy club, but you're the only act, the place filled with hard men. It's a setup, isn't it?'

Having fixed his eyelashes, Duchess fluttered them at Coffin and pouted. Coffin took a step towards to him and Duchess tottered away on his high heels, almost going over again.

'You're wound too tight, Joe, you need to relax,' Gosling said. 'Sit down, have another drink.'

Stilts was back at the table, handing out pints of beer off a tray. He had another whisky for Coffin. The girl was with him, but now she was up close, he could see she was older than he had thought. She looked like she tried to keep in shape, but the weight had started gathering on her hips and backside. She looked vaguely familiar to Coffin, in her denim dungarees and her spiky hair, until he realised she resembled the members of eighties girl pop group Bananarama.

To Gilligan and Shaw, Coffin said, 'Get up, we're leaving.'

'Already?' Gosling said. 'But we're just getting to know each other.'

'I know enough,' Coffin said.

'All right, Joe, don't be so hasty,' Gosling said. 'Sit down and I'll tell you what's going on.'

'Forget about it, I'm not interested.'

'What about a cool two million in cash?' Gosling said. 'Would that interest you?'

Coffin hesitated.

'Yeah, I thought so,' Gosling said, and grinned.

'You're bad news, Gosling,' Coffin said. 'I get involved with you and it'd be like giving you an invite to fuck me over and then some. I told you, I'm not interested.'

Coffin left, pushing his way past hard men carrying pints of beer back to their tables, Shaw and Gilligan scrambling to catch up with him.

THAT HORSE-FACED BITCH

Emma's insides tightened at the sight of the Metropole Tower, home to the *Birmingham Herald*. It had been Barry's suggestion that they meet here. Emma had wanted to tell him no, let's meet somewhere else, somewhere I don't have to face old ghosts. But she couldn't get the words out, and then he had said his goodbyes and rung off.

So here she was, standing in the lobby, concentrating on steadying her breathing. Listening to the pulse thud in her ears and feeling the warmth of the morning sunlight on her back still as it streamed through the wall of window panes on the Metropole Tower's front.

'Can I help you?' the man at the desk said.

'No, thank you,' Emma said. 'I know where I'm going.'

If only that were true, she thought.

She punched the button to call the lift. Standing facing the metal doors, she could feel the man's gaze on her. As though he was checking her out.

You're being paranoid, she thought. *Of course he's not checking you out.*

But it wasn't that silly an idea, was it? After the news broke of the vampires escaping last night, the city was back to living in fear.

Seemed the respite from the vampire threat had been far too brief. And yet, for most people, this was a completely new threat, something they had never had to fear before. Something they were struggling to get their heads around.

The lift arrived, and the doors slid open. Emma stepped inside, pushed the button for the top floor.

As the doors slid shut, she thought back to the days when she worked here and she used to run up and down the stairs during her lunch break.

Why do you have to do your training here, anyway? Why the hell can't you join a gym like everybody else? Karl Edwards, the former editor of the *Birmingham Herald*, had said.

Emma smiled, remembering her reply.

Gyms are for wimps.

Her smile faded.

Karl Edwards was the reason she was back at the *Birmingham Herald* offices today.

The lift was fast and smooth and it was only moments before the doors were opening once more. Emma stepped out of the lift and into the open plan office space that was the *Birmingham Herald*.

This place felt so familiar to her it was strange to be returning as a visitor. The clatter of keyboards being tapped, the electronic hum of printers spewing out paper, the constant stream of news from the massive TV monitor on the wall and over it all the chatter and hum of people talking.

Barry, sitting at his desk, waved to her and stood up.

Emma headed straight for him, acknowledging waves and nods of heads from staff members she remembered from her days on the paper. There weren't many, lost amongst many more faces that she didn't recognise.

'Bloody hell, Barry,' she said. 'Who are all these new people? I hardly recognise anybody.'

Barry raised his eyebrows, glancing towards the editor's office. 'Yeah, our esteemed editor, Ms Lockridge, decided to have a change of staff, to liven things up, she said.'

'Nice,' Emma said. 'She allowed to do that? Just sack whoever she wants?'

'When you don't have a permanent contract, yes,' Barry said.

He pulled up a chair from a vacant desk. Emma sat down.

'You doing okay?' Barry said, sitting next to her.

'Yeah, I'm good. How about you?'

'Still got problems with rotating my right shoulder, but other than that, I'm good too. The doctor who treated me at the hospital said I was lucky not to have broken my neck.'

'Did you tell him you almost had it bitten off?'

'No, I left that bit out.'

Emma placed a hand on Barry's arm. 'Seriously, I am never going to forget seeing you lying at the bottom of those stairs. I thought you were dead.'

'I thought I was dead, too,' Barry said. 'You see the news this morning?'

Emma nodded. 'It's all starting again.'

Barry took a deep, ragged breath. 'And I'm guessing that's why you're here, right? Thing is, Emma, I can't get involved again. I'm not too ashamed to admit I'm scared, and as soon as that big yellow orb in the sky starts setting, I'm heading inside and locking the doors and windows and not coming out again until daybreak.'

'No, it wasn't the vampires I want to talk about. It's Karl.'

'Karl? Really?'

'I know who murdered him.'

Barry sat back in his chair, staring silently at Emma.

'But keep it to yourself, all right?' Emma said. 'I've got no proof.'

'How do you know he did it?' Barry said.

'I accused him and he admitted it to my face.'

'Oh shit.' Barry leaned forward again, elbows on knees. 'You're telling me this scumbag knows that you know?'

'Afraid so, yes.' A brief image of Gilligan standing in front of her as she sat on her bed, him unzipping his trousers and pulling out his engorged cock, flashed through her mind. She pushed it out of her thoughts. 'Don't worry, I'm fine, he hasn't tried anything.'

'Not yet,' Barry said. 'Who is it?'

'An Irishman goes by the name of Gerry Gilligan. He's part of the Slaughterhouse Mob.'

'Does Coffin know about this?'

'No. Thing is, me and Joe aren't exactly best buds right now.'

'That's what happens when you're a celebrity,' Barry said.

'Believe me, it's nothing to do with that,' Emma said. 'Joe will hate being in the limelight.'

'I suppose you're right. Did you hear that Jonathan Ross invited him on his show for an interview?'

Emma couldn't help but smile. 'I would love to see that, but it isn't going to happen.'

'Have you told Nick about this Gilligan fella?'

Emma leaned forward in her chair. 'No, and you don't tell him either. In fact, you don't tell anyone, got it?'

Barry put his hands up. 'Okay, okay, I won't.'

Emma leaned back again. 'But there is something you can do for me. I want you to do some digging on him, find out everything you can. I know he's got connections with the Real IRA, and he was mates with Brendan Kavanagh, used to be landlord at O'Donoghue's before somebody took a dislike to him and murdered him.'

Barry was shaking his head. 'Bloody hell, Emma, you've been mixing with some right lovely types, haven't you?'

'Just get me some info on this piece of shit, all right? Gerry Gilligan, you got that?'

'Yeah, yeah, I got it.'

'Good,' Emma said. 'We need to put this bastard behind bars for what he did.'

'Can I help you, Miss Wylde?'

Emma jumped at the sound of the voice from behind her. She spun round, standing up at the same time. Came face to face with Frances Lockridge.

'You startled me,' Emma said.

That wasn't quite true. Lockridge had scared the crap out of her. Emma's heart was still racing, and she had to fight to keep her breathing under control.

'Maybe that's because you have a guilty conscience,' Lockridge said.

'What?' Emma said, taking a step closer to Lockridge, who took another step away.

'Don't you try and intimidate me, young lady,' the editor said. 'I know your type.'

'My type?' Emma said, almost spitting the words out. 'What the fuck is that supposed to mean?'

Barry stood up. 'Hey, let's all calm down, shall we?'

Lockridge glared at Barry. 'I'm perfectly calm, thank you. And I would ask you to escort this woman off the *Birmingham Herald* premises. She no longer works here and so is trespassing, and I will call the police if I have to.'

'I see I'm not the only one who doesn't work here anymore,' Emma said. 'You having a clean out, getting the yes people in?'

Lockridge's cheeks coloured a little. 'And your attitude, young woman, was the reason why Karl Edwards gave you your notice.'

'Yeah, right,' Emma snapped. 'I don't believe Karl gave me the sack, and even if he had been planning on it, he would have talked to me first. Let me ask you one thing. Are you investigating who murdered him?'

'The police have that matter in hand.'

Emma stepped up close to Lockridge, got right in her face. The editor tried backing away again, but she was up against a desk and had nowhere to go.

'If something like this had happened while Karl was here, he would have had the entire newsroom investigating,' Emma said, her voice low. 'And he wouldn't have let anybody off the hook, himself most of all, until he got the murdering bastard's name and face plastered all over the front page.'

'As I said—'

'Yeah, I know, the police have the matter in hand.' Emma laughed, and even to her ears, it sounded like the sharp bark of a crazy woman. 'The fucking cops have got nothing but their dicks in their hands right now. And all the while you're sitting here turning the Herald into a cheap gossip mag. You should be ashamed of yourself.'

Frances Lockridge snapped her mouth shut and turned to face Barry. 'Please escort this woman out of my newsroom before I call security and ask them to escort you off with her. And if I have to resort to that, believe me Barry, you will not be coming back.'

'You should go,' Barry said.

'Yeah, I'm out of here,' Emma said.

Emma strode through the newsroom, aware that all eyes were on her. The lift doors opened immediately when she pushed the call button. Barry stepped into the lift with her. As Emma stood inside the lift, waiting for the doors to close, she could see Lockridge standing and watching her. Staring at her, chin tilted up, so that she appeared to be looking down her nose at Emma, and that colour still in her cheeks.

The lift doors slid shut, breaking their eye contact.

'Bloody hell, Emma,' Barry said. 'You still need to work on your people skills, you know that?'

'You're telling *me* I need to work on *my* people skills after we both just got talked down to by that horse-faced bitch?'

'Hey, don't take your anger out on me, I'm trying to help you here!'

'By escorting me off the premises?'

'That's right, Emma. I don't know if you noticed, but I was being threatened with the sack up there, and if that happens, I'm not going to be able to help you nail this murdering bastard Gilligan. You need me in the *Birmingham Herald*, not out looking for a job.'

'All right, all right,' Emma said.

The lift doors slid open.

'Go home and calm down,' Barry said. 'I'll call you later.'

'You promise?'

'Absolutely.'

Emma stepped out of the lift. Turned and faced Barry as the doors began to close. 'Hey, thanks.'

The doors shut before Barry could reply.

EMMA WALKED THROUGH THE CITY, down New Street. She had to pause whilst a tram trundled past before she could cross Corporation Street. The city centre was busier than ever, it seemed. Like the entire population of Birmingham was out, getting done what they needed to do before darkness fell.

Before the vampires came out.

Birmingham, always aching to catch up with London and become a city of importance in UK culture, had suddenly found itself in the news after all. But not in a way the city councillors wanted. The vampires were big news now. The television debates and programmes about vampire folklore and history that had been a nightly fixture since they first became public were only going to intensify now that a group of them had escaped.

Emma stepped off the kerb and hurried across the wide road before another tram arrived. She walked up the narrow New Cannon Passage until it opened out at the top. Birmingham Cathedral dominated the city here, sat amongst one of the few green spaces in the centre.

Emma scanned the Cathedral grounds as she walked. Many people used it as a shortcut from Colmore Row down to New Street, whilst others sat on the park benches or gathered in groups to sit on the grass. She spotted Mitch pushing the baby buggy with Louisa May fast asleep inside it.

'How did it go?' Mitch said.

'Yeah, fine,' Emma said. She squatted down and looked at Louisa May. 'Her cheeks are red, is she all right?'

'A bit restless, I think she might be teething.'

Emma gently stroked her daughter's cheek with the back of her fingers.

'She feels hot.'

Mitch squatted down beside Emma. 'That's what happens when they're teething. Honestly, Emma, don't worry.'

'I'm going to take her home,' Emma said. 'You're going to Angellicit now, aren't you?'

'I don't know, I'm still not sure it's such a good idea.'

'Aww, come on Mitch, what do you mean you don't think it's a good idea?'

'You know exactly what I mean, I'm not so sure anymore that it's such a good idea, and I think you should go to the police.'

'They don't want to know, I told you that.' Emma stood up, looked around her. 'They're too busy thinking about vampires.'

'Well, I can understand that,' Mitch said.

'Are you going to do this? For me?'

Mitch stood up. 'All right, Emma, enough of the emotional blackmail. I'll keep on him for a while longer.'

'Good. Thank you.' Emma took hold of the buggy's handles. 'I'll see you tonight. Make sure you get inside before dark.'

'Don't worry, I will,' Mitch said.

Emma stood up and kissed him lightly on the lips. 'Be safe.'

———

MITCH HEADED FOR ANGELLICIT. As he walked, he kept up a constant surveillance of his surroundings, glancing over his shoulder, checking out the faces in the crowds. He cut down a few side streets, took the long way around past the Bullring, down the wide stone steps towards Digbeth before backing up on himself and cutting through New Street Station.

Mitch was pretty sure he wasn't being followed, he couldn't see any reason why he would. But he wanted to be sure.

Especially as he was the one who was going to be doing the following soon.

When he finally arrived at Angellicit, he hung back, on the opposite pavement and out of sight of the entrance. The club was still closed up, too early in the day for it to be open and doing business. Even so, he didn't want to be spotted hanging around. Acting suspicious.

At least that's what he told himself.

The way his insides tightened up at the sight of the club, his prison for several days, told him a different story. The ones who had held him captive, the ones who had tortured him, they were gone now. Merek Guttman, Steffanie Coffin, those two Chinese bastards, that fake doctor, Shaddock, they were either dead or in prison.

Except for Steffanie. She was still out there, somewhere. Unaccounted for.

But the men in there now? Joe Coffin and his Slaughterhouse Mob? They had done nothing to hurt Mitch. In fact, they had been instrumental in rescuing him.

But still, the sight of that building, that doorway.

Mitch stepped back into the shadows where he couldn't see it anymore.

And he waited for Gerry Gilligan to make to make an appearance.

CHELSEA AND MADISON

Something had changed.

The city centre emptied of people as darkness fell. Steffanie watched them scuttling inside like the cockroaches they were, but instead of the light it was the dark that startled them. And from up here, they looked like insects. Some nights Steffanie felt that if she opened the window and reached out she could scoop the tiny figures up and cram them into her mouth, and she could chew on them and crunch their bones, their hot blood running over her lips and down her chin.

Michael grunted as he chewed on the carcass, sucking every last drop of blood he could manage from it. Steffanie ran her hand over his head, through his unwashed, tangled hair. Her boy had long since bled the dog dry, but still he sucked on it. He was desperate for blood, they both were.

But they had to stay hidden. They couldn't venture too far from their hiding place, couldn't take too much risk in their need to feed. If they were discovered now, in their weakened states, they would be caught.

Steffanie watched as two young women left a bar and climbed into a taxi. Both of them laughing. Probably with a combination of fear and excitement. Steffanie knew that feeling well. The fear of stepping onto a stage under the bright spotlights, her bare flesh glistening with oil, the excitement of knowing all those men were watching her.

Devouring her.

Steffanie placed a finger in her mouth, ran the nail over her tongue.

She needed blood.

She needed sex.

This was no life, hiding from people when they should be out hunting. When the people, the cattle down there, should be hiding from her.

Steffanie had discovered the empty building shortly after escaping from Angellicit the night Joe Coffin murdered Merek Guttman. Downstairs, the ground floor was being redeveloped as a bar, another one to add to the long line of clubs and pubs that already ran down both sides of Broad Street. But on the first and second floor, they were left alone. None of the builders or labourers ventured upstairs.

During the daytime, Steffanie and Michael were disturbed by the noise of drills and hammers, of shouted curses and laughter. But at night, the place was theirs and they were free to roam at will.

Most evenings she sat at the window and watched as the revellers outside grew steadily drunker and rowdier. She almost envied them. That loss of self-control as the alcohol flooded their systems, their inhibitions flung away like the shackles that they truly were.

Steffanie had picked off one or two of them over the last couple of months, brought them back here so that Michael could drain them completely dry, make sure they never turned. But she had to be careful. The last thing she wanted was to draw attention to herself and Michael. With just the two of them, they were vulnerable and she didn't want the police, or Joe, to discover their hiding place.

And so they had stayed hidden, feeding when they could on the occasional human. But tonight it looked like even that was becoming denied to them as suddenly the human cattle seemed to have grown wary of the night. Why was that? Why did they all scuttle from the protection of their taxis and straight into the clubs and the bars?

Usually they roamed Broad Street, shouting and laughing and screaming, sometimes in delight and sometimes in anger.

Easy pickings.

Especially the ones so intoxicated they could hardly stand, the ones who wandered off the main thoroughfare and found themselves down an unlit side street.

But tonight the atmosphere was different. The pubs and the clubs still throbbed with music and the sound of people getting steadily drunker. But the streets, they were empty. Everyone was staying indoors.

Michael was still sucking at the body of the dead dog, his face buried in its carcass. There was no blood left in the body. Why didn't he realise that? It had long been sucked dry.

'Stop it!' she hissed, pushing him away.

Michael fell on his back on the dusty concrete floor. He gazed up at Steffanie, his face blank, his eyes dark.

'Mummy?'

Steffanie turned away, looked out of the window again. That one word was all he ever said to her. Drove her mad.

Another taxi drew up and stopped outside Moochers. Two girls and two men climbed out of the taxi, took a quick look around and ran, almost sprinted, inside. As though they were scared of something. Something that only came out at night.

Like vampires.

Could it be true? Were there more vampires at large? Steffanie had thought that she and Michael were the last ones. After all, the others were dead now. She had watched from her hiding place as the Noonan brothers, and Harry and the others, were dragged outside into the sunlight.

There were none left.

Joe Coffin had made sure of that.

Hadn't he?

Steffanie looked back at Michael, who had returned to the dog carcass and was sucking at its chest cavity. It was a risk, but she had to leave him alone for a little while. She had to go outside and explore. Find out what was going on.

There was no point telling him what she was doing. The boy had limited intelligence. Barely knew any words besides 'mummy'. The rest of the time, he made do with hooting and grunting. He seemed to live by instinct alone, apart from when Steffanie was giving him commands. That was different, and most of the time he was proving to be very pliable.

What pleased her most of all was his hatred of his father. That was something she hadn't taught him.

Steffanie crept downstairs, her eyes sharp in the darkness, picking out the steps with ease. Pausing in the bar area, Steffanie saw that a carpet had been laid today. At one end of the room were stacks of tables and chairs, the chairs wrapped in opaque cellophane. Steffanie hadn't realised the project was this far along. Once the bar opened for business, she didn't think they would be able to stay hidden for very long.

They had to get out, find somewhere else to hide.

Steffanie eased open the window at the back of the building and climbed outside. She could smell Indian cooking, exhaust fumes, and hundreds of human scents all mixed together. Some of them were man made, like body sprays and perfumes, but underneath all that were the intoxicating odours of flesh and sweat and the merest hint of blood.

Steffanie crept past the skip overflowing with plasterboard and splintered wood. She ran down Sheepcote Street to where it met Broad Street.

It was deserted.

She stopped running, straightening her back and shoulders, fluffing her fiery red hair out and began walking down Broad Street as though she owned it.

THE CITY HAD GROWN. It was full of light and shone in the dark. Chitrita had never seen anything so beautiful or magical in all her days. She walked around the perimeter of the garden roof, gazing out at the city below her, marvelling at the wonder of it all. She lifted her hand and reached out as though gathering up the flickering lights.

This city could be hers.

The wind tugged at her hair and at the ivory dress splashed with scarlet blood. The full moon bathed her in an unearthly light, strong enough to cast a faint shadow across the rooftop. She stepped up onto the lip of the roof and held out her arms, her hair blowing in the wind.

Ten stories high above the city, if she fell off the edge, she knew she would die.

But Chitrita had no fear of death.

She had already died twice and returned to life. The first time when Guttman had taken her in his arms and pierced her flesh with his teeth. Chitrita had let him take her, had abandoned herself into his embrace. The second time she had died had been her one hundred year sleep.

But now she was awakened, and this city could be hers.

After the escape from the police station, the other vampires had scattered. They were like scared sheep, with no purpose other than to run away from their captors. But they were her children now, they owed Chitrita their lives and once they had overcome their fear, they would find her and return to her.

Dark shapes hurtled through the night sky, gathering and swirling around Chitrita. They came quickly, darting this way and that before settling onto Chitrita's arms and shoulders and on her head, nestling in her hair.

More bats gathered, hovering above her where they could not find space to settle on her. Hundreds of them, thousands.

Chitrita closed her eyes and let the night take her.

STEFFANIE HAD NOTICED them before the sounds of retching reached her. Two young women in a bus shelter, one of them spewing up the contents of her stomach. The steam from her vomit frosted the bus shelter window in a small, opaque circle.

Why were they outside? Had they no fear? Or were they simply too stupid, or drunk, to realise the danger they were in? Steffanie would teach them a lesson, but one they would not live long enough to benefit from.

She strode down Broad Street towards the bus shelter. The one girl was leaning over, her hands on her knees whilst her stomach ejected yet more alcohol and half-digested food. Her friend rubbed her back with one hand, murmuring comforting words. But her head was turned away, her face twisted out of shape with disgust.

Steffanie would take her first. Rip open her jugular whilst her friend was too preoccupied with vomiting still. Once Steffanie was satisfied that the young woman was going nowhere, she could leave her to bleed out on the pavement whilst she took care of her companion. It was too easy. There would be no thrill in the kills. But the hot, steaming blood spilling onto the cold ground would be satisfaction enough for tonight.

The vomiting woman's friend stepped out of the bus shelter and looked up.

'Oh my God, Chelsea, you've gotta look at this, it's like something out of a horror film!'

Chelsea retched again, splattering chunks of vomit on the ground and against the bus shelter window.

Steffanie halted. Looked up to the skyline where Chelsea's friend was looking.

'Oh my God, it's amazing, you got to look Chelsea, quick. Stop puking and look.'

'I can't stop puking, can I Madison?' Chelsea wailed, and vomited again.

Madison was right.

It was amazing.

The full moon, brighter and more intense than Steffanie had seen it before, hovered above the Library of Birmingham. And on the top of the library, silhouetted against the moon's light, stood the figure of a woman, her arms outstretched as though embracing the night. But even that startling sight wasn't what caught the attention.

A massive cloud of bats hovered and flitted across the roof, alighting upon the woman and then darting away again. And there were more of them converging upon the roof, so many of them they began to blot out the light of the moon.

'Bloody hell, where's my phone? I've got to get a picture of this!'

Steffanie's attention was caught by Chelsea's friend once more. The young woman had found her mobile and was swaying as she held it up and tried to focus on the spectacle high above. Even Chelsea had managed to stop spewing and craned her head back as she wiped at her lips with the back of her hand.

Madison squinted at her phone, the glow from the screen illuminating her face.

'I've got to put this on Facebook,' she said.

Steffanie flew at the young woman, who looked up from her screen at the last moment and screamed. She was holding the phone up and the flash went off, momentarily blinding Steffanie. The vampire raked her fingernails across the woman's face, splattering droplets of blood over the bus shelter window. Madison howled as Steffanie sliced open her throat, and the howl turned into an anguished gurgle.

Chelsea stood up straight, her eyes round and wide and brimming with tears. She stared at Steffanie through the blood and vomit splattered glass, her puke flecked lips trembling.

Steffanie let go of Madison, who collapsed on the cold pavement. Blood pooled on the ground, in between the gaps in the paving stones, and then ran over the side of the kerb and into the gutter. Chelsea backed up, never once taking her eyes off Steffanie. Her back hit the opposite plexiglass wall of the bus shelter.

Steffanie stepped over Madison's corpse. Licked the blood off her fingers and smiled at Chelsea.

Chelsea made a run for it, dashing out of the bus shelter.

Steffanie scrambled up the side of the bus shelter and squatted for a moment on the roof, watching as Chelsea staggered drunkenly away. Broad Street was deserted still, apart from a car approaching from the city centre. Steffanie leaped from the bus shelter. The cold night air swept over her face and her hair. For a moment she was flying, before she landed on top of Chelsea, knocking her to the ground.

Chelsea screamed as her face scraped against the pavement, ripping the flesh away.

Steffanie turned Chelsea over onto her back and pulled at her top. The buttons pinged as they scattered across the ground and Steffanie ripped the fabric apart, exposing Chelsea's chest and stomach.

Steffanie raked her fingernails across the young woman's torso, drawing scarlet lines of blood. The sight of the blood, the young woman's exposed flesh, overwhelmed Steffanie's senses. She sank her teeth into Chelsea's left breast and began sucking greedily.

She lost herself in the warm, sticky blood flooding her mouth, running over her lips and down her chin. The blood smeared over Chelsea's breasts and abdomen and she screamed, thrashing and kicking and pulling at Steffanie's hair.

Steffanie grew bored with the noise. Yanking Chelsea's head back and fully exposing her throat, Steffanie fastened her teeth around the soft flesh and clamped her jaws together. She dragged her head back and tore a glistening chunk of flesh from Chelsea's neck. Blood pumped on to the cold ground.

Steffanie spat the chunk of flesh out and began lapping at the pool of blood like a dog. She was feverish, desperate for the hot, fresh blood.

Her surroundings faded from view, from her senses. She could have been anywhere, nowhere.

There was nothing but the blood.

A gossamer thin caress across her face and her back. Reminded her of her days stripping when her clothing fell from her.

Another.

More brief touches, like fingers made of wedding gowns.

Steffanie's senses slowly returned as the caresses increased in frequency. She lifted her head from the puddles of blood on the ground. Her hair was sticky with it.

She looked up.

The moon was no longer visible. Neither were the street lights.

The darkness moved, shifted this way and that.

Undulated like a black sea.

The bats.

They had come down from the library rooftop and were gathered around Steffanie, darting to and fro in crazed, angular paths.

Steffanie watched them, totally entranced by their dark beauty.

And then they parted, and revealed a woman in a pale, blood spattered dress. The woman gazed at Steffanie, and no words were needed.

Come, she was saying.

Come with me.

A WOMAN AND A DUCK WALK INTO A BAR

'Bloody nice place you've got here, Joe,' Gosling said. 'If you ever need a comic on the act, talk to Stilts, funny as all hell he is.'

Coffin glanced down at Stilts. The dwarf stared back at him, silent as always. Stilts was dressed in a tailor-made suit and tie, shiny black shoes, hair combed in a neat side parting. Looked almost comical, he was so well turned out today.

But one look at his eyes was enough to get the message across that Stilts was no comic.

'Can't see it myself,' Coffin said.

Gosling laughed. 'Don't let his tough guy attitude faze you. I've seen him reduce grown men to tears of laughter. And the ladies, well, you just wouldn't believe it if I told you. Casanova had nothing on this little fella.'

'What do you want to drink?' Coffin said to Gosling.

'Whatever you're having is fine by me, Joe.'

'What about him?' Coffin said, gesturing at Stilts.

'Stilts doesn't drink, not a drop. Interferes with his digestion.'

Coffin held up two fingers to Stut behind the bar. Pulled out a chair and sat down. Indicated that Gosling should do the same. Gosling joined Coffin at the table. Stilts stood beside him.

Even sitting down, Gosling was still taller than Stilts.

'Thought we might be doing business in your office, Joe,' Gosling said.

'No, we can talk here,' Coffin said. 'We won't be disturbed.'

'This where you always do business, is it?' Gosling said.

'No.'

'You're a man of few words, Joe, I like that.'

Stut arrived holding a glass of whisky in each hand. He placed them on the table.

Gosling said, 'A man walks into a bar and sees a dog in the corner licking its balls. He says to the bartender, 'I wish I could do that.''

Stut looked at Gosling and then at Coffin.

Gosling said, 'The bartender replied, 'You can, but you'll have to pet him first.''

Stut started laughing. Stilts didn't react at all, looked like his face had been carved out of stone.

Stut left, shaking his head, and still chuckling.

'Don't you appreciate a good joke?' Gosling said to Coffin. 'A big man like you, all the stress you must be under, you should laugh more.'

'Why don't you tell me more about this robbery?' Coffin said.

Gosling pulled a white handkerchief out of a pocket and dabbed at his forehead, shiny with sweat. He had been wearing a jacket when he came into the club, but had taken it off. There were dark stains under his armpits, and his shirt bulged against his belly, straining at the buttons.

'Straight to the point, that's what I like,' Gosling said, stuffing the handkerchief back in his pocket. 'But tell me, Joe, are you in? I need a good man like you on the job.'

'Tell me more first,' Coffin said.

'Shaw said you were interested, said you were in.'

'Shaw should keep his mouth shut,' Coffin said. 'He might have talked me into letting you tell me a bit more about this gig last night, but that doesn't mean I'm in.'

Gosling sighed. 'Bloody hell, Joe, you're making me work for this, aren't you? All right then, have it your way. You remember Stuart Ullman, don't you? Managed that band in the 1970s, bloody rip-off of the Beatles, can't remember their name now. Well, they had a couple of hits before they sank without a trace, but earned Ullman enough that he could set himself up as a nightclub owner. Owned a string of them all over the West Midlands. Most notorious one was Mr T's in Stourbridge.' Gosling paused, took a swallow of his whisky. 'He was a mean fucker, by all accounts. But he made himself an absolute fucking mountain of money before he died.'

'I remember Ullman,' Coffin said.

'Took a bullet in the belly,' Gosling said. 'Long, painful way to die, that is.'

Coffin picked up his whisky glass, studied the dark amber liquid. 'He deserved it.'

Gosling pulled his handkerchief from his pocket and dabbed at his forehead again. 'Know him, did you?'

'Know him?' Coffin tossed the whisky back and slammed the glass down on the table. 'I was the one put that bullet in his gut.'

Gosling paused, his hand holding the folded handkerchief against his forehead. 'Bloody hell, Joe. You're full of surprises, aren't you?'

'Keep talking,' Coffin said.

Gosling resumed dabbing the handkerchief at his forehead, then his cheeks and his top lip. 'Well then, you'll know his old lady survived him and ran the clubs for a few more years before the clubbing scene changed and she lost touch. But by then she'd earned enough money that she was sitting on a mountain of cash and ready to retire.'

Gosling looked at his empty glass.

Coffin looked over at the bar and caught Stut's eye, held up his hand, indicated two more drinks.

'The old biddy's living in a huge pile on the Staffordshire border, just her and her security firm.'

'Security firm?'

'That's right, but they only have one job and that's looking after Mrs Ullman and her big stash of money.'

Stut arrived with two more drinks. Placed them on the table.

'A woman and a duck walk into a bar,' Gosling said, eyes flitting from Coffin to Stut. 'The bartender says, "Where did you get that pig?" The woman says, "That's a duck, not a pig."'

A half smile hovered on Stut's lips as he waited for the punchline.

'The bartender says, "I wasn't talking to you, I was talking to the duck."'

Stut laughed and shook his head as though it was the funniest joke he had ever heard.

Stilts stared at Stut, the expression on his face unreadable.

Stut noticed, and his laughter died. 'Wh-wh-what's his f-f-ffffucking problem?'

'You've got a stutter,' Gosling said. 'I knew a man once who had a stutter. He went to the doctor's about it, and the doctor says, "Your problem is your penis is four inches too long and the strain is pulling on your vocal chords." So the man says, "What can I do about it?" And the doctor tells him he needs an operation to remove the extra four inches. Six months later he comes back and says, "Doctor, the operation was a success. I don't stutter anymore, my confidence has grown, I've got a new job and I feel great. Thing is, my wife misses the great sex, and I was wondering if I could have the extra four inches put back on." And the doctor says, "N-n-no, I d-d-don't think th-th-th-that's p-p-p-possible."'

Stut was laughing again, ignoring Stilts.

'All right, cut the comedy routine,' Coffin said. 'Stut, go back to the bar.'

Gosling leaned forward, his belly squashed up against the table. 'The widow, I was telling you she's sitting on a big pile of cash in her country house. When I say sitting on a pile of cash, that's exactly what she's doing. The old biddy's got this fear that the banks are robbing her, so a couple of years back she cashed in all her investments and savings plans and took all her money out of the banks.'

'And she keeps it in her house?' Coffin said.

Gosling nodded. 'Had a safe room built specifically for the purpose of keeping her cash safe. Has thirty million in twenty-pound notes stacked in briefcases in there.'

'And you're planning on taking it from her?'

'That's right.' Gosling leaned back in his chair and it creaked beneath his weight. 'Be like taking candy from a baby.'

'How will you get into the safe room?'

'That's where Stilts comes in. He might not look it, but this little fella is a master safe breaker. Isn't that right, Stilts?'

Stilts said nothing, showed no sign that he had even heard Gosling mention his name.

'Is he deaf as well as mute?' Coffin said.

'No, I told you, he can talk, he just chooses not to,' Gosling said.

Coffin took a swallow of his whisky. Turned the glass around and around in his hand, watching the light play on the cut edges. 'I don't know. The Slaughterhouse Mob isn't really a breaking and entering type of firm. Not something we've ever done before.'

'Always a first time,' Gosling said.

Coffin kept turning the glass around. 'I don't get it. Why do you need me? Sounds like you got it all sorted.'

'We need your manpower, Joe. The old bird's got security patrolling the house twenty-four hours a day. Thing is, at the moment she's down a man. One of her crew left last week, disappeared without a word. It's going to take her another week or two to replace him, so now's the time to strike to while she's short-handed.'

'You have anything to do with that?'

'Nope. She loses a man every once in a while.'

Coffin stopped turning the glass around in his hand. 'It's happened before?'

'Two or three times now, yeah.'

'And no one knows why?'

Gosling dabbed at his forehead. 'You know what these people are like, they're always moving on to other jobs.'

'I don't know,' Coffin said. 'Not sure I like it.'

'What's not to like?' Gosling said.

'A safe room? A security firm? Disappearing security guards? Sounds wrong to me.'

'Come on, Joe, where's your sense of adventure? I've heard the stories, and not just the one where you carved that old guy up with a chainsaw and char-grilled the body parts. I heard you pulled yourself off a meat hook just a few months back, now that takes some balls, that does. And I heard the story about your father too, about how you caved his head in when you were just a kid.'

'Where'd you hear that from?' Coffin said.

'Let's just say I've got my ear to the ground and I get to know about lots of things. Why'd you put a bullet in Ullman's stomach, though? That I don't know.'

'We had a disagreement.'

'Really? For fuck's sake, I'm staying on your good side then. What do you say? Are you in?'

'No.' Coffin stood up. 'I'm going to have to refuse your offer.'

'Are you sure about that?' Gosling said, looking up at Coffin. 'It'll be the biggest payday you've ever had. You're not going to make that kind of cash squeezing Pakis for protection money.'

'Like I said, I'm refusing your offer.'

Gosling climbed to his feet. 'I'm sorry to hear that.' He held out his hand. 'But if you change your mind, you know where to find me.'

'I won't change my mind,' Coffin said, ignoring Gosling's hand.

Gosling held his hand out a moment or two longer and then let it slowly drop to his side. 'Right, come on then Stilts, I think we've outstayed our welcome.'

Coffin watched as the big fat man and his tiny companion walked away. Gosling seemed huge enough that he wouldn't fit through the doorway into reception, but he did. Stilts, following behind, paused at the doorway and looked back at Coffin. His face remained as still as it had the whole conversation, his eyes dead, unreadable.

Coffin was on the point of asking the little man if there was a problem when Stilts abruptly turned and followed Gosling out of the door.

SHAW WAS in the car park round the back of Angellicit, sitting in the passenger seat of the Stig's car. The Stig was in the driver's seat, talking on his phone. Gilligan was standing behind the car, also on his phone. Gilligan had been sitting in the back, but then when his mobile started buzzing he'd scrambled out of the car pretty quick.

Shaw didn't like it. After their talk in the Punchline the other night, Gilligan had seemed preoccupied. Shaw had thought Gilligan would want to talk some more about the situation, about taking Joe out. But the Irishman hadn't mentioned it since. Shaw was glad about that, to be honest. Him and the Stig, they'd decided that taking over the Mob right now probably wasn't the best idea in the world. And since their visit to Scotland, Shaw had begun to lose interest in the game, anyway. Over and over he kept seeing Shocker's kid on the floor, leaking blood.

Poor little bastard. It wasn't right.

Shaw watched as Gosling and Stilts left Angellicit and got into a car. As the car doors were pulled open, the interior light came on. The yellow glow picked out someone sitting in the driver's seat, but Shaw couldn't make out who it was. Might have been the transvestite, what was his name?

Duchess Swallows, that was it.

Duchess and Stilts, the Bananarama reject and a Bernard Manning wannabe. They made for a freaky bunch. Scarier than the vampires in a way.

Or maybe not.

'What do you think that fat bastard wanted?' Gilligan said as he climbed back into the car.

'Probably to talk about that job he was going on about,' Shaw said.

'What do you think?' Gilligan said. 'Do you think Joe will bite?'

'Dunno,' Shaw muttered.

The Stig finished his call and watched as Gosling's car was driven away. 'Was that Gosling?'

'Yeah, the funniest comedian in the West Midlands,' Shaw said.

'In his own head, more like,' Gilligan said.

'Any luck?' Shaw said to the Stig.

'Nah, wherever Shanks Longworth is, he's hiding low, and I don't blame him. He must be crapping his pants knowing that Joe's after him.'

'I dunno about that,' Shaw said. 'I never met the bastard, but I've heard he's a complete and utter psychopath. I wouldn't be surprised if he's out looking for Joe.'

'Well, if that's the case, we need to keep our eyes peeled, don't we?' the Stig said.

The back door to the club opened and Stut walked outside, letting the door slam shut behind him. He walked over to the car, pulling on his trademark black leather jacket.

'What's happening?' Shaw said, lowering his window.

'Joe t-t-turned Gosling d-down,' Stut said. 'He's in a stinking m-mood, he's k-k-keeping the club cl-closed tonight.'

'Bloody hell, the place is going to fold at this rate,' Gilligan said. 'Hasn't the man got any idea of business?'

'And you have, have you?' the Stig said.

Gilligan leaned over the Stig's seat from the back. 'I know enough that you close your doors often enough, then business is going to go elsewhere.'

'All right, Paddy, calm down,' the Stig said.

'You want to jump in the back?' Shaw said to Stut. 'We might as well go for a drink.'

Stut climbed in the car and sat down next to Gilligan in the back.

'Is that Mitch I see over the other side of the road?' the Stig said.

'Bastard!' Gilligan hissed, leaning forward from the back seat again, so he could get a good look through the front windscreen. Mitch was standing beneath the glow of a street lamp. He was looking up and down the street, seemed unsure what he wanted to do. 'That miserable fucking soldier boy has been following me around the last week or two, he has. What the fuck does he think he's playing at?'

'What makes you so special?' the Stig said. 'Could be he's keeping an eye on all of us, scoping out Angellicit.'

'And what the hell would he be doing that for?'

'I bet it's that reporter,' Shaw said. 'The one that was balling Joe before he blew her off. I bet she's hired him, now that she can't use Coffin as an excuse to hang around anymore.'

The Stig turned around and looked at Shaw. 'Seriously?'

'What?'

'You're telling me that Joe was shagging the reporter?'

'Had to be, didn't he?' Shaw said. 'Why else would he keep her around?'

'You think the kid's his, as well?' the Stig said.

Shaw shrugged. 'Probably.'

'I wouldn't touch the dirty skank with a barge pole,' Gilligan said.

Shaw and the Stig both twisted around in their seats and stared at Gilligan.

'I think someone's protesting a little too much,' the Stig said.

'Yeah,' Shaw said. 'You got the hots for her or something?'

'No, she's just on my case the whole fucking time, ever since I showed Joe that video she had of him killing Terry Wu.'

'Nah, I don't think that's it,' the Stig said, winking at Shaw. 'You've got a boner for her, haven't you? Want to take her back to yours and slip her one, right? And I can see why you might want to, she's an attractive looking woman from what I've seen. Even when she was looking ready to pop a kid out, she was a looker.'

Gilligan kept his eyes on Mitch, who was walking away around the front of Angellicit and then out of sight.

'You got it all wrong,' Shaw said. 'Look at him, it's Mitch he wants to pork, can't keep his eyes off him.'

'Well, whatever the two lovebirds want to get up to is their business,' the Stig said. 'I hear it's all legal now anyways.'

'You two are a laugh a minute, you know that?' Gilligan said. 'Almost as funny as that fat bastard, Gosling.'

'Oooh,' the Stig said. 'Someone's a little touchy.'

'Fuck you,' Gilligan said. 'Fuck the pair of you.'

The Stig laughed and started the engine up.

'Let's go get that drink,' he said.

Shaw realised he had meant to ask Gilligan who he had been talking to on his mobile, but he had forgotten. He thought about asking him now, but decided he couldn't be bothered.

It was probably nothing worth worrying about.

DRUNK

Coffin sat in the darkened club alone.

In his right hand he held a cigarette, the smoke curling upwards.

In his left he held an empty whisky glass, his hand almost engulfing it. On the table stood two bottles.

The Jack Daniels was now half empty. Coffin stared at it, thinking about pouring himself another slug.

Not sure if he wanted to.

The other bottle didn't have a label.

But Coffin knew what it was called.

Del Maguaya Pechuea Mezcal.

Leola had found it behind the bar. Said it looked like someone had been drinking it, and recently too. She told him all about how it was made, how it was distilled three times with skulls and blood. She'd held that bottle in her hand and looked at it for a long time, like maybe she wanted to twist the cork off and put the bottle to her mouth and upend it. Just swig that foul looking shit down in one go.

In the end she had simply put it back where she found it and turned to Coffin and said, 'I heard it tastes rank.'

Coffin had been sitting alone in the club for an hour or two. He wasn't sure how long, he'd lost all track of time.

When Gosling and his pet dwarf had left, Coffin had sent the others home too.

Stut had said, 'Wh-wh-what about the cl-cl-club?'

Coffin had said, 'The club's closed tonight.'

Mort would have had a heart attack if he'd heard Coffin saying that. Angels, as it was named back when Mortimer Craggs owned it, never closed. Some nights there was barely anybody in here, the place was deserted except for some bare ass girl on the stage gyrating around a pole and trying not to look bored.

Thing was, Coffin was starting to think he knew how she felt. Being leader of the Slaughterhouse Mob wasn't exactly as much fun as he had thought it might be. Only a few months in, and after he had declared that he was going to take the Mob back to its glory days, and Coffin was bored and restless.

More worryingly, the takings were down at all the clubs that the Slaughterhouse Mob owned and Coffin's heart wasn't in the protection racket anymore and he was thinking of closing that part of the operations down.

Then there was the huge pile of money that Craggs had left the Mob owing to various outfits, none of them legal and all willing to take the matter into their own hands if Coffin couldn't pay back what was owed.

Coffin put the cigarette between his lips and picked up the Jack Daniels. He poured himself a generous serving. He had a buzz on already and maybe he would keep drinking until he fell unconscious.

It wasn't just the Mob that was bringing him down, he knew that.

Hunting down and killing Shocker Stronach had been a big deal for Coffin. Shanks Longworth was next.

Coffin intended to pay them both back for kidnapping him and delivering him to that bastard Stone and his psycho wife.

Coffin took a deep pull on the cigarette and held it for a moment, letting the smoke scorch his lungs before releasing it.

Coffin downed the Jack Daniels in one and poured more into

the glass.

If he drank enough tonight, he thought maybe he could blot out the image of the boy lying on the floor, blood leaking from his gunshot wounds.

Coffin, Gilligan, and the Stig, they hadn't mentioned the boy once since that day. But Coffin saw him every day, every time he closed his eyes.

He regarded the Mezcal again.

Leola had said it was made in some shitty little village in Mexico and there was nowhere else in the world it could be bought. And yet there it had been, sitting behind the bar. Coffin knew Mort hadn't bought it, which meant Guttman had acquired it during his brief stint as manager of Angellicit, alongside Steffanie.

Coffin picked up the bottle and turned it around, staring into the dark liquid.

Fucking vampires.

He downed the glass of Jack Daniels and slammed it on the table. He twisted the cork off the bottle of Mezcal.

Poured himself a shot. Stared at the dark liquid in the glass.

He'd got himself a proper buzz going on now.

He picked up the glass and downed the drink.

The Mezcal was thick and scummy in his mouth. It tasted of death and blood and rotting flesh and when he swallowed it, it crawled down his throat like a living thing. Coffin hit the table top with his fist and ground his teeth together, fighting his body's reflexive urge to regurgitate the drink.

There, it was down and the need to vomit it back up was fading.

Coffin pushed the cork back into the bottle.

The room was spinning a little. He pushed the bottle away. Leola had been right, the stuff tasted like shit.

Coffin pulled a crumpled pack of cigarettes from his pocket, and a silver lighter. The lighter was the classic style, with the flip back top and the mechanism inside. Coffin flipped open the top and flicked the striker with his thumb. A long, yellow flame flowered from the lighter and Coffin lit his cigarette and snapped the top shut.

He put the lighter and the cigarette packet back in his pocket.

Standing up, Coffin had to steady himself with a hand on the table as the empty club swayed and tilted. What the fuck was wrong with him? He could drink more than this. It was that Mezcal, had to be.

He looked across at the stage.

Steffanie was there.

Naked.

Swaying to music that only she could hear. Hands on her hips, slowly running them up her torso and over her flat, perfect stomach. Over her breasts and up her neck, her fingers becoming entwined in her long hair. She pushed her hair up until it cascaded down her back and she arched her spine, jutting her chest out, one leg up on the tips of her toes, her knee bent.

It was her classic striptease pose. She held it whilst she gazed at Coffin.

'Get the fuck out of my club,' Coffin said, the cigarette wobbling up and down in his mouth as he spoke.

He blinked, and she was gone.

Coffin rubbed his forehead with the back of his hand. Realised he was holding the open Jack Daniels bottle when some whisky slopped out and down his shirt. He pulled the cigarette out of his mouth and let it drop to the floor. He ground it out beneath his heel. He put the bottle to his lips and took a swig.

What the fuck was the matter with him?

He looked around the empty club. Place was full of fucking ghosts, that was the problem.

Coffin looked at the Jack Daniels bottle. It was empty. When had that happened? He placed the empty bottle on the table.

Headed to the rear of the club.

Took the stairs carefully.

At his office, Mort's old office, he paused at the closed the door. The office doubled as his bedroom, too. Since coming back to the club, he hadn't been able to return home. Hadn't even wanted to sleep anywhere else at all. Every night he bunked down on the sofa, tossing and turning all night, trying to get comfortable because the damn thing was too small. He could have slept in one of the fuck rooms, but the water beds would have made him queasy.

Besides, sleeping in the office, not having a proper bedroom to go to bed in, it felt right somehow.

Like he wasn't intending to stick around for too much longer.

Coffin opened the door.

He felt it immediately. Something was wrong, something was different.

He took a step inside. Another one.

Movement. A rush of air.

Coffin stepped sideways. A blur of motion, another rush of air and something whistled past Coffin's shoulder.

The man stepped back and lifted his sword from where it had struck the floor. He held the sword before him in a double handed grip, the double-edged blade pointing straight up. He was wearing a black, loose fitting outfit, resembling a karate uniform.

He scowled at Coffin. His shaved scalp and face were tattooed with Oriental letters and dragons.

'What the hell is this, Halloween?' Coffin said.

The man said nothing. He raised his sword and stepped forward, lunging into a crouch as he swung the blade down in a swift arc. Coffin jumped back out of the way and stumbled when his legs hit a barrier. It was the sofa, and he sat down on it, the sword swooshing past him and slicing open the cushion. The stuffing burst free from the slash.

Coffin half rolled, half fell onto the floor. The room was spinning, bile rising in the back of his throat, and he imagined this was how it must feel to be seasick.

The man stepped forward, raising his sword once more. Coffin kicked out at his legs, but his attacker easily stepped to one side, driving the sword down hard as he dodged Coffin's kick. Coffin rolled, and the sword nicked his shirt, drawing blood on his shoulder.

Coffin kicked out again with both feet, this time connecting. The man stumbled and dropped to one knee. Coffin scrambled out of the way, his movements clumsy and a little sluggish. Behind the settee, he saw an electrical cord running up to a bookshelf. On the shelf was a lamp, the base of which was a figurine of a naked woman, painted gold like Jill Masterson in Goldfinger.

Coffin had never liked that lamp.

He pulled the lamp from the shelf as the warrior leaped over the sofa, swinging his sword. Coffin smashed the bulb and the pendant off the top of the figurine's head and thrust it at his attacker. The live electrical wires connected with the man's chest. With a loud crack, as though somebody had just flicked a giant whip, and a brilliant flash of light, Coffin's attacker jerked away and hit the floor.

Grabbing the back of the sofa, Coffin dragged himself upright. He had to hold on tight as the room tilted. The floor seemed to be balanced on top of a giant ball and every move Coffin made sent it wobbling precariously.

The man propped himself up on his elbows, the confusion clearing from his face. Coffin needed to shock him again, quick. Put him out of action for good. He jabbed the figurine at his attacker, but it pulled up short without making contact.

Coffin looked back. The cord was too short.

'Shit,' Coffin grunted.

The assassin was climbing to his feet and looking for his sword. Coffin saw it, the other side of the sofa. He lunged for it but sprawled drunkenly over the back of the sofa and rolled onto the floor. His attacker wasn't faring too much better, still recovering from the electric shock.

Coffin grabbed the sword handle and hauled himself back up on his feet. The man was on his feet now, too. Coffin swung the sword at him, but he misjudged its weight. It felt unbalanced and unwieldy in his hands. The sword swung wildly out of his control and twisted from his grip, landing on the floor with a heavy thud and skidding across the office.

Coffin's attacker smashed across the side of his head in an open handed karate chop.

Coffin hit the floor hard. Fireworks exploded inside his head. Brightly coloured flashes of lights, shooting stars, loud bangs and fizzing, spinning wheels.

'Get up, you fucker,' Coffin told himself, his voice slurred.

The warrior punched him in the face using the heel of his hand, whipping Coffin's head to back. More explosions and pain this time, even through the numbing effect of the whisky.

Coffin blinked blood out of his eyes. Everything looked blurred. He was floating in space, looking down at planet earth.

How was that possible? Was he dead?

If he was dead, why did he hurt so much?

He needed to get back down to earth and finish this fight off. He couldn't let this costumed freak get away.

Coffin sat up.

Reached out to the world. The globe atlas that Mort had loved so much.

Coffin lifted the top half of the world to reveal the bottles of whisky, brandy, rum, all of them a decent vintage.

Seemed a shame to waste them like this.

Coffin grabbed a bottle at random, a dark rum, and twisted round. The man had walked across the other side of the office and picked up his sword. Looked like he was about ready to finish off Coffin for good.

Coffin threw the bottle at him.

The man deflected the bottle with the sword. The bottle smashed and showered him with rum and shards of glass.

Coffin picked out another bottle. The fifty-year-old Glenfarclas. Threw it at his attacker, who smashed it with his sword. He was drenched with the whisky.

The bastard was drawing closer.

Coffin tipped the whole globe of drinks over and staggered away. The office was still spinning. Coffin had to support himself with a hand against the wall. The Mezcal was rolling around in his stomach, like a ball of thick, scummy oil. Coffin's hand found a door handle, and he twisted it and pushed the door open. Fell into the en-suite bathroom.

'Shit,' Coffin muttered. He'd thought it was the door out. Now he was trapped.

He spun around to face the doorway and lost his balance. Sat down heavily on the toilet.

The assassin filled the doorway.

Coffin stood up, grabbed at the medicine cabinet above the sink for balance. Wrenched the door off.

Threw it at the warrior, who easily batted it away.

The sweet smell of rum and whisky filled the bathroom.

The man raised his sword.

Coffin pulled his lighter from his pocket and flipped the cap open.

The assassin paused, his eyes widening.

Coffin's thumb flicked the wheel, and the wick flamed into bright orange light.

He threw the lighter at his attacker.

With a soft, almost gentle explosion, the man's chest and head burst into yellow flame. He immediately began beating at his clothing as the flames spread swiftly.

He dropped the sword.

Coffin lunged for the sword, missed, and fell on his side on the floor.

He got up on his hands and knees, grabbed at the sword, and swung it at the man's legs.

The sword bit deep into his shins.

The man howled and fell to his knees, the flames licking at his throat.

Holding the sword with both hands, Coffin drove the double-edged blade up and into the soft flesh beneath the man's jaw. He kept going, pushing all his weight and strength behind the movement, lifting the man off the floor as the sword bit deeper. The assassin's head was angled back, his face contorted in a grimace of pain.

With a roar of anger, Coffin gave the sword one last powerful shove. The man's body flipped over and the sword's point popped through the back of his skull and skittered against the wall.

Coffin sat down on the floor, breathing heavily. He watched the flames as they died down.

And then he doubled over and threw up the stinking Mezcal.

EPISODE FOURTEEN

LET GO, BABY

The bed creaked and groaned with each thrust of her hips on top of him. His hands massaged her huge breasts, his thumbs rubbing at her erect nipples. The temptation to sit up and place his teeth around one of those nipples and bite it off was strong.

But he was better than that.

He slid his hands down over the undulating mass of her pale flesh and gripped her hips.

'Ooh, you like this, don't you?' she said, her voice flat and dispassionate.

Tightening his hold on her hips he guided her movements, urging her on to go faster. Somebody thumped at the wall behind his head, and shouted, 'Stop it! Stop it! I'll call the police, I will!'

'Shut your fucking mouth you stupid bitch!' she screamed back, not missing a stroke. 'I'll do what I want in my own flat, you nosey cow!'

He arched his neck, his head flattening the thin pillow. He could smell the damp in it, he could hear the microscopic creatures scurrying through the material.

'You ignore her now,' she said, breathlessly, her breasts bouncing as she increased the rate of her rhythm. As if she needed to finish this, to bring him to climax so that she could get him out of her dirty little flat and bring in her next customer.

'Jesus!' he screamed as he came. 'Praise Jeesuuuuusssssss!'

The woman giggled, the first genuine sound she had made since she brought him up here.

He burst into tongues. 'Koodabashantamalicondunalamanason-tacoolalmalashanti!'

She lifted herself off him and climbed off the bed.

'What are you doing?' she said. 'What's all that gibberish?'

He couldn't reply, the Holy Spirit had overcome him and taken control. He lay on his back, raising his arms up and out in supplication as the Spirit rolled through him and the words flew from his mouth.

'Stop it! Stop that noise! I'm calling the police now!' the woman screamed from the flat next door, thumping furiously on the wall.

'Go on then, call the pigs, see if I care!' she yelled back.

He slowly lowered his arms as the euphoria ebbed away, leaving him drained but satisfied.

The woman giggled again. 'I've never heard anyone praise the Lord after I finished fucking them.'

'You done good, girl,' he said. 'You done real good, but you need to repent o' your sins, that you do.'

'Are you a Jesus freak?' She pulled on a faded bathrobe, tied it around her stomach. 'You don't look like a Jesus freak, all those tattoos. You just look like a freak.'

He sat up on the bed, leaning his back against the wall. 'We all freaks, girl. Freaks and sinners, that's what we be. But we also be children of God, and one day we gone meet God and he gone say, 'Child, come here, come here and tell me, have you repented o' your sins?' That's what he gone say, and you gone need your answer ready, you done want to be cast down into the pits of Hell.'

She put a cigarette between her lips and lit it as she gazed at him, running her eyes over his nakedness. 'You really are a freak, aren't you? A weird freak. Where'd you get all your tattoos done? Even your dick's tattooed.'

He stuck out his black tongue. 'Even my tongue, girl. Ever last inch o' me is inked with my sins so I can be pure o' heart before the good Lord.'

She blew out a plume of smoke and sat down on the edge of the bed. 'You gonna have to get yourself another tattoo because you fucked me?' She rested her fingertips on his thigh, running them up and down the length of it. 'There's no room left for any more tattoos.'

'I ran out o' space for my sins a long time ago,' he said. 'I just ink over the top o' the old ones.'

She sucked on her cigarette and let the smoke trickle out from between her lips as she talked. 'I don't believe in God. And if he exists, well, I guess I'm going downstairs, right? But that's all right, I think they have the best time down there. I bet it's boring in heaven, sitting on a cloud, playing a harp.'

'You don' know what you're talkin' about, girl,' he said, plucking the cigarette from her fingers and taking a deep drag on it. 'You gone be in hell and you gone be tortured day an' night by the demons down there. An' they gone have fun with you, an' they gone use their teeth and claws on you, an' worse, girl, they got worse things than their teeth and claws.'

She took the cigarette back from him. 'Nah, that doesn't sound like fun.' She ran her fingers up his thigh. 'But what about you? What if you sinned one time and then forgot to get another tattoo? Or you didn't have time, like maybe the tattoo parlours were all closed?'

'I ain't got no need of no tattoo parlours,' he said. 'I ink myself.'

'But you're covered in tattoos!' She placed a hand on his shoulder and pushed him forward so that she could see his back. 'There ain't no way you could get everywhere with a needle.'

He took her hand off and leaned back against the wall again. 'I told you, I ink myself.'

Her eyes ran over his nakedness. 'Everything, every last inch of you is black. Do you even know what your tattoos are? What they look like? They've all bled into one another, it's impossible to see them. Except . . .' She paused, taking another drag on her cigarette. 'Except, if I keep looking at you, it seems like your skin moves, like the tattoos are alive. Like, what do you call it? One of them optical illusions.'

'Done look too close at the tattoos girl,' he said. 'You stare too hard they gone suck you in an' your heart will be as black as midnight.'

'You are so weird.' She placed a hand on his flaccid cock and began massaging it. 'You want to go again? Yeah, you do, you're getting hard already.'

She stubbed the cigarette out in an ashtray on the bedside table and climbed on top of him, straddling him. He was already stiff, and she rubbed herself up against him and let out a little moan. Of course she was acting, he knew that. He'd fucked enough of them over the centuries to know when they were genuine and when they were pretending.

He sat there, his hands grabbing at the bed sheet, his fingers curling up and pulling the sheet into his fists. She paused in her movements, leaned across him and grabbed a tube of lubricant. She squirted a blob in her palm and then smoothed it over his erection.

'Hmm, you like that, don't you?' she whispered.

He knew what she was doing. She could charge him twice now. She would work him, bring him to climax quickly so that she could get him out before her next client arrived. But that wasn't how he wanted to play it.

'How long you got girl, till your next trick?'

'As long as you want, baby,' she said. Her voice had turned into a caricature of a sexually aroused woman, a Hollywood version of lust and sexual heat. He almost felt sorry for her.

Grabbing her by her ample hips he pulled her off and turned her on her back on the bed. He ran his hands down her body, over her breasts and her stomach and down between her legs.

She still had her hand around his cock, sliding up and down, up and down. A heat was building inside of him. Screwing his eyes shut he panted, trying to keep control.

'Let it go, honey,' she whispered. 'Let it go, it's all right.'

He jerked his head from side to side. *No! No!*

The sex was supposed to release him, give him relief from the urges that sought to consume him. But here, right now, it wasn't working. He was falling into a delirium, a feverish nightmare of blood and torn flesh. He could smell the blood, he could taste it.

Let go, baby.

Let go.

His eyes snapped open. He saw her chest heaving, her large, red nipples standing erect. He sank his head into her breasts, his mouth finding a nipple. She moaned in false ecstasy, her hand still pumping up and down on his cock.

The woman next door thumped on the wall again screaming, 'Stop it! Stop it now!'

He lifted his head. The air was buzzing with insect-like creatures, formless evil things chittering around his head. He could taste death in the room with them. He should have tattooed himself after her fucked her, not wasted time talking. He should have sought redemption.

Instead he was edging closer to losing himself, to letting the demon take over and consume him.

He pulled away from the woman and just as he did so he ejaculated over her hand and onto the bed sheet.

'What's wrong, mister?' she said. 'Wasn't that nice?'

'Stay away from me,' he whispered, as he climbed off the bed. 'I gone an' sinned an' I gone sin some more if'n I don' find no redemption.'

She sat up in the bed and began wiping her hand clean with tissues. 'You're weird, you really are.'

He crouched on the floor, naked and trembling. He reached for his travelling bag and pulled out a black box. He opened it up and began removing bottles of black ink and needles.

'What are you doing?' she said.

'I got to tattoo mysel', purge the evil from me,' he replied, not even sparing a moment to look up at her.

'Oh no you don't,' she said. 'I've got another customer coming soon, you need to pay me and get out of here.'

His head snapped up and his lips peeled back from teeth suddenly grown long and sharp.

'Let me be, woman, before I rip you open and drink your blood!' he hissed.

She pressed herself up against the wall, the breath catching in her throat.

And she watched him silently as he began tattooing black ink over his already blackened skin.

CATS

The cat jumped on his knee, looked like it was getting ready to make itself comfortable. It was a mangy tabby, one ear chewed off in a fight a long time ago, a couple of old scars on its nose.

Shanks Longworth pushed it off his lap with a vicious shove. The cat squealed as it hit the floor and dashed away, disappearing through an open door.

Longworth brushed cat hair off his trousers and then wiped his hand on his shirt. Disgusting bloody things, cats. Problem was, this house was full of them. Prowling in and out of the rooms, snaking around his ankles, getting into sudden, shocking little scraps which ended as soon as they had begun.

He pulled a handkerchief out of his pocket and sneezed into it. What now? Was he bloody allergic to the buggers, too?

A tall, stooped man entered the living room. His trousers and shirt were stained and covered in cat hairs.

'It's all there,' he said.

'I bloody well told you that to start with,' Longworth said.

'You expected me to check it, didn't you?'

'Yeah, I suppose.'

'When do you need the hardware, then?'

'Tonight,' Longworth said. 'That going to be a problem?'

The man's face was gaunt, and he had dark shadows under his eyes. Looked like his whole life was a problem, a problem he kept attempting to fix but kept failing at. He flopped down in an armchair, his long legs and bony knees sticking out at wide angles.

'Tomorrow night,' he said eventually. 'You can collect the gear tomorrow night.'

'That's too late, I need it tonight.'

The man gazed at Longworth with watery eyes. 'That's too bad. I'll go and get your money for you, you can take it and find somebody else to get what you need.'

'I was told you were the best at this, that you could get me whatever I needed,' Longworth said.

'I am the best,' the man said, reaching for a crumpled packet of cigarettes on a table by his chair. He peered inside the packet and then crumpled it up and dropped it on the floor. 'But I'm retired now, have been for a few years.'

A scrawny cat, its hair matted in clumps, sat at Longworth's feet and looked up at him. Longworth kicked it away.

'So why are you supplying me?' he said.

'Your mate, your contact, I owed him a favour.' He'd found a bent cigarette from somewhere and it dangled from his lips as he spoke. 'That's why.' He struck a match, the flame flaring range against the cigarette end. 'Now, your collection is tomorrow night. Take it or leave it.'

'All right, old man,' Longworth said. 'I'll take it.'

A cat yelped and dashed out of the living room, another one hot on its tail.

Longworth glanced around the room, at the threadbare furniture, the dirty rug and worn carpet, the cat litter trays deposited in all the corners and the cats prowling round and around.

'How the hell do you live like this?' Longworth said. 'Don't the evil bastards give you nightmares? They would me.'

'You get used to them,' the man said.

Longworth kicked out at a black cat snaking around his ankles.

It darted across the room and laid its teeth into another cat that had been sitting washing itself.

'What do I do, come back here tomorrow night and pick it up?' he said.

'No!' the man said. 'Don't come back here. I'll give you an address, you'll be met.'

'Who by? You?'

The man chuckled softly. It sounded more like an asthmatic wheeze. 'No, not me. Like I said, I don't really do this sort of work anymore. Let's just say I'm having to outsource the actual procurement and delivery of the goods.'

'Is that why the price was so fucking high?'

The man nodded. 'But don't worry. You'll get what you need.'

The two cats were facing each other off, crouched with hackles raised. They were both making a low growling noise, like nothing Longworth had ever heard before.

It sent shivers through him.

SHITHOLE

He took a left, walking fast down Corporation Street and away from Angellicit. There, that would confuse the stupid bastard. He knew his type, British Army was full of idiots like him. Gilligan had grown up listening to his father's stories about life in the IRA, and the stupidity of the British soldiers. He loved telling stories, did his old man. Even near the end, when he could hardly get the words out in between the racking coughs, his handkerchief spotted with flecks of blood, he kept on telling the stories.

Gilligan crossed Corporation Street, dashing in front of the path of a tram approaching its stop. He turned left on the corner and began walking up New Street.

The urge to take a quick glance over his shoulder and check that Mitch was still following him was strong, but Gilligan knew better than to give in to it. That would be a dead giveaway to Mitch that he had been rumbled.

Birmingham. What a shithole it used to be. Now it was trying to be all modern and sexy and culturally relevant, whatever the fuck that meant. But if you walked far enough, you could still find the shitty parts.

Walk far enough in any city and you could find the shitty parts.

Gilligan took a right at the end of New Street and cut through the Bullring. Down the broad stone steps and past St Martin's Church.

On towards Digbeth.

The buildings were more industrial down here. The brickwork dark from years of pollution. Gilligan ducked down a side street. There were no houses here, no shops, just manufacturing units.

Gilligan stepped just inside the cover of a brick archway and waited. Made sure to keep his shoes out of the black puddles of oil.

When he saw Mitch, Gilligan grabbed him and hauled him into the archway. Shoved him up against the cold brick wall.

'What the hell do you think you're doing then, eh?' Gilligan hissed. 'You've been on my bloody tail the last few days, following me everywhere like I'm a bloody mother hen. Now just what the fuck are you up to?'

Mitch wrenched himself free of Gilligan's grip. 'Feeling a little paranoid, are you, Gerry?'

Gilligan stepped back, eyed Mitch warily. 'Now what gives you the right to use my first name, like we're all friends or something?'

Mitch straightened his jacket. 'What would you rather I called you? Peaceful?'

'Where'd you get that name from?' Gilligan said.

'It's amazing what you can find out these days, especially if you know where to look.'

'And what the fuck does it matter to you what my name is?' Gilligan took a quick glance at the street behind him. He'd been stupid, confronting Mitch like this. For all he knew, Mitch wasn't the only one tailing him. And how did he know his old nickname from his days back in Belfast?

'Ah come on, Peaceful, relax,' Mitch said. 'It's not like you've got a guilty conscience or anything, is it?'

'What are you talking about, soldier boy? You're not making any sense now, are you?'

'It's just a shame you haven't got your old mate Brendan with you, maybe you'd act like a man then instead of a fucking pussy,' Mitch said.

Gilligan eyeballed Mitch, but he was shorter than the ex-soldier and had to look up to keep eye contact. Mitch was using his size to gradually force Gilligan out of the shadows of the archway and onto the street.

'You're talking out of your arse, soldier boy, making noise and nothing else,' Gilligan said.

'Is that right?' Mitch said, leaning in closer, his voice low. 'How about this for making noise, then? I know you murdered Karl Edwards, and I'm going to keep on your tail until I've got enough I can go to the cops and get you put away for a long, long time.'

Mitch shoved Gilligan out of his way and began walking away.

Gilligan stared at his back, imagining holding up a gun and shooting a single bullet into the back of Mitch's head. How the fuck did he know about the newspaper editor? And what was it to him?

Emma Wylde. It had to be. That stupid bitch had hired Mitch, like he was some kind of private detective, to find the dirt on Gilligan. But how did she even know him?

Angellicit. They were both there that morning, soldier boy even went and rescued her, like some fucking prince in shining armour. No, she hadn't hired him, they were an item, weren't they?

'Oi, soldier boy,' Gilligan shouted.

Mitch paused, turned around.

'When you see your girlfriend tonight, why don't you ask her how she enjoyed having my cock in her mouth? And think about that when she's tonguing you.'

'What did you say?' Mitch shouted, walking back down the alleyway towards Gilligan.

'You heard me,' Gilligan said. 'Your girlfriend's a slut, but she gives good head, I'll tell you that.'

Mitch threw a punch at Gilligan, who dodged it. He didn't see Mitch's other fist coming for him until it smashed into his nose and sent him reeling backwards on his heels. He staggered, thought he was about to fall as his world grew dark and warm blood poured from his nose and over his lips and chin. Mitch saved him from falling, grabbing Gilligan by the shirt and punching him in the face again.

This time he did fall over, skinning his hands on the rough tarmac and banging his elbows. Mitch got in close, raising a foot to give Gilligan a good kick in the side. This time, Gilligan was ready and hooked his feet around the leg Mitch was standing on. The ex-soldier hit the ground hard next to Gilligan.

Before Gilligan had a chance to take advantage, Mitch was up on his knees, his one hand at Gilligan's throat and the other raised and clenched into a fist.

'Go on then, soldier boy,' Gilligan said, spitting flecks of blood as he talked. 'Go on then, give it all you've got.'

The fist descended, shooting towards Gilligan, filling his vision.

A moment of pain, shooting stars and vivid yellow and orange explosions before everything went dark.

SHAW AND STUT were dragging the body down the stairs. They had already wrapped it up in heavy duty tarpaulin. The corpse's head banged against every step as they dragged it down by its feet.

Coffin watched them from the top of the stairs. He held a cigarette between his fingers, the white smoke trailing up and slowly dispersing.

'Shit, this bastard weighs a fucking ton,' Shaw said.

Thunk, thunk, thunk, went the head as it hit each and every step.

By his side, Coffin held the sword. He had cleaned the blood and flecks of brain and bone from it.

'What are you going to do with that?' the Stig said.

Coffin took a drag on the cigarette. 'Keep it. Put it on the wall to replace the one that used to be in there.'

'You used to have a sword in your office?'

'Mort did. A Japanese Samurai sword. I killed a vampire with it.'

'Oh yeah, I heard about that,' the Stig said.

'Where's Gilligan?' Coffin said.

'Don't know, nobody's seen him this morning.'

'Get hold of him, we need to meet, talk about this Gosling situation. Tell Shaw, too.'

'You going to go in with him?' the Stig said.

'Just get the others together,' Coffin said.

THE NOISE of the door slamming shut made Emma jump, and she accidentally flicked a blob of nappy cream from her finger and onto her top.

'Shit,' she muttered and grabbed a wipe and started scrubbing at the spot. Something else to go in the wash before the cream left a greasy stain.

Louisa May lay on her back on the bed, kicking her bare legs and chewing on a fist. Her cheeks were a fiery red again this morning, but she seemed reasonably settled, at least. Emma grabbed the baby's feet and lifted her up enough to slide a nappy under her bottom.

'Hi Mitch,' she shouted, as she fastened the nappy together. 'I'm upstairs!'

Emma sat Louisa May up, holding her around her torso. The skin felt rough beneath her finger tips. Emma took a closer look. More eczema. She ran her fingers over Louisa May's soft skin and the patches of dry blemishes.

'Why didn't you tell me?'

Emma picked up her baby, holding her against her shoulder, and turned around.

'Mitch! What the hell happened?'

He stood in the bedroom doorway. A vivid bruise discoloured his left cheek, and the eye was swollen partially closed and bloodshot.

'Why didn't you tell me, Emma?' he said.

His knuckles, too, Emma noticed. Bruised, bleeding in places.

'Tell you what?'

'He raped you, didn't he? That bastard Gilligan, he raped you and you never told me.'

'No, no.' Emma shook her head. Her instinct was to go to him and hold him, but she had Louisa May in her arms, and she hadn't washed her hands after changing the nappy, and she didn't like the look in Mitch's eyes, like he had lost his sense of what was normal, what was right and wrong.

'He told me,' Mitch said. 'He told me every fucking detail. Until I made him stop.'

Emma glanced at his knuckles, bleeding again.

'What did you do to him?' she whispered. 'Is he…?'

'No, the bastard's alive.'

Emma started breathing again. 'Mitch, he didn't rape me, he's messing with you, that's all. He… he tried to rape me, but I fought him off.'

Mitch continued staring at Emma, his brow furrowed.

'You fought him off,' he said after what had seemed like an eternally long pause. 'You think that makes it all right then? You think he should just get away with it?'

'No, of course not.' Emma clutched Louisa May a little tighter. 'It's just, I don't understand, did he attack you?'

'No,' Mitch said, and wiped the back of his hand across his nose, smearing blood over his cheek. 'I went after him.'

'You can't do that, you can't just go assaulting people, you'll end up in jail.'

Mitch looked at the blood smeared across the back of his hand. 'I'm going to have a shower.'

Once he had left the room, Emma had to sit down on the bed before her knees gave way. The violence had radiated off him like a physical heat, like he might explode with fury at any moment.

Like he might have assaulted Emma?

No. No, he wasn't like that. Mitch had rescued Emma from the vampires at the club. Had come for her despite the infection raging through his body, despite his wounds and the likelihood that he might die by attempting to save her.

Hurt Emma?

No, he wouldn't do that.

THEY WERE BACK in The Punchline. Coffin, Shaw, the Stig and Gilligan.

Gilligan's face was covered in scrapes, his nose red and swollen and his left eye was covered in an angry looking bruise and swollen almost completely shut. Coffin didn't ask him what had happened. It wasn't his business, and besides which he wasn't interested.

Gosling was there, his bulk dwarfing the chair he was sitting on. The rolls of fat on his neck spilled over his collar, and his fat face was slick with sweat. But his eyes darted around the room constantly, taking things in, assessing the situation, never still.

'What made you change your mind, Joe?' Gosling said.

Stilts arrived at the table with a tray of drinks and a bottle.

As the little man was handing out the drinks, Coffin took the bottle and said, 'I'll take care of this.'

Stilts regarded him in silence for a few moments before turning and walking away.

Coffin topped his whisky up with the bottle. 'Not that it makes any difference to you, but the situation has changed. Looks like the Seven Ghosts are intending on coming back and making a play for Angellicit.' He took a sip of the whisky. It was good. 'And they intend to take me out as well.'

Gosling chuckled. 'Is that why your man over there looks like he tried shagging a two hundred pound gorilla? Or maybe that's just his wife?'

Shaw looked at Gilligan and burst out laughing. Gilligan stood up.

'You watch your fucking mouth, now,' he said.

'Sit down,' Coffin said.

Gilligan remained standing for a couple of moments, the tendons in his neck standing out, his dark purple bruises standing out against his pale skin. Finally, he sat down.

'Like I said, it's none of your business,' Coffin said to Gosling. 'You wanted manpower, you got manpower.'

'The thing is, I need to know what kind of manpower I've got,'

Gosling said. 'I need to know you can do the job and looking at Paddy over there, I'm not so sure of that anymore.'

'You want me to come over there and show you what I can do?' Gilligan said. 'You might be a big man, but you're all lard, I could take you down in a second, I could.'

'See what I'm talking about, Joe? The man's got a hair trigger temper.'

'Gerry, go take a walk outside,' Coffin said.

Gilligan stood up, looking like a petulant child. Coffin was about to tell him again to go when Gilligan turned and walked away.

'He's got a temper on him, hasn't he?' Gosling said.

'Tell me about the job,' Coffin said. 'Tell me how we're going to do it.'

Gosling regarded Coffin for a long moment. 'All right, Joe,' he said, finally. 'It's simple, really. Widow Ullman lost another of her security firm last night. Walked out on her in the middle of the night. Not a surprise, I suppose, as I'm guessing she pays them peanuts. And if you pay peanuts you only get monkeys, am I right, Joe?'

Coffin said nothing. He wasn't in the mood to chat.

'So that leaves her with three rent-a-bodyguards. One to keep a presence inside the house, reassure the paranoid old biddy that there aren't hordes of masked men beating the doors down or climbing through the windows.'

'Seriously?' Shaw said. 'Is she that bad?'

'Absolutely,' Gosling said. 'Nutty as a fruitcake is what she is. That leaves two more, who would normally be patrolling the outside of the house and through the gardens. I say normally because with two men down she has no one to attend the gated entrance, and no one to sit in the safe room with her cash.'

Shaw was shaking his head, grinning. 'This is going to be like taking candy from a baby.'

'You think so?' Gosling said. 'You might be surprised. All these men she hires are ex-mercenaries, soldiers of fortune. They're tough bastards, sharp too.'

'I don't get it,' Coffin said. 'Why would these men be working for next to nothing? If they're so pissed off about the pay that they walk off the job in the middle of the night, why would they take it in the first place? It doesn't make any sense to me.'

'Bloody hell, Joe, that's the most you've said all morning,' Gosling said, chuckling. The rolls of fat around his neck quivered as he laughed. 'You must be exhausted, have another drink.'

Coffin scowled at Gosling.

'Seriously, Joe, I don't know why the stupid sods are leaving. Maybe the old biddy is asking them for sexual favours, but does it really matter? The point is, they're two men down right now and we can't afford to miss the opportunity to go and get all that money that's just sitting there waiting for us.'

'All right, so we get past the security, take them out, whatever. How do we get inside the safe room?' Coffin said.

'Stilts here is our man,' Gosling said, indicating the dwarf as he approached the table, as though he had been summoned. 'Stilts can get us in anywhere, he's world renowned for his locked room cracking skills. He once broke into the Zurcher Kantonalbank in Switzerland, ranked number one in the league tables of safe banks in Europe. He didn't take anything though, just the opposite, in fact. He left a deposit. Smack in the middle of the vault, a steaming pile of crap.'

Coffin looked at Stilts. 'Comedian, safe cracker, you're a multi talented man.'

Stilts returned Coffin's stare. His features could have been carved from stone, they were so still.

Gosling laughed. 'He says even less than you, I'm surprised the two of you aren't best mates by now.'

Coffin turned his gaze back upon the big man. 'You're full of shit. You expect me to believe all this?'

Gosling clutched his chest and rolled his eyes. 'Joe! You're breaking my heart! Would I lie to you? Maybe I was exaggerating a little about the Zurcher Kantonalbank, but the rest is true. This little fella, he can get you in anywhere you want.'

Coffin threw his whisky back and poured himself another. 'If you can get in, then why do you need us?'

'Muscle, Joe, I need you for the muscle. If we get into a fight, I need someone I can count on, someone tough like you. Stilts, he can kick people in the shins, but that's about all he's good for in a scrap, and Duchess just flounces around screaming. But you, Joe. You and the Mob. You're the ones I need on my side.'

'What do you think?' Coffin said to Shaw.

'Come on, Joe, we've faced worse than a few ex-mercenaries for hire. This'll be a piece of piss.'

Coffin looked at Gosling again. Drummed his fingers on the table.

When it came down to it, he didn't have a choice. The Slaughterhouse Mob needed the money.

'All right, we're in,' he said.

AN EMPTY GRAVE

Steffanie gasped as Chitrita brought her to climax. She gripped Chitrita's head between her hands, the vampire's hair tangled around her fingers, shuddering with delight as Chitrita licked at her.

Michael stood passively watching them, gazing blank eyed at their writhing, naked bodies.

Steffanie cried out and Michael flinched at the sound of her voice.

Chitrita lifted her head and looked at the boy. Michael gazed back at her.

'Does he never say anything?' she said.

Steffanie, breathing heavily, turned her head to look at her son. 'No, he only knows a few words. He was too young when he turned.'

Chitrita crouched on her hands and knees and looked down at Steffanie. 'We should get rid of him. Kill him.'

'Why?' Steffanie said.

'He slows you down, he will slow us both down.' Slowly, Chitrita stood up. She walked towards Michael, her bare feet making no noise on the hard floor. 'I don't know why you keep him around.'

Steffanie yawned and stretched, her breathing slowing. Outside, a girl screamed and then burst into a fit of giggles. A man joined her, laughing hard.

'He does what he's told, and besides, me having Michael tears Joe apart.' She smiled. 'And anything that torments Joe is worth having.'

Chitrita circled the boy, running her hand through his hair and down over his face. 'Joe Coffin. Ever since I was pulled from the ground, I've been hearing his name. Those two freaks who kept me in a cage and fed me never stopped talking about him.'

Steffanie sat up. 'Stump and Corpse?'

'Yes, do you know them too?'

'They used to do jobs for the Slaughterhouse Mob sometimes.'

Chitrita continued circling Michael, trailing her hand over his shoulders, round his neck and then up through his hair. 'One day soon I'm going to kill them for what they did.' She paused, her hand resting on the top of Michael's head. 'Except, they did dig me up and bring me back. If not for them, I suppose I would still be under the ground. When I kill them, I'll do it quickly, I suppose I owe them that much.' She looked down at Michael, placing a finger under his chin and tilting his head up so that he was looking at her, and she smiled. 'Or maybe not. Maybe I will enjoy myself, let them suffer. Depends how I feel at the time.'

More screams and laughter from outside. Steffanie pulled back a heavy tarpaulin, crusted with plaster and dust, and looked out of the window. Two couples, the men in tight fitting, white shirts and jeans, the girls in short, low-cut dresses.

They were drunk, obviously. Daring each other to see who could stay outside the longest. A game, a stupid game. Trying to scare each other. Even from up here, Steffanie could see their fear. It would hardly take anything to send them scurrying inside the nearest bar.

'And what about Joe?' Steffanie said.

'He most certainly needs to die,' Chitrita replied. 'All the time I hear people talking, saying Joe Coffin this and Joe Coffin that. So very boring.'

'He's hard to kill,' Steffanie said, watching the couples wandering up Sheepcote Street towards Broad Street, still laughing. Still scared.

'No one's that hard to kill,' Chitrita whispered, bending over Michael, her face only inches from his. 'Shall I show you? Shall I kill the boy?'

Steffanie let the tarpaulin drop back into place and turned to Chitrita. 'No. I like having him around. I told you, it rips Joe apart. When we kill Joe, I want him to be looking at Michael as we do it.'

'Do you still have feelings for the boy?' Chitrita whispered. 'Don't tell me there is still a tiny part of his mother left inside you.'

'No, I told you. It gives me satisfaction to know that Joe is tearing himself apart thinking about Michael, wondering where he is, and how he can cure him.'

'Cure him?' Chitrita stood up straight and tossed her head back, her laughter echoing around the empty room. 'There is no cure for this!'

'Joe thinks there is. Merek told me about Leola and the Priest, about the tattoos and their faith in God.'

'Leola is a silly little girl. She's weak, pathetic.' Chitrita spit the words out. 'And the Priest is a deluded old man, nothing more.' Chitrita began walking around the empty space. 'We need to find somewhere else to stay. We are too vulnerable here.'

Steffanie followed Chitrita's movements, watching her as she prowled through the shadows, like a large cat. The vampire moved beautifully, gracefully. Her flesh was white and unblemished, her limbs long and slender and yet containing such power. Chitrita was beautiful in a way that none of the other vampires were. Even Merek and Abel, although they had both exuded power and a hungry sexuality, a certain heat that attracted Steffanie, they hadn't been beautiful in the way Chitrita was.

'Where can we go?' Steffanie said. 'The house has been demolished and Joe is back in Angellicit.'

Chitrita stalked the perimeter of the room until she closed in on Steffanie once more. She ran her fingers through Steffanie's long, tousled hair and over her face, over the ragged hole in her cheek.

Steffanie embraced the naked vampire, sliding her hands down her back, over her buttocks.

Chitrita kissed her, and Steffanie opened her mouth, accepting the long, sinuous tongue, the heat rising once more in her belly.

And Michael watched them.

ONCE THE MEETING with Gosling and his gang of weirdos and freaks had finished, Coffin took off on the Fatboy. He told the others he was heading back for the club. Once he was on the bike, he changed his mind.

He headed out of the city, opening up the throttle and letting the bike take the lead. He had no destination in mind, nowhere to go other than back to Angellicit. The place wasn't just his club now, along with the others scattered around Birmingham and the surrounding area, but it was his home. The house where he had lived with Steffanie and Michael had sold quickly. The opportunity to own a place where the notorious Joe Coffin had once lived, where there had been a gruesome murder, was too much to resist for some people.

Coffin was glad to be rid of it. His memories of the time spent there were soured now. When he thought of Steffanie, he thought only of her betrayal with Terry Wu, and who knew who else? And when he thought of Michael, he couldn't see his son anymore. Only the monster he had been turned into.

The light from the bike's headlamp cut through the darkness, illuminating the black tarmac of the road. He sped past the occasional car, but mostly the roads were clear.

Coffin's head was filled with questions, the thoughts tumbling over one another, jostling for space in his mind. The voices crowded his head, demanding to be heard, wanting answers to questions until they turned into so much white noise. This was why he needed to get out on his own, away from everyone.

Seemed like everyone wanted a piece of him now. Stut and Shaw and the others, always looking to him for a decision on something. The cops wanting his help with the vampires, and the public looking to him like he was a celebrity. The Seven Ghosts were still after him, seeking revenge and a piece of the action in Birmingham. Stump and Corpse, who he owed a favour to, and God knew what form that would take.

And Steffanie. Wherever she was right now, she wouldn't rest until she'd put Coffin in the ground. Permanently.

Coffin let his unconscious take the lead as he rode the bike out of the city and then gradually back in again. Thinking over the events of the last few days, he was only half aware of where he was.

But then he realised and pulled the bike over to the side of the road.

The graveyard.

Coffin climbed off the bike and removed his helmet. He walked into the graveyard, his boots crunching on the gravel path the only sound in the night. He found their graves quickly, even though they weren't there anymore.

Coffin stood at the spot where his wife and son had been buried. Where Michael had been, there was now a new gravestone.

Ethel Wilkinson, Born 5th May 1932, Died 23rd June 2018. Rest in Peace Nanny Ethel.

Fresh flowers had been placed in a vase on the grave.

The other plot where Steffanie had been buried was an open grave, waiting for a new occupant. Yellow hazard tape cordoned off the hole. A spade, its blade thick with clumps of soil, lay beside it.

Did they still use spades to dig graves? Coffin thought they would have used mini diggers, or something similar.

Coffin leaned over the hole, looked down inside.

His chest tightened up at the thought of seeing Steffanie lying at the bottom, grinning up at him.

The grave was empty.

Coffin took a deep breath and looked around at the dark shapes of the gravestones and angels silhouetted against the night sky. The air was cool on his face. He noticed a flurry of movement around the top of the church tower.

Bats.

Was it his imagination or were there more bats than usual around at the moment? Or perhaps he was just noticing them more.

What was he doing here? There was nothing for him in this place, apart from memories. Bad memories. The funeral, Steffanie and Michael being lowered into the ground. And then his return to this spot, with a spade, to dig up their graves. To prove to himself that they were still dead, still in the ground where he had seen them buried.

Coffin watched the bats spiralling around the church tower. He could just make out their winged shapes against the clear sky, tumbling and darting sharply around and between each other.

Coffin heard the movement at the last moment, just before his skull exploded with pain. At that instant where he had realised someone was approaching him, that they were in fact right behind him, he had begun moving. He hadn't managed to get out of the way of the blow to his head, but he had moved enough that it hadn't fully connected.

From the force of the blow, Coffin was sure he would have been dead if he had received the full impact.

Coffin fell to the damp ground and rolled over. His assailant was standing over him. Clad in black leather biker's gear and wearing a helmet, the visor obscuring his face. In his right hand, he held a baseball bat. The end was dark with a splash of blood.

The biker bent down, raising the baseball bat above his head. Coffin kicked out, but the attacker moved swiftly out of the way. The baseball bat hurtled towards Coffin, his attacker driving all his force and weight behind the movement. Coffin deflected the blow with his arm and the bat smacked into the soft ground, throwing the man off balance.

Coffin used his assailant's momentum to push him to the ground. Coffin got to his feet. Blood was running down the back of his skull and onto his neck. He felt dizzy and sick.

Coffin's attacker had jumped to his feet. He crouched in front of Coffin, holding the baseball bat, the featureless helmet pointed Coffin's way.

Coffin picked up the spade lying by the side of the open grave.

The biker lunged for him, swinging the baseball bat. Coffin smashed the spade against the bat and it went flying from his attacker's hand. It tumbled through the air, end over end, and disappeared in the darkness.

Coffin smacked the spade into the biker's head. The impact made a loud crack and the biker's head snapped sharply to one side. Coffin drove the spade into his chest and the man staggered and fell into the open grave. He landed at the bottom of the pit on his back.

Coffin jumped down after him, his feet crunching into the man's chest as he landed on top of him. Coffin heard a muffled grunt of pain from inside the bike helmet. Slivers of dirt ran down the grave's walls as the biker struggled to fight Coffin off.

Kneeling on his attacker's chest, Coffin gripped the bike helmet with both hands and yanked it off. The man gasped with pain.

As Coffin had expected, the man was Chinese.

'Stop struggling,' Coffin growled, throwing the helmet to one side and picking up the spade. 'Who are you?'

The Chinese man, eyes wide and face damp with sweat, spat at Coffin.

Coffin raised the spade. 'Tell me what's going on, or I'll cave your head in.'

Coffin's attacker started talking rapidly in Chinese.

'Don't you speak English?' Coffin said.

The man jerked his head from side to side, still talking. Coffin thought he heard a couple of words he understood. Maybe not.

Coffin sighed.

He smashed the spade into the man's face and silenced him.

He climbed out of the open grave.

He didn't need answers, he already had them.

The Seven Ghosts were back, and they wanted Coffin dead.

PUT SOME CLOTHES ON

Archer sat in his car, the windows steaming up as he sipped at his coffee. The engine was silent, the lights off. He was parked half on and half off the pavement outside his house. He still thought of it as his, even though he didn't live there anymore.

A car sped past him. Had to be doing at least 45mph even though they were in a 30mph zone.

Archer picked up his mobile from the space between the seats and scrolled through his messages. Nothing. This was an annoying habit of his that he had developed in the last couple of months. Somehow, he seemed to have got it fixed in his subconscious that Emma would have messaged him. He had no idea why she would message him, other than banal day-to-day stuff, but still.

He had this compulsive need to check his messages.

And once he had checked, and seen there was nothing from her, he had to steel himself against messaging her. What good would it do? He had nothing much to say to her.

Except that one thing.

About kicking Mitch out of the house.

Archer didn't like him. Didn't trust him.

Archer knew if it wasn't for Mitch that Emma might not be alive right now. He knew that. But it didn't make any difference. He still didn't like the man.

Archer had had one of his people look into Mitch's background. There was nothing much there. His excellent record as a soldier. The divorced wife. That dodgy website that was supposed to help people make life choices and win the lottery was about the most muck against Mitch that Archer's colleague could scrape up.

Still, Archer didn't like him.

Wasn't even sure he trusted him.

Archer took another sip of his coffee, looked at the house through the partially steamed-up window. The light was on in the bedroom. Archer wondered if Emma and Mitch were in there right now, making love.

Archer shifted in his seat.

Nothing he could do about it even if they were.

Archer placed his coffee cup in the holder and placed both hands on the steering wheel. *Just go,* he thought. *I don't even know what the hell you are doing here in the first place.*

Protecting Emma and Louisa May, that's what. With all these vampires on the loose once more, Archer had thought it might be prudent to check up on Emma every night. Keep a look out for a while. Make sure they were safe.

Bullshit, Archer thought. *You know why you're here and it's got nothing to do with vampires.*

Archer picked up the coffee again and took another sip.

The light in the bedroom switched off.

'Shit,' he muttered.

He could imagine them in there right now, under the covers. Embracing, their naked limbs entwined with each other. Archer sipped more coffee. His hand was shaking. His teeth were clenched tight.

Putting the coffee down, he laid his head against the seat back.

Closed his eyes.

Got to relax, he thought. *Just take a moment, calm down and then get the hell out of here.*

A knocking on the passenger side window broke through his thoughts and he snapped his eyes open.

'Can I help you, Detective Archer?'

Mitch, leaning with one hand on the car roof, peering through the misty glass.

Fuck.

Archer stabbed at the button to slide the window down, forgetting that the engine was turned off. He twisted the key in the ignition to switch on the electrics and the window slid smoothly down. Once Archer could see Mitch clearly, without the steamed-up window obscuring him, he noticed the bruising and swelling on his face.

'What happened to you?' Archer said. 'Get into an argument with someone?'

'I'm more interested in knowing what the hell you're doing outside…' He paused, as though he had been about to say *outside my house,* and thought better of it. 'Surely it's not good police protocol to be stalking your ex?'

'I'm not stalking anyone,' Archer replied. 'But as a police officer, I do need to ask you again, and you are required to answer. What happened to your face?'

'Oh crap, you're not going to pull this on me, are you?' Mitch stood up straight so that Archer couldn't see his face anymore.

Archer climbed out of the car, forcing Mitch to back up as the door opened. Slammed the door shut and stood in front of Mitch.

'You've obviously been in a fight, which means someone else got hurt. You want to tell me about it here, or do I have to take you down to the station?'

'Don't do this, Detective Archer,' Mitch said. He glanced towards the house.

Archer saw the glance. And all of a sudden, it became totally and absolutely clear to him what had happened. Mitch had had a fight with Emma. He knew what she was like, had lived with her for long enough. That temper of hers was like a firework. It might spark and fizz for a long time, it might even go quiet enough that you could think it had gone out, but then she would explode. That was what had happened. They'd got into an argument and Emma had lost it big time.

And Mitch had hit her.

Emma wouldn't have held back. That was where he got his bruises from when she hit him. Then she kicked him out, and now here he was trying to worm his way back into her home, into Archer's house.

The question was, how badly had he hurt her?

And what about Louisa May?

'Turn around and put your hands on the car roof,' Archer said.

'Are you serious?' Mitch said.

'Just do it,' Archer said, reaching for his cuffs.

'What the hell's going on? You're arresting me?' Mitch stepped up a little closer to Archer, puffing his chest out.

'Turn around and put your hands on the car as I asked you, sir, before you get yourself into more trouble than you're already in.'

Mitch stood his ground for a moment longer, long enough that Archer wasn't totally sure which way this was going to go. If Mitch wanted to fight this out, Archer wasn't sure he could take him on. He tensed up, ready.

Mitch stepped down, almost seemed to deflate.

'This is fucked up,' he said, turning around and placing his hands on the car roof.

Archer frisked him, then said, 'Put your hands behind your back.'

'This is so fucked up,' Mitch said.

He lowered his arms and placed his hands behind his back. Archer cuffed him quickly and efficiently.

Pulling open the rear door, Archer said, 'All right, in the car. We're going down to the station.'

He placed his hand on top of Mitch's head and guided him into the back of the car. Slammed the door shut and locked it.

Mitch looked up and glared at Archer at the sound of the central locking mechanism clunking into place.

'Hey!' he shouted, his voice muffled behind the glass. 'What the fuck is this? You said you were taking me to the station!'

Archer turned his back on the car and walked up the drive to his house. Nobody was going anywhere until he had made sure that Emma and Louisa May were all right and unharmed.

It took over a minute of knocking on the door and waiting until Emma finally opened up.

'What's going on?' she said. Her hair was wet, and she was wearing a dressing gown. Archer saw a trail of damp footsteps across the floor.

'Are you okay?' Archer said. 'Did he hurt you?'

'Did who hurt me? Nick, what are you talking about?'

'I'm talking about Mitch, about the fight you had.' A high pitched buzzing had started up in Archer's ears. There was something wrong here, but he couldn't work out what.

'What fight?' Emma said, pulling the dressing gown a little tighter. 'We haven't had a fight. Where's Mitch? What have you done with him?'

'Don't lie to me, Emma, don't try and protect him. I know you hit him back, I saw the bruising, but you were protecting yourself. You've got nothing to worry about.'

Emma stood on her tiptoes and looked over Archer's shoulder. 'Oh God, is that Mitch in the back of the car? Have you arrested him?'

'He refused to answer my questions, I had to arrest him.' This conversation was spiralling out of his control. It wasn't meant to happen like this.

'Nick, let him out of the car!' Emma hissed. 'Mitch hasn't done a thing.'

'What about the bruising and the swelling all over his face, then? Huh? How the hell did that happen? And don't tell me he walked into a door.'

'He was mugged,' Emma said.

'Did he report it?'

'No, I don't think so.' Emma looked around Archer, down the drive. 'Are you going to let him out of the car?'

'No,' Archer said. 'I'm not convinced. I want to question you both some more.'

'Fuck, Nick!' Emma hissed. 'Do I look like I've been in a fight? Do you see any bruises?'

'No, not on your face, but you might have other bruises, I know what these bastards can do. They know to punch their victims in the body where no one can see the bruises.'

Emma undid her dressing gown and opened it up, pulled it off her shoulders, and let it fall to the floor. She stood, completely naked, glaring at Archer. Her skin was pink from the hot water of the shower, soft and unblemished. She turned and showed him her back.

Archer looked away. He felt sick with desire.

'Satisfied now?' Emma said.

'Put some clothes on,' Archer said, his voice thick and heavy.

'Let Mitch out of the car.'

Archer walked back down the drive, his feet crunching over the gravel. His limbs felt heavy and his stomach turned over, like he was going to throw up. He couldn't get Emma out of his head, standing naked in front of him.

Archer let Mitch out of the car. Uncuffed him.

Mitch threw a punch at Archer. Smacked him in the face and knocked him to the ground.

Emma screamed.

Archer lay on his side on the gravel, listening to Mitch walk away. Heard Emma shouting at Mitch, the two of them arguing.

He hauled himself to his feet, climbed in the car and drove away.

PUMPER-UPPED

'What happened to you?' Leola said.

Coffin was standing over the sink, bare-chested, washing dried blood off the back of his head. The water running down the bowl and into the plughole was stained pink.

'Got smacked over the head with a baseball bat,' Coffin said. 'Looks like I'm on the Seven Ghosts' hit list still.'

Leola took the flannel from Coffin and began bathing the wound. 'Did you kill him?'

'What do you think?' Coffin said, leaning over the sink.

Leola held the flannel under the warm running water and squeezed it, rinsing out the blood.

'I think you need to be more careful,' she said.

Leola dropped the flannel in the sink and turned off the water. She picked up a towel and began gently patting dry the wound on Coffin's head. She finished drying Coffin's scalp and draped the towel over the towel rail. Coffin stayed where he was, leaning over the sink.

'That's the second time the Seven Ghosts have sent an assassin after me. The first time was here, at the club. But this time? I was back at the church, at Steffanie's grave. How the hell did he know I was there?'

Coffin turned around to face Leola. She was wearing a simple summer dress, revealing expanses of inked skin.

'Don't you ever get cold?' Coffin said.

'No.' Leola placed a hand on Coffin's arm. Looked up at him.

'What's wrong?'

'I'm leaving. I'm going home.'

'When?'

'Soon, the next couple of days.'

Coffin touched her cheek, gently ran his fingers back through her hair. 'You want to talk about it? Tell me why?'

Leola smiled, shook her head.

'What?'

'Talk about it? That's not you, Joe. You're not a talker, you're a doer.'

'Yeah, I suppose you're right.'

Leola nuzzled her head into Coffin's hand, like a cat enjoying the attention. 'You ever think about talking, Joe? About *really* talking? You carry a lot of baggage inside of you, anyone can see that.'

'What, you mean like to a therapist or something?'

'Yes, exactly that.'

'No.'

'Good,' Leola said. 'Don't ever talk to anyone, Joe. All that shit you carry around inside of you, all the crap that's happened to you, don't ever talk to anyone about it.' Leola placed a fist against her breasts. 'You've got to keep it all locked up in here. Without it you'll lose that rage, you won't be Joe Coffin anymore.'

Coffin had been looking at that fist, and now his eyes were drawn to the tattoos running across the top of Leola's chest and down under her dress. Desire stirred deep within him.

'Why do you need to go?' he said.

'There's nothing for me here, I need to get back home.' She paused. 'I only came back because of Guttman, because he needed destroying. You've done that. There are no more of the old ones left, except those still buried in the ground.'

'You were all for digging them up the other day, you couldn't wait to get started.'

'I was bored, I'm always bored. Those two vampires left, it's probably best just leave them where they are. Nobody's going to dig them up now.'

'We can go do it now, if you like,' Coffin said. 'And what about the vampires that escaped the other day?'

'They're nothing, you can deal with them all by yourself.' Leola smiled and placed a hand on Coffin's chest. 'Oh Joe, I'm not even sure why you want me around. Do you even know?'

Coffin pushed past her, out of the bathroom and into the office. He poured himself a whisky. Drank it down in one. Leola followed him.

'Are you angry?' she said.

Coffin put the empty glass down. 'Why would I be angry?'

'I think I know how you feel about me.'

Coffin thought about having another drink. Decided against it.

Leola said, 'You enjoy me, my body. I can give you what you need. But you hate me, too. Sometimes when you look at me, I know it's not me that you see.'

'Is that right?' Coffin said.

'Yes,' Leola said. 'You see Steffanie.'

Coffin said nothing.

Someone knocked at the office door.

'Joe?' It was Shaw. 'You've got visitors.'

'Yeah? Who?'

'Those two freaks, Stump and Corpse.'

'Shit,' Coffin muttered. And then, louder, 'I'll be right down.'

He pulled on a T-shirt. Looked at Leola.

'You coming?'

They headed downstairs. The club was empty apart from two girls gyrating on the stage to a pounding beat. The music echoed around the big, empty space. Corpse was standing by the front of the stage, his head titled up as he stared at the girls. One of them, wearing nothing but a G-string, was teasing him by leaning over him and giving him little flicks of her long hair in his face.

Corpse had a vacant grin on his gaunt face, his head bobbing up and down on his scrawny neck as he followed the girls' movements. As usual, he was wearing his stained, threadbare suit, the sleeves and legs too short for his lanky frame.

Stump stood a little further away from the stage, watching Corpse, not the girls. She had on her long, black leather jacket and her wraparound sunglasses.

'Hey, can someone turn that shit down?' Coffin shouted. 'I can hardly hear myself think!'

Shaw flicked the music off completely and the two girls stopped dancing.

'Aww, we were enjoying that,' the one girl said.

'Quit moaning,' Coffin said. 'We'll be opening up soon and then you'll be complaining about being on stage all night.'

The girl who had been teasing Corpse bent down until her breasts were level with his face. He didn't look up at her, just stared at her naked breasts.

'I'd like to say you're cute,' the girl said. 'But you're not, you're just creepy.'

She straightened up and the two girls ran off the stage, giggling.

Corpse watched them until they had disappeared through the back and then he turned to face Stump. He had a stricken look on his face, as though he was in pain. His trousers bulged at the crotch. Seemingly not knowing what he was doing, he shoved a hand down his trousers.

'Stop that, Mr Corpse!' Stump said. 'This is neither the time nor the place.'

Something switched on in Corpse's face and he removed his hand from inside his trousers.

'What do you two want?' Coffin said. 'I'm opening up soon and I need you two off the premises. You'll scare the punters away.'

Stump's head slowly swivelled towards Coffin, as though she were a robot. 'Really, Mr Coffin, after all the hospitality we have shown you.'

'Yeah, and you'll be making me pay for that,' Coffin said. 'So cut the crap, tell me why you're here and then get lost.'

'If that is how you want to be, then this is our favour,' Stump said. 'Mr Corpse and I need you to kill someone.'

Coffin thought about this for a moment. Leola and Shaw watched him, along with Stump and Corpse, waiting for his reply.

'It's not that simple, is it?' he said, finally. 'You want someone killed you could do it yourself. Why me?'

'It's a vampire,' Stump said.

'I don't do that anymore,' Coffin said. 'Go and see the Old Bill, I'm sure they'd be more than happy to talk to you.'

Stump began stroking her mannequin's hand with the tips of her fingers. The plastic was shiny and yellow with age.

'But Mr Coffin, you are so much more skilled in this area than the police,' she said.

'And what about you?' Coffin said. 'There's no reason you can't go using that blade you have hidden inside that plastic hand. Is it true? Do you really have a knife attached to your stump? Why don't you show us? We've been wondering about that for years, haven't we fellas?'

There was a soft murmur of assent from the others.

Coffin stepped a little closer to Stump. 'But there's something you're not telling me. You could call in a bigger favour than this. What's going on?'

Stump kept stroking her plastic hand. Corpse was pulling at the crotch of his trousers, readjusting himself.

'Mr Corpse and I dug this particular vampire up,' Stump said. 'I believe her name is Chitrita.'

Leola groaned and tipped her head back.

'What?' Coffin said, swivelling around to face her.

'Chitrita is one of the old ones,' Leola said. 'She was with Guttman and the others when I first met them, back when they turned me.'

'Great,' Coffin said, and turned back to Stump. 'You're telling me you dug one of those monsters up and then, what? Kept it as a pet?'

Stump said nothing. Just looked back at Coffin, her pudgy face impassive, her eyes hidden by the dark sunglasses.

'When Guttman was pulled out of the ground, he was weaker than a newborn kitten and looked like a bag of bones. I'm guessing this, what did you call her? Chitrita, I'm guessing she looked the same. You fed her, didn't you? Let her build her strength back until she could escape. Shit.'

Stump said nothing.

Corpse was looking at the bulge in his trousers as though utterly perplexed by it.

'We took you in, Mr Coffin, when you needed help,' Stump said. 'We found you medical care when you needed it and nursed you back to strength.'

'Yeah, and I'm grateful and everything, all right,' Coffin said. 'In fact, I'm so fucking grateful you get a lifetime's free entry into the club, both of you, and the drinks are always on the house. But I'm not killing vampires anymore. Now go get yourself one of those free drinks or fuck off out of my club.'

Stump stared at Coffin. Pursed her lips together.

Coffin wanted to snatch those sunglasses off her face, see her eyes for once.

Stump was still stroking her plastic hand, but her movements were quick and insistent. She stopped and gripped the mannequin's hand.

Coffin braced himself. He'd never seen the blade rumoured to be hidden beneath the false hand. He wondered how long and sharp it might be. If the blade was clean and shiny or stained brown with the dried blood of all her victims.

Stump relaxed her grip and let go of the hand.

'Come, Mr Corpse, I think we have outstayed our welcome here,' she said.

Corpse looked up at Stump. He had his hand back down his trousers again. He looked as though he might be in pain.

'The dancer girl, she pumper-upped my pencil, Mrs Stump,' he said. 'It's hurting.'

'Joe?' Shaw said. 'We need to open up.'

'Yeah,' Coffin said. 'Do it, these two freaks were just on their way out.'

Stump turned and headed for the exit without another word. Corpse followed her, shuffling awkwardly as he tried to catch up, his hand still down his trousers.

'I think you lost a couple of friends there,' Leola said.

Coffin grunted. 'They were never friends. Definitely a problem though.'

'You've got a bigger problem than those two,' Leola said. 'And its name is Chitrita.'

JULIE

She had been surviving on the blood of rats and stray cats. It wasn't enough; it didn't satisfy the need for more blood, for fresh, warm, human blood. But it helped.

She knew she had to keep a low profile, that if she was discovered, she would be caught and possibly murdered. But, despite this, she had taken to wandering outside in the evening, late enough that it was dark but early enough there were still people around.

She couldn't explain it, why she did that. The risks were obvious, the benefits not so. And yet here she was every evening, wandering through Brindley Place, beside the canal. Up and down the towpath and then through the pedestrianised streets lined with restaurants and bars and art galleries.

The hardest times were when she could smell blood. Someone might have cut themselves earlier that day, a plaster placed over a finger or a thumb. Or a woman might pass her and she was menstruating.

And the blood lust would wash over her and she had to hold tight and resist the urge to pounce, and to bite and rip and shred and drink.

She had to hold her head a certain way, so that her long hair hung slightly over her face, masking the deformity of her teeth and jaws, hiding them from view.

The way she walked, the way she held herself, nobody ever paid her any attention. Young people, old people, couples, groups, they all did their best to act like they couldn't see her, like she was invisible. And yet they still managed to see her well enough that they got out of her way on the paths and the streets.

She was just like the homeless people she saw every evening. At least *they* saw her. Noticed her.

They were outsiders too, just like she was. But there was no loyalty within their ranks. She saw the drug and alcohol fuelled fights, and the arguments over possessions.

She made no attempt to make friends with any of them, and they kept their distance from her. Apart from that one old man, his beard a filthy matted grey, his long hair plastered to his scalp, his face lined and pockmarked.

But his eyes, they were a startling blue, and she had a feeling he had been handsome once.

It had been obvious what he wanted, and she had let him lead her away, somewhere out of sight of the couples and the groups of people out having a good time. She had thought about sinking her teeth into his throat, feeding on his warm blood. She changed her mind when he began clumsily groping her. Up close, the stink of his unwashed flesh and the cheap alcohol on his breath turned her stomach. When he exposed himself to her, she snarled at him and he turned and fled, stumbling along the towpath as he zipped up his trousers.

That had made her laugh.

There had been one young man, sitting on the towpath under a bridge, a sleeping bag and a tiny rucksack his only possessions who didn't look like the other homeless. He was still clean shaven, hair trimmed neatly. He looked like he might have lost weight recently, but he didn't appear to have been on the streets as long as the others.

She used to pass him every night, along with the tide of

humanity that managed to walk within feet of him and yet still ignored him, pretended that he was not there.

She thought about him a lot. She wasn't sure why.

It seemed to her that since she had died and then returned to the world of the living, not only her senses had sharpened, but her view of life too. She could now see the absurdity of how she had once lived, of how the cattle she surreptitiously mixed with were still living. The futility of their days made her laugh.

But when she saw the young homeless man in his sleeping bag, she experienced a pain in her chest and her stomach. At first she couldn't explain it, but as the evenings passed, and it happened every time she saw him, even every time she thought of him, she began to remember.

She had desired him.

Not his blood. Him, his presence, his touch.

That first time she had approached him and tentatively sat down next to him, her heart had pounded as though she was on a first date. He hadn't said anything, not at first. He had given her a smile. Let her have time, space to make the first move.

She had held her head in that slightly odd way of hers so that her hair hung over one side of her face just so. But as the evening wore on she had slowly adjusted her position so that her hair fell away, revealing her slightly elongated jaw, the slight protrusion of her teeth.

I was born this way, she had explained.

She had allowed him to touch her jaw, just lightly with his fingertips.

Does it hurt? he had said. *Is it uncomfortable?*

No, it's fine. I hardly notice it.

On the second night she had sat down next to him, he had offered her his sleeping bag, and they had cuddled up together inside it. She almost lost all of her self-control that night. To feel his body warmth, his touch, to smell his breath and sense the throb of his heart inside his chest.

She would have ripped his throat open in a moment if not for those other desires at war with her need for fresh blood. The desire for his company, for the touch of his skin upon hers.

Very human desires.

A sense memory of her life before this life.

She couldn't remember that much about it now. There was a gap between the two, a huge chasm of darkness. She knew she couldn't go back. This was her life now, feeding on the blood of others.

And yet…

Still she had flashes of memories, of feelings, of what it had been like to be that other person.

What's your name? he had asked her on their second night together.

And she'd had to stop and think.

Her name.

Yes, she'd had a name once.

I'm sorry, he'd said, once the silence had stretched out between them. *You don't have to tell me if you don't want to.*

Julie Carter, she said, the name dropping into her mind even as she was speaking it.

Later, after he had fallen asleep, his arms wrapped around her, she had to fight the tide of memories flooding her mind. She had lain under the bridge, eyes wide open, thinking of her family, her mother, her Uncle Frank and the night she was taken by that man and kept captive on the narrowboat with the child vampire.

And the other woman, she remembered her too. It was the woman's fault that Julie had been turned into a vampire. If not for her, the man who had abducted her might have let Julie live.

But as the memories returned of her previous life, it seemed they turned sour and rancid. As though there had always been something dreadful about that life.

As though by becoming one of *them*, she had been set free.

She had left her new friend in the early hours of the morning before the sky began to grow light. After peeling herself slowly and carefully from his sleeping embrace, she had gone back to her hidden spot where she could stay safe from the sun.

She told herself not to go back to him.

She told herself that the next time she saw him, she might not be able to help herself.

That she would kill him.

The following evening, as night slowly replaced day and the city lights blinked into life, she awoke from dreams of blood. She stretched, cat like. The hunger was strong within her.

What had woken her?

Something gossamer thin, a sensation on her face, a brief touch, a caress almost.

There, again. The briefest of touches, a dark shape darting past.

Another one.

She could see now.

Bats.

More of them, gathering like a cloud of wings and fur and teeth and dark, shining eyes.

They gathered around her, hanging from the iron railings, from the arched brickwork. More and more of them. Filling the dark of the evening with an even blacker night.

She felt no fear. She felt almost at one with these creatures.

The canal water glittered dark beneath the lights of the city.

She was curled into a dank corner, away from prying eyes. But there was somebody there now, a figure amongst the bats flitting through the air, watching her. Standing quite still, unconcerned by the winged creatures swarming around her.

Yes, it was a woman, she could see that now as she approached.

The bats had filled the space now, seemed like they were part of the air, part of the fabric of being. A hand reached out of the darting, flickering mass and she reached up herself and she took hold of the hand.

The woman pulled her to her feet.

Leaned in close until her lips were brushing her ear.

'Julie,' she whispered. 'Your name is Julie and you are one of us.'

A fountain of heat bloomed in Julie Carter's stomach, spreading into her chest and neck, flushing her pale face.

'You are a beautiful creature, Julie,' the woman whispered. 'You are one of us, one of the night creatures.'

She ran her fingers down Julie's face.

Down her neck.

The bats dived and turned and skittered over and around them. As though they could sense the excitement, the tension in the air.

'Go,' the woman whispered. 'Go and be with him and then come find me.'

The woman lowered her hand, and it brushed over Julie's chest and her abdomen, and then she stepped back and disappeared into the mass of bats.

Moments later and the bats had gone, and Julie was left on her own.

A crowd had gathered on a footbridge overlooking the canal. Julie stared at them and they stared back.

'Are you all right?' someone shouted.

She ignored them and turned away.

Once again, she wandered up and down the tow path and through the crowds, and she knew that this was the last time she would do this. The desire, the need, for blood was too strong. And what was the point? Why did she torture herself in this way?

Had it been simply an unconscious longing to go back to who she had once been?

The hours crept by as she trudged up and down, up and down. She avoided walking by her new friend's spot. She knew she couldn't see him anymore. She had to leave, find somewhere else to feed and hunt. Find others like her.

But finally, in the early hours of the morning, after all the bars and the clubs had closed, and the streets were empty, she found herself standing by his slumbering form. The night had grown colder, and he was curled up in his sleeping bag, a hat pulled down low over his head.

He was the only one since that night she had been kidnapped and then murdered who had shown her any kindness.

She had sat down beside him on the cold floor.

He had stirred. Smiled when he saw her.

Where have you been? he had whispered.

She had shushed him and climbed into the sleeping bag with him.

She had held him.

He said, *You're trembling? What's wrong?*

Nothing, she had replied, and clamped her teeth on his throat and ripped it open.

YOU A MONSTER

'Hey, girl, it been a while.'

Leola froze. She couldn't see him, but she knew him right away. She would know that voice anywhere.

She was standing outside Angellicit. The club was throbbing with people inside, but out here, on the street, she was alone.

At least she had been.

The Priest stepped out of the shadows as though he was materialising from the darkness. No, as though the darkness was creating him, bringing him into the world.

Even in the light of a street lamp, he was still barely visible. With his black overcoat and chimney stack hat, his black, tattooed skin and eyes and teeth, he was more of a shadow than the shadows around him.

It was as though he was an empty, man shaped space in the fabric of reality.

'What are you doing here?' Leola said.

'I done gone travelled halfway round the world to come see you, girl,' he replied. 'Ain't you got nothin' more to say to me than that?'

'You never leave the Bayou,' Leola said. 'You never go anywhere, not anymore. Not since…'

'Thought it was 'bout time I saw somethin' o' the world again.' He chuckled softly. 'It's been a long time.'

He drew closer. His clothing rustled. He held a black leather bag in his right hand.

Leola knew what was in there. His tattoo equipment. The Priest carried that bag with him everywhere.

'Don't lie to me,' Leola said. 'You never go anywhere, you said you never would, ever again.'

'Things change girl.' The Priest grinned. 'The times, they change. Ain't nothing no one can do 'bout that, that's for sure.'

He looked behind her, at the club doors, the door handles formed into angel shapes.

'Angellicit,' he said, and breathed deep. 'Now ain't that a name to toy with the mind. I 'magine all manner o' shit goes on in there.'

'You can't go in,' Leola said.

The Priest cocked an eyebrow. 'Ain't you gone introduce me to Mr Joe Coffin? I heard so much 'bout him, I just dyin' to meet him.'

'No.'

Leola took the Priest by the arm, the fabric of his coat sleeve stiff to the touch. She led him away from the doors, away from the eyes of the bouncer who had been watching them from just inside the open doorway.

'Why are you here?' she whispered as they walked. 'You never leave, you never go anywhere. How did you even make it here, this far?'

'You 'shamed o' me, girl? Is that it?'

Leola stopped walking, turned to face him. 'No. But I came to you when I needed you. After I killed that man, Stone, I came to you and you tattooed me and gave me absolution. So why are you here?'

'Like I said, things they are changin'.'

'What does that even mean?'

The Priest leaned in close. She could smell aniseed on his breath.

'Ain't you felt it?' he whispered. 'Somethin' big happennin'. Somethin' gone change everythin'.'

'What?' Leola said, and for the first time in over a hundred years, she felt a chill running up her back and along her shoulders.

The Priest leaned back and chuckled. 'I don' know, girl. If'n I knew already, I wouldn't need to git on one o' those big iron birds an' fly here now, would I?'

He adjusted his hat, grinning all the while.

Leola shook her head, still unable to believe her eyes and her ears. 'I don't even know how you got through customs, how you weren't even noticed and stopped.'

'Oh, I's stopped all right,' the Priest said. 'I's stopped lots, an' they searched me an' they axed me questions, that's what they did. Axed me so man' questions it like they want to perplex me, but I didn't get perplexed. I just answered their questions until they let me go on my way.'

'Where are you staying?' Leola said.

'Oh I gots mysel' a room in the city,' the Priest said. 'It gone turned out to be an entertainin' stay already, that's for sure. I should travel more often, I kinda forgot how interestin' it could be.'

'What does that mean?' Leola said.

The Priest chuckled. 'No don' you go worryin' your pretty little head, girl. I ain't gone break the faith, you know better'n that.'

Leola looked up and down the street. It was deserted, as it had been since the vampire breakout. The only time it was busy was when young people arrived in taxis, or were dropped off by family or friends in cars. And then it was straight from the waiting vehicle and into the club.

People were stupid. Didn't they realise the vampires could go anywhere? Including in clubs and pubs and bars.

Being inside was no protection.

'You can't stay here, you should go.'

'Go where, girl? Where's I got to go that worth being?'

'Home, go home back to the Bayou. Back where you belong.'

The Priest sighed. 'I don' belong nowhere, you know that. You don' belong nowhere too.'

Leola sighed. 'Come on, let's walk.'

They stepped back out onto the main road and began walking.

The city centre was eerily silent, shop windows ablaze with light. Leola's ears picked out laughter in the distance, the hum of chatter from the bars. A single car cruised past, the driver looking left and right out of his windows as though looking for someone or something he had lost.

'Did you know Chitrita is back?' Leola said.

The Priest stopped walking and grabbed Leola's upper arm. 'You gon' tell me that again, girl.'

Leola pulled free. 'What's wrong with you?'

Even through the ink, the Priest's face suddenly looked drawn and tight. 'What you said, girl, I'm axin' you again, you gon' tell me that once more.'

'Chitrita, she's back,' Leola said.

'She dug herself out o' her grave?' the Priest said.

'No, Guttman was paying to have all the old ones exhumed. Bring them back, give them life again. Joe finished them off, thought he had killed them all, but Chitrita.' Leola paused. 'She's alive, she's young again.'

'You seen her then?'

'No, but I know.'

'That's what I bin feelin', what's bin gettin' me so antsy these last few months, like spiders crawlin' an' chewin' at me. That's the change, sho' 'nuff.'

Leola peered into the Priest's dark eyes. She had never seen him this rattled before. 'What do you mean?'

'Chitrita, she one o' the old ones, one o' the powerful ones. That feelin' o' mine, it bin growin' while she bin gettin' stronger.'

They walked some more in silence. A taxi drew up full of people, young men and women spilled out of the vehicle giggling and chatting, and ran into the nearest bar. Two bouncers stopped them, got them to open their mouths so they could inspect their teeth before letting them inside.

'People, they ain't go no sense,' the Priest said. 'Cattle gone die soon, that's for sure.'

Leola sighed. 'I was about to come back, I told Joe that very thing today. There was nothing for me here anymore.'

'You bin sleepin' with that man name o' Coffin?'

'Yes.'

'This Coffin, he know all `bout you?'

'Yes.'

'An' yet he still puts his cock in you, like you a normal woman, like you ain't infected. Why he do that then?'

Leola stopped walking. Closed her eyes. 'I don't know. He trusts me. Sort of.'

'You should stay away,' the Priest said. 'You a monster, girl. The good Lord's forgiven you an' absolved you o' your sins, but you still a monster.'

Leola opened her eyes, looked up at the Priest. 'Is that true? Is that what we both are? Monsters?'

'Sure, girl. You know that, you don' need me to tell you.'

'Then what makes us any different from the others? From Chitrita and Guttman?'

'They don' know they're monsters,' the Priest said. 'But we do.'

'Take me back to your place,' Leola said. 'Show me where you're staying.'

They started walking again.

'You sure you want to do this?'

'Yes, I'm sure.'

'What about Mr Coffin, ain't he gone wonder where you gone?'

'That doesn't matter,' Leola said. 'Doesn't matter at all.'

GILLIGAN

Gilligan didn't give a fuck about vampires. He'd seen them, seen what they could do. Once you'd seen something, once you'd been in the thick of it, been scarred by it, it didn't matter anymore.

So Gilligan wasn't scurrying like a frightened rabbit from bar to bar. He owned these fucking streets, he did. Not some half dead creature from a fucking Hammer Horror flick.

The first bar he'd tried getting into after he left Coffin and the others at the Punchline he'd been stopped at the door by a big gorilla in a suit, the lower half of his face covered in black, thick hair whilst his scalp was shaved smooth. The bouncer had placed his hand on Gilligan's chest and told him to open his mouth. Gilligan had resisted the urge to spit in his face and did what he was told. After a quick look at his teeth, the bouncer let him inside.

This was what it had been like, every bar he went to. People looking suspicious at you if you weren't part of a group. How quickly the city had been plunged back into living in fear.

But not Gilligan.

A bloody vampire could drop down in front of him right now and he would break its fucking neck.

Gilligan knew he'd drunk too much. Knew he should head back, sleep it off.

That wasn't going to happen. Twice today he had been fucking humiliated. His face still burnt with the shame of it, even now with all the drink inside of him.

That fucking soldier boy had been faster and stronger than Gilligan expected. Easy to get a reaction out of, fucking pitiful how easy it had been. But Gilligan hadn't expected the beating that the soldier boy had given him.

Gilligan couldn't let that go, couldn't let that slide. A thing like that, it followed you around the rest of your life. A monkey on your back, taunting you, shaming you. A thing like that, it got out, folks wouldn't let you forget it. Make a person a laughingstock, it would.

Like that fat bastard Gosling. He didn't know what had happened, but he knew, he knew enough just from looking at Gilligan. The others did too. That fucker Shaw, laughing at him.

Bastard.

Gilligan had to put it right. If he didn't, then he would never get that monkey off his back.

Gilligan's mobile buzzed.

He pulled it from his pocket, glanced at the screen.

Shaw.

Was this the call Gilligan had been waiting for?

'Yeah?' he said.

'Where the fuck are you? Joe's in a foul mood.'

'And?'

There was a moment of silence on the phone, and then Shaw said, 'Joe's been attacked again, at the cemetery this time.'

'Seriously? Fuck.'

'You should come back. The job's happening, we've got to get ready.'

'When's it happening?'

'Tomorrow night.' Silence again, just for a moment. 'Get yourself back here, Gilligan. Joe's going to have a fit if you don't.'

'Yeah, I'm on my way,' Gilligan said, finishing the call.

He slipped the mobile back in his pocket and wiped his sleeve across his forehead. All of a sudden, he was sweating. It was the booze, and the stress.

Fucking Joe Coffin, why wouldn't the bastard just die? The man had more lives than a fucking cat.

Wait a minute, though. This could be the opportunity he had been waiting for. After his humiliation at the Punchline earlier, Gilligan needed to get revenge. To put things right, show them who was boss. Show Gosling and Coffin and Shaw and all the others that he didn't take shit like that from no one.

If the robbery was happening tomorrow night, that would be a perfect opportunity. Coffin, Gosling, the transvestite and that midget, the Stig and Shaw too, all of them would be there. All together in one spot, out in the middle of the countryside, where no one was going to disturb them. And, if he timed it right, he could not only get those bastards out of his life, but he could walk away with a pile of cash too.

Gilligan retrieved his mobile.

'Hey,' he said when they picked up. 'What the hell are you playing at? That bastard Coffin is still alive.'

Gilligan listened.

'Yeah, well, you get another chance tomorrow night. But there's going to be more people there, and they'll all need taking out.'

Gilligan listened some more.

'Fuck all that fancy ceremonial sword shit. Just get some guys to take some guns along.'

He listened some more.

'Yeah, I'll get back to you with details of exactly where and when.'

Gilligan finished the call, slipped the phone away.

Forget the Mob and its debts, Gilligan was walking away with a ton of cash.

Before he did that, he had to finish off his unfinished business with Mitch. Teach him a lesson he'd never forget, if he survived in the first place.

But it wasn't just Mitch, was it? It was that fucking bitch, that stupid fucking bitch who thought she was some big shot investigative reporter. She was the one really needed teaching a lesson, needed putting in her place she did. Who the fuck did she think she was? Gilligan had killed her editor, he should do the same to her, too. Do her in before she went to the coppers. He could do both of them, her and Mitch. Do both of them, but she needed teaching a lesson first. She needed putting in her place, and Gilligan could do that. Yeah, he'd enjoy doing that.

Gilligan wiped at his mouth. His head was fogged up with too much drink, but he still knew what he had to do. And he could do it, as well, he could do it tonight, right now. He didn't need to be sober for something like this because Gerry Gilligan was a sly fucker.

All he needed was the opportunity, and he wasn't going to get that by getting well and truly shit-faced in the city.

Gilligan pulled himself up a little straighter, like he had made a decision.

Fucking soldier boy Mitch.

And that bitch, that slag.

She needed teaching a lesson.

EMMA LOOKED DOWN at Louisa May, fast asleep in her cot. In sleep, she looked so very peaceful, so beautiful. At moments like this, Emma found it hard to believe still that she'd given birth to this child. That this tiny human had grown inside her.

Emma reached down and gently stroked her daughter's soft cheek.

Thought about Nick, standing on the doorstep, accusing Mitch of having hit her. Thought about Nick lying on the gravel after Mitch had punched him.

Emma took a deep, slightly ragged breath. If she thought about it too much, she might start crying. But not for herself, perhaps, more for Louisa May. It seemed to Emma that Lou should have a father in the house. No, not a father, but her father.

Nick Archer.

How would Emma's daughter react when she was older and

found out that it had been Emma who had finished the relationship with Nick? Would it matter to her? Would it be something she could dismiss? Or would she blame her mother for not having a father around as she was growing up?

The guilt tugged at Emma.

What had she been thinking when she disrobed in front of Nick? Had it just been about showing him, giving him proof that there were no bruises? That Mitch hadn't been hitting Emma?

Or had it been more?

Look at me. This is what you had once, but now you've lost it.

Emma took her hand from Louisa May's cheek, straightened up. She shouldn't have done that with Nick. It had been wrong and mean-spirited.

Emma heard Mitch moving around in the bedroom next door. He was stopping the night again, but Emma wasn't sure if she wanted him to anymore. Everything had moved so fast between them after he had rescued her at Angellicit. Her counsellor had warned her against it. Told her that her emotions for Mitch were too strongly tied in to how she felt about him in his role as her rescuer.

Knight in Shining Armour Syndrome, the counsellor called it. That the emotion went both ways, that there was a bond between them now, but that didn't mean it was a good thing.

Emma knew she was right, suspected that Mitch had had the same advice too, but neither of them spoke about it. Getting together, becoming intimate, just seemed the most natural thing to do after what they had been through.

How could anybody else hope to understand it?

Maybe, though, that didn't matter as much as she had thought it did. They needed more than a shared trauma to grow closer together.

A police siren in the distance cut through the silence of the house. Emma wondered what had happened. Whether it was a regular police call or if it had something to do with vampires.

Emma could hardly believe the nightmare was starting again.

How could it just keep happening over and over? If only they could be exterminated once and for all.

Emma heard Mitch swear at something.

He was still tense, wound up over the confrontation earlier. Every little thing was winding him up. Emma barely knew what to say around him. After the argument they'd had outside, the two of them had barely spoken a word.

Nick hadn't deserved any of this. The taunting, the beating.

It was all just so fucked up.

Tomorrow, yes tomorrow, Emma would call Nick. Apologise. And tell him, tell him that she had kicked Mitch out, that he was no longer living in Nick's house. Not that she was going to invite Nick back in to her life. Might be a good idea to just stay away from men for a while.

Emma quietly stepped out of Louisa May's bedroom, closed the door softly behind her.

Mitch was standing in the doorway of their bedroom.

Looking at Emma.

'What's wrong?' she said.

'Everything,' he said.

They continued to look at each other in silence, and it seemed to Emma that Mitch understood, without her having had to say a word.

They both jumped at the sudden pounding on the front door.

'Who the fuck is that?' Emma said.

'Let me go check it out,' Mitch said.

Emma touched him on the arm as he passed her on the landing. 'Be careful.'

'Yeah.'

Mitch ran down the stairs. Emma stayed at the top, where she could see the front door.

Mitch paused at the door and bent down to peer through the spy hole.

'Who is it?' Emma said.

'Can't see anyone,' Mitch said.

'That's good, right?'

Mitch stood up, looked at Emma at the top of the stairs. 'No, it's very bad. Whoever is out there doesn't want to be seen.'

They both flinched at the sound of shattering glass from the rear of the house.

'Don't open that door!' Mitch said as he ran towards the kitchen and out of Emma's view.

Emma turned back to the baby room and opened the door a crack. Louisa May was still sleeping soundly. Emma shut the door again.

Louisa May was safe up here.

Emma took the stairs two at a time as she bounded down them.

She put her face to the door, her eye to the peephole. No one there, just like Mitch had said. But then she saw a dark shape scurrying past, and she recoiled as it pounded on the door.

'Shit!'

Her heart was pounding.

More glass shattering, another window gone.

Where was Mitch?

Emma ran through to the back of the house, into the kitchen. She shivered in the cool breeze flowing through the house. The patio door was wide open.

'Mitch?'

She slowly approached the open door. Stepped outside.

The floodlight should have come on, triggered by her movement, but the garden stayed shrouded in darkness, apart from the pool of light cast from the kitchen. As she made that realisation, her feet crunched over broken glass on the patio. She looked at the glass and then up and saw the broken light hanging from the wall.

'Mitch?' she whispered.

Silence, apart from the soft whispering of the trees at the bottom of the garden, the movement of their branches in the breeze just discernible in the dark.

This was stupid, she needed to get back inside and call the police.

Emma turned back to the house and screamed as a figure lunged at her from the darkness. A pair of hands reached out and grabbed onto her, fingers snagging at her clothing. She tried to pull away but her attacker was on top of her, his weight dragging her down.

Losing her balance, Emma staggered backwards a few steps and then toppled off the edge of the patio and onto the damp, cold grass. The man had fallen on top of her, his weight pinning her to the ground. Emma kicked and screamed and managed to push him off.

He rolled over onto the ground and lay still.

Emma pushed herself up and onto her knees.

Looked at the prone form lying next to her.

'Mitch?' she said.

His head had been bashed in, the side of his skull, a mangled, scarlet mass of matted hair.

Somewhere in the distance, another siren began to wail.

BLUE SKY

Steffanie eyed her companions uneasily. The girl, Julie Carter, she remembered seeing on the news when she disappeared. That had been Abel Mortenson, the vampire who had originally turned Steffanie and Michael. And the black woman, the maid from the Travelodge on the motorway where she had been hiding with Merek Guttman.

But the others she didn't recognise. Victims of Abel's probably.

Chitrita had been roaming the city throughout the night, finding these lost vampires and drawing them to her, bringing them back here. For the most part, they were a sorry-looking group. Emaciated and dirty. They needed fresh blood. They needed to learn how to hunt.

And Chitrita was about to give them their first lesson.

Michael kept close by Steffanie's side. He wasn't at all sure about these new members to their 'family'. He watched them constantly, and if one of them happened to shuffle too close, he growled at them. The only one he allowed near was the girl, Julie.

She seemed to have a calming effect on him.

The room above the bar was crowded now, with all these

vampires. It was obvious they couldn't stay here much longer. With so many of them, they would be discovered soon.

And besides, the renovation downstairs was almost complete, and the new owners had been upstairs earlier in the day, before Chitrita had begun gathering the other vampires, talking about their plans to extend up here.

Steffanie and Michael had hidden with Chitrita and listened furtively as they talked. Steffanie had been all for opening up their throats, but Chitrita had urged caution.

It seemed she had another plan in mind.

But what that plan was, she was keeping quiet about.

As soon as the sun had set, Chitrita had left to search out the stray vampires and bring them back. Steffanie and Michael had watched from the window as Chitrita led her band of shuffling, abject looking followers to their hideout.

But she hadn't brought them inside.

Instead, she had called Steffanie and Michael down and out onto the street. It was gone three in the morning and the city was finally fully asleep. The vampires walked, shuffled and ran up Broad Street, away from the city centre, with Chitrita leading. Bats flitted overhead, their dark shapes almost invisible against the night sky.

They walked up the centre of the road. A solitary car appeared coming towards them, its headlights growing larger and brighter, even as it slowed down. The driver sounded his horn, but Chitrita paid no mind and kept walking.

What a sight we must make, Steffanie thought. *Do we look like zombies from a late night horror film? Or ghosts perhaps?*

The driver obviously had similar thoughts as he suddenly turned off down a side road and drove away.

Chitrita continued to walk, leading the way for her ragtag band of vampires. She hadn't even told Steffanie where they were going or what they were doing.

Trust me, she had whispered in Steffanie's ear.

And Steffanie did.

As they approached Five Ways Island and the underpass, Chitrita turned off down a side road. They all followed her obediently. Chitrita halted, and they gathered outside a large building, one of the old Georgian houses. There was a large sign at the driveway's entrance which said it was now the Blue Sky Care Home.

And Steffanie knew what they were here for.

Chitrita walked up to the large front door, lifted the ornate brass knocker, and let it fall. Then she saw the metal intercom attached to the wall beside the door and she pressed the buzzer.

Steffanie stayed behind with the other vampires, out of sight of the door. They waited in silence.

Chitrita lifted the brass knocker once more and rapped out a quick succession of three short, sharp knocks.

They waited again. The vampires shuffled in and around each other as they grew restless, waiting. Steffanie had to keep herding them back into position, out of sight of the front door. The bats were darting around the house, swooping and diving, whilst others had roosted in the eaves.

The vampires' heads snapped up at the sound of movement behind the door.

'Who is it?' a muffled voice called out.

'Please, can you help me?' Chitrita said. 'The battery on my phone is dead, and I need to call my husband, he'll be wondering where I am.'

Steffanie was impressed. Chitrita had learned a great deal about this new, modern world since she escaped from Stump and Corpse.

Steffanie watched from behind her hiding place as Chitrita took a small step back from the door. There was a peephole in the front door, and Chitrita was letting the woman inside take a good look at her, and let her see that she was on her own.

'He'll be so worried,' Chitrita said. 'I should have been home hours ago, but I took the wrong junction off the motorway and I don't know how I've ended up in Birmingham.'

More movement behind the door.

'All right,' said the woman.

The sound of a lock turning was followed by the door slowly opening.

The look of horror on the woman's face as Steffanie and the

others stepped into view was wonderful. Chitrita had her foot in the door and her hand over the woman's mouth before she knew what was happening.

The vampires crowded in behind Chitrita and Steffanie shut the door.

The woman was crying silently, long trails of tears running down her cheeks and off her chin.

Chitrita held the woman close in an embrace and licked the tears away.

'Don't cry,' she whispered as she arched the woman's head back, exposing her throat. 'You're going to wake up a new woman.'

Chitrita sank her teeth into the woman's fleshy throat.

As the other vampires began wandering, Steffanie took Michael's hand and led him up the stairs.

'Come with me,' she whispered. 'Let's find something to drink.'

Michael hooted softly with excitement and anticipation.

They padded softly along the landing, past closed bedroom doors, tables with vases of flowers, paintings of lakes and blue skies and mountains on the walls. They stopped outside a door and Steffanie placed her palm against it. She pressed an ear to the door and listened.

She grasped the door handle and turned it softly.

The door opened quietly into a darkened room. A small, curled up form lay under blankets on a bed. Steffanie could hear a soft wheezing and snoring.

They crept into the bedroom. Steffanie had hold of Michael's hand and she could feel his excitement building. They stood by the bed and looked down at the huddled old lady, her jaw slack and revealing her wasted gums in her mouth.

Michael was trembling.

Steffanie let go of his hand.

The boy climbed on the bed and pulled the covers back to reveal the old lady's wasted, frail body. She stirred, moaned a little. Sounded like she was muttering something, saying someone's name.

Michael, hunched on all fours on the bed, lowered himself down and sniffed at the old lady's throat. Had he been too long without hunting? Was he unsure what to do?

The little boy rotated his head, like an automation, and smiled.

'Blood,' he said. 'Blood.'

His smile grew wider, revealing his fangs. He turned back to the old woman and sank his teeth into her throat. Her eyes snapped open and her whole body stiffened as the boy began drinking her blood. The slurping noises he made grew louder as the scarlet liquid ran from his mouth and over the woman's wrinkled, scrawny neck and pooled on the bed sheet.

Steffanie watched silently as Michael fed. The old woman's body began to relax as the life force drained from her.

Steffanie left Michael feeding and wandered along the hallway. Doors to rooms had been left open and Steffanie could hear scuffles from some as the occupants struggled to fight off their attackers. A shrill, cracked scream rang through the home and was abruptly cut short.

The black maid from the Travelodge staggered drunkenly from a bedroom, blood running from the corners of her mouth and over her chin. She saw Steffanie and gave her a little wave and a goofy smile.

Steffanie ignored her.

She picked a closed door at random and opened it up, sliding silently inside the bedroom. The old man in the bed lay on his back, his huge belly a large mound beneath the bedsheets. The only sound in here was the man's snoring.

Steffanie closed the door.

Saliva flooded her mouth at the thought of his hot blood on her tongue.

She stood by the side of his bed, savouring the moment, the anticipation.

Another muffled scream.

Every single pensioner in this home would be dead within the hour.

And when they woke up once more, changed, immortal, Chitrita would have an army of vampires on her side.

The man's eyes fluttered open.

'Mary? Mary, is that you?' he said, his voice thick with sleep. 'Oh, I had such a vivid dream, a nightmare. I dreamt I had grown old, and that you were dead. It was a dream, wasn't it?'

'Yes, all a dream,' Chitrita whispered, and placed a hand over his eyes. 'Now go back to sleep.'

He tried to fight her when her teeth pierced his throat, but his struggles were weak and half-hearted, as though he knew what was happening and had resigned himself to it.

His warm blood flowed over her tongue and she swallowed greedily. She kept her hand in place over his eyes, and it was only later, once all the old people and the staff in the home were dead, that she wondered why she had done that. What had possessed her to make that pathetic attempt to hide the horror of his situation from him? And that single thought that had blossomed in her mind as she drank his blood.

That she was depriving him of the right to join his wife in death. This old man would soon begin his new existence, life eternal. But without his beloved Mary.

The vampires sat and lay in various rooms in the home, blood staining their mouths and splattered in their hair and on their faces, satisfied for the first time in a long while. Chitrita wandered amongst them, whilst the bats thudded at the windows, the sound of their wings beating at the glass panes a victory drum roll.

Some old people would wake as vampires soon, whilst for others the process would take longer, days even.

And soon enough, Steffanie and Chitrita would have the beginnings of a vampire army, with which they could take the city.

EPISODE FIFTEEN

JEREMY

Emma sat and waited.

Her left eyelid twitched in short bursts.

Too much black coffee had her nerve endings firing constantly. She snapped her fingers, clicked her teeth, Couldn't keep a thought in her head for more than a second or two.

She thought about Joe.

That wasn't right, was it? Mitch, Mitch was the one on the table in the operating room. Not Joe.

She waited and waited. They'd told her she had to wait downstairs, told her to get herself a coffee.

While she waited.

The nurse, the nice one. Young, pretty. She'd said they could be awhile. Said the surgeons had to investigate first, find out how much damage had been done to Mitch's skull. How much, if any, had been done to his brain.

Hadn't she read somewhere once that approximately half of the brain could be cut away and it would make hardly any difference to a person's personality or ability to function?

She didn't believe that. Surely that was an impossibility.

She picked up her phone. Googled, 'can you live without half of your brain?'

Apparently, it was true. Something to do with something called neuroplasticity.

Emma put her phone down. Picked it up again.

Thought about contacting Nick.

The police had arrived at the house with the ambulance, and Emma had been questioned some more at the hospital, too. But no sign of DCI Archer.

Was he that pissed off at her that he couldn't even come and see her now?

And what about Joe?

If she phoned him and told him what happened, would he come?

He would have done once.

Emma scrolled through her contacts, found his number.

They hadn't spoken since that night at Angellicit. He still believed she had betrayed him. And in a way, she had, hadn't she?

When she first got hold of that video of Joe murdering Terry Wu, it had been with the intention of taking it to the police, of writing up a huge expose of Coffin and Craggs and the Slaughter-house Mob. Get that publishing deal, make a name for herself.

As time had gone on, though, her feelings had changed, and she had seen the situation grow more complicated.

Emma had realised that Joe was more complicated than she had first thought.

But still she had held on to her evidence.

'Hey.'

Nick sat down next to her.

Emma switched off her phone and placed it face down on the table, wondering if he had seen Joe Coffin's name on her display.

'Hey yourself,' Emma said.

'They leave you on your own down here?' Nick said. 'There should be an emotional support officer sitting with you.'

Emma smiled thinly. 'I think they're a little bit stretched at the moment.'

'Even so, I'll be having words with someone,' Nick said. 'Sorry I couldn't get here sooner, no one thought to tell me what was going on until Amrit heard about it. How is Mitch?'

'I don't know,' Emma said. 'He's in theatre right now, having the back of his skull put together again.'

'You see who did it?'

Emma shook her head. 'No, I found Mitch outside, whoever attacked him had gone.'

'Yeah?'

Emma glanced at Nick, looked away again. He knew she was lying. And really, why was she not telling him about Gilligan? Why hadn't she told the police woman earlier when she asked the same question?

Emma took a deep breath.

'Have you heard of a man by the name of Gerry Gilligan?'

'Gilligan? Yeah, he's a petty crook with IRA connections. He's in with Coffin and the Mob now. He was there that night at Angellicit.'

Of course he was, Emma thought.

'Why? Are you saying he attacked Mitch?'

Emma nodded, unable to speak for a moment as an image of Gilligan flashed into her head as he unzipped his trousers.

'What the fuck for?' Nick said. 'What's going on, Emma?'

Emma swallowed, and her dry throat clicked painfully. 'If I tell you, you promise to not get all angry and shouty?'

Nick placed his hand over Emma's, resting on the table. 'I'll promise to try my best.'

Emma took another deep breath, organised her thoughts. She couldn't tell him everything. Some of it had to stay her secret.

'Gilligan murdered Karl,' she said.

'You got proof?' Nick said.

'No, but I confronted Gilligan about it and he admitted it to me.'

'Bloody hell, Emma, why didn't you come to me with this?'

'Because I thought you would get all shouty at me.'

Nick squeezed her hand. 'I don't believe you. You were going after him yourself, weren't you? What was this, some kind of Death Wish revenge thing? Did you get Mitch involved? That's why Gilligan attacked him, isn't it?'

'Slow down, that's too many questions, Detective Inspector Archer,' Emma said.

Archer sighed. 'What the hell am I going to do with you? Every time I turn my back, you're digging yourself deeper and deeper into the shit. Is there anything else I don't know?'

'No, that's everything.'

'I don't believe you.'

Emma pulled her hand away from Nick's. 'I knew I shouldn't have said anything. This is turning into a police interrogation now, and I'm feeling like the suspect.'

'Oh for fuck's sake, Emma!' Archer hissed. 'You don't have to go into a hissy fit every time I ask you a question. Have you ever stopped to think that I ask you this stuff not because I'm a cop, but because I actually care about you?'

Emma said nothing.

'I care about you, and your safety, and Louisa May. You think I ask you this shit because I want to make your life hell? Or because all I ever think about is work and my arrest record? Is that it?'

Emma shook her head. 'No.'

'Then stop attacking me every time I ask you something. I'm trying to help you here.'

Emma took Nick's hand. 'I know. Thank you. And, I'm sorry.'

'Just tell me what's going on.'

'You're right, I wanted revenge on Gilligan for what he did. I got Mitch involved, got him tailing Gilligan wherever he went. Gilligan spotted him and they got into a fight. Mitch left Gilligan in a right state and I guess Gilligan wanted revenge himself.'

'And that's it?' Nick said.

Emma looked Nick in the eyes. 'That's it.'

'All right, thank you for telling me. Right, I'll call this in, get a search on for Gerry Gilligan. We'll find him, and we'll put him behind bars. But you're out of this now, okay? Leave Gilligan to us.'

Emma saw a nurse approaching them. A sudden panic squeezed

her chest tight, and she struggled to catch her breath. Looking at that nurse as she drew closer, seeing the expression on her face, Emma knew what she was going to tell them.

I'm sorry, the surgeon did everything he could. Mitch is dead.

Emma stood up, still gripping Nick's hand.

Nick stood with her.

'Mitch is out of theatre and he's been moved to ICU,' the nurse said. 'You can come up and see him for a few minutes.'

'How is he?' Emma said.

'There was some swelling in the brain and the surgeon had to release some fluid, but after a couple of days in ICU he should be a lot better and we'll be moving him onto a regular ward.' The nurse stroked Emma's arm. 'Don't worry, he's going to be fine.'

'Thank you,' Emma said.

'Right, I'm going to head back to the station,' Nick said. 'Keep me updated.'

'I will,' Emma said. She touched him on his elbow. 'And Nick, I'm sorry about earlier, at the house, when you came by.'

'Forget about it,' Nick said.

Emma watched him walk away.

'He looks like he's been in a fight too,' the nurse said.

'Sorry?' Emma said, momentarily confused.

'That bruise on his face, how did he get that?'

'He walked into a door,' Emma said. 'Can we go see Mitch now?'

'Of course.'

They went up in the lift. The hospital corridors were quiet, apart from cleaning staff out with huge, floor buffering machines which hummed softly as they were swept over the floors. Emma had lost track of time, but it had to be the middle of the night, maybe early morning.

As the nurse swiped them into ICU, Emma remembered this was where she had paid Charlie 'Stut' Boyd a visit after he shot himself in the leg.

Mitch was tethered to a machine and a drip, his head swathed in a mass of white bandages. His eyes were dark, bruised.

Emma had never seen him look so helpless, not even at Angellicit.

As she sat down next to him, his eyes fluttered open.

'Hi,' Emma said.

'Hi,' Mitch croaked.

'How do you feel?'

'Never better,' Mitch said.

'That's good,' Emma said. 'I thought maybe we could go out for pizza in a bit, have a few drinks, party the night away.'

'Sure,' Mitch whispered. 'Just give me a minute, okay?'

'The doctor says you're going to be fine,' Emma said.

Mitch had closed his eyes again.

'I think maybe we should leave him to get some sleep,' the nurse said. Emma hadn't realised she had been standing there. 'It would probably be a good idea for you to go home and get some rest, too. We'll look after him.'

Emma stood up. 'Yes, of course, thank you. I'll come back tomorrow.'

The nurse smiled. 'I think you mean today.'

There was a clock on the wall. It said the time was three-twenty.

Emma took the stairs back down to the ground floor. There was a security guard at the main hospital entrance. Took Emma a moment to remember why.

It was still night time. He was checking for vampires.

Emma felt sorry for him. If even just one vampire turned up, that security guard didn't stand a chance. It seemed no one fully understood the danger they were in.

Not yet, anyway.

Emma ran for her car and climbed inside. She didn't start the engine but instead pulled out her mobile and opened it up. Joe Coffin's name was still on the screen in her contacts folder.

She hesitated only a moment and then scrolled past him until she reached Barry's contact details.

'Sorry, Barry,' she whispered.

It took him a while, but he answered eventually, his voice slow and groggy sounding. 'Emma?'

'Hey, Barry, sorry to wake you,' Emma said.

'What's wrong? Are you all right? What's going on?'

'Gilligan attacked Mitch earlier this evening, bashed his skull in.'

'Oh shit! Seriously?'

Barry was awake now.

'Mitch has had to have surgery, but he's going to be fine,' Emma said. 'I just wanted to let you know, you should be careful. Gilligan's a psychopath.'

'You don't know the half of it,' Barry said.

'What do you mean?' Emma said. 'Have you found something on him?'

Emma could hear movement on the other end of the phone.

'Hold on a sec, I'm just getting up. What's the time, anyway?' Pause. 'I was going to phone you anyway later this morning. Hang on.' More movement. 'Here we go. Have you heard of a company called the Jiangchi Corporation?'

'No,' Emma said. 'Should I?'

'Not necessarily. They're a Chinese entertainments company, they run casinos, betting shops, clubs and bars, restaurants, they've even got a TV channel. They are pretty big in China but nobody's ever heard of them because all of their subsidiary ventures are run under different names.' Barry yawned. 'Sorry, I don't think I've ever been up so early before.'

'You're kidding me,' Emma said. 'You've never done the grave-yard shift on a paper?'

Barry laughed. 'I've only ever worked on local rags, and they don't do graveyard shifts. More like down the pub by eight o'clock shifts.'

'So, this Jiangchi lot? What have they got to do with Gerry Gilligan?'

'Maybe nothing,' Barry said. 'But the Jiangchi Corporation is known to have some dodgy funding paths, and one of those is with the Real IRA faction that Gilligan is a member of.'

'Barry, I'm a little lost right now,' Emma said. 'Are you telling me that the Real IRA buy weapons from the Jiangchi Corporation?'

'That's right,' Barry said. 'But here is where it gets really interesting. The Jiangchi Corporation is also the legal front for a certain Triad faction.'

'The Seven Ghosts,' Emma said.

'Correct, go to the top of the class,' Barry said.

'This doesn't make sense, though,' Emma said. 'The Seven Ghosts made a deal with the vampires to take on the running of Angellicit, whilst Gilligan was with Coffin, trying to take it back. Just whose side is he on?'

'My guess is, whoever has got the upper hand, Gilligan is with them.'

'Maybe you're right,' Emma said. 'Look, Barry, be careful, all right? I don't want anyone else getting hurt.'

'Don't worry about me, Careful is my middle name.'

Emma smiled. 'Yeah? I thought it was Jeremy?'

Barry was silent for a moment.

'How the hell do you know that?' he said.

'Bye, Barry,' Emma said, and hung up.

WIZZTINKLING HIS KNICKALOONS

The scream ripped through the empty corridors and rooms, up and down the stairwells, and echoed around every last corner and crevice. It went on and on, drawn out seemingly beyond all human capacity for such a scream, and when it finally faded away, there was a crash of metal and another scream.

Corpse kept to the shadows as though aware that he should make as little movement and disturbance as possible. His small, dark eyes watched Stump as she threw her arms wide and screamed again.

The man in the cage was crouching low, his hands over his ears, making himself as small as possible. His jacket and shirt were stained with dirt and sweat and blood. His nose was swollen and red, his eyes puffy and bruised from when Stump had smashed the cricket bat into his face.

Corpse didn't think he would last much longer and then they would have to go and get another one of their playthings. It could get so boring down here without anything to play with.

Stump kicked out at a wooden kitchen chair, sending it skidding across the floor and toppling over onto its back.

'I want him dead!' she screamed, red faced and sweaty.

Strands of her hair, always so severely tied back, had come loose and were hanging over her face. She stood there, her round frame shuddering as she gasped for breath, and eyed Corpse through hooded lids. Even for Corpse, it was unusual to see her eyes, so often they were hidden behind dark sunglasses.

'Mr Coffin is burduous to murdinate,' Corpse said.

A low growl began building in Stump's throat. Corpse didn't like the sound of that growl. It hardly sounded human.

'We should kill him ourselves,' she said. 'We should slice him open and pull out his guts, all while he watches. We could have so much fun with him.'

She started growling again.

The man in the cage had removed his hands from his ears, but he was still crouched down, as though hiding in a tight space. No, he definitely wouldn't be around for much longer.

The growl suddenly escalated into a scream and Stump lashed out at nothing, swinging her arms as though hitting someone. She howled and kicked and leapt up and down and stamped her feet.

And she stopped, breathless once more.

And she noticed the man in the cage, and she blinked her eyes.

Realising he had been noticed, the man tried shrinking even further into himself, looked like he was trying to make himself invisible.

'You,' Stump said, her voice slightly husky and hoarse from all the screaming. 'You.'

The man placed his hands over his head and looked up at Stump as she slowly approached the cage.

He began shaking his head. 'No, no, not me, no.'

'Yes, you,' Stump whispered. 'You need to pay, you need to pay for all of it.'

'Pay for what?' the man said. A tear rolled down his swollen, filthy face. 'I don't know what you're talking about. Whatever it was, I didn't work for her then, I wasn't there, it wasn't anything to do with me at all.'

'It doesn't matter,' Stump said. 'You work for her now.'

'No, not anymore I don't. Let me go, let me go and I'll get out of here, I'll go far away, you'll never see me again.'

'Look at him, Mr Corpse. Isn't he pathetic? So full of bravado when we first brought you here, but now?'

'I ruminink he mightbe wizztinkling his knickaloons soon, Mrs Stump,' Corpse said. 'I'm not determinating to disinclean that, it's whiffouly.'

Stump pressed her enormous bulk against the cage and peered through the wire mesh at the man cowering against the other side of his tiny prison. She enclosed her hand around her mannequin's wrist.

'I can give you money,' the man whispered. 'So much fucking money you wouldn't believe it.'

'I very much doubt that,' Stump said.

'No, it's true, I can! Mrs Ullman, she keeps all her cash in a safe room in her house. Briefcases full of it just lying around to be taken. Isn't that what you've been after all along?'

Stump looked at the man in silence as though she were thinking hard about what he had just told her.

'What do you mean?' she said, finally.

The man looked over at Corpse. 'The fucking undertaker over there, he told me all about it, about how you kidnap one of the security team every now and then. We all thought they just upped and left, because Ullman's widow is so freaky-deaky, like danger-ously screwy, that she couldn't keep anyone employed for longer than a few months. But it's you, you've been picking us off, one by one.'

Stump sighed and looked at Corpse.

'I'm sorrogetic, Mrs Stump,' Corpse said. 'I didn't contemnate to, I was growling disinattentivated, and you were divertitating your-self. I desiraved jabberwocking.'

Stump turned back to the man. 'You're wrong, I'm afraid. The money has never been a consideration.'

'Oh fuck,' the man sobbed, and covered his face with his hands. 'What's this all been about then? Why are you keeping me here?'

'To hurt you, Mr Morel, why else?'

'Hurt me? But what the fuck for? What the fucking hell have I ever done to deserve this, *this*, from you?'

'You work for that bitch!' Stump hissed. 'Isn't that enough?'

Morel lifted his face, his eyes wet and pleading, a line of tear tracks running through the filth on his cheeks. 'Then why the fuck don't you kidnap her and keep her in a cage instead of me?'

'Because this is more fun,' Stump said.

Stump grinned as she gripped the mannequin's hand even tighter, her knuckles turning white under the pressure.

'Fuck's sake, I know the combination! I can get you in, and all that fucking cash is yours!'

Stump relaxed a little.

'All of it?' she said.

'Yeah, all of it, every last fucking penny.'

'In exchange for your life, is that right?'

The man bowed his head. 'That's right. All that money, in exchange for my fucking life.'

Stump remained silent for a few seconds as she considered this. The money would come in useful. And taking it would be another way of getting revenge on Mrs Ullman.

Stump stepped away from the cage and let go of the mannequin hand.

'Well, Mr Corpse, it looks like we shall be paying Mrs Ullman a visit very soon, doesn't it?'

Corpse nodded his head, and it bobbed up and down on his scrawny neck as though under the control of a mad puppeteer.

Corpse did so love trips outside for adventures.

POT KETTLE BLACK

C offin's mobile vibrated in his pocket. He pulled it out, took a look at the screen.

Emma Wylde.

He thumbed 'Ignore' and slipped the mobile away again.

'Important call?' Gosling said.

'No,' Coffin said.

'Stilts here, he doesn't say much on the phone either,' Gosling said, and chuckled.

Coffin twisted around in his seat, looked at Stilts sitting in the back of the car with Gosling. 'He takes the piss out of you all the time. Why do you put up with it?'

Stilts said nothing, just stared blank faced at Coffin.

Coffin turned back to the front. As usual, he'd had to jam himself inside the car. Gosling had watched him and said it was like watching someone pack a sleeping bag back into its bag. But then Gosling had struggled to get in the back of the car too.

The Stig was driving.

Shaw, Gilligan, Stut and the Duchess were in the car behind.

They took the Hagley Road out of Birmingham and headed for Stourbridge. The Stig swore when he took the wrong turn off the

Stourbridge ring road and had to turn back on himself. Gosling laughed.

They left Stourbridge and headed out to the countryside. By the time they got to the Ullmans' place the sun was low on the horizon. The Stig drove right on past the gated entrance, followed by Shaw. They parked up in a pub car park half a mile further down the road. Two For One, the pub sign said. No name, nothing else. Just Two For One.

The Stig climbed out of the car and lit up a cigarette.

The Duchess, wearing black, figure hugging lycra, joined him. Any doubts that Coffin might have had about the Duchess's gender had been dispelled at the sight of the skin tight outfit and what it revealed. Duchess wasn't wearing a wig tonight, revealing his shaved head. But he was still wearing eyeliner and garishly bright yellow lipstick.

'Fucking hell, Duchess,' Gosling had said when he'd seen him. 'You're going to announce our arrival by lighting up the whole house wearing that shit on your lips.'

Duchess had laughed and blown Gosling a kiss before tottering off in his high heels. At least he had changed into sensible shoes before they left.

The Stig and Duchess stood and smoked together. The Stig didn't seem at all fazed by Duchess's appearance, and Coffin watched as the two men chatted quietly together.

'Penny for them, Joe,' Gosling said.

Coffin grunted, looked out of the window. Watched the cars driving by on the dual carriageway.

After ten minutes or so of waiting, a car pulled into the car park and parked next to Coffin's car. The black window slid down.

Gosling opened his window.

'There's just two of them on tonight, and one in the safe room,' a craggy faced man said, all skin and bone and sharp cheeks.

'Numbers are down again,' Gosling said.

'Yeah, Morel did a runner last week, and the old biddy hasn't got around to replacing him yet.'

'Morel?' Gosling said. 'I thought he was one of your more reliable employees?'

'So did I,' the man said. 'Appears I was wrong.'

He passed a slip of paper through the open windows. 'That's the number for the gate at the entrance. Once you're in the grounds, make sure you close the gate again and park somewhere out of sight of the main road.' He passed a second slip of paper through the window. 'You're going to have to bust your way into the house, but once you're inside, that's the number for the burglar alarm. You have twenty seconds before it activates and calls a private security firm. If Stilts there wants to get his trousers down to do his customary crap in the vault, I suggest disarming the alarm.'

'This private security firm, they any good?' Gosling said.

'They're better than good, and if you happen to be there and they make a visit, I hope you have a funeral plan in place, is all I'm saying.'

'They any connection with you?'

'Nope. Mrs Ullman trusts no one, and she has different people handling different aspects of her business, especially when they overlap. When are you going in?'

Gosling checked his watch. 'Another half hour.'

'I'd leave it a little longer. The old witch has been antsy tonight, like she knows something is up.'

'I don't like it,' Coffin said. He'd been looking out of his window, watching traffic shoot by while listening to the conversation. But now he leaned over so he could see the man in the car.

'What's not to like, Joe?' Gosling said. 'Old witchy bitch Ullman is a couple of men down, we've got the number for the burglar alarm and Stilts the master safe cracker.'

'And don't forget Duchess,' the man said. 'Every crack breaking and entering squad needs a transvestite to run around screaming while the real men get on with the job, right?'

'You just said you lost another man, one of your best,' Coffin said. 'And you don't know where they're going or why? It makes no sense.'

'To be honest with you, Mr Vampire Killing Joe Coffin, I don't give a shit,' the man said. 'I'm out of this game from tonight on, which is why I'm helping out Jim here.'

'You're giving him a cut of the money?' Coffin said.

'Don't get your knickers all tied up, Joe,' Gosling said. 'There'll still be plenty to share around, don't you worry.'

'And Ullman's widow, you said she's suspicious,' Coffin said.

'No, I said she's antsy,' the man said. 'She gets like this sometimes. Besides, she's an old biddy, what's she gonna do? Run you over with her zimmer frame?'

The man and Gosling laughed.

'I'll get you your cut tomorrow morning,' Gosling said.

'Yeah,' the man said, and his window hummed as it slid up, obscuring his features once more.

'You're wound too tight, Joe,' Gosling said. 'You should relax, this is going to be like stealing candy from a baby.'

Coffin's mobile vibrated with another call. He took a look at the screen.

Emma again.

Coffin tapped 'Ignore' and put the phone away.

'Someone's keen to talk to you, Joe,' Gosling said.

'When we've done this and I've got my share of the money, I don't ever want to see you again,' Coffin said.

Gosling clutched his chest in mock pain. 'Joe! Does this mean you're leaving me? And here I was thinking we had something special going on.'

'You're nothing but trouble, Gosling,' Coffin said. 'And I should just walk away from this job right now.'

Gosling leaned his bulk forward so his head was just behind Coffin's right shoulder. 'But you can't, can you? You need the cash, just like I do, and that's why you're here.'

'Like I said, after tonight, we go our separate ways,' Coffin said. 'In fact, it might be a good idea if you leave Birmingham and go open one of your comedy clubs somewhere else, like maybe Brighton, or Portsmouth, somewhere far enough away I won't ever have the bad luck to run into you again.'

'You hear that, Stilts?' Gosling said. 'Anybody listening to this might get the impression Joe doesn't like us much.'

Stilts said nothing.

Duchess appeared at Gosling's window. 'I'm bored. An' this outfit keeps a'ridin' up between me arse cheeks.'

Gosling stretched his arm out of the window and slapped Duchess on the backside and cackled with laughter.

'Once we've got that money I'll kiss your arse if you want me to!' Gosling turned back to Joe. 'Let's go, Duchess is bored and I'm bored too.'

'Your man said we should wait a little longer,' Coffin said.

'Sod that for a game of soldiers,' Gosling said. 'My blood's up, I can't sit in this bloody car any longer.'

The Stig climbed back in the driver's seat. Glanced at Coffin. One look was all Coffin needed to see the Stig didn't much like it either.

He put the car into first and they rolled out of the Two For One car park and back onto the dual carriageway, where he put his foot down.

Within a couple of minutes, they were back outside the gated entrance to the Ullman house. On the other side of the black, cast iron gate, a gravel drive wound its way up a slight incline between trees and disappeared from view. The house couldn't be seen from this vantage point, but Coffin had been here before.

He knew what the house looked like, inside and out.

Last time he had been here, he had left a dead body on the living room floor, bleeding into the carpet.

'Go type in the access code,' Gosling said to Stilts.

The little man climbed silently out of the car, holding the slip of paper with the numbers on it, and walked up to the gate. He peered at the slip of paper and then up at the key pad. He reached up, stood on his tiptoes, but still the key pad was out of his reach.

Gosling chuckled in the back of the car.

A car door slammed behind them, and Gilligan came striding into view.

'For the love of god, is this a fucking joke or what?' he said, and snatched the paper from Stilts' hand.

He punched in the numbers and the gates began their slow, electronic swing inward. The Stig inched the car forward and crawled through the gap as it widened, the tyres crunching over the gravel. He pulled over to the side and waited for Shaw to pull up behind him.

Stilts got back in the car.

'It's a shame for you, isn't it?' Gosling said, still chuckling. 'Never mind, when you crack that combination on the safe, nobody will be laughing then, will they?'

Gilligan walked past, muttering.

'Where's your man going?' Gosling said.

Coffin climbed out of the car.

'Hey, over here,' he said, and pointed into the cover of the trees. The drive was lined with mock Victorian gas lamps, shedding harsh electronic light everywhere.

Beneath the cover of the trees, it was dark.

'I'm glad I day wear me stilettos,' Duchess said as he shut his car door. 'This gravel'd 'ave bin murder on me ankles.'

Shaw opened the boot on his car and pulled out a bag. He carried it over to the trees where everyone was gathering and pulled back the zipper.

'Take your weapon of choice,' Coffin said.

The Stig and Shaw went for the handguns. Gilligan, Gosling, and Stut went for the sawn-off shotguns. Stilts didn't take anything.

Duchess had a good look at the remaining weapons. Picked out a handgun.

Coffin said, 'Shaw, Stig, go round the back of the house. You'll lose the cover of the trees before you get there, so be careful. If there's security round the back, take them out as silently as possible. The hardware's your last resort, and this goes for everyone. If anyone discharges their weapon, we call the whole thing off and get the hell out of here. Am I clear on that?'

Everyone nodded and murmured agreement, apart from Duchess and Stilts.

'Gilligan, Stut, you come with me and we'll take the front.'

'What about us, Joe?' Gosling said, grinning like he was having the best time in the world.

'I don't give a fuck what you clowns do,' Coffin said. 'As long as your master safe cracker is there to get us in when we need him.'

Coffin took the lead whilst Shaw and the Stig crossed the gravel drive and entered the gloom of the tree covering on the opposite side. Gosling and his companions followed Coffin.

They trod carefully and slowly between the trees, their feet sinking silently into the mowed grass. In daylight there wouldn't be much cover here as the trees were spaced out enough to allow sunlight for the grass to grow, but at night it was perfect. As they drew further away from the driveway, Coffin caught glimpses of the house between the trees. Security lights illuminated the front patio.

Coffin caught a glimpse between the trees of a body slumped over a garden table on the patio. He signalled the others to stop. He drew closer whilst taking care to remain under the cover of the trees. The man was sitting in a garden chair, his upper body lying face down on the table. There was a cigarette on the table. Most of it was one long column of ash. It had to have been there for a while, burning down on its own.

'Now what do you think happened here?' Gilligan whispered.

'Looks like someone beat us to it,' Coffin whispered back.

'Is he dead?'

'Don't think so, I think I can see him breathing.'

'You think they're inside now?'

Coffin shook his head slowly, staring at the unconscious security guard the whole time. 'Don't know.'

'What's the holdup?' Gosling said. He hadn't seen the man at the table.

Coffin turned and held up his hand to shush him.

'Now what's the little bastard up to?' Gilligan hissed.

Coffin turned back. Stilts was walking across the illuminated lawn as though he had every right to be there. He climbed up onto the raised patio, grabbed the security guard by his hair, and lifted his face off the table.

The man started moaning, his eyelids fluttering.

Stilts produced a knife from seemingly nowhere and drew it across the man's throat. Scarlet blood spurted from the slash in the guard's neck and splattered noisily over the patio table. His hands jerked and twitched, and his feet kicked the flagstones as he died.

Coffin leapt from his hiding place and strode across the lawn. Grabbing Stilts by the shoulder, he dragged the little man away.

'What the fuck do you think you're doing?' he hissed.

Gosling was right behind Coffin, chuckling softly.

'You think this is funny?' Coffin whispered, turning on Gosling. 'He was just a kid, he was barely old enough to shave!'

'Aww, come on, Joe!' Gosling said. 'Isn't this a case of pot calling kettle black?'

Coffin grabbed Gosling by the throat and shoved him up against the patio table. Its feet scraped against the ground and blood poured over the edge and splattered on the flagstones.

'I ought to take that knife off Stilts and shove it in your guts,' Coffin hissed.

'You're not focusing on the right things, Joe,' Gosling said. 'Think about the money. Think about all that bloody money just waiting for us.'

Coffin held onto Gosling for a few seconds and then let him go. He took a step back, glanced at Gilligan and Stut standing on the lawn behind Gosling.

'You know how much I dislike your man here, but he's right, we need to focus,' Gilligan said.

Coffin held up his hand, palm out, and put a finger to his lips. Apart from the sound of cars on the road, there was silence.

They were exposed right now, out in the open in the glare of the security lights. Were they being recorded by CCTV, too? Maybe they had already triggered a silent alarm and that other private security firm was already on its way.

And even if they weren't, it looked highly likely that there was already another outfit in the house. But who? And were they after the money too, or something else?

'Are we going to stand here all night, Joe?' Gosling said.

'Because I don't know about you, but I'm starting to feel like a rotisserie chicken in a supermarket under this spotlight.'

'Hey, Joe!'

It was the Stig, walking onto the lawn from around the opposite side of the house, followed by Shaw.

'He give you trouble?' the Stig said, gesturing at the body slumped across the table, still leaking blood.

'No,' Coffin said.

Where was Stilts? He'd done another disappearing act and Coffin was afraid of what he would do next. Coffin had underestimated the little man. As well as all his other attributes, he was obviously a psychopath too.

'Where's the other security guard?' Coffin said.

'We found him out cold around the back of the house,' the Stig said. 'Looks like somebody else had the same idea as us.'

'Yeah,' Coffin said. 'You think they're still inside?'

'There's a white van parked around the back. Might belong to the firm guarding this place.'

'Or it might belong to the firm breaking in,' Coffin said, scanning the outside of the house for any signs of a break in.

Duchess appeared in the glare of the security light, pulling at the black, stretchy Lycra around his backside. 'Ooh, I'm goona 'ave plenty 'o skid marks in this thing afower the night's out, I can tell ya.'

'Where's the dwarf?' Coffin said.

Gosling wheezed with laughter. 'Did you hear that? Joe's about as un-PC as I am.'

'We're wasting time out here,' Coffin said. 'And for all we know we've been spotted already, standing out here under the spotlight.'

He shook his head and began walking up to the front door. Once on the patio, he saw Stilts. The little man was standing at eye level with the lock, his lock picking tools scattered around his feet. He was absorbed in his work and paid no attention to Coffin.

The rest of the crew gathered on the patio and watched Stilts.

'Fuck it, we're wasting time,' Coffin said.

He spotted a garden gnome and picked it up, raising it to shoulder height to throw at the window beside the door.

The front door swung open.

An insistent beeping started up in the cavernous hallway.

Gosling pushed past Coffin and into the house. He keyed in the number on the white keypad on the wall and the beeping noise stopped.

Coffin placed the gnome back on the patio. Stilts joined Gosling inside the house.

'You think she heard all that noise?' Coffin said.

Duchess pushed past him. 'Quick, sumboddy show me weer the pisser is, mar bladder's big as a beach ball.'

Coffin stepped over the threshold.

'All right, let's take a look around,' he said. 'And if we're on our own, let's go find that safe room, see if there's anything left worth taking in there.'

YOU CAN'T HURRY ART

The sweat was pouring off Stilts as he worked. His face was shiny with it and his shirt stained dark on his back and under his arms. He was standing in front of the safe room door, hidden behind a floor to ceiling bookshelf that swung out at the touch of an invisible catch.

Coffin had expected an old-fashioned dial on the front of the safe room door, had pictured Stilts twisting the dial one way and then the other as he listened to the mechanics of the bolts inside the door with a stethoscope.

It wasn't anything like that. The lock was an electric one and Stilts had brought an array of cables and black boxes with him and a laptop. Coffin had no idea what he was doing, or if Stilts even knew what he was doing. By now Coffin was beginning to wonder if this whole thing was just a setup of some kind, a charade for Coffin's benefit. It seemed like there was something else going on, and whatever it was, Coffin was missing it.

Whilst Stilts worked, Gosling had helped himself to whatever he could find in the kitchen, and was now sitting in an armchair eating a massive sandwich of ham and pickles and drinking a pint glass full of Coca Cola.

'It's well known the old biddy's got a sweet tooth,' he said, and let out a huge belch. 'Bloody hell, it doesn't half gas me up though. I'll suffer with my IBS tomorrow, I bloody will at that.'

Stut was at the door, keeping a lookout. They had scouted out the ground floor and quickly determined that they were on their own. There was no sign of a disturbance of any kind, no sign of a forced entry. Coffin didn't like it, not one bit. But they were here now. They needed to get the money and then get the hell out.

Coffin had sent Shaw upstairs to double-check there was nobody there and to make sure Mrs Ullman wasn't going to cause any problems.

Now it was a waiting game while Stilts did his part.

Coffin looked at the unlikely safe cracker, at his sweat stained back, and said, 'How much longer is he going to be?'

'Relax, Joe,' Gosling said through a mouthful of ham sandwich. 'Stilts isn't just a safe cracker, he's an artist, and you can't hurry art now, can you?'

Duchess pulled at his suit around his bottom and crotch areas. 'I'm tellin' ya, I'm goona 'ave sum bluddy awful chaffin in mar nether regions termorra mornin'. I shoulda vaselined oop.'

'We've been here too long,' Coffin said. 'And I don't know if you've forgotten, but we've got a dead body lying on the lawn. If anyone comes by, we're fucked.'

Gosling stuffed more sandwich in his mouth. 'You worry too much,' he said, his voice muffled through the half eaten food. 'You should get yourself something to eat, sit down and take the weight off your feet. I'm sure I spotted some beer in the fridge too, have a drink, take the edge off.'

'Bloody hell, Joe, you still think this is a good idea?' Gilligan said quietly in Coffin's ear. 'This is like something out of a comedy, and we're the butt of the joke.'

'Speak up, Paddy, I can't hear you,' Gosling said, and belched.

Coffin saw a muscle twitching in Gilligan's bruised jaw as he ignored the taunts.

Stilts started up a drill, the sound of its high pitched whining filling the room. He placed the tip of the drill against the metal door and began drilling into it.

'What the fuck is this?' Coffin shouted.

'Do I look like the safe cracking expert?' Gosling shouted back, spraying gobbets of chewed food over his belly. 'Ask the man himself.' He laughed. 'Oh yeah, sorry about that, I forget sometimes he can't talk.'

Stilts stopped drilling, plunging the room back into silence. He fed a metal probe attached to a black wire through the hole and then tapped at the keys on the laptop.

There was a beep followed by a muffled clunk from inside the door, which swung open a fraction.

'At bloody last,' Gilligan muttered, casting a glance at Coffin.

'Open her up, Stilts,' Gosling said. The sandwich had disappeared from his hand and been replaced with a gun.

Stilts reached up and grasped the single metal handle and pulled. The door swung open easily and silently.

Coffin had the shotgun ready. If there was somebody in there, and Gosling said there always was, then they would have heard all the work Stilts had been doing on opening up the door, they would be ready and probably armed.

The door swung wide open and came to a halt.

The room's interior was stark and plain, revealed beneath harsh lighting from ceiling lights. In the centre of the room was an upright metal cage on wheels. Inside the cage was a man. His wrists and ankles had been secured to either side of the cage with plastic ties, forcing him to stand in one position, his arms raised like he was a sacrifice. His mouth was hidden with a gag. His eyes bulged with terror as he stared at Coffin.

Coffin took a step forward, clutching the shotgun. 'What the—'

'Please, put down the gun, Mr Coffin,' Stump said as she walked into view. She was holding her own gun, resting across her mannequin's arm.

Coffin sighed. 'I don't believe this.'

Stump smiled. 'Oh, do believe it, Mr Coffin. Now, put down your gun.'

'No,' Coffin said.

'Oh I ruminink you should,' Corpse's voice came from behind Coffin.

Coffin's shoulder blades tingled with anticipation of a bullet in his back.

'All of you, lay down your weapons,' Stump said. 'I think we should have a little chat, but I can't talk with all this weaponry pointing my way. It doesn't do for a clear mind, not at all.'

Coffin said nothing.

'Joe?' Gilligan said. 'The freak's got his gun trained right on you. He'll take your head off if you're not careful.'

'You got a chance to take him out?' Coffin said.

'Not a chance in hell, you'll be dead before I can make a move.'

Coffin gazed at Stump the whole time he was talking. Gosling was on the periphery of his vision, but Coffin couldn't tell if he was still holding his gun or not.

'Gosling, what about you?'

'I've put my gun down, Joe. I think you should do the same,' Gosling said.

'All right then,' Coffin said, and lowered his gun slowly to the floor.

'Now, isn't this nice, everyone together,' Stump said. 'It's like a family reunion.'

'What are you doing here?' Coffin said.

'The same reason as you,' Stump said. 'The money.'

'And you just happen to turn up the same night as us?' Coffin said. 'That's one big coincidence.' He looked at the man in the cage, and a memory stirred, of seeing something similar once. 'What's the deal with him?'

'One of our playthings, Mr Coffin, we like to collect them,' Stump said. 'Unfortunately, our last one had to be put down, as he had lost his usefulness to us.'

Coffin noticed the body lying on the ground behind the cage. A man, looked like he'd been beaten up pretty bad.

And then shot in the head.

'You two freaks have been picking off Ullman's security guards, haven't you?' Coffin said. 'I remember now, when I had that fever, that infection, and you got that doctor in to treat me, I remember I went wandering at one point and I found someone, a man, in one of those cages. I thought it was a fever dream, but it wasn't, was it?'

'Bloody hell, Joe, there you go again making a speech,' Gosling said, and chuckled. 'I think you might have said more in the last two days than in the rest of your life.'

'Hello Mr Gosling,' Stump said, rotating her head to look at the fat man in the chair.

'You know each other?' Coffin said.

'Only by reputation,' Gosling said. 'What's the deal with taking Ullman's security? Wouldn't stamp collecting be easier?'

'But a lot less rewarding,' Stump said.

'Stump and Corpse hate the Ullmans,' Coffin said, talking to Gosling but not taking his eyes off Stump. 'I thought you'd given up on your vendetta since I put a bullet in the old man.'

'You know us better than that, Mr Coffin,' Stump said, smiling.

'So what now? Are you going to shoot us all and take your money? Seems like everyone has to stand around talking all the time rather than just getting on with the job.'

'So impatient, Mr Coffin,' Stump said. 'But yes, of course, let's get on with the main act, shall we?'

'Would you mind if I finished my sandwich first?' Gosling said and took a bite. 'Bloody nice piece of ham this is.' His voice was muffled and thick with chewed food. 'You should try some.'

UPSTAIRS, Shaw stiffened when he heard the drill start up. Took him a moment to realise what it was. He relaxed a little. Not that his nerves were going to let him off the hook too easily. He was wound up tighter than he thought possible.

This whole setup stank to high heaven, as far as he was concerned. And he knew the others, including Coffin, felt the same. The thing was, the potential payday at the end was too big to ignore.

Much too big.

Shaw opened the next door he came to along the landing. A bathroom, bigger than his living room at home. No toilet in here, simply a rolltop bath set in the middle of the bathroom, ornate brass fittings, shelves lining the walls filled with toiletries and pot-pourri. Stank like a whore's boudoir.

A thin layer of dust coated all the surfaces and thick, filthy strands of cobwebs hung in corners and from the ceiling. The old biddy probably hadn't used this bathroom in years. Probably too feeble to get in and out of the bath.

This was the second bathroom Shaw had discovered. The other one had a shower in it and a toilet and sink. That one was obviously still being used.

Shaw closed the door and continued his search. He needed to find the old lady. All the noise of the drill from downstairs could be waking her up.

He opened the next door he came to, taking it quiet and slow. Although with the sound of that drill downstairs, he wasn't sure why he was bothering.

A massive, four poster bed tried to dominate the room, but failed. There were too many other distractions. The scarlet drapes hanging from the walls and billowing beneath the ceiling for one. The paintings, portraits mainly and all of the same, stern, pompous man. Shaw was no art expert, his idea of culture was reading the Metro newspaper instead of the Sun, but he could see these paint-ings were crudely done.

Who the hell was the subject of those portraits? Stuart Ullman, perhaps? Shaw had heard of him before, back when he owned that string of nightclubs, but he'd never seen a photograph of him.

Shaw closed the door behind him. Got his iPhone and switched on the torch. Shadows danced in the corners as he walked towards the bed.

The thick carpet seemed to swallow his feet with each step he took. Either side of the four poster were two huge chests, like the old trunks he'd seen in those black and white films his mother used to watch.

Shaw approached the trunk nearest to him. The light from his mobile illuminated the objects placed on top. A skull, with a fat candle placed on top, rivulets of melted wax running over the pale bone. Another skull, black hieroglyphs carved into its features. An open book, small, illegible text on one page and an illustration of a horned, cloven footed naked man on the other, his impossibly huge penis standing erect and proud.

'What the fuck?' Shaw whispered.

The writing in the book was so tiny Shaw had to bend close to read it. The words were strange, a language he didn't recognise.

He cast the light of the mobile over the bed. Mrs Ullman was a shrunken figure, outlined beneath the blanket covering her. Her long white hair was splayed across the pillow. The harsh light of the mobile's torch cast deep shadows into the fissures of skin on her face.

Shaw couldn't help but shudder as he looked at her. The sickly yellow of her flesh gave her the appearance of death. Only the slight rattle in the back of her throat gave away the fact that she was breathing.

Shaw noticed the trunk on the opposite side of the bed. More skulls and candles on its top, and something else too.

Something that made Shaw shudder again.

Surely it couldn't be.

His eyes had to be playing tricks on him in the light from his mobile.

Shaw walked around the bed. As he drew closer to the trunk, his feet seeming to grow heavier and slower as he approached it, he realised he had been right.

Lying between the skulls and the candles was a severed hand. It looked to be old, the flesh yellowed and dried out. In fact, Shaw was pretty sure it wasn't real. Just some stupid prop or joke, that was all.

Still, it gave him the creeps.

A memory of a story his mother told him surfaced. About the body of the woman found in the tree nearby here. Except for her hand, which had been removed and buried several yards from the tree.

The Hand of Glory, his mother had called it. Some sort of witchcraft ritual.

Shaw couldn't take his eyes off the severed hand.

It had to be a prop.

Had to be.

He reached out and picked it up.

The flesh felt dry and repulsive, and it seemed to squirm in his hand. Shaw dropped it like it was a red hot coal.

It thudded on the trunk and Shaw glanced at the old lady in the bed. She mumbled a little, murmuring words he couldn't catch the meaning of, and then she was silent again apart from that rattle in the back of her throat.

Shaw wiped his hand on his trousers.

He was creeped out good and proper now.

The drilling stopped.

Thank fuck for that, Shaw thought.

He backed up, away from the trunk and that hand lying on top, away from the bed and the old lady. He turned and opened the door. Once he was outside of the bedroom, back on the landing, he felt like he could breathe again.

They had to get out of this place. Just grab the fucking money and run.

Shaw took the stairs quietly even though he had seen the old lady sleeping through the noise of the drill. The house, everything he had seen, spooked him out. It was as if by moving as quietly as possible, he could avoid disturbing something that was still sleeping.

Something that he absolutely did not want to wake up.

Shaw stopped outside the living room door. It was ajar, but Shaw was standing to one side of it. He couldn't see inside, but he could hear voices.

And one of those voices he recognised as that freak's Stump's.

Shaw gripped his gun a little tighter. Listened some more, trying to pinpoint where people were in the room by the sound of their voices. It was too difficult, he couldn't do it.

He would just have to step into the doorway and hope for the best. He hadn't heard that other freak Corpse say anything yet. Was he there, or was it just the mad bitch, with that filthy mannequin's hand attached to her arm?

Thinking of Stump's missing hand reminded Shaw of the hand lying on Mrs Ullman's bedside table. Bloody thing had to be fake, right?

It had to be.

Shaw shoved the thought away and stepped into view. Corpse was standing right in front of him, his back to him. Shaw lifted his gun and placed the barrel against Corpse's head.

'No one move, or I'll blow the fucking undertaker's head off,' he said.

THAT'S MY GIRL

Coffin ignored the urge to turn around. He needed to keep his eyes fixed on Stump. If he turned his back on her, he was certain she would shoot him.

'Is that you, Shaw?' he said.

'Yeah, Joe. I've got Corpse covered, anyone moves, I'll stick a bullet in the back of his head and then he really will be a corpse.'

Coffin kept on looking Stump in the eyes. She hadn't moved, her face hadn't shown any expression at all.

'I think you should put your gun down,' Coffin said.

Stump said nothing. And yet, despite the lack of expression on her face, it seemed to Coffin that her eyes betrayed her. That he could see in there her hatred of Joe Coffin, and how desperate she was to pull that trigger.

Coffin had never had much time for diplomacy or subtleness. Maybe it was a skill he needed to start learning.

Like, right now.

'You caught me in a bad mood at the club the other night,' Coffin said. 'I was wrong to say what I did.'

Stump continued staring blank faced at Coffin. It was as though she were in a trance.

'After everything you did for me when I was wounded, you're right, I should be repaying that debt.'

'I think you are bargaining for your life, Mr Coffin,' Stump said.

'No, *you're* bargaining for Corpse's life,' Coffin said. 'You shoot me and Corpse will be dead before I hit the ground. And then everyone else in this room will turn their guns on you.'

'But I am expected to believe that you are going to let us go?' Stump's face twisted into a sneer. 'And that you will then carry out the favours you owe me?'

'Yes,' Coffin said.

'Why should I believe anything you say?' Stump said.

'You know me, I say it how it is.' Coffin kept his gaze fixed on Stump. 'If I say I'm going to do something, I do it.'

The sneer of disbelief slowly left Stump's face as she relaxed a little. She regarded Coffin a little longer and then slowly lowered the gun.

Coffin realised he was clenching his fists, digging his nails into the soft flesh of his palms. He unclenched them, let the tension ease from his body.

Stump raised the gun again.

'Easy,' Coffin said, as he heard movement behind him, everyone raising their guns once more.

'What about the money?' Stump said.

'What about it?' Coffin said.

'Mr Corpse and myself, we were here first. We should take the money.'

'No,' Coffin said. 'You leave the cash here. It's ours.'

'But that hardly seems fair, Mr Coffin,' Stump said. 'You were being so reasonable just a moment ago, but now you are demanding to keep everything.'

'I don't know what's going on between you and Mrs Ullman, or the history you had with the old man, but I know how much you hated him, and still do.'

'You saved us once from him,' Stump said.

'That's right, I did,' Coffin replied. 'And you know I didn't do that for you, I was there to kill him, nothing else. After all those things that bastard had done, he deserved to die.'

'This is fascinating, Joe,' Gosling said, his mouth full of sandwich. 'Are you going to tell us more?'

Coffin ignored him.

'And then we repaid the debt we owed you,' Stump said.

'Yes, you did, but I never saw it that way, I never thought of you owing me a debt, a favour. But now I see how important that is for you, and I promise you I will repay the debts I owe you.' Coffin paused, trying to think through what he was going to say. 'But taking all that cash, for you it's just an act of spite, a fuck you to Mrs Ullman. But do you actually need it? I don't think so. The thing is, you want me to pay back some favours, I need that money.'

Stump slowly lowered the gun again.

'Mr Corpse?' she said. 'You can put down your weapon. We're leaving now.'

'Bloody hell, Joe,' Gosling said. 'You ever get tired of the criminal life you could work for the United Nations.'

Coffin turned around. 'All right everyone, put down your guns. Stump and Corpse are leaving.'

Corpse weaved his way past Coffin, his head bobbing up and down on his neck, and joined Stump. Together, they took hold of the cage on wheels and began pushing it out of the safe room and through the living room.

'Hey, no, no,' the man in the cage said. 'No way, you can't take me with you, you said I could go free. What the fuck is this? You said I could go free!'

Coffin stepped to one side as Stump and Corpse pushed the cage past him. They struggled to keep it moving over the soft carpet, and the cage halted by Coffin.

'Don't let them do this!' the man hissed at Coffin, his face pressed against the wirework of the cage. 'They're going to kill me. Please don't let them do this!'

With some effort, Stump and Corpse got the cage moving again. Coffin watched as they rolled it through the doorway. The man inside the cage fell silent, as though resigned to his fate.

The tiny wheels snagged on another piece of carpet. Corpse gave the cage a good shove to try to get it moving, but it toppled instead. The man screamed as the cage fell over and landed on its side, the metal frame rattling as it hit the floor.

The man inside the cage began crying.

'Oh, Mr Corpse, less haste and more speed, please,' Stump said.

'I'm sorrologise, Mrs Stump, but I just desirating to vamoosepart,' Corpse said, whimpering a little.

'Give me a hand,' Coffin said to Shaw.

They bent down either side of the cage and lifted it back upright. The man in the cage had split his cheek open where it hit the wire mesh, and a small flap of skin hung open, bleeding slowly.

'Let's help them get this thing outside,' Coffin said.

'Fucking hell, Joe, are you serious?' It was Gosling. He was eating his sandwich still, but standing up now. 'We should be taking the money, not helping out these two retards.'

Coffin ignored Gosling.

With Shaw's help, he manhandled the cage out into the hall.

'That your van out the back?' Coffin said.

'Yes, indeed,' Stump replied.

Together they manoeuvred the cage into the kitchen where the going was much easier on the slate floor. Stump opened the patio doors. The slate floor was a seamless level surface from the kitchen out to the garden, apart from the metal rails inset into the ground for the runners on the doors. Coffin and Shaw were able to roll the cage outside with no problems.

Stump opened up the back doors of the white van and said, 'I will have to start the engine to operate the ramp.'

'Forget that,' Coffin said. 'We'll lift him in.'

Coffin and Shaw both got a good grip on the cage and lifted it into the back of the van. The man inside the cage stayed silent the whole time.

Gosling, Stilts, Duchess and Giligan had gathered at the patio doors to watch. Gosling had finished his sandwich and was licking his fingers, one by one. When he'd finished, he wiped his hands on his trousers and disappeared back into the house.

Stump and Corpse got in the van's cab. The exhaust coughed blue smoke when they started the engine.

As Coffin watched them drive away, Shaw said, 'What was that all about? Shouldn't we have just shot them both?'

'Maybe,' Coffin said. He looked back at the house. 'Let's get back inside, before Gosling takes all the money.'

Duchess emerged from the kitchen, a cigarette hanging from his lips, glossy with lipstick. He was still pulling at his tight outfit.

'This thing keeps aridin' oop me crack,' he said. 'I'm neva wearin' one o' these agen. I doe no how Catwoman does it.'

Coffin walked past Duchess without saying a word to him, followed by Shaw. Inside the house Gosling, Stilts, and Stut were piling stacks of money into bags. Gilligan was watching them.

'Where's the Stig?' Coffin said.

'He's out the front,' Gilligan said. 'He wanted to make sure Freaky and Deaky left and didn't just park round the front and come back in to shoot us all.'

Gosling straightened up, gasping for air. 'Bloody hell, Joe, look at all this money. Let's get it in the cars and get out of here before the coppers turn up.'

Coffin opened his mouth to answer Gosling, but his answer was cut short by the sound of motorbike engines. The glow from their headlights swept across the living room wall.

'Now what?' Coffin muttered.

Stilts and Stut stopped shovelling money into bags.

Coffin went and joined the Stig at the open front door. Five black-clad figures on motorbikes, their completely black visors turned to face Coffin, sat on motorbikes, revving their engines. As if at a prearranged signal which Coffin couldn't see, they all reached behind their backs and pulled out short, snub-nosed semi-automatics.

'Oh shit,' the Stig said.

The two men hit the ground, scrambling for cover as the gang of bikers unleashed their firepower. A hailstorm of bullets slammed into the house, shattering windows and thudding into the walls.

Coffin crawled back into the living room. Everyone was on the floor, hugging the carpet. The curtains were billowing into the room as though they were caught in a gale, one that was also ripping them to shreds. Stuffing sprang from chairs and wood splinters flew like missiles. A cloud of plaster dust whirled through the room as bullets smashed into the walls.

'What the hell's going on?' Gosling shouted, his face a blotchy red and shiny with sweat.

'Members of the Seven Ghosts is my guess,' Coffin shouted back.

Gosling had his gun out again. 'We've got to take the fight to them!'

'And how do you expect us to do that?' Coffin shouted. 'They've got us pinned down!'

The gunfire stopped.

The sudden silence seemed more deafening than the gunfire had been.

Coffin risked pulling himself up to peer out of the window. All five of the bikers were reloading their weapons with swift, practised movements. Coffin thought about standing up, letting loose with both barrels of his shotgun.

Remembered he didn't have it to hand.

They had finished reloading now. They were raising their weapons.

Coffin was about to get back to hugging the carpet when he spotted movement amongst the trees behind the bikers. Duchess Swallows stepped from his cover of the trees and up behind the biker nearest to him. He had a small handgun, and he slipped it under the biker's helmet and pulled the trigger.

The biker jerked upwards, arching his back. Blood poured from beneath his helmet and over his outfit. With what looked like practised ease, Duchess grabbed the semi-automatic with his free hand whilst dropping the handgun from the other.

Before the other assassins had even fully comprehended what was happening, Duchess turned his new weapon on them and began strafing them with bullets. As the bikers kicked and jerked and collapsed under the onslaught of his weapon, Duchess began screaming and whooping, his red painted lips parted in a huge, crazy grin.

'That's my girl,' Gosling said, standing beside Coffin.

Once the last of the bikers had collapsed under the hail of bullets, Duchess stopped firing. He lifted the muzzle of the gun to his lips and blew it, like a cowboy in a wild west B-Movie.

'Stig, get out there and gather up their guns,' Coffin said. 'And let's get that money and get out of here before we have any more visitors.'

GIRL'S GOT NO STYLEEE

Shanks Longworth walked along Lozells Road, past the Indian and Thai takeaways and the fish and chip shops. Shazanz Kebab House, Dixy Chicken, Aziz Pizza, Saqib Kebab House, The Plaice.

He'd been instructed to look out for a kebab shop called McDoner's, and there it was, across the road and behind a barrier of a portable metal fence. The signage aped the McDonald's brand, but no one was going to be fooled.

Longworth crossed the road and dodged through a gap in the metal fence. He pushed at the door and it opened stiffly.

The young, bearded man behind the counter nodded at Longworth and tilted his head toward another door at the rear of the shop. There were no customers, but the kebab meats were already hot and dripping grease on their skewers behind the counter.

Longworth pushed through the door and entered a small room with four tables, each with four chairs pushed under them. The strip lights on the ceiling were off, but Longworth could see enough from the light spilling out of the window cut in another door at the opposite side of the room. He walked towards it. The indistinct sound of chatter grew louder as he walked closer.

The glass was opaque, like a bathroom window. Through the glass, Longworth could see vague, distorted shadows moving around.

He pushed the door open.

A group of Arabic looking men were sitting around a large table. There was nothing on the table, but there were wooden crates stacked up haphazardly along one wall. Arabic writing had been stencilled on the sides in black ink.

One of the men stood up. He was wearing a black leather jacket and jeans and he was clean shaven. He looked westernised. Not like the others, all wearing traditional thawbs. They looked nervous as hell.

'Yeah?' he said, his eyes and posture radiating hostility.

'You know what I'm here for,' Longworth said.

'You got to tell us that,' the man said. 'You got to say it.'

'I'm picking up some hardware.' Longworth scanned the room. All he could see were the wooden crates.

'Yeah? What hardware, man? We don't do no hardware, we do kebabs, you in the wrong place.'

'Cut the routine, we both know that's not true,' Longworth said.

The man glanced at his companions, zeroed in on one. 'Pat him down, yeah?'

The young man stood up, approached Longworth slowly. He reached out and began patting his hands over Longworth's chest, his touch light and hesitant.

'Not like that, you mong,' the man said. 'Tell him to hold his arms up and give him a good feel, like you're touching him up.'

Longworth held out his arms, and the young man patted him down a little more forcefully.

'Tell him to spread his legs, yeah, and pat his legs down. Don't forget his balls and his arse, all right? Give them a good squeeze.'

Once the physical search had been finished, Longworth lowered his arms. The young man's face was scarlet as he stepped back.

'All right, good, yeah,' the man said. 'Where's the money?'

'What money?' Longworth said.

'The money for the fucking hardware, man. We ain't no charity, right? Yeah?'

'I already paid,' Longworth said.

'Not me, man. You gots to pay me or you don't get no hardware, yeah?'

Longworth scanned the room again. His gear had to be in one of the wooden crates. There was nothing else in the room.

He dropped his gaze on the leader once more, meeting that hostile, aggressive stare of his. Longworth guessed he was showing off, asserting his authority with the newbies in the room. Maybe trying to prove how clever he was. He'd already been paid to deliver the goods, but acting like he hadn't been was a way of getting some extra cash.

Longworth knew he could play it one of two ways.

He could either give the man what he wanted, the money and the prestige that he needed to show these young kids he was boss. Longworth had the cash on him, that was no problem. And loss of face was no problem either. Not when he didn't expect to survive the night.

Still, it pissed him off.

So that left the other way.

Longworth took one long, swift step forward, bringing his other foot up and burying it in the man's crotch.

The man doubled over, screaming. Longworth grabbed him by the back of the head and brought his knee up, smashing it into the man's face.

The scream turned into a gurgle.

Longworth spun him around and slammed the man's face into the table and wrenched his arm up behind his back.

The others shifted away, eyes darting between each other, wondering what they should do.

Longworth had one hand on the back of the man's head, pressing his face against the table top, and his other hand forcing the man's arm up behind his back.

'Any of you want to have a go, be my guest,' Longworth said.

'You won't get far before I rip his arm off and use it to beat you all to death, am I clear?'

The young men, wide eyed with fear, all nodded.

Longworth leaned in close to the man, their faces only inches apart. Snot and blood bubbled out of the man's nose.

'Now then, Cupcake, where's my gear?'

'In the crate, the one nearest to the door.'

Longworth let go of him and he slid to the floor, moaning and clutching his balls.

The top of the crate was loose. Longworth pulled it off. There was a holdall bag inside. Longworth unzipped it and inspected the contents.

Satisfied, he zipped it up and hefted it over his shoulder.

He walked out of the shop and down Lozells Road without a backward glance.

EMMA PROWLED THE KITCHEN. The walls seemed to be closing in on her, the air tasted stale, like there wasn't enough oxygen in it. Once she would have relished time on her own in the house, away from the buzz of the office. Times like that were when her articles began to form in her head, and when she sat down at the computer to type them out, they arrived fully formed, with little in the way of editing needed.

But tonight wasn't like that. Tonight she was going crazy.

With Mitch in the hospital and Louisa May at her mother's house, Emma knew she should have been taking advantage of the quiet. Should have gone to bed, caught up with some much needed sleep.

Even if she hadn't been too wired for sleep in the first place, all that coffee she had drunk would have kept her awake through the night. The conversation Emma had had with Barry kept running through her head.

Gilligan's ties to the Jiangchi Corporation.

That night, at the club, the members of the Seven Ghosts, they had to have seen Gilligan, surely. He was supposed to be on their side, and yet he had detonated that nail bomb.

Or maybe they had never met him, maybe they never even knew the name Gerry Gilligan. Just because the Real IRA faction Gilligan was a member of and the Jiangchi Corporation were doing deals for arms, that didn't mean Gilligan had ever met any of them personally before.

And what was Gilligan doing here? Was he still a member of the Real IRA? Did he intend to use his connections with the Slaughter-house Mob to plant Real IRA cells in Birmingham? Emma could never see Joe allowing anything like that.

At the thought of Joe, Emma had to bite back a scream of frustration. That man was driving her mad. Why the hell wouldn't he take her calls? Surely he'd seen her calling enough now that he would realise something was up?

Emma picked up her mobile, looked at the screen as it bloomed into life.

No missed calls, nothing at all.

The big, ignorant gorilla. She needed to tell him about Gilligan, explain the situation.

She glanced around the kitchen. Yep, those walls were definitely closing in on her.

She needed to get out. Do something.

Anything.

Nick would want her to stay inside, keep out of trouble. So would Mitch.

Damn. It was hard enough having one fella looking out for her, trying to nanny her and keep her wrapped up in cotton wool, but two of them?

Forget that.

Slipping the mobile in her pocket and grabbing her keys off the kitchen table, Emma headed out. She took the car and drove into the city centre.

Angels, or was it Angellicit again, she couldn't keep track. Whatever the hell it was called now, that was where the action was. Where it always was.

Emma parked up a couple of streets away. The city centre streets were quiet, the only sign that the city was alive, the music pounding from the clubs, the shop windows ablaze with light. Everyone huddled indoors or clubbing and drinking the night away, believing they were safe.

Emma locked the car and hurried down Williams Street. Kept a look out as she ran. There was the club, a bouncer standing in the doorway, checking customers at the door. A second bouncer stood by him, looking bored.

Emma ran across the street and joined the tiny queue at the entrance. As she approached the door, the bouncer checking everyone looked at her and shook his head.

'What's that supposed to mean?' Emma said.

'You're not coming in dressed like that,' he said, his voice thick and deep.

'Are you shitting me?' Emma took a look over her shoulder at others joining the queue. The girls were in high heels, crop tops revealing skinny midriffs, shorts so tiny they exposed butt cheeks.

Emma was wearing jeans, trainers, and a hooded top.

'You can't wear jeans in here,' the bouncer said.

'All right, I guess I'm not dressed for a night out—'

'Or trainers.'

'What about the top, does that pass?'

The bouncer gazed at her, his face dead.

Emma blew her cheeks out in frustration, resisting the urge to swear at him.

'Will you let us in?' a girl shouted from behind Emma. 'We wanna get inside before we get bit.'

'Bite me, baby!' a male voice shouted and everybody laughed. Nervously.

'Look,' Emma said, turning back to the bouncer. 'I don't even want to come into your scuzzy club, I've already spent more than enough time there.' She leaned in close, dropped her voice a little. 'I need to see Joe, that's all.'

'Joe who?' the bouncer said.

'You're taking the piss, right?' Emma said.

'The only way you're coming in this club is if you're wearing the right outfit.' His eyes scanned her from head to toe and back again. 'You ain't wearing the right outfit.'

Emma turned and stalked off.

'Girl's got no styleeee!' someone shouted.

More laughter.

Emma's face burned with frustration and embarrassment. All right, so she was old enough that she could have been their mother, but seriously? To be mocked like that by a bunch of teens?

With a swift glance back to check if anyone was watching her (they weren't, everyone was too intent on getting inside the club) Emma scooted around the side and into the club's parking space. If the neanderthals on the front weren't going to let her in, maybe she could sneak in the back.

As soon as she saw the fire escape door, she knew that wasn't happening. Blank, featureless, it was firmly shut.

'Shit! Fuck! Bugger!' she hissed.

There had to be a way of getting inside and seeing Joe. She had to tell him about the stuff she'd found out, about Gilligan.

Maybe then, when she'd done that for him, he would start talking to her again.

She toyed with the idea of calling him, or maybe texting him. At the very least, he should see her text on his home screen. But even if he knew she was standing outside Angels, would he even think about letting her inside?

Depending on how pissed with her he was, he might even send those two gorillas on the front door to see her off.

Two pairs of headlight beams cut through the shadows, illuminating the side wall. Two cars pulling into the parking area.

Emma shrank into a corner, hiding in the shadows.

The cars pulled to a halt side by side.

Coffin got out, followed by a big, fat man she didn't recognise.

'Bloody hell, Joe, but that were fun, weren't it?' the man said.

Coffin walked around the back of the car. More men were getting out of the cars. The Stig, Shaw, Stut and someone else she didn't recognise. A woman, no that was wrong, a man dressed in women's clothes, all made up like a drag queen.

Emma clenched her teeth when she saw the midget appear as he walked around the front of the car.

What the hell was going on?

They started pulling holdalls out of the cars and dropping them on the floor. The holdalls bulged and looked like they were heavy. One of the holdalls rolled on its side when it hit the ground and something fluttered from the partly open zip.

It was money.

The man dressed as a woman shrieked and ran after it and the others laughed at him.

Had Joe robbed a bank?

That didn't make any sense. The Slaughterhouse Mob had never taken such a high risk venture before. It just wasn't their style. Maybe Joe was doing things differently now that Craggs was gone.

Somebody opened up the fire escape door from inside and they carried the bags in. Coffin paused at the door, the last one to enter the building, and turned and took a long look around the car park.

Emma shrank back into the shadows, willing herself invisible.

Coffin entered the building and pulled the fire escape door shut.

Emma started breathing again.

She walked over to the two cars, their engines ticking as they cooled down.

Bending down, she cupped her hands around her eyes and peered through the passenger window. The interior was spotless, the car looked as though it had just rolled off the forecourt.

'Hey, girl, you lost somethin?'

Emma jumped and turned around. A tall, thin man in a long overcoat and a stove-pipe hat stood and grinned at her. Emma had never met him before, never even seen a photograph, but she knew him immediately.

'You're the Priest, aren't you?' she said.

The Priest grinned, showing off his black teeth. 'Now girl, I'm impressed. How'd you know that?'

'Leola told me all about you.'

BATS

Archer ignored the stares as he walked through the station. Amrit would ask him what had happened, but nobody else would. Seemed like he was invisible these days, he was ignored so steadfastly by everyone. Sure, no one made it obvious they were ignoring him. No one outright refused to talk to him or listen to what he had to say. But he didn't have that same respect anymore that he once held. No one reported to him much anymore, or sought his advice.

The station was buzzing. Extra manpower had been drafted in to cope with the escape of the vampires. Of course, most of their time was spent fielding telephone calls about vampire sightings that turned out to be nothing of the sort.

And the tension between the Birmingham coppers and those from out of town was thick in the air. That old us and them mentality. Everyone thinking they knew better than the other guy.

The police drafted in from other stations had no idea what they were up against. They hadn't been here last time. Most of them were still having trouble believing that vampires were real.

They would find out soon enough, Archer was sure of that.

'Hey, Boss, what happened to you?' Choudhry said.

Archer flopped down in the chair next to Choudhry. 'Walked into a lamppost.'

Choudhry grinned. 'You had an argument with Emma, didn't you? And she hit you.'

Archer grunted.

'That why you stayed away all day? I was wondering where you were.'

'I'm here now, aren't I?' Archer said.

'Hey, you should see this,' Choudhry said, turning back to his computer and hitting the space bar on the keyboard. The monitor sprang into life, revealing a photograph, a selfie of two young women. They looked excited, happy. From what Archer could see of the background, it looked like they were in a nightclub or a bar.

'Who are these two?' he said.

'Chelsea Orme and Madison Hughes,' Choudhry said. 'These are the two girls murdered on Broad Street.'

'And you took these photos off their phones and uploaded them onto your computer?' Archer said. 'You're a sick puppy, Amrit, getting your jollies off like this.'

'Takes one to know one,' Choudhry said. 'This is evidence.'

'We're thinking a vampire attack, right?'

'Wrong. We *know* it was a vampire attack. Look at this.'

Choudhry clicked on to the next photograph. It was blurry, the mobile obviously hadn't been held still, and the flash had left streaks of light across the image.

'Oh shit,' Archer whispered. 'Steffanie Coffin.'

She had been caught in mid lunge, mid pounce. Even through the blur, Archer could see her, could see the open mouth, the teeth, the look of crazed hunger on her face.

'We always knew she was out there somewhere,' Choudhry said.

'I know, but I was hoping she might have died, or found God or something.'

'What about the boy, Michael Coffin?' Choudhry said. 'You think he's out there still, too?'

A wave of exhaustion washed over Archer and he rubbed a hand over his face and flinched as he touched the bruised area.

'What did Emma hit you with, a rolling pin?' Choudhry said. 'I thought Parvit had a temper on her, but your lady is a tigress.'

'Emma didn't hit me,' Archer said. 'It was her boyfriend, Mitch.'

'You want me to go and arrest him, Boss?' Choudhry said. 'We can't let him get away with punching a policeman.'

'How come you didn't suggest that when you thought it was Emma who had hit me?'

'That's different. I couldn't arrest Emma, I like her too much.'

Archer sighed and turned to look at the busy station. 'You think there's much chance of anything constructive happening here?'

'You're joking, right? Talk about the right hand not knowing what the left hand is doing.'

'All right, then. Download that photograph of Steffanie Coffin onto my phone, and then how about you come with me and we pay your friend and mine Joe Coffin a visit?'

'I'm in,' Choudhry said, hitting the computer keys. 'Anything to get out of this place.'

When the download onto Archer's mobile was complete, the two men stood up. Choudhry grabbed his jacket. As they were walking through the station, they were halted by a shout.

'Archer! Choudhry!'

Archer groaned quietly.

Superintendent Nielsen waved them over to his office. Normally he didn't work in the Birmingham station house, but with the case being such an important one, and multiple forces needing to cooperate and pool resources, he had been tasked with working on site and supervising.

'There's a disturbance down on the Hagley Road, near Fiveways,' Nielsen said, pulling the office door shut behind Choudhry. 'I need you two to go and find out what's happening.'

'Sir, we were just about to go out—'

'This takes priority,' Nielsen said.

'Is it vampires?' Choudhry said.

'It might be,' Nielsen said. 'We're not sure yet, that's why I need you two down there, scout out the situation before we commit men we can't spare to it.'

'Sounds more like a job for a PC,' Choudhry said.

'No, I want you two on it.'

'Sir, what's happening?' Archer said.

Nielsen sighed. 'The problem is, Detective Archer, bats. A whole hell of a lot of them, by all accounts.'

'Bats,' Archer said, and looked at Choudhry.

THE BATS WERE MASSING, swirling around in tight, seemingly random little movements until, at an unspoken command, they dispersed before regrouping only a few seconds later. Spectators had gathered on the streets despite the risk of a vampire attack to watch the spectacle. Cars had stopped on the usually busy Broad Street. People stood in silence or sat in their cars, eyes following the bats as they swooped and dived and tumbled through the night. The silence was broken only by the blaring of horns from further down Broad Street as drivers, unable to see what was going on, grew impatient to get moving.

No one paid any attention.

No one moved.

That is until the bats began swooping at the groups of men and women. The crowds broke, screams shattering the silence that had accompanied the spectacle. The bats dived between people, nipping at faces and necks before flapping away again. The dark shapes flitted here and there, darting away before they could be grabbed or swatted at.

Leola watched the commotion from her hidden spot on the canal, clinging to the side of a bridge over the dark water. Her fingers were laced through the iron latticework, holding her in place as she watched the bats.

All day she had been prowling the city, creeping through its shadows and dark corners, watching, listening.

Waiting.

She had left the Priest asleep on his bed, his tattooed body lying prostrate and naked on top of the covers. He would've slept through most of the day, only stirring when the sun had begun to set. Even though he was 'cured' of his vampirism, he seemed unable to shake off the last of the traits of being a vampire. Sunlight worked no harm on him, but still he preferred to sleep during the day. The night invigorated him, sharpened his senses, and his intelligence.

Leola had no real preference. Day or night, it was all the same for her. And she could easily go a week without sleeping.

So she had left the Priest alone in his rented room. At first, she had thought of returning to Angellicit. Maybe Joe would ask her where she had been, or maybe he would not have even noticed her absence. Either way, they needed to talk. Leola had decided she was returning to Haiti, but the news that Chitrita was alive now had placed a seed of doubt over that decision.

And now the Priest was here.

Although he was keeping quiet about why, and maybe he didn't even fully understand why himself, she could see that he was worried.

Frightened even.

Today, exploring the city's hidden places, the nooks and crannies where evil lurked just beneath the surface, she had shared in the Priest's fear.

As the sun had begun to set, the sky growing darker and lights springing on in the office buildings, Leola saw the first of the bats.

At first it had been the odd, small groupings flying aimlessly between the tower blocks. As the sky grew darker and darker, more bats joined them and they began to mass. That's when people on the streets had begun to notice them.

Leola had followed the bats as they started moving with a much more distinct sense of purpose. This was something she had never seen before.

Finally they had settled here, on Broad Street. Leola had studied them from her hiding place, clinging to the bridge over the canal.

Now the bats were growing ever more frantic. What were they doing? Why were they acting like this? Something was happening, something very bad. Were they simply agitated about something?

Or were they acting under the influence of something outside of their control?

Beneath her, on the towpath, people were running past. Cafes and bars, already crowded with onlookers, opened up their doors and let the men and women fleeing from the bats inside to safety. Faces and hands were pressed against the glass doors of the International Convention Centre, eyes and mouths open wide in awe and fear.

A narrowboat chugged past beneath Leola. Its doors and windows were firmly shut and much of the boat was hidden by the dark, winged shapes of the bats.

A small grouping of bats broke away from the chaos on the street and darted upwards and then along Broad Street, away from the city centre. Leola could see that they were keeping tight together, flying with a purpose.

Leola climbed over the railing and onto the bridge.

She began running after the dark, winged cloud.

She dodged through the crowds of screaming people. A body barrelled into her, almost knocking Leola off her feet. She shoved the man out of the way with a snarl and continued after the bats.

'Help me, oh God help me!' a man screamed, his voice high pitched and descending into a wail.

Leola kept on running. She ignored everyone and everything.

More of the bats were breaking away and following the original group. They swooped along Broad Street, flitting over the heads of men and women cowering on the tarmac road.

Leola kept on running. Single minded in her pursuit.

Until she saw someone else doing exactly the same thing.

Following the bats with no regard for what else was happening.

A young black woman, looked like she was wearing a tattered and stained outfit, a single garment like a shroud. She didn't look to be in very good condition herself. Her arms and legs like sticks, her cheekbones like carved pieces of granite.

A vampire.

Leola kept her in sight, ignoring the bats for the moment. The vampire was intent on pursuing them anyway, so all Leola had to do was follow her instead.

They ran further down Broad Street, towards the Five Ways island. Dodged between cars, windows and doors closed, their occupants staring wide eyed at the spectacle before them.

The bats suddenly swooped down a side street. A dark trail of blurred wings and bodies.

The vampire ran between the cars, pounding at the windows and leaving behind smears of red. Had she attacked someone? Or was it her own blood?

Leola watched as the vampire followed the bats down the side street.

Where were they headed?

Running between the stationary cars, Leola followed the vampire down the side street, but keeping her distance. The bats had paused in their flight and seemed to be drawing together, closing in on something.

Leola saw the cloud of bats were gathering outside a large house. They landed on the roof and clung to the walls and the windows. Turning the inanimate building into a living, breathing, monstrous thing.

The vampire had slowed down as she approached the house, which was gradually disappearing beneath the mass of dark, fluttering bats. Except for the doorway.

Leola stayed back, out of sight of whoever was in that house.

More bats flitted over her head, catching up with their companions.

They ignored Leola.

It seemed they had lost interest in everything else apart from that one building.

Or what was inside it.

The skeletal vampire in the tattered clothes paused outside the house, head arched back as she gazed up at the bats clinging to the brickwork.

A figure appeared in the doorway, beckoning the vampire closer. Leola's chest tightened at the sight of it. There was something very familiar about that person, framed by the bats clinging to the sides of the building.

Before Leola could follow that thought, try to pinpoint that feeling, that recognition, her attention was distracted by movement from across the street. Another vampire, slinking out from behind the Ikon art gallery. A man, shuffling awkwardly, as though still growing used to the new way his body moved. He was tall and gangly, older than the black woman. His skin was pockmarked with wounds and sores.

A bat zipped past Leola, and its teeth had nipped at her cheek before she even realised it had been there. Shocked, she touched her cheek. It was wet. Blood glistened on her fingertips.

That was twice now she had been attacked by a bat in the last few days. It wasn't right.

Leola returned her attention to the vampires approaching the bat covered building. There were two figures standing in the doorway now, beckoning the others on, drawing them closer.

Leola risked moving closer herself, wanting to get a good look at these two. If only they weren't standing in the shadows so much. As if they didn't want to be seen. Usually Leola's vision was sharp enough that she could pick out details of form hidden by the dark. But tonight she was having problems.

Tonight, something was wrong.

She scurried down the road, keeping to the shadows, and found a hiding place in the entrance to a multi story car park. She crouched, waiting.

Peering at the figures in the doorway as the other two vampires drew closer.

Concentrating so hard on working out why that female figure seemed so familiar that she did not hear the scuffle of feet behind her, or feel the rush of air until it was too late.

Leola's attacker was on top of her before she even realised what was happening. Leola whipped around, snarling, teeth bared. Her attacker was too strong, too fast. The vampire swiped a clawed hand at Leola's face, opening up a red split in her cheek.

She staggered, dropped to the ground on her back. The vampire was a blur of motion, a clawed hand slashing another raw wound in Leola's abdomen.

Leola scrabbled backwards, desperate to find herself some space to move, to defend herself. The vampire was too quick, on top of Leola again before she could find enough space to return the attack. The bats swooped down low, obscuring Leola's sight, and began nipping at her flesh. A bright red slice of pain pierced her shoulder as the vampire slashed open another wound in Leola's flesh.

Hands yanked at her hair, clawed at her arms and legs. Too many hands. Leola felt like she was suffocating, drowning in darkness and fluttering wings.

The bats lifted from her, darting up and away. Leola lay on her back on the cold ground, her arms and legs pinned down by strong hands. The vampire who had attacked Leola was leaning over her, bedraggled hair hanging over her face. Leola recognised her. The missing girl, Julie Carter.

'Bring the bitch inside.'

Leola twisted her head.

That voice, she hadn't heard it in over a hundred years. But she recognised it immediately.

Chitrita.

A LONG QUEUE

Stut, Shaw, and Gilligan carried the bags of cash upstairs. Coffin told them to dump them in his office.

Gosling nudged open the door leading into the club and gazed at the girls dancing on the stage.

'Now this is what I call entertainment, Joe,' he said. 'I've been thinking maybe I should get some girls meself. Who wants to see a fat bastard like me standing up all night telling shit jokes, eh?'

'I wouldn't know,' Coffin said.

Gosling tore his eyes off the girls and let the door close. 'How about we have a drink, Joe? A toast to our success.'

'How about we just count the money and split it like we agreed?' Coffin said. 'You can be on your way then.'

Gosling chuckled. 'Have it your way.'

They took the stairs, Gosling puffing and panting with each step. When they walked into Coffin's office, they found everyone standing around the open bags of money, staring silently at their haul.

'Bloody hell, I've never seen this much cash in my life,' Shaw said softly.

The beat of the music pulsed through the floor. Duchess's hips twitched slightly, in time with the beat. 'There's enuff theer ter keep me in 'eels an' lippy fer the rest o' me loife.'

'Let's count it out, divide it into two halves,' Coffin said.

'Now, is that what we agreed, Joe?' Gosling said. 'I thought it was more like a sixty-forty split, seen as I told you about the money in the first place, and seen as how Stilts did all the hard work of breaking into the safe room.'

'Is that right?' Coffin said.

Gosling smiled. 'After all, your men mostly provided the muscle. I provided the brains and the know-how.'

'An' doe ferget the glamma,' Duchess said, and blew Coffin a kiss.

'It's a fifty-fifty split or nothing,' Coffin said.

'That's right,' Shaw said. 'You couldn't have done this without us, and you know it. Doesn't matter who were the brains and who were the muscle, you needed us.'

Stilts looked up at Shaw. Stared at him, his eyes dead.

'What are you looking at, you freak?' Shaw said.

'Now, now, I'm sure we can settle this amicably,' Gosling said. 'No one wants a disagreement, do we? Not after we worked so well together this evening.'

'It's straight down the middle,' Coffin said. 'Or it's nothing.'

'Sound like you're desperate for some cash, Joe,' Gosling said. 'You in trouble, are you?'

'Doesn't matter what I need the money for. That's how it is.'

'We could always take the money, Joe. All of it.'

Gilligan pulled a gun out of his jacket and pointed it at Gosling's head. 'I fucking knew it!'

Stilts and Duchess both pulled guns, Duchess seemingly out of nowhere, and trained them on Gilligan. Shaw, Stut and the Stig pulled their guns on Stilts and Duchess.

'All right, everybody calm down,' Gosling said. 'There's no need for us to go all Reservoir Dogs on each other.'

No one moved.

'I said, put your guns down,' Gosling said.

Stilts and Duchess slowly lowered their guns. Coffin nodded, and the others did the same.

All except Gilligan.

'Gilligan, lower your weapon,' Coffin said.

'He's going to shaft us, Joe,' Gilligan said. 'He's been screwing around with us this whole time and he isn't finished yet.'

'Put your gun down,' Coffin said.

Gilligan refused to lower the gun. Gosling stared at him, his face blank.

'Put away the gun, Gilligan,' Coffin said. 'Now.'

Gilligan finally lowered his weapon. He was breathing hard, like he'd just finished running.

'Now that were fun, weren't it?' Gosling said, his voice soft. He was still staring at Gilligan. There was a slight sheen of sweat on his face.

'Go outside, cool down,' Coffin said.

'Seems like you're always telling me to get out, ever since we met this fat bastard and his band of freaks,' Gilligan said. He was still eyeballing Gosling.

'Just leave,' Coffin said.

Gilligan broke eye contact with Gosling and pushed past Coffin as he headed out of the door. He slammed it shut behind him.

'He's a hotheaded one, that one,' Gosling said. 'You should get rid of him, Joe, before he does something you'll regret.'

'I'll deal with my own men,' Coffin said. 'Let's count this money.'

EMMA STARTED SHIVERING. Since when had it got so cold? Or was it something else making her shiver?

Like plain and simple fear.

The fire escape door to Angellicit looked as formidably feature-less and impregnable as before. There was no way she was getting in there. Except, the Priest, he'd told her to wait by the door. Said he would get her inside.

And then he had left her, waiting alone in the dark of the parking area behind Angellicit.

Was that why she was shivering? After all, if what Leola had told her and Joe was right, the Priest was a vampire. He might have taken a vow, or whatever it was he was supposed to have done, to refrain from taking bites out of people and drinking their blood, but what was that worth?

Especially if he saw a nice, juicy throat ready and waiting for the taking.

Had it been Emma's imagination, or had he been gazing long-ingly at her exposed neck whilst they talked?

Whatever, he was gone now, and supposedly to make his way inside Angellicit and then to let her in through the fire escape. How he was going to get past the bouncer dressed in his long, black coat and his battered top hat, Emma wasn't sure. But then again, he wasn't wearing jeans or trainers, so maybe he would sail right through, no questions asked.

Except for his teeth, of course. The bouncers were all checking everybody's teeth before allowing anyone inside a club. Did the Priest have pointed fangs? Even though his teeth were the most visible part of him in the dark, Emma hadn't noticed if they finished in sharp points. Didn't Leola file her teeth down? Maybe he did the same.

Emma stared at the door, willing it to open.

If the Priest was good to his word and let her in, she had to waste no time in finding Joe. Gerry Gilligan was inside that building and as soon as he saw Emma, that would be the end of her attempt to get to Joe, to talk to him. The bastard was probably sticking close to Joe. She had to separate them somehow, get Joe on his own. How she was going to do that when Joe didn't trust her anymore, wasn't even talking to her, Emma didn't know.

But she had to try.

There was a metallic clang from the other side of the fire escape door and then it began opening out.

Emma stepped back to give it room.

The Priest looked at her.

'You gone stan' there all night?' he said. 'Or you gone come on inside where it warm, bout as warm as the doorway to hell.'

'You sure know how to impress the girls, don't you?' Emma said.

'I done got no need to impress the girls,' the Priest said. 'I done got no need to impress no one.'

'I suppose not,' Emma said, and stepped inside Angellicit.

The Priest pulled the door closed behind her. The corridor they stood in was dark, the only light spilling from the opposite end of the hall. The throbbing pulse of the music from the club next door shivered through her chest. How loud did they need to turn that shit up? Surely it wasn't good for you? A whole generation of kids were going to grow up not only addicted to smartphones but deaf as well.

Or maybe Emma was just getting old.

'You seen anyone yet?' she said.

'You talkin' bout the sheep outside, I seen them and they done know it, but they headed for the slaughterhouse like the cattle they are,' the Priest said.

Emma raised her eyebrows. 'You know something I don't?'

'You done know nothin', girl,' the Priest said, and chuckled.

'What the hell are you doing here, anyway?'

The Priest grinned, exposing his teeth. 'I's lookin for Leola, what about you, girl?'

'Yeah, well, I'm looking for someone too. Joe Coffin, you might have heard of him.'

'Oh yeah, I's heard o' him. He's the dead man walking, got a Coffin for a name an' waitin for a coffin in the ground.'

'Yeah, whatever,' Emma said.

She started walking down the corridor, towards the light. The Priest followed her. He was mumbling to himself. Emma couldn't make out what he was saying, but it sounded almost like a chant or a prayer.

The club was obviously in full swing, but Emma didn't want to go in there. She wasn't dressed for it, for one thing. No, Joe and his goons would be upstairs, no doubt counting their money. She looked up the stairs, thinking about the last couple of times she had been here. Both of them with Merek Guttman.

She shivered again.

He was dead now. Joe Coffin had made sure of that.

Guttman wasn't coming back.

Ever.

'What's wrong girl, you got the heebie-jeebies on you?' the Priest said.

'Shush!' Emma hissed.

There was someone coming down the stairs.

Emma shrank back into the shadows, the Priest with her. All that black, tattooed skin was where he had an advantage over her. Put him in a darkened room he was invisible. Up close, she could smell him, a faint whiff of something like sweet cloves. No garlic, though.

Gerry Gilligan stepped into view, his back to Emma and the Priest.

He muttered something, but Emma couldn't catch what he said. He lit up a cigarette and dropped the match on the floor.

He pulled out his mobile and held it to his ear.

'Yeah, it's me,' he said. 'I know, I was fucking there, remember?'

Emma held her breath. She could only just hear him over the pounding of the music.

'Yeah well, those jokers almost took my fucking head off too, didn't they?'

Gilligan listened some more.

'Of course not, are you mad?' he said. 'I was the one who set this up, right?'

Emma realised she was still holding her breath and let it out slowly.

'Aww, fucking hell, seriously?' Gilligan listened again. 'No, I don't want to have a fucking meet up. What have you got in mind? Team-building activities? Or something else?'

As he listened on his mobile, Gilligan walked down the corridor and pushed his way outside through the fire exit.

The door clanged shut behind him.

Good, at least that was him out of the way.

But what was he saying? Had he been talking to someone from the Seven Ghosts, perhaps? Or his Real IRA contacts?

Right now, that didn't matter.

Emma took the stairs fast, wanting to get up there before she met anyone on the way down. Although she couldn't hear him, she could sense the Priest right behind her.

She knew where she was going. If Joe was going to be anywhere, it would be in his office. The problem was, who else was going to be in there with him?

When Emma reached the office, she paused outside the door. The Priest hovered beside her, listening to the rumble of indistinct voices from inside.

'You gone go in first, girl?' he whispered, grinning at her and revealing his blackened teeth.

'How about you do it?' Emma whispered back. 'You're going to distract them from me, that's for sure.'

Still grinning, the Priest nodded. He pushed the door open and stepped inside.

The conversation halted and for a brief moment, there was silence.

Then there was hurried movement, shouted orders for the Priest to stay right where he was.

Emma peeked round the doorway. The office was filled with men and they all held guns, arms extended and pointed at the Priest.

'What the bloody hell is this, then?' the fat man said. 'The circus left town a long time ago.'

'You're Leola's friend, aren't you?' Coffin said. 'The Priest.'

'An' you're the mighty Joe Coffin,' the Priest said. 'I's been looking forward to meeting you.'

COFFIN LOWERED HIS GUN.

'Emma,' he said. 'You can come out from behind the freak.'

'I don't know,' Emma said. 'All those guns are making me nervous, pointed in my direction like that.'

'Everyone, lower your guns, it's all right,' Coffin said.

'Bloody hell, Joe,' Gosling said. 'My men's guns are up and down more often than a tart's knickers. Can't we just shoot him?'

'You gone be in a heap o trouble you shoot me,' the Priest said.

'What the hell are you doing here, Emma?' Coffin said.

'I need to talk to you,' Emma said. 'Please, can you tell your men to put down their guns?'

Coffin couldn't take his eyes off the Priest. Leola had described him perfectly, but it was still a shock to see him. His long, black overcoat, his battered stove-pipe hat, and his skin, inked black. Even his eyes and his teeth.

'Look like you seen a ghost, Mr Coffin,' the Priest said.

'I don't know what I'm looking at,' Coffin said. He waved his gun, indicating that the Priest should step inside the office. 'Go over there, sit down.'

The Priest walked languidly over to the sofa and sat down, stretching out catlike, his arms resting across the back. All the guns followed him, as though pulled by a magnetic force.

Coffin lowered his gun. 'Stut, keep your gun on him.'

Everyone else lowered their guns. Coffin grabbed Emma by the arm and pulled her out of the office, into the corridor.

'What the hell are you doing here?' he hissed. 'Didn't I tell you I didn't want to see you again?'

Emma yanked her arm free of his grip. 'Hey, you're hurting me. And what's with the goon squad in there?'

'That's not your business.'

'And the money, I guess that's none of my business too, right?'

'Yeah, right.'

'You robbing banks now, Joe? I didn't think that was your style.'

Coffin leaned in close. 'Like I said, it's none of your business. I trusted you, Emma, and you betrayed me. I'm not making that mistake again.'

'Oh shit, Joe, can't you just let me explain about all that?' Emma said.

'There's nothing to explain, I know everything I need to know.'

'Is that it? After everything we went through and you're ready to just take that snake Gilligan's word against mine? Did you ever stop to wonder how the fuck he got hold of that video? Huh?'

Coffin kept quiet.

'Has he ever talked to you about that? You don't trust that bastard, I know you don't. He's trouble, Joe, and he's going to get you killed if you're not careful.'

'Yeah, well, he's at the back of a long queue,' Coffin said. 'There are a whole hell of a lot of people out there who are likely to get me killed one way or another.'

'The thing is, Gilligan's probably helping most of them,' Emma said.

'What the hell's that supposed to mean?' Coffin said.

'That guy's a—'

The sound of gunfire from downstairs cut Emma off.

FUZZY WARM FEELING

Angellicit was throbbing with music and people. It seemed to Stut that the place was more popular than ever, especially since the latest breakout of vampires. Even the stage acts had taken on the theme of vampires. Right now, there were two girls and a guy gyrating up there. The girls had false vampire teeth jutting out from between their ruby red lips and they were both all over the guy who was pretending not to enjoy it, but not doing a very good job.

All three were pretty much butt naked and oiled up. They had the poles to writhe around, and chains to wrap around each other, and fake blood dribbling from their mouths. Even the guy which made no sense to Stut, none at all.

But then the punters didn't come here for logic and sense. They came to get off their heads to some hardcore music whilst half-naked bodies gyrated on the stage.

Stut preferred working down at Edwards No. 9. He couldn't say why, it weren't like the crowd were any different, but the mood at Angellicit had changed since Joe took over. For one thing, Stut couldn't work out why Joe hadn't changed the name back to Angels.

That's what Craggs would have done.

And what the fuck was the reason for letting all the youngsters in? That was what Edwards was for. Angels had always been a gentleman's club, not a grungefest, which was what Joe had turned it into.

Mortimer Craggs was probably spinning in his grave.

Not that Stut cared about Craggs anymore. Not since the bastard had betrayed them, right here in this very room. How could he have done that, just handed them over to those vampire fucks without batting an eyelid?

And was it true that Craggs had left a load of debt behind?

It was a sad fucking end to his life, that was for sure. Reputation was in tatters now.

Looked like a sad end to the Slaughterhouse Mob, too. Why Joe got involved with that fucker Gosling and his crew of freaks, Stut didn't know. Surely the Mob could have taken the old lady's money without that fat bastard and his dwarf. And Duchess just freaked Stut out. He could barely look at him without feeling ill.

Stut hated it when Joe sent him packing, off on some stupid errand just to get him out of the way. But for once, when Joe had told him to come downstairs and look after the club, Stut had been happy to oblige. All that arguing over the cash and now that freak the Priest, and that reporter sticking her beak in again.

It was a mess, and Stut wanted nothing of it.

Stut gazed around the club, throbbing with music and heaving with young people, when he spotted a young woman staggering towards him. The throng of clubbers parted to let her through, like she had some invisible force field around her that was pushing everyone out of the way.

Stut saw why. She had a stream of vomit down her chest and top.

And she was crying.

Stut grabbed her by the arm and guided her towards the toilets. She let him take her.

In her other hand, she was clinging onto a full, unopened bottle of red wine.

Inside, exposed in the glare of the lights and the white tiles and mirrors, she looked even worse. And she stank, too.

She stood at the sink, looking at herself in the mirror, and began crying even harder. She placed the bottle of wine on the counter next to a sink. Her hand was shaking, and the bottle made a clattering noise as she put it down.

Stut grabbed a wad of paper towels and threw them at her. 'S-s-soak them in w-w-w-water and cl-clean yourself up.'

She looked at the paper towels scattered over the sink in front of her as though she didn't know what they were. Then she lifted her eyes and looked at her reflection.

'I should never have drunk so much,' she said, between racking breaths. 'I was just trying to impress him.'

Stut was standing across the other side of the bathroom, trying to keep his breathing shallow, not inhale too much of her stink.

The door opened and a man in a tight top showing off his muscular chest and arms tried coming inside.

'Get l-lost,' Stut said.

The man looked as though he was about to argue the point, but then Stut saw the recognition dawning on his face as he realised who he was talking to.

He backed away, letting the door swing shut.

Stut looked back at the girl. She hadn't moved. He had to admit, if you could forget the stink and the vomit down her front, she looked pretty tasty. Nice arse on her, that was for sure.

'You c-c-can't stay here,' he said. 'This is the m-m-men's toilet.'

He thought about taking her back to his, offering to let her clean up there. She looked good for a shag, but the thought of all that vomit put him off. Besides, even if she scrubbed up good, he didn't want that mouth of her on his, that tongue of hers round his tongue. She'd have to give her teeth a good scrub first, and Stut wasn't going to let her use his toothbrush.

No, the more he thought about it, the more he decided it was a bad idea.

'Come on,' he said. 'It's t-t-t-time you f-fucked off out of here.'

They both flinched at what sounded like explosions on the other side of the bathroom door. The girl hiccuped and abruptly stopped crying.

Stut could hear screams outside. The music was still throbbing through the walls, but Stut could hear the screams..

The bathroom door burst open and a group of men and women barged inside, just as Stut heard another explosion. No, not an explosion.

Gunfire.

'What's happening?' Stut shouted.

One of the girls had blood leaking down her arm and flecks of it on her face. Like she'd been cut by flying shards of glass.

More people running inside the bathroom, seeking somewhere to hide, some protection. Stut pushed past them. Got to the door.

Looked out.

'Oh, f-f-f—'

COFFIN TOOK THE STAIRS FAST, with Shaw close behind him.

Another burst of gunfire, the sound of glass shattering.

'Sounds like there's a fucking tank out there!' Shaw said.

'Shit, this is all we need.'

'What are we gonna do, Joe?' Shaw said.

Coffin didn't know. This was all getting too weird.

'Go back upstairs, tell Gosling and the others we've got a situation down here. Tell them... just fucking tell them what's going on.'

Shaw turned and headed back up the stairs.

'And tell them to bring their guns!' Coffin yelled.

He spun around as the door leading to the main part of the club crashed open and a mass of terrified men and women flooded through.

More gunfire and this time Coffin heard the bullets smashing through plasterwork and bricks, heard tables and chairs disintegrating beneath the onslaught.

Coffin pushed against the tide of people running screaming past him.

'Coffin! Get out here now!'

Coffin stood to one side of the open door and took a quick look around. Tables and chairs had been smashed into splintered pieces of junk littering the floor. The bar had been riddled with bullet holes, the bottles of drink on the wall behind it had disappeared, and the air reeked of sweet alcohol. Bullet holes had been punched in the walls. A flickering light cast manic, dancing shadows over everything.

And then Coffin saw people on the floor. He couldn't be sure how many were alive still and how many dead. He could see some lying completely prone and hugging the floor, hands over heads, waiting to die or be rescued.

'Coffin! Get the fuck out here, you coward!'

Shanks Longworth, standing in the middle of the devastation he had wreaked. A massive automatic gun cradled in his arms.

Coffin pulled back out of sight.

Where the hell was Shaw with those guns?

And what about the others? Where the hell were they?

Coffin heard movement, footsteps crunching over broken glass and splintered wood. Longworth, heading this way, towards Coffin.

Any second now, and Longworth was going to start spraying bullets everywhere again. That gun looked powerful enough that the bullets would punch right through the wall and into Coffin's head and chest.

He moved, heading for the back door. Get outside and around the front, maybe surprise Longworth that way. It was a shit plan, but about the best Coffin had right now.

Coffin froze when he heard the metal clunk of the gun's mechanism.

'Stay right where you are,' Longworth said. 'Just stay right where you fucking are.'

Coffin slowly raised his hands out to the side.

'I know you want revenge,' he said, his back tingling at the thought of the gun trained on it. 'But did you have to murder those people out there?'

'Feeling all high and mighty and self-righteous, are you?' Longworth said. 'Didn't stop you putting a bullet in Shocker's kid now, did it?'

'That was an accident,' Coffin said.

'Makes no difference to the kid, does it?' Longworth said.

'No, I suppose not,' Coffin said.

'Turn around. Turn around and look at me.'

Slowly, slowly, Coffin turned around on the spot, keeping his hands out by his sides where Longworth could see them. Beads of sweat were pouring down Longworth's face, and he had to keep blinking to get the sweat out of his eyes. He was holding the massive gun pointed at Coffin's chest.

On the edge of his vision, behind Longworth, Coffin thought he detected movement. He kept his eyes focused on Longworth's.

'What now?' Coffin said. 'Are you going to kill me, or kidnap me, or just stand there and look at me all night until I die of boredom?'

'I'm going to rip you to pieces with this gun,' Longworth said. 'This thing's full of metal jacketed bullets, pierce a tank's hide they would, so they'll go through you like a knife through hot butter and tear you to shreds.'

'Nice,' Coffin said. 'And then what? You walk out of here with a nice, fuzzy warm feeling inside? Like you got revenge, and now that's it?'

Longworth hefted the gun a little higher.

Coffin's insides tightened as he waited for the bullets to rip through him.

Stut smacked Longworth across the head from behind with a full bottle of red wine.

Longworth staggered, and the gun went off in his hands. The bullets ripped through the floor and the walls, the gun veering wildly from side to side. Coffin lunged out of the way.

Stut hit Longworth again across the top of the head, trying to bring him down, put him out of action.

Longworth swung the gun around, still firing.

Coffin barrelled into him and they both hit the floor. The gun went silent.

Coffin raised his fist and smashed Longworth in the face.

And again.

Longworth moaned and spat a bloody tooth out.

Coffin pulled the gun off him and shoved it to one side. He climbed to his feet and kicked Longworth in the side.

Stut smashed the wine bottle against the door frame and the hall filled with the smell of red wine.

'Let me glass the b-b-b-bastard,' he said.

Coffin shoved him out of the way. Shaw had arrived.

Coffin reached out and took the handgun that Shaw offered him.

He turned back to Longworth and put a bullet through his head.

TWERKY

Emma shrank against the wall as the gunfire ripped through the club downstairs. It had been a mistake coming here. Why on earth had she thought Joe would actually listen to her? Of course he wouldn't. He'd made up his mind about Emma, and there wasn't a fat lot that was going to change it.

More gunfire. Violence followed Joe Coffin around like a faithful dog, always at his heels. And for some stupid reason, Emma was always following him around, too. Why was that? What the hell was she after?

A single shot from downstairs followed by silence. Whatever was going on, Emma had the feeling it was over with now.

She was standing in the hall outside Joe's office, her back against the wall. She could hear the fat man inside talking.

Emma decided it was time to get going. There was no way Joe was going to listen to anything she had to say right now. He was too wound up, there was too much shit happening. Emma pulled herself away from the wall and ran down the stairs. She used the fire escape exit to get outside. She could hear sirens in the distance. Definitely time to get away before the place was crawling with police.

Go home. Think about what to do next.

Out on the pavement at the front of the club, people were pouring out of the doors. Nobody was in charge, nobody to direct people to safety. Emma mingled in with the crowd, let the flow carry her until she was able to duck down a side alley and make her way back to her car. Just as she climbed inside her car and slammed the door shut, her mobile began buzzing.

She looked at the screen.

It was Barry.

'Hey, Barry, what's up?'

'Are you watching the news right now?'

Emma frowned. Now what? 'No, should I be?'

'There's a huge colony of bats gathering on Broad Street, not far from where those two girls were murdered.'

'And they think these bats are something to do with the vampires?'

'No one's confirmed that yet, but yeah, that's what everybody's thinking.'

'Okay, thanks Barry.'

Emma called up the news app on her phone. It was the top item. Birmingham and its vampire problem was national news these days.

Emma threw the mobile onto the passenger seat and started the car.

It wasn't time to go home just yet.

She didn't notice Gerry Gilligan emerge from the shadows, watching as she drove away. With a brief glance back at the club, Gilligan climbed in his car and followed Emma.

GOSLING DABBED AT HIS FACE, mopping up the sheen of sweat. The Stig was still holding his gun on the Priest, who was sitting on the sofa and grinning like a loon. Duchess and Stilts were sitting at Coffin's desk, Stilts in the chair and Duchess on the desk, his legs crossed. He was examining his fingernails.

'Well, this is a pretty pickle, isn't it?' Gosling said.

The holdalls of cash were on the floor, stacks of money poking out of the opened tops.

'What the fuck are you grinning at?' Stig said to the Priest.

'I's just grinning,' the Priest said. 'You gots to laugh at life some days, else it drag you down into the ground and you ain't never gone get up again.'

'You find that in a Christmas cracker?' Gosling said. 'Me, I hate all that life advice shit. Much prefer the jokes. Here's one. Two snowmen were standing in a field. One says to the other, "Can you smell carrots?"'

Duchess doubled over and screamed with laughter. No one else said a word.

'No?' Gosling said. 'How about this one then? What did Santa do when he went speed dating? He pulled a cracker.'

The Stig glanced at Gosling. 'You're fucking loony tunes, you know that? All of you, you're fucking fruitcakes.'

'You don't look so good,' Gosling said. 'The pressure getting to you?'

'Don't worry about me,' the Stig said. 'I'm fine. Just as soon as Joe gets back, we can finish counting this money and then you three can fuck off back to the loony bin where you belong.'

Gosling chuckled. 'Is that what you think?'

The Stig glanced at Gosling again, quickly returning his attention to the Priest. 'What's that supposed to mean?'

'All that gunfire downstairs, you think it hasn't been noticed? The coppers are probably on their way right now, and once they're here and they've got this situation contained, they'll be going through here with a fine-tooth comb. And I'm betting once they find all this money they're not going to let us keep it.'

The Stig looked at Gosling again.

'I'd keep an eye on Baron Samedi over there, he looks like he wants to give you a kiss.'

The Stig snapped his attention back to the Priest.

Stilts opened up a drawer in the desk and started rifling through it.

'Hey, what the fuck do you think you're doing?' the Stig said.

Stilts ignored him.

'Hey, you fucking deaf as well as dumb?' the Stig yelled.

'What does Miley Cyrus have for Christmas dinner?' Gosling said.

The Stig, his gun still trained on the Priest, whipped his head around to look at Gosling.

'What?' he said.

'Twerky,' Gosling said, and lifted the gun he had been holding down by his side and shot the Stig in the head.

Before the Stig had hit the floor, Gosling was turning his gun on the Priest.

The sofa was empty.

'What the bloody hell?' Gosling whispered.

''E's beoind ya!' Duchess screamed.

Gosling spun around, crouching as he moved. The Priest was a blur of movement. The office door opened and then slammed shut.

Gosling fired, a hole splintering in the door beneath the impact of the bullet. Straightening up, Gosling ran for the door and yanked it open. There was a hole in the wall where the bullet had smacked into it. Gosling looked up and down the hall.

It was empty.

He returned to the office and shut the door behind him.

'Right, you two, let's get this cash out of here before Coffin comes back.'

Duchess jumped up and down, squealing and clapping his hands.

Stilts jumped down from the chair and joined Duchess, zipping up the bags.

Gosling called a number on his mobile.

'What the bloody hell's going on?' Gosling said. 'There's been a bloody firefight at Angellicit tonight, is that anything to do with you?'

Gosling listened, and then said, 'All right then. Yeah, don't worry about it. Coffin will be dead soon enough.'

'We've got problems,' Archer said, finishing his call with the station.

'You know, one day you're going to tell me, hey, everything's fine, the station just called to see how we are,' Choudhry said.

They were standing by the car. Traffic had ground to a halt as they had drawn closer to Broad Street. The two men had been about to carry on towards the cluster of bats on foot when Archer's phone had rung.

'There's been a shootout at Angellicit,' Archer said. 'All units are being sent over there.'

Choudhry threw his hands in the air. 'Seriously?'

'It's worse than that,' Archer said. 'There are other tiny pockets of bats gathering all over the city and attacking people. We've got units going there too.'

Choudhry looked at traffic behind them. Their car was blocked in both directions.

'So what are we meant to do? Head over to Angellicit or one of these bat attacks or what?'

'No, up ahead on Broad Street is still the largest gathering of bats and they're not attacking yet. We should go find out what we can and then touch base with the station again.'

'You do realise it's not a gathering of bats, don't you?'

'No, and do I look like I give a shit what it's called?'

'It's a colony of bats,' Choudhry said, undeterred by his partner's disinterest. 'A pity we're not dealing with crows, then it would be a murder.'

'A murder?' Archer said. 'What are you talking about?'

'That's what you call a group of crows, a murder,' Choudhry said.

'Great. Next time we're in a pub quiz you can be on my team. Right now, we need to get moving.'

Angellicit had emptied out. Now that the danger was obviously over, people had begun milling about on the street outside. No one seemed sure of what they should do. Sirens had been heard approaching, but now they had fallen silent.

Inside the club, Coffin grabbed Shaw and Stut.

'Anyone seen Gilligan?' he said.

Both men shook their heads.

'All right, you two get upstairs and look after the cash. You need to stash it somewhere before the cops get here.'

As the two men headed for the stairs, Coffin took a swift look around the club. As far as he could see, nobody had been shot. Longworth had to have been aiming over everybody's heads when he came in, all guns blazing. Coffin had been the one in his sights, nobody else.

Coffin looked down at Longworth's body. He had to decide what to do with that next, and he had to make that decision quick. On the one hand, he could leave it there. After all, there were enough witnesses that Longworth had come into the club armed to the teeth and with intent.

On the other hand, Coffin had shot and killed him.

That was going to kick up an almighty stink.

There was no way Coffin could get rid of the body in time though, and besides which, there were all those witnesses.

Best just to leave things as they were and deal with the shit when it hit the fan.

'Joe?'

It was Shaw. He looked pale, a little sick.

'What?' Coffin said.

'The Stig, he's dead.'

'What the fuck?'

'He's been shot.' Shaw swallowed. 'In the head.'

'Where are the others?' Coffin said.

'They're gone, all gone,' Shaw said. 'The money too.'

Coffin turned away. Clenched his hands into fists, digging his fingernails into his palms.

Someone outside screamed, quickly followed by someone else screaming.

What now? Coffin thought.

He walked through reception and looked out of the door. A huge, black cloud was hovering low over everyone gathered outside Angellicit. Men and women were running, screaming, colliding with each other as the cloud seemed to attack them. It took Coffin a moment to realise what his eyes were seeing. That the cloud was in fact a mass of bats swirling around each other. Every so often, a bat darted from the black mass and attacked someone.

A young woman wearing sparkling thigh length boots, shorts and a cropped T-shirt ran screaming at Coffin as two bats clawed at her scalp. Coffin grabbed her and hauled her inside. Swiped at the bats and threw them to the ground and kicked them to death.

Someone else ran for the open door, the safety of the club.

More joined him.

'Joe?' Shaw said. 'What about the cops? They're on their way.'

'No, they're not,' Coffin said. 'I don't know what the hell is going on, but I don't think we'll be seeing the Old Bill tonight. Get these people inside.'

Stut joined them. With the help of the bouncers, they started herding people back into the club, whilst others took off screaming down the road. The bats swirled and dived and darted, scratching and biting at the crowd. Once the last person was in, Coffin slammed shut the club doors.

Some of the clubbers were crying, whilst others just stood in shocked silence. Shaw and Stut looked at each other, unsure of what to do next.

'Oh God, they're all over the city,' a young man said, staring at his mobile.

Coffin walked over and took the phone off him. There was a video playing. It was hard to see what was going on in the dark and whoever was filming couldn't keep their phone still, the picture was wobbling all over the place. But Coffin could hear the screams and the shouts, and he could see enough to make out the clouds of bats.

'Where is this?' Coffin said.

'I don't know, it's someone on Facebook, they're live.' The young man leaned over and pointed at the bottom of the screen. 'They're on Broad Street, look it tells you there.'

Coffin's mobile buzzed against his thigh. He pulled it from his pocket and looked at the glowing screen. It was Leola.

He thumbed the accept call button and said, 'Where the hell are you?'

'Hello, Joe.' Coffin recognised that voice immediately.

It was Steffanie.

'Follow the bats, Joe, if you want to see your bitch again.'

COFFIN GUNNED the Fat Boy into life. The streets of Birmingham were deserted of pedestrians, but traffic was heavy. Coffin ignored the underpass and continued up to the traffic light junction, mounting the deserted pavement to bypass the stalled traffic.

Coffin opened up the throttle, speeding along the pavement between lamp posts and illuminated shop windows. The slow moving traffic ground to a complete halt as he drew closer to Broad Street, and the pavements had begun to fill up with bystanders, forcing him to slow down and finally come to a halt.

Coffin pulled his helmet off.

And saw the dark cloud of bats hovering in the distance, a moving shadow against the night sky.

There had been small pockets of bats all over the city, but this colony at Broad Street was the largest by far. When Steffanie had said follow the bats, this was what she had meant.

Coffin watched the massive cloud of dark, fluttering shapes. He could hear the screams of people as they were attacked.

'It's like something out of a film,' a young woman standing next to Coffin said to her friend.

Despite the crowds on the pavement and the gridlock on the road, Coffin could see he would have more freedom of movement a little further on. All the spectators were keeping their distance from the main action. Most of them looked spooked and ready to run at a moment's notice.

Coffin put the helmet back on. Turned the collar of his thick leather jacket up.

Getting bitten by a bat didn't worry him too much.

But there were bigger things with teeth than bats out there.

Coffin began slowly pushing the Fat Boy through the crowd, snarling at everyone to get out of his way. Soon the crowd had thinned out and Coffin was able to speed up again. He rode the bike along the pavement up Broad Street, beside the cars stuck in a queue on the road. Frightened faces peered out at him from the windows.

A young woman ran towards Coffin, screaming and beating her hands at her head. A bat was darting around her, nipping at her face and neck and scalp. Coffin skidded the bike to a halt. He climbed off it and intercepted the woman running blindly into him.

Coffin snatched the bat off her and crushed its tiny body in his fist. He dropped it to the ground, a crumpled mass of wings and fur.

The woman started running again. Coffin watched her for a moment and then turned to look back up Broad Street. To his right were a row of bus shelters, and across the other side of the road the Rep and the Library of Birmingham.

Some of the cars headed out of the city, and into the cloud of bats, had managed to turn and cross the divide onto the opposite carriageway. But then a bus had tried that and got itself stuck halfway across, its chassis jammed against the concrete rise between the roads. That had effectively blocked off any cars beyond that point that were trying to make an escape. Behind the bus, closer to the city and where Coffin was currently standing, there was a divider between the two carriageways preventing any other drivers from making the same attempt to cross onto the opposite road.

Coffin decided to walk from this point on. He didn't like the idea of one of those bats flying straight into his visor and causing him to crash. But he decided to leave the helmet on for the moment.

As he walked closer to the panic and the chaos, another woman ran past him being tormented by a pair of bats, and then a man sprinted past him, roaring and waving his hands in the air.

Coffin ignored them. He couldn't rescue everyone, and besides, that wasn't his job.

He needed to find Steffanie.

And then kill her.

As Coffin walked, he drew nearer a crowd. Incredibly, some people who weren't being attacked had not left and were taking photographs or videoing the chaos. What looked like a news crew was there, too.

Coffin had to start pushing past bodies, elbowing people out of the way. Parts of the crowd were moving, flowing down Broad Street. A couple of bodies lay on the ground, bleeding. Some people milling around looking shell shocked and seemingly not sure what to do.

There were less bats here than Coffin had thought there would be, although still quite a sizable cloud of them. Some bats broke away and darted down Broad Street in the same direction as the crowd.

Coffin followed them.

EMMA HAD SKIRTED around the city centre and tried approaching Broad Street from the opposite direction, but had to abandon her car at Five Ways. From what she could see, it looked like almost every road around Broad Street was grid locked, and the ones that weren't had been cordoned off by the police.

Except not quite because the police were still setting up road-blocks. Looked like they had only just got here. Maybe, if she was quick, she could get onto Broad Street from a road they hadn't blocked off yet.

Emma ran down Islington Row Middleway, one of the major arteries off Five Ways island and then took a left down Tennant Street. She knew she had to move as fast as possible. Halfway down Tennant Street, she took another left down St. Martin's Street. Here she met a small group of panicked people streaming towards her.

'Don't go down there!' one young woman yelled at Emma as they passed each other.

Emma ignored her. St. Martin's Street was a dead end for cars, but a narrow passageway continued down onto Broad Street. Emma had been right. There was no police cordon here. Not yet.

Emma sprinted down the alley, bracing herself for the chaos she had seen on the news report. When she exited onto Broad Street, she pulled up short.

The relative silence was the first thing that struck her. There was the steady rumble of car engines idling, but none of the blaring of horns that you would expect in a traffic jam. There were very few pedestrians left now. One or two braver souls had hung around, helping others up off the ground. Most of the faces she could see peered from car windows, eyes searching for something up above.

Bats, of course.

Of which there seemed to be very few. One or two solitary bats flying drunkenly around here and there, their dark shapes just discernible against the night sky and the lights on Broad Street.

What the hell had happened? Where were they?

Emma walked towards the city centre. Ducked as something swooped past her, briefly disturbing her hair.

'Shit!' she muttered. That was scarier than she had expected.

'Hey, get in the car,' someone hissed.

Emma turned. A young man, all grooming products and attitude, had opened his window, arm out, gesticulating at Emma.

'Where did all the bats go?' Emma said.

'Get in the car, before they come back!'

Emma approached the car. 'Tell me where the bats went.'

'She's crazy, Steve, just close the window,' a young woman sitting next to Steve said.

'They went down there,' Steve said, pointing. 'Are you a policewoman?'

The young woman leaned into view and giggled. 'Are you going to arrest all those bats?'

Emma walked away, heading to the side street Steve had pointed at. Sheepcote Street.

Emma began jogging towards it. Another bat swooped past her, snagging at her hair. Had it nipped at her scalp with its teeth?

Emma touched her head and paused in her running to look at her fingertips.

No, there was no blood.

Emma turned at the sound of car doors opening. Now that almost all the bats had gone, a few brave souls were deciding to climb out of their cars, heads twisting as they searched the sky for more winged creatures.

A lone bat skittered towards a woman who screamed and hurriedly got back in her car, slamming the door shut. The bat slammed into the window and then flew away.

The back of Emma's neck began tingling as she realised that someone, or *something*, was standing right behind her.

She turned and then recoiled in shock.

'Fuck!' she hissed. 'You scared me!'

Joe Coffin scowled at her.

'I should have known you'd be here,' he growled.

SHIT EATER

Standing in front of Emma, looking down at her, Coffin realised that he had been unconsciously rehearsing what he might say to her if he ever saw her again. He knew he thought about her too often. He knew the hurt of her betrayal still cut him.

There were many things he could say to her, accuse her of. In Coffin's world, you only betrayed a person once. There was no get-out clause, no second chances. That was the code that Mortimer Craggs had lived by, had run the Slaughterhouse Mob by.

Betray me once and I find out, you're a dead man, was what he used to say.

Coffin lived by that code too.

Emma should have been no different.

Coffin stood in front of her, his fists bunched by his sides, his jaw clenched. It was like his mouth had been glued shut.

'So, you gonna say something, or what?' Emma said. 'Or are you just going to stand there like a big ape and stare at me?'

Coffin loosened his jaw, took the pressure off his teeth. Felt like he was grinding them down to nothing.

'What the hell are you doing here?' he said. 'Have you got a death wish or something?'

'I could say the same about you,' Emma said.

Coffin shook his head in frustration. 'Does your boyfriend know you're here?'

'Mitch, no, he's still in hos—'

Emma clamped her mouth shut.

Coffin raised an eyebrow. 'You and Dirty Harry no longer an item?'

'It's complicated,' Emma said.

'I wish people would stop saying that every time I ask a question. It's like everyone thinks I'm stupid or something.'

'No, it's not that.'

'I shouldn't even be talking to you.'

A bat flew by. Coffin ducked.

'I'm glad you are,' Emma said. 'I want to explain, tell you—'

'No, not now,' Coffin said. He looked behind him, then back at Emma. 'You planning on following all those bats down Sheepcote Street.'

'Yeah.'

'What if I told you to stay here, let me do the investigating?'

'What do you think?' Emma said.

Coffin sighed. 'Yeah, that's what I thought.'

'How about we go investigating together? It'd be like an episode of Cagney and Lacey.'

'I guess I can't stop you,' Coffin said, turning and heading down the street.

Emma followed him.

Coffin walked slowly. Street lamps were on all the way down the road, as were lights from shops and bars and offices. But down towards the end of the road, there was a dark, shifting mass. As though a hole had been punched in reality, or a black veil had been thrown over a section of the street.

A bat flew close by Coffin's face, its wingtips brushing his cheek. His hand automatically rose up to swat it away, but it had already gone.

Another bat flew past and then back again.

'There's more of them down here,' Emma said.

Coffin raised a hand to shush her.

He could see the dark, undulating mass a little clearer now. A single building covered in them. There were too many to cling on to its sides and so the others were hovering as close as possible, like the building was some kind of bat magnet.

Whatever had attracted them there, they didn't want to leave.

There was a sign outside at the front, The Blue Sky Care Home.

'Fuck, that's so weird,' Emma whispered.

'Yeah,' Coffin said.

'We gonna go closer, or hang back here?'

'I'm going inside that building,' Coffin said. 'You should stay here.'

'You know I won't,' Emma said.

'I know, but you go in there you're on your own. I'm not looking out for you.'

'Yeah, whatever,' Emma said.

Coffin hugged the shop fronts as he walked further down Sheepcote Street, and closer to the bats. He knew he was illuminated by the light from the shop displays, but the alternative of walking down the middle of the road felt more dangerous somehow.

Emma scooted up beside him. 'What do you think is inside, then? The bats are there for some reason, right?'

'I already know what's inside,' Coffin said.

'You going to tell me or do I have to interrogate you to get an answer?'

Coffin looked at Emma, raised an eyebrow. 'It's Steffanie.'

Emma stopped walking. 'Are you serious? How do you know that?'

'I just do,' Coffin said, and kept on walking.

Emma caught up with him. 'And you're planning on just walking in there?'

'Nope. I'm planning on killing her too, just after the bit where I walk in there.'

They were drawing closer to the bat covered building. Coffin saw some scaffolding, a skip. Bats were clinging to the scaffolding poles and clambering over the rubbish in the skip.

'Have you got a plan for that?' Emma said.

'What, the walking in there part, or the killing Steffanie part?'

Emma snorted. 'I see you've lost none of your stupid sense of humour.'

'It's easier to be funny when you actually know who is knifing you in the back. Not knowing was killing me.'

'Like I said, I can expl—'

'Like I said, not now.'

Coffin turned his back on her. Whatever she might try to say, whatever explanations she could think up, none of it changed the fact that she had kept secrets from him, that she had been digging into his life, looking for dirt.

That she had been intent on writing an expose about him, of shopping him to the coppers with that film of him murdering Terry Wu.

If it was anybody else, anybody other than Emma, they would be dead by now.

Coffin knew this, and the thought bothered him.

He pushed the thoughts away, forced himself to concentrate on what was happening right now. He had been flippant when he answered Emma about walking in there, but the truth was he had no other plan.

Maybe, for once in his life, he should come up with one. Get out of here, get the others and come back in force. Coffin had no idea what Steffanie had been up to in the last few months. And what was it with all the bats? They were a completely new development and Coffin didn't like it.

'Joe?' Emma said.

'Quiet, I'm thinking,' Coffin said.

He expected a smart reply to that, but Emma said nothing.

Coffin dismissed the idea of leaving and gathering the others. Not his style. Steffanie was inside that building, he didn't know how he knew that but he did. And that meant Coffin had to act now. By the time he got back with Stut and Shaw and the others, she might well be gone.

All of Coffin's anger, seemed like everything he had ever raged about or railed against, was now focused on the bat covered building, on that front door. He needed to get inside there and rip that woman apart, destroy her completely like he had done with Abel Mortenson and Merek Guttman.

After he had finished with Steffanie, when he knew she was out of his life forever, he could deal with Michael.

'Joe?'

Coffin stirred, felt like he had zoned out there for a moment.

'This is no way to be, skulking in the shadows,' he said. 'Fuck it, I'm going in.'

He walked out into the middle of the road and towards the doorway. Several bats detached themselves from the wall and flew towards him and then up and over his head.

Coffin stepped up to the front door. Now he was closer, he could see it was one of the older buildings in the city, renovated and restored and given a new purpose.

A cloud of black, shifting shapes swarmed from the doorway and over Coffin. The flapping of their wings brushed against his face, their claws scratching his flesh, teeth nipping at him.

He roared, swinging his arms, punching at empty space. The bats nipped at his hands, at his arms. Coffin couldn't see a thing, he'd been thrown into darkness, his ears filled with the sound of rustling wings and tiny limbs.

He opened his hands and grabbed at the mass of bats, grabbing a bat in each of his fists. He squeezed, the tiny bones crunching in his hands, the blood squirting from beneath his fingers.

The mass of bats cleared, the last of them rushing past him and out of the door.

Coffin blinked. A woman stood just inside the open doorway. For a moment Coffin thought it was Steffanie. The way she held herself, poised like a cat, perfectly still and yet looking ready to spring at any second.

But it wasn't Steffanie.

She was a vampire though, Coffin could see that.

'Steffanie, where is she?' Coffin said.

The woman smiled. Her teeth were huge, seemed to envelop her lower jaw as the smile widened until her face resembled a skull.

'Joe,' she said. 'I'm so very pleased to see you. Steffanie has told me all about you.'

'I'll bet she has,' Coffin said. 'And all of it bad, right?'

The smile grew impossibly wider. 'She said you were good in bed.' She paused, her tongue flicking out to lick her red lips. 'Sometimes.'

'Who are you?'

'Chitrita.'

'Shit eater?' Coffin said. 'Stupid name if you ask me.'

Chitrita tipped back her head and laughed. 'Steffanie never told me you were so funny!'

'She never had much of a sense of humour. Now we've got the introductions out of the way, why don't you tell me where the hell she is?'

Chitrita placed her hands on her cheeks. 'Ooh, Joe. Are you getting angry? What a temper you have!'

Coffin unclenched his fists and let the mangled bats drop to the floor with a soft splat. He took a step further inside and closer to Chitrita.

The smile switched to a snarl, and she growled.

Coffin stopped.

'What was that, are you a dog now?' he said.

The toothy smile returned. 'I didn't say you could come any closer.'

'I suppose vampires must like their personal space,' Coffin said, and took another step forward.

Chitrita growled again, peeling her lips back to reveal the tips of her fangs. Her entire body, without having moved or shifted position, had taken on a shivering tension. Coffin sensed her power, knew that when she did move, it would be fast.

Far too fast for him, for his reflexes to kick in.

'Really, Joe, you should stay where you are. You'll be dead soon enough, so why rush the moment?'

'I'm not very patient, never have been,' Coffin said. 'Never could wait for anything.'

There was movement behind Coffin. Before he could turn to see what was happening, he heard Emma.

'Get your freaking hands off me, you toothy bastard!'

A cadaverous vampire was dragging Emma into the house by her hair. She was on her knees and kicking and screaming and struggling to stand up, but the vampire just ignored her and continued dragging her inside.

He let go of her and she fell, her palms making a soft smacking noise as they hit the floor.

'Didn't I tell you to stay where you were?' Coffin said.

Panting, Emma looked up at Coffin, her hair corkscrewed across her face. 'To be honest, I think the last thing you said was, fuck it, I'm going in.'

'Let's go upstairs,' Chitrita said. 'Steffanie will be so pleased to see you both.'

Coffin held Emma by the arm and helped her up on her feet.

Emma sucked in her breath. Another vampire had entered the large reception area.

'Julie,' Emma said.

Julie Carter stared dead eyed at Emma and Coffin. If she recognised Emma, she showed no sign of it.

'I told you to stay where you were,' Coffin muttered. 'Now look at the mess we're in.'

BATTY

Archer and Choudhry abandoned their car and ran. Archer's guts were tight with tension. Seemed for a while they almost had a handle on this vampire situation and now it was spiralling out of control once more. They were like a disease. You thought you had stamped them all out apart from maybe one or two, but that wasn't good enough. You had to exterminate every last single one of them or else they would replicate.

If the vampires weren't stopped now, they would be colonising the city soon. And then what?

'Looks quiet, Boss,' Choudhry said.

He was right. There were people milling around, looking confused, dazed. Some were lying on the floor, being treated by paramedics or looked after by friends, or maybe strangers.

Archer couldn't see any ambulances parked nearby, and he guessed the paramedics must have got here the same way as he did, on foot.

'Where the hell have all the bats gone?' Archer said.

A paramedic looked up.

Archer pulled out his ID. 'DCI Archer, where did the bats go?'

The paramedic pointed. 'Down there, but I'd stay away if I was you.'

'Yeah, you'd be batty to go down there,' the other paramedic said.

Choudhry rolled his eyes. 'Everybody's a comedian these days.'

'Come on, let's see what's happening,' Archer said.

As soon as they turned down Sheepcote Street, they pulled up short. There was a crowd in front of them. Photographers, reporters, curious bystanders.

'What is it about people? They know what those bats can do and now they're following them?' Choudhry said.

'People are stupid,' Archer said. 'Haven't you realised that yet?'

They began pushing their way through the crowd.

'Police! For your own safety, head back onto Broad Street!'

The crowd kept moving forward.

'That's the trouble with people these days, no respect for the police,' Choudhry said, shaking his head.

They shoved their way forward until they reached the front of the crowd. There seemed to be an invisible barrier across which no one was prepared to cross.

Archer immediately saw why.

The building in front of them had become a living, breathing thing. A dark, evil mass of shifting, pointed shapes. Archer had to fight the urge to turn and run. To go back to his house and find Emma and hold her tight.

To lie to her and tell her that everything was going to be all right.

'Bloody hell,' Choudhry whispered.

Archer twisted his head, scanning the crowd. 'Why the hell are we the only police on site?'

'Probably sat in the traffic jam wondering what to do next,' Choudhry said.

'Get on your radio, find out what's happening.'

Archer swallowed. His mouth and throat were dry. The need to turn and run, escape the nightmare in front of him, was now battling with an insane desire to approach the bat infested building.

He could see an open door, thought maybe he even glimpsed a figure inside, some movement.

The bats shifted and folded their wings, and the building itself appeared to tremble.

Why the hell was it covered in a mass of bats? What was the attraction for them?

'Control says they've got no one to spare,' Choudhry said, breaking into Archer's thoughts.

'The fuck they have,' Archer said, the anger rising inside his chest.

'Apparently, there's loads of bat attacks happening all over the city. Each one is pretty small scale, but there's too many happening.'

'Yeah? And what about here? Haven't we got a bat problem here?'

Choudhry shrugged. 'That's what I said, but apparently because this one has calmed down, because the bats aren't actually doing anything at the moment, we're a low priority.'

'Stupid bastards,' Archer said. 'All the other bat attacks, they're a distraction. Keep everyone busy, away from here.' Archer studied the shifting mass of bats. 'But this is the main attraction, inside there is where it's all going on, I bet.'

'You're talking like the bats know what they're doing,' Choudhry said.

'I think they do,' Archer replied.

'Hey, are you two cops?' a voice from the crowd said.

Archer turned, spotted a young lad, spiked hair, acne covered face, no way he was old enough to be out drinking.

'Yeah, you know something?' Archer said.

'Yeah, Joe Coffin's in there, I saw him go inside. And all these bats flew out, it was sick, like something out of a horror film.'

'Why doesn't it surprise me that Coffin's involved?' Archer muttered.

'And then there were this woman with him, she went in too.'

Oh shit! Emma?

CHITRITA, Julie and the male vampire took Coffin and Emma through the home. There were other vampires, too, hanging back in the shadows, watching them. Had to be all the vampires who had been kept in the mortuary on Steel Lane. But not just them, there were others. Had to be residents of the old people's home. Had the vampires turned them all?

Coffin clenched his jaw, his eyes flicking around the room. They took Emma up ahead of him, the man dragging her along, his long fingers wrapped around her upper arm.

Emma was struggling, pulling away from him.

'Stop fighting him,' Coffin said. 'You're wasting your time, he's too strong.'

'I can't help it,' Emma said. 'He stinks like something the cat dragged in and left behind the fridge, I can hardly breathe here.'

Coffin could smell him too, the ugly sweet stink of death and putrefaction.

The vampires took them along the landing and past bedroom doors, all of them wide open. Coffin couldn't help but glance into the rooms as they walked by. They were all bedrooms or bed-sitting rooms. Some of them were empty, in others he saw corpses lying on beds. Faces pasty white, flesh sagging from bones, arms hanging over the sides of the beds.

Some corpses were twitching.

Returning to life, of a sort.

How many residents had there been in this home? Had they all been turned?

'Please, keep moving, Joe,' Chitrita said, her voice purring with pleasure. 'Your wife is waiting for you.'

Coffin grunted.

An ancient looking vampire limped past them. He bared his long, yellow teeth at Emma, but her captor shoved him away.

'They're all growing hungry,' Chitrita said, and sighed. 'It's growing ever more difficult to keep them penned up in here, I'm going to have to do something about that soon.'

'How about you let me take care of them?' Coffin said.

'You are so funny,' Chitrita said, and gently placed a long fingered hand on his shoulder.

Coffin tried shaking her off, but her grip grew tighter. They were still walking, drawing towards a closed door. Emma was struggling again, like she had an idea what might be behind that door, and she wanted nothing to do with it. The tall vampire gripping both her arms looked like a walking skeleton, but he was obviously strong. He held her tight and pushed her on.

Chitrita opened the door and ushered them through. They were in a communal living space. Easy chairs and coffee tables were dotted around the large room. Paintings of landscapes and dogs and cats hung from the walls. The wallpaper was an elaborate flower design and there were lamps on tables.

It might have looked nice but for the blood splattered over the walls and furniture, like Jackson Pollock had been asked to decorate using an open artery instead of a paint brush.

Sitting in a wingback chair, looking like she was pretending to be a queen, was Steffanie. She was wearing an old wedding gown, its trail winding out in front of her. At her feet sat Michael. His hands were scarlet with blood and his face splattered with it. He was playing with a toy car on the carpet.

He didn't even look up as they entered.

Sitting in another wingback chair next to Steffanie was Leola. She had been tied to the chair with strips of bed sheets, wound around and around her torso and arms and legs so that she was completely immobile. Another strip of bed sheet had been wrapped across her mouth and around the back of the chair, tying her head in place. Her eyes were wide and round, but not with fear.

With utter fury.

Emma was fighting again, struggling against the vampire's grip.

'Let her go,' Steffanie said in a bored voice.

The vampire released Emma, who jumped away from him and began rubbing her arms where he had held her.

'You should tell toothy there he needs a bath,' she said. 'That man stinks like a mouldy old chicken carcass.'

'Easy,' Coffin said, holding out his hand to placate Emma.

'It's good to see you, Joe,' Steffanie said.

'Really?' Coffin replied. 'How come I always get the feeling I'm the last person you want to see?'

Chitrita laughed as she sauntered across the blood flecked carpet to a third wingback chair next to Steffanie.

On Steffanie's other side, Leola continued to stare at Coffin.

'You never told me he was so funny,' Chitrita said.

She sat down, placed the tip of her finger to her lip. Her lips were full and scarlet, looked almost like they were swollen with blood and about to pop. Her fingernails were long and curved.

Steffanie reached over and took Chitrita's other hand in hers. 'It's good to see you, because that means I can watch you die.'

'Charming,' Emma said. 'You always attract such a high class kind of girl, Joe?'

Steffanie flicked a hand at Emma. 'Who's this?'

'Hey, you don't remember me?' Emma said. 'I'm the reporter you talked to about sending your husband up shit creek without a paddle. You remember, all those lovely chats we had in country pubs, somewhere you wouldn't be spotted.'

Steffanie gazed at Emma for a couple of moments.

'No,' she said. 'I don't remember you at all.'

'Shall we kill her?' Chitrita said.

'That would be fun,' Steffanie replied. She looked down at the boy sitting at her feet. 'Why don't we let Michael do it? He needs the practice.'

Steffanie stroked the boy's cheek, and he looked up at her. Bending down, she whispered in his ear and pointed at Emma.

His eyes grew large and round, and his mouth opened in a smile.

'No,' Coffin said, taking a step toward Steffanie.

A vampire stepped in front of him. The flesh on his face was saggy and wrinkled and his hair had been combed over his scalp in thin wisps. Despite his appearance, he radiated power.

Coffin stayed where he was.

Michael stood up.

'Steffanie, don't do this,' Coffin said.

Michael had started growling, and his lips were contorting into a snarl, baring his pointed teeth.

'Oh, fuck,' Emma whispered.

Chitrita leaned forward in her chair. 'This is going to be fun.'

'Steffanie, do not do this thing,' Coffin said.

'Go get her,' Steffanie hissed in Michael's ear.

With a full throated snarl, Michael leapt to his feet. He immediately squatted down again, getting on all fours, and scuttled across the carpet towards Emma. She turned and sprinted for the door, to be stopped by the tall, thin vampire. He grinned at her.

Coffin planted his hand on the old vampire's chest and shoved him out of the way. Before Coffin had even taken two steps, the vampire was on him along with a second one and they were pulling him to the ground.

'Keep hold of him!' Steffanie yelled. 'But get him on his feet again. I want him to watch.'

Michael was circling Emma, growling continuously. His lips were pulled right back, showing his teeth and his gums. He looked more like a crazed animal. Emma kept her eyes on him constantly. At the moment she let her guard down and looked away, the boy vampire would be on top of her.

She moved slowly across the room, stepping sideways away from the vampire blocking the exit. Perhaps she could escape through one of the windows. But would she have time to open it before Michael was on top of her?

Emma doubted it.

But right now, that was the best idea she had.

Coffin was on his feet again, a vampire standing either side of him, their hands on him.

'Michael, Michael,' Coffin said. 'Look at me son, look at me, it's Daddy.'

Michael ignored Coffin. He only had eyes for Emma. A long strand of saliva drooled from his bottom lip.

Emma's thigh hit a table. She stopped moving.

This was no good. What did she think she was doing? Where was she going?

On the periphery of her vision, she could see a vase with some wilted flowers on the table she had walked in to. Slowly, she reached out her hand and placed her fingers around its neck. She picked it up, turning it upside down to empty out the flowers and the water.

Michael watched, fascinated.

'Michael,' Coffin said again, raising his voice.

The boy ignored him.

His growling grew in intensity, and then he leaped at Emma.

She swung the vase at him, connecting with the side of his head. The vase shattered and Michael hit the floor and rolled over. He jumped up onto all fours again and shook his head.

Emma had run to another table, another vase of flowers.

Coffin hung his head. He had to look away, even if just for a moment.

Michael was growling again.

Steffanie and Chitrita, still holding hands, watched intently.

Emma held the vase out like a weapon. It was a long, thin glass vase. The boy eyed it uneasily. Being hit over the head with the other vase obviously hurt him.

'Joe, you got any ideas?' Emma said.

Coffin looked up.

'Try smashing the vase,' he said. 'You can use the broken end as a weapon. Go for his eyes, his mouth, his throat.'

Emma stared at him, horrified.

'He'll kill you, unless you kill him,' Coffin said. 'You've got to at least disable him.'

'I don't think I can do that,' Emma said. 'He's just a child, he's your child.'

Michael's growling was growing in intensity again. He was getting ready to attack.

'You've seen what he can do,' Coffin said. 'He's not my boy anymore, he's a monster.'

Michael sprinted across the room. He was squealing and waving his arms. Emma knocked the end of the vase against the table, but it simply bounced off.

Michael jumped on Emma, clawing at her clothes and her hair.

They both staggered and almost fell over. Emma hit Michael on the back of the head in an attempt to dislodge him. Coffin could hear the sickening thump of glass against bone across the other side of the room.

The boy let go of Emma and scurried away behind her. She spun around, trying to keep him in her sights at all times.

The boy ran away and behind the wingback chairs, whimpering and rubbing his head.

Steffanie rolled her eyes and sighed. 'That boy is such a disappointment.'

Chitrita let go of Steffanie's hand and stood up. She lifted a hand and curled her fingers in a come here gesture. More vampires appeared from the shadowed corners of the large room. Coffin hadn't realised they were there.

Any ideas he'd had about fighting his way out of here disappeared. There were too many. His only hope was to wait it out, see what Steffanie and Chitrita were planning. If they had intended killing Coffin and Emma, surely they would have done that by now.

No, Coffin had an idea that Steffanie in particular wanted to see Coffin suffer.

'Take them,' Chitrita said. 'Tie them to the chairs.'

Coffin saw Micheal peeking out from behind the two winged back chairs.

Steffanie and Chitrita stood up.

Two vampires each guided Coffin and Emma to the chairs. More vampires appeared, carrying lengths of ripped bed sheets.

They were prepared, they'd thought this through. Planned it.

The vampires shoved Coffin into the chair and began winding the ripped sheets around him, tying them together until he was completely immobile. His wrists were tied together and then his hands pulled up and behind his head where another length of ripped sheet was tied to his hands and then pulled down behind the chair and underneath it where the other end was tied to his ankles.

He felt like a turkey trussed up for Christmas.

They tied Emma's arms to the chair armrests and left her feet free.

She twisted her head and looked at Coffin.

'It's okay,' he said. 'We're going to get out of here.'

Steffanie laughed, flicking her fiery red hair off her face. The ruined side of her face was in shadow, but Coffin could still see the empty eye socket, the holes in her cheek and the chipped, ruined teeth.

She drew closer to him, bending down over him. She ran her fingers up his thigh.

Coffin felt completely exposed.

'What are you doing?' he said.

'Having some fun,' Steffanie whispered.

Her hand left his thigh and travelled up his abdomen, up to his chest. The touch of her long fingernail was soft. Steffanie's hand hovered at his throat, her fingers barely touching his flesh. She looked into his eyes, and Coffin could see nothing in that gaze.

Nothing human, at least.

Steffanie drew closer. Behind the chair, Michael squirmed to get a better view of what was going on.

Steffanie was close enough now that Coffin could feel her breath on his cheek. His arms and his back were starting to hurt from the position he had been pulled in to. Steffanie's hand left his throat and began travelling down his torso again, her single finger tracing a path down to his abdomen.

'How would you like to be one of us, Joe?' she whispered. 'You and me, back together? Michael, your son once more. We could be a family.'

The stink of decay filled Coffin's nostrils. He could smell death on her breath, on her flesh. Her empty eye socket was crusty with dried blood. The torn edges of her flesh where the shotgun pellets had ripped her cheek apart were green and rotten.

'I'd rather try fucking a lion,' Coffin said. 'I'd fancy my chances more.'

Steffanie chuckled. Her hand had reached his trouser belt now. She undid the buckle and slipped the belt free.

'We'll see,' she whispered.

One handed, she popped the button undone at the top of his trousers and then pulled his zip down.

She slipped her hand down inside his pants.

Coffin inhaled sharply.

'Hmmm,' she murmured.

Coffin twisted his head away. There was a cold fire in the pit of his stomach, burning bright. He closed his eyes and ground his teeth together as she slowly massaged him.

'Do you like this?' Steffanie whispered.

Coffin said nothing, the stink of death in his nose, at the back of his throat. He could feel her crawling through his mind, opening him up, exposing him.

Steffanie withdrew her hand and Coffin gasped.

He opened his eyes, saw her gathering up the wedding dress, folds and folds of it bunching in between them.

She straddled him. Placed her hands on his shoulders and her forehead against his and lowered herself on him.

Coffin turned his head away again, trying to avoid the rancid smell of death.

He grunted as she slid herself on to him. She was cold, so cold.

Steffanie began moving up and down on him, her hair falling over his face, her foul breath caressing his cheek.

Coffin screwed his eyes shut and clenched his jaw so hard he thought he might fracture his teeth. There was a scream building inside of him, but he couldn't let it out.

He couldn't.

WHY DO YOU ALWAYS HAVE TO SPOIL IT, JOE?

Archer and Choudhry had to crouch and run to get through the mass of bats.

The bats nipped at their scalps and their hands, any spot they could find that was bare flesh. At times the air was so thick with the bats that Archer and Choudhry were running blind, relying on their memory of the road and the house ahead of them to get them there. Archer panted with the effort of running. It was hard to breathe. His leg hurt and his limp hindered him, but he couldn't stop. Not now he was in the thick of all the bats.

Archer collided with Choudhry, who had stopped, doubled so far over his head was almost between his knees.

'I think we've gone too far!' he shouted.

Archer could only just hear him over the noise of the bats darting around and above them. The rustling of wings beating against the air was magnified to such a degree that it was a physical wave washing over them. And Archer was sure he could hear the clicking of the bats that was supposedly beyond human hearing.

Archer grabbed Choudhry by the arm. 'Which way? I've lost my bearings!'

Choudhry got hold of Archer. They were almost embracing and doubled over still.

'This way, I think!'

They ran, keeping low to the ground, Choudhry pulling Archer along. It felt like they were in a black cloud of beating wings and hurtling bodies. Of teeth and claws. Archer thought he might go mad if he spent much longer here.

Choudhry tripped and fell and Archer went with him.

'It's the kerb!' Choudhry shouted. 'We tripped over the kerb, we're back on the pavement.'

Archer hadn't even realised they had left the pavement and been running down the middle of the road. On all fours, they crawled forward until they got to a brick wall. Choudhry grabbed Archer again and pulled him close.

'I know where we are!' he hissed. 'We need to keep moving down this way. The house is down here.'

Archer nodded. Choudhry began crawling again and Archer followed him. Something warm dripped into Archer's eye. He wiped at it. In the darkness created by the mass of swirling bats, he couldn't see what was smeared over his fingertips, but he was pretty sure it would be blood. The bats were attacking with increasing ferocity as Archer and Choudhry got closer to the house.

Nothing was going to stop Archer from getting in there. Not if Emma was in there, and potentially in danger.

'Here!' Choudhry motioned at Archer to follow him and they crawled through an open gateway.

Archer thought he saw a glimmer of yellow light, from a window perhaps. His leg was on fire now where Michael had bitten him. Archer wasn't even sure if he would be able to stand up again once they got inside the house and away from the bats.

Choudhry crawled up a step and Archer followed him. They shuffled through a doorway and inside the house. The bats followed them, darting into and around the reception hall.

Choudhry kicked at the door. It slammed shut. The bats outside slammed into the door, making thudding noises like a crowd of children were throwing tennis balls at the house.

Archer gasped. It suddenly felt like he could breathe again. He looked anxiously up at the bats, but they were darting to and fro high up near the ceiling. They didn't seem to like being inside and came nowhere near Archer and Choudhry on the floor. They flew over to the window where the bats outside were gathering.

The two men looked at each other.

'You're bleeding,' Choudhry said, touching his forehead.

'So are you,' Archer replied, indicating his cheek.

'What the hell was that?' Choudhry said.

'It's the vampires, it's got to be. They must have the bats under some kind of control.'

Choudhry ran his hand through his hair. 'I thought we were going to die out there.'

Archer got up onto his knees and then onto his feet. His leg hurt, hot spikes of pain shooting through his thigh, but he could stand.

'You all right, Boss?' Choudhry asked as he stood up.

'Yeah, I'm fine.' Archer glanced around. 'We need to keep our eyes peeled. We don't know who might be in this place.'

'What do you think it is, some kind of old people's home?'

'Maybe,' Archer said.

The two men jumped and turned as a drumming sound started up. The bats were hurling themselves at the windows. The glass panes shivered beneath each impact.

'You think they're trying to get in?' Choudhry said.

'I don't know. Maybe.'

Movement behind them. The two men turned their backs on the windows. A frail old lady in a dressing gown stood by the reception desk. Her white hair was long and tied back, the ponytail draped over her right shoulder. She had a hand on the desk to steady herself. Her fingers were swollen with arthritis and the back of her hand covered in liver spots.

Archer and Choudhry glanced at each other.

'Don't be frightened, we're police officers,' Archer said.

He pulled his ID out and flipped the plastic wallet open.

The old lady regarded him silently through watering, rheumy eyes.

'Are you the only one here?' Choudhry said. 'Are there others?'

The old lady hobbled a few steps closer. Her bony legs protruded from a pair of large slippers. The fronts of the slippers had big, yellow bobbles for eyes and fur underneath, like her slippers were a face with a moustache.

'Miss?' Archer said.

The old lady opened her mouth, revealing red, raw gums empty of teeth, and hissed at the two men.

'Oh shit,' Choudhry said.

'Keep out of her way,' Archer said. 'Chances are she can move faster than you think.'

'You don't have to tell me that,' Choudhry said. 'I was there when the vampires escaped from the mortuary.'

The old lady hobbled closer. Reached out a swollen hand towards them. Her fingers clawed stiffly at the air.

Archer and Choudhry separated, so that they were on either side of her.

'Do you think she's just pretending to be slow?' Choudhry said.

'No,' Archer said. 'If she was fast enough, strong enough, she would have been after us by now, I'm sure of it.'

'I'm still keeping my distance.' Choudhry glanced at Archer. 'What do you want to do?'

'You distract her and I'll sneak up behind her and cuff her.'

Choudhry raised an eyebrow. 'And how do you expect me to do that?'

'Get closer to her, let her think she has a chance of catching you.'

'Didn't I just say I was keeping my distance?' Choudhry sighed. 'You never listen to me, do you?'

Archer was round behind the vampire now. All of her attention was focused on Choudhry.

'Hey, nice doggie, come here, there's my good girl,' Choudhry said, smiling at the old lady and waggling his fingers at her.

The vampire smacked her gums together. They made a wet, slapping noise.

'Ugh, you really are disgusting,' Choudhry said. 'But what are you going to do if you catch me? Gum me to death?'

Archer had his cuffs out and ready. Even though the vampire looked frail, even though she had no teeth, he knew she could still be dangerous.

'Could you get a move on, Archer? This old girl is starting to freak me out.'

Archer lunged, grabbing her wrist and snapping the metal bracelet around it. The vampire turned, moving faster than he had thought she was able, and fastened her mouth on his throat.

'Get her off!' Archer screamed, pushing at her.

Her gums slid over his neck as she made disgusting sucking noises. Choudhry pulled her off and slapped the other cuff around her free wrist. She rolled onto her back on the floor, struggling to free herself from the restraints.

'That was horrible,' Archer said, wiping his sleeve on the slime dripping from his throat.

'It's just a good job she didn't have her false teeth in,' Choudhry said. 'Then you'd have been in trouble.'

'Tell me about it.' Archer looked around the reception area. 'What do you think? Shall we go exploring?'

The bats were still hitting the windows with their wings and their bodies.

'No, I think we should call in backup,' Choudhry said. 'You really want to go looking through this place all by yourself? There are probably blood sucking monsters hiding in every corner.'

Archer thought of Emma, of the kid who'd said he saw the woman coming in here with Coffin.

Choudhry held up his hands before Archer said anything. 'I know, I know, you think Emma might be here.' He sighed. 'Let me call the station, get some help down here. Once I've done that, I'll come exploring with you..'

Once Choudhry had made his call, the two men walked slowly and quietly deeper into the home. Archer stopped at the first door that was open, standing out of view of whoever might be in there. He slowly looked around the corner and sucked in his breath.

'What is it?' Choudhry whispered, standing next to Archer.

Archer signalled him to come and take a look. An old man lay on the bed, the covers pulled off him. His pyjamas were splattered with crimson blood. His skin was white with red blotches.

And he was moving, twisting his head from side to side as though he was having a nightmare.

The two detectives crept into the room and watched the old man as he continued snapping his head from one side to the other.

'That looks painful,' Choudhry whispered.

'I think he's turning into a vampire,' Archer said.

'What are we supposed to do, shove a wooden stake through his heart? I mean, look at this guy, he's got teeth.'

'No, that would be murder,' Archer said.

'Murder? But these things aren't even alive, are they?'

'Doesn't matter, we can't just go shoving pointed stakes through their hearts.' Archer looked at Choudhry. 'Are you prepared to do that?'

'I don't know,' Choudhry said. 'If I see one of them charging at me with its teeth bared and I have a stake to hand, then yeah, I suppose I might.'

'Let's get out of here,' Archer said.

They stepped back outside the bedroom. Archer looked up and down. Everything was quiet, too quiet.

Why was that?

JOE COFFIN OPENED his eyes again as Steffanie climbed off him. The vampires were all gathered around, watching. He took a deep, ragged breath. Seemed like the room was full of vampires, standing there in complete silence. Like they had just witnessed something sacred.

A foul, ugly, obscene tribal ceremony. A display of power.

'One last time, Joe,' Steffanie said, trailing a finger across his cheek.

Coffin's back and shoulders were on fire. He wasn't sure how much longer he could hold this position they had tied him into, but he also knew he had no choice. He would be kept there for as long as they wanted to keep him there.

Coffin looked at Emma. She was slumped in the wingback chair, her head hanging down as though she had fallen asleep.

'Hey, you okay?' he said. His voice was hoarse, almost a whisper.

'What do you think?' she said, without looking at him.

Steffanie held out her arms and twirled around on the spot, her wedding gown trailing behind her.

'So how was it for you, Joe?' she said, and laughed. She slowed to a halt, facing Coffin. 'We used to have a good time, didn't we? In the bedroom at least.'

'Is that right?' Coffin said. 'So how come you decided to start shagging Terry Wu?'

Steffanie dropped her arms and pulled a sulky face at Coffin. 'Why do you always have to spoil it, Joe? Here we were talking about the good times and you had to bring up Terry.'

'You were the one had an affair. You were the one set me up to kill Terry and film me doing it.'

Steffanie smiled. Or at least half of her face smiled, the half that didn't have holes in it.

'Don't forget, your girlfriend was part of that, too. She was ready to throw you to the wolves on the front page of her newspaper.'

'I told you she remembered me,' Emma muttered.

Coffin shifted position, trying to ease the pain in his back and shoulders.

'What was your problem, Steffanie?' Coffin said. 'Can you even remember now? When I first met you, you wanted to get out of the stripping game. Then when we got married, you went straight back into it. What the hell did you marry me for? Why'd you agree that we should have a child? None of it makes sense to me.'

Steffanie tilted her head back, looked at the ceiling with her one eye. 'I don't know. Sometimes it's so hard to remember now.' She looked at Coffin again. 'I think I was just bored. That's all. Bored.'

'Are you two going to argue all night, or are we going to have some fun?' Chitrita said.

Steffanie pushed both hands through her hair, holding it up and off her face.

'All right, who's next then?'

The vampires whispered amongst each other and began shuffling forward.

Julie Carter stepped out from amongst them and walked up to Coffin.

'Me,' she said, smiling slyly. 'It's my turn now.'

The vampires gathered behind her, nodding, grinning.

Julie undid her dress and let it fall to the floor. She stepped out of it.

She was naked.

Slowly, she eased herself onto Coffin's lap. Her mouth hovered over his throat, her lips and teeth brushing his flesh.

Coffin could smell her. Decay. Disease. Death.

She pressed herself up against him, slowly rubbing her body up and down against his.

Coffin ground his teeth together, his head turned away. The vampires crowded around him began a low murmuring, building in intensity as Julie Carter's undulations increased in speed and intensity.

The murmur grew into a chant.

'THAT DOESN'T SOUND GOOD,' Choudhry said.

Archer stared at the closed door. Whoever, whatever, that noise was, it was coming from behind that door.

'When are we getting backup?' Archer said.

'Soon as they can tear themselves away from all the other shit that's happening in the city right now,' Choudhry said. 'I think it's just you and me for the moment, brother.'

'Great,' Archer said.

He crept up to the door and placed his ear against it. The

chanting had stopped, but he could hear movement inside and the murmur of voices. Sounded like there were too many in there for Archer and Choudhry to go barging in without help. Archer crept back to stand beside Choudhry.

'We can't go in there on our own, we'll be slaughtered within minutes.'

'That's what I've been trying to tell you,' Choudhry said.

'We need a diversion.'

Archer had a quick look around, trying to find something, anything, he could use to draw the vampires out of that room. The incessant drumming on the windowpanes reminded him of the bats outside, trying desperately to get inside. It seemed like they were following Archer and Choudhry through the home, beating themselves against the glass.

'Let's open the windows,' he said.

Choudhry turned and stared at the swirling mass of dark, winged bodies throwing themselves against the windows.

'Are you mad?' he said. 'We just escaped from those flying rats a few minutes ago. Now you want to set them on us again?'

'We can use them as a diversion,' Archer said.

'Uh-uh, you have gone loopy-loop. I don't know if you noticed, but those things out there are vampire mascots. Didn't you ever read Dracula? We open the windows, those bats are coming straight for us and nobody else.'

'Doesn't matter,' Archer said. 'We open the windows and then we run in there, where the vampires are. The bats will follow us and there are so many of them it will be chaos.'

Choudhry eyed Archer uneasily. 'I don't know, sounds like a crazy plan to me.'

'You got any better ideas?'

'Yes, we wait for backup!'

'That's not an option,' Archer said. 'Who knows when, or even if, we'll get any kind of backup at all. Meanwhile, Emma could be in there and those blood sucking bastards could be doing God knows what to her.'

Choudhry ran his hand over his face. 'Why do I do this? All right, let's do it.'

The two men ran to a separate window each and took hold of the window opener.

'On three,' Archer said.

'Three!' Choudhry shouted and flung his window open.

Archer was right behind him and the bats flooded into the home, an endless stream of darkness flowing through the open windows.

Archer and Choudhry ran for the door. The hallway was already filled with bats and more were flying in.

Archer got to the door first and grasped the door handle. Choudhry slammed into the door beside Archer. The bats were over them already, nipping at their scalps and their hands.

'You ready?' Archer shouted.

'Just do it!' Choudhry shouted back.

Archer opened the door.

SWALLOWED UP BY DARKNESS

The Priest was covered in bats. He looked like he was made of dark, fluttering wings. Only his face showed, but even that was hard to see in the dark.

He had been squatting on a low wall across from the care home, watching everything that was going on. Earlier he had seen Coffin and Emma enter the building, and then he had watched as the two policemen followed them.

Now he was waiting to see what would happen next.

He wasn't the only one.

The man thought he was hidden well in his dark corner, but the Priest could see him. The Priest recognised him too. He had seen the man earlier at Joe Coffin's club. But what was he doing here? What was his interest in the vampires?

Whatever it was, the man was wise to stay hidden for the time being.

Even the Priest knew better than to enter the care home on his own. The bats might be his friend, sensing that innate vampirism deep within him, but the vampires inside that building wouldn't tolerate him. Chitrita was in there, he knew that much. He could sense her presence, and if she wasn't so distracted with whatever it was she was up to, she would be able to sense his. In fact, if she knew the Priest was here, she would probably be trying to kill him right now.

Another good reason to stay outside.

To bide his time.

Coffin and Emma, the two policemen, they were foolish. So frail, these humans, and yet at the same time so convinced of their own invincibility. They had to be, that was the only reason he could think of that they would risk their lives in this way. Once a person was bitten, once that person had become immortal and seen the universe how it truly is, all pretence dropped away. And your eyes were truly opened for the first time.

The Priest knew that life after death was a curse, not a blessing. Even the life eternal promised by Christianity, by his Lord Jesus, was something to be scared of, not welcomed. The Father God was a harsh, demanding parent. A jealous father who demanded complete and unconditional love and devotion. Heaven was little more than an eternity of servitude to a slave master.

And yet, and yet. The Priest had been saved from his curse by his devotion to God, and he had been given a blessing and saved from the eternal fires of Hell. The Father in Heaven deserved unconditional love for saving even a sinner as debased as the Priest.

He shifted slightly on the wall and some of the bats rose into the air and darted around in erratic movements above his hat. The Priest could hear the bats talking to each other. He was one with them, and yet apart from them at the same time.

The bats were here to keep intruders out of the vampires' way.

Chitrita had a plan, and the bats were part of it.

The Priest continued watching.

As did the man hidden in the darkness.

THE DOORS to the large communal room opened and bats flooded in. Seemed like every bat in the city had congregated outside the door as more and more of them darted inside, turning the room dark with their beating wings.

Coffin kicked at the floor, trying to turn his chair over. It was too heavy, and with Julie Carter on top of him, he could only just get it moving a little. The bats swarmed towards him. Coffin glanced at Emma. She had her head down and her knees drawn up to her chest.

Julie, aware of the commotion, was climbing off Coffin.

And then she disappeared, swallowed up by a dark cloud of beating wings as the bats flew over them and everything turned black. They nipped at Coffin's face and his scalp, at his arms stretched painfully over his head and barrelled into his chest and stomach. They covered him, crawling over him, their wings beating against him, their teeth on his face and his neck and arms.

Coffin bellowed and arched his back, but it did nothing to shake any of the bats off. There were so many of them he couldn't catch his breath, like the bats were sucking all the air out of the room. He kicked out, twisting as much as his restraints allowed him to. The room was filled with the noise of the bats, of their wings. It was as though the air itself had taken on physical form and become agitated, violent.

Coffin twisted and kicked out again, writhing in the wingback chair.

He felt something loosen.

A knot in the sheets somewhere. Coffin let himself go loose, relaxed for a moment and then jerked his body hard and straight. There, something was giving, he had a little more movement now. He did it again, tautening every muscle in his body and twisting one way and then another.

The bats continued beating at his face and his chest, at his arms and legs, everywhere that was exposed to them.

He thought he heard a scream, but he couldn't be sure.

The sheets began unravelling. Coffin pulled his arms free, and a hot, searing pain shot through his shoulders and down his back. He dragged himself to his feet, beating at the cloud of bats darting around him.

And then he fell to his knees as pins and needles weakened his trembling muscles. The bats descended upon him, sensing a weak prey. Coffin beat at them, creating swirls and eddies in the movement of the bats.

As his legs recovered movement and feeling, Coffin managed to stand up, using the wingback chair for support. He gave himself another precious couple of moments and then launched himself towards Emma. It was only when he was right next to her that he saw her. Bats were entangled in her hair, biting and flapping their wings. Emma had curled herself up as much as she could into a tight ball in an attempt to protect herself.

Coffin pulled at the sheets tying her to the chair until they began unravelling.

'Down on the floor!' he shouted as he pulled her out of the chair.

Emma flung herself face down onto the floor and Coffin joined her, wrapping a protective arm around her.

'We're going to get out of here,' he said, his lips up close to her ear.

She nodded.

Coffin looked up just in time to see the bats parting and Steffanie stepping through the gap. Bats hung from the folds in her wedding dress and off her veil. Coffin jumped to his feet, a red rage falling over him. He reached out, his hands curled and ready to grab at her throat, to strangle the life out of her. And if that wouldn't kill her, then break her neck and set fire to her. He would do whatever it took to rid himself of that woman.

Before his hands found her throat, she had gone, disappeared into the swirling cloud of bats.

Another figure appeared, crawling along the floor, covered in bats.

'Emma!' it shouted.

Archer. Coffin got down beside the detective. 'She's all right. Get her out of here as fast as you can.'

Archer nodded. Emma pulled herself up onto her knees and they began crawling.

They swiftly disappeared into the cloud of beating wings.

Coffin crawled over to where he thought Leola would be, keeping his head down as the bats flew at him, their teeth nipping at his back and his scalp. He found Leola covered in bats, tangled in her hair, crawling over her face. Coffin grabbed at them, plucking them from her and throwing them away. Leola gasped as he pulled the sheet from her mouth.

More bats landed on her.

Leola snarled and shook her head, dislodging bats from her hair.

Coffin pulled at the sheets, tying her to the chair. When they began unravelling, she was able to quickly free herself.

'Joe!' she hissed.

Coffin turned just in time to see Chitrita emerging from the cloud of bats. Arms outstretched, she grabbed him and sank her long fingernails into his flesh.

Coffin snapped his head forward, smashing his forehead into her nose. She let go as cold blood splattered over Coffin's face.

Coffin shoved at her and she disappeared once more into the mass of flying bats.

'Let's get out of here,' Coffin said, taking Leola's hand and pulling her along with him.

More clawed hands reached out, grabbing at Coffin and Leola. Coffin kicked and punched, Leola slipping free from him and disappearing. Coffin lashed out, trying to pull free of the fingers clawing at him, but more hands were on him now and there were too many of them. They pulled Coffin to the floor. He saw faces intermittently between the bats darting past. Sneering, snarling faces, mouths open, exposing pointed teeth and red tongues.

Coffin kicked and lashed out but there were too many vampires clawing at him, crawling over him. He roared as their teeth sank into him. They were biting any piece of flesh they could find. His arms, his legs, his torso.

He tried rolling over, but he could hardly move. The vampires had him pinned to the floor.

And they were draining the blood from his body. Even over the sound of the bats' wings beating the air, he could hear the vampires slurping and sucking as they drank blood from whatever part of his body they could find.

Coffin's world began turning grey.

'ARE YOU OKAY?' Archer said.

Emma nodded. They were sitting in the back seat of a police car with Choudhry, the three of them squashed together. The quick response unit vehicle had been the first, and so far, only one to turn up. Two policemen sat in the front.

They made it clear that they had been ordered to wait for more units to arrive.

'Did Joe make it out?' Emma said, wiping at her face with some hand wipes that somebody, she couldn't remember who, had given her. After having all those bats crawling over her, she felt dirty. Diseased.

'I don't know,' Archer said. 'He told me to get you out, and that was the last I saw of him.'

'You've got to go back inside and help him,' Emma said.

'Are you serious?' Choudhry said. 'You know what it's like in there, we'd be suicidal to even think about a thing like that.'

'We'll go take a look for him in a minute,' Archer said.

Choudhry said something under his breath that nobody caught and shook his head.

'I'm coming with you,' Emma said.

'No, you're not,' Archer replied. 'Coffin's a big boy, he can look after himself. We'll go in, take a quick look around, but if we can't see him or if it's too dangerous still, we're getting out of there and taking you to hospital. All right?'

'But what about all the vampires in there? What are we going to do?'

'There's nothing we can do, not right now. Not without more men, preferably armed.'

Emma started to speak, to argue, but Archer cut her off.

'I'm not discussing this any more, Emma. We need to get you to hospital, get you some shots or something. For all we know, those bats have rabies.'

Emma nodded, too tired to argue anymore.

Archer turned to Choudhry. 'You ready?'

'For that lowlife Coffin? Are you serious?'

'We can't just leave him there.' Archer looked at the two policemen in the front of the car. 'Besides, we've got backup now.'

Choudhry snorted. 'Oh yeah, I hadn't noticed. We'll be fine.'

Archer opened his door. 'Stay here, Emma. Do not leave the car.'

Emma watched as they all climbed out. The vehicle was an armed response unit and now they each had a gun.

They headed back for the care home.

A wave of tiredness swamped Emma. She looked at the tiny packet of hand wipes she had been given. It was empty, she'd used them all. What she really needed was a shower. Emma closed her eyes, rested her head against the seat back.

Don't be long, she thought, as she started to drift off to sleep.

Moments later, or it could have been minutes, Emma started as she heard the rear door opening up.

'Nick?' she said, opening her eyes. 'Did you find him—?'

Gerry Gilligan grinned at Emma.

'You and me, we have some unfinished business,' he said.

EPISODE SIXTEEN

ARCHER AND CHOUDHRY

When the sun finally rose over the city, it seemed to lack its usual power. Grey, drab daylight illuminated the devastation caused by the bats during the night. Bat attacks all over the city had brought the roads to a standstill in many places. Car wrecks still blocked some streets, and everywhere there were signs of destruction, smashed windows, rubbish strewn across the pavements and roads, and early morning commuters wandering dazed through the mainly empty streets.

DS Amrit Choudhry, clutching a strong, black coffee with plenty of sugar in it, surveyed the destruction from his car. He'd had no sleep the previous night, and now he was running on caffeine. As far as he could see, there wasn't going to be much opportunity for sleep anytime soon.

Nick Archer climbed in the passenger seat and stared grimly out of the front windscreen.

'No luck,' Choudhry said. It wasn't even a question.

Archer slammed his fist onto the dashboard. 'No, nothing. Barry hasn't seen her for a couple of days and said the last time he spoke to her was on the phone last night when he told her about the bat attacks.'

Choudhry sighed. 'You want to try the club, see if Coffin turned up yet?'

'What the hell happened, Amrit? I told her to stay where she was.'

'Yeah, I know,' Choudhry said. 'We were hardly gone anytime at all. I don't see how she could have got far.'

Archer smacked his fist against the dashboard again. 'We couldn't find her though, could we? Someone or something must have taken her. It's the only explanation.'

Archer and Choudhry hadn't managed to get very far into the care home. The air had been thick with bats still, although they seemed to be paying less attention to humans at that point. The old people's home seemed to have become a dark, living, breathing being it was so full of bats.

They had decided to return to the car, but when they got there, they found it empty.

Emma had gone.

Archer and Choudhry had spent the rest of the night looking for her, making phone calls, talking to anyone who might have known where she was.

It seemed like they had started off with nothing and now they had even less.

Once the bats had begun dispersing all over the city, they had returned to the care home with an armed backup force. Apart from a few feeble vampires who struggled to move, the home had been empty. Even Coffin had gone.

'Let's go and visit Angellicit,' Choudhry said. 'Who knows, Coffin might be there now.'

Archer just nodded.

Choudhry drained his coffee.

When they got to Angellicit, they parked across the street and made their way slowly to the entrance, keeping an eye out for bats or vampires. Both men were on edge and it wasn't light enough yet that either of them felt they could relax their guard. Archer pounded on the door.

'Police! Open up!'

It took a few minutes, each one dragging by, but the door was finally opened.

'Wh-wh-what is it?' Stut said.

'Where's Coffin? We need to talk,' Archer said.

'He's n-n-n-not here,' Stut said.

'Perhaps we should come in and have a look around,' Choudhry said.

'What f-f-f-for, I told y-you, he's n-n-not here.'

'Maybe we don't believe you,' Archer said.

'You n-n-need a warrant,' Stut replied.

Archer and Choudhry passed a glance to each other.

'Are you hiding something?' Choudhry said.

Stut shook his head.

He looked guilty as hell.

Archer stepped up close, got in Stut's face. 'If you like, we can take you down to the station for questioning while we dig up a warrant. Could take a while though, but I've got lots to ask you, so that'll be all right. Or, you could let us in, we can make sure Coffin's not here like you say, and I'll save my questions for another day. What do you think?'

Stut eyeballed Archer, his jaw flexing.

Archer planted a hand on his chest and shoved hard. Stut tottered and fell over on his back.

Before he could get back up on his feet, Archer and Choudhry were inside, the door slammed shut behind them.

'You c-c-can't do that!' Stut yelled.

Archer grabbed a fistful of Stut's shirt, hauled him to his feet and slammed him up against a wall. 'No, you're right, I can't. But I'm doing it, anyway. Want to know why?'

Stut nodded.

'Because you're a pathetic, nasty little piece of shit who should have been behind bars a long time ago. But I'm willing to overlook that if you work with me for the moment. Now tell me, is Joe here?'

Stut shook his head again. 'N-n-no one knows wh-wh-where he is.'

Choudhry had walked over to the doors into the main part of the club and opened them up.

'What the hell happened here?' he said. 'Looks like a war zone.'

Archer let go of Stut and joined Choudhry. 'Someone shot the place up. Who was that?'

'S-s-s-someone out to get Joe,' Stut said, straightening his shirt. 'Barged in h-here last n-n-n-night armed to the teeth.'

'How come that never got called in?' Archer said.

'The b-b-bats kept everyone here,' Stut said.

'You got any idea at all where Joe might be?'

'N-n-n-no,' Stut said. 'He's not answering h-h-his phone or anything.'

'You believe him?' Choudhry said.

Archer grimaced. 'Unfortunately, yes.'

'He's n-n-n-not the only one m-missing,' Stut said. 'N-n-n-no one can find G-G-Gilligan either.'

Archer looked at Choudhry.

'Oh fuck,' he said.

YOU LOOK FINE

Flashes of memory. Faces, mouths, teeth, clawed hands.
Bats.
Darkness.

They dragged him down into the darkness. Took him with them. Their teeth, all over him, biting him, their mouths sucking at him, bleeding his life away.

More flashes of memory.

Leola over him, her mouth moving but no words.

And the other one, her friend, the man known as the Priest.

Lifting him, pulling him to his feet. His arms over their shoulders.

Darkness again.

Light.

Dark.

Monsters.

No, not monsters, not anymore.

A bed.

A needle.

Pain.

Darkness.

A buzzing sound, like an angry wasp. And pain too. Was he being stung?

Coffin struggled from sleep, from unconsciousness. He was lying on a bed. Looking at a ceiling stained with damp, the edges of the wallpaper curling at the corners, hanging in tiny, cobwebbed strips.

His eyes were gummy, and he had to close them.

The buzzing started up again, and a wasp stung him.

'What the hell?' he growled, slapping at his chest where the pain still lingered.

'No, no, you gots to lie still, Mr Coffin,' a voice said.

Coffin rubbed at his eyes and opened them. The Priest was sitting on the edge of the bed. Leola sat on Coffin's other side. The Priest was holding something. Looked like a needle.

Coffin pushed himself up into a sitting position, his back against the wall. Brushing his fingertips against his chest he felt the bumps, the tenderness.

'Are you giving me a tattoo?' he said, his voice thick with sleep still.

'I had to do it, Mr Coffin,' the Priest said, holding up his hands. 'You done gone lost a lot o blood to those unrepentants, an I don't wants you turnin, I surely don't.'

The Priest pushed a button, and the needle started buzzing again.

'Get that thing out of my face,' Coffin growled.

The Priest switched off the tattoo machine.

'It's for your own good, Joe,' Leola said.

'Why?' Coffin said. 'You saying I'm a vampire now?'

Leola looked down at her hands, curled in her lap, and back up again. 'Probably not, but the Priest just wanted to be sure.'

Coffin ran his fingers over the small lumps where his skin had swollen under the needle. 'What do you mean, probably not?'

'You didn't die, Mr Coffin,' the Priest said. 'My girl here, she got to you, she saved you.'

'Steffanie, Chitrita, the other strong vampires, they left as soon as the bats began to disperse. That left the weak and the old ones, the ones who had only just turned, they were feeding on you. I was able to start pulling them off and then the Priest came in and helped me.'

'We gots you here to my place, Mr Coffin.' He cackled. 'You almost in a coffin tonight!'

Coffin kept running his fingers over the tattoo on his chest. 'You got a mirror?'

'I ain't finished yet,' the Priest said. 'You wants to see a work of art before it been done? That ain't right.'

Coffin looked at Leola, the question in his mind unasked.

Leola nodded, almost imperceptibly. 'Let him finish.'

Coffin leaned back against the wall. 'This better be the right thing to do.'

The Priest began his work again, leaning over Coffin, the needle piercing Coffin's flesh whilst it buzzed.

When he had finished, the Priest straightened up and admired his work.

'You gots to be free of sin, Mr Coffin. You should give your life to the good Lord Jesus.'

'Get me that mirror,' Coffin said.

He sat up and swung his legs off the bed. The room began to spin and Coffin gripped the edges of the mattress until it had passed.

'Are you all right?' Leola said.

'Yeah, I'm fine.'

The Priest returned with a handheld mirror. The glass was scratched and rust had gathered in the corners, but Coffin could see the light bouncing off it. For a moment, before looking at the tattoo, Coffin considered the myth that vampires could not be seen in mirrors. If that was true, and Coffin could see himself in the mirror, then that meant he was still human.

He held the mirror up. The first thing he saw were the bite marks. Puncture wounds over his chest and abdomen, on his shoulders. They had started crusting over, but they still looked fresh and raw.

Next, he looked at the tattoo on his chest. It was swollen and red, the skin around the markings bruised, but he could make it out.

Black lines and hieroglyphs, shapes that almost seemed to move if he looked just to the side, but stopped as soon as he focused on them.

'How does this help?' Coffin said.

'It will help you repel your vampiric instincts,' Leola said. 'Help to keep them under control.'

Coffin lifted his gaze from the mirror. 'You said I'm probably not a vampire.'

'You're probably not,' Leola said. 'This is… I don't know how you say it.'

'Better safe than sorry?'

'Yes, that's it.'

Coffin dropped the mirror on the bed and stood up. The bed sheet fell from him. He was naked.

A wave of dizziness washed over him again, but not as powerful as before. His legs trembled slightly. He was still weak from loss of blood.

'Are you okay?' Leola said.

'Yeah,' Coffin replied, but he remained standing where he was, unable to trust that he wouldn't fall down if he tried walking. 'Did Archer get Emma out? Is she safe?'

'I saw her being taken outside. Detective Archer and another man were looking after her.'

'Good.' Coffin thought for a moment. 'I need to get back to the club. We've got problems.'

'You should stay here,' Leola said. 'You're weak from loss of blood.'

'I told you, I'm fine,' Coffin said. 'Where are my clothes?'

Leola and the Priest exchanged a glance.

'We burnt them,' the Priest said. 'They was contaminated with bad blood.'

Coffin said to Leola, 'You need to go back to the club, get me some fresh clothes.'

Leola smirked. 'I think you look fine as you are.'

Coffin scowled. 'Just get me some fresh clothes. I've got things to do.'

Once Leola had returned with a fresh set of clothes, and because he was feeling stronger, Coffin walked back to where he had parked the Fat Boy the previous night. To his surprise, it was still there.

He rode back to Angellicit, parked around the back.

Stut and Shaw were cleaning up when he walked inside.

'Joe!' Shaw said. 'Where the hell have you been?'

'Never mind that,' Coffin said. 'What's going on here?'

'Archer came by,' Shaw said.

'What the hell did he want?' Coffin said.

'He d-d-d-didn't say,' Stut said. 'H-h-h—'

'He seemed to be looking for Gilligan,' Shaw said.

'Yeah?' Coffin looked at the bottles lined up behind the bar. He felt like he could murder a drink, but he turned away. He had to stay sharp. 'What's he want with Gilligan?'

'He didn't say,' Shaw said.

'Anyone seen the Irish bastard?'

Stut shook his head.

'What about Emma? Did Archer say anything about Emma?'

'No,' Shaw said. 'Is something wrong, Joe?'

'No, everything's peachy,' Coffin said. 'We still got Stig's body upstairs?'

'Yeah, and we put Longworth's carcass down in the cellar.'

Coffin sighed. 'Which means we're going to have to carry the bastard back up again.' He thought for a moment. 'Okay, maybe best for now if we stick the Stig down there, too. Anyone heard from Gosling?'

The two men shook their heads.

'All right. I'm going to pay him a visit at his club. You two are coming with me.' He paused, looked at the bar again, at the drinks. 'We're going to need arming up, too. We got some artillery at the moment?'

'Yeah, we're good,' Shaw said.

'All right. Get some stuff and then meet me down here in five minutes.'

Coffin went into the back and took the stairs two at a time. He paused outside his door, just for a moment, and then swung it open.

The Stig lay on his back on the floor, a pool of dark red blood surrounding his head like a demonic halo.

Coffin walked around the body, scanning the room. Not a single scrap of money had been left behind. Gosling had to have had this planned all along. Except, it didn't quite make sense. Gosling had taken advantage of the attack by Shanks Longworth downstairs, distracting Coffin and the others. Had he known Longworth was on his way? Had they planned it like that?

No, that didn't make sense either. Gosling had to have decided to act on the spur of the moment, which meant he'd had something else planned originally.

But what?

Coffin headed back downstairs. Shaw and Stut already had a duffel bag stuffed with guns waiting for him.

Coffin picked up the bag and headed for the door. Paused and looked back.

Shaw and Stut hadn't moved.

'What?' Coffin said.

'We've, um, been thinking, Joe,' Shaw said.

'Yeah?' Coffin said.

'Yeah.' Shaw paused, thinking for a moment. 'We were talking, you know, while we were getting the guns together. We were thinking, like maybe it's not such a good idea, going to the Punchline right now.'

'Is that right?' Coffin said.

Shaw looked at Stut, but Stut wasn't saying anything. Looked like Shaw was the spokesman.

'Yeah, I mean, things are, you know, not the same anymore.'

'And how's that?' Coffin said, placing the bag on the floor.

'Well, you know, since we lost Mort and stuff, things have gone south pretty fast.'

Coffin strode over to Shaw and grabbed him by his shirt collar, shoving him up against a wall.

Coffin got his face right in Shaw's.

'You think I don't know that?' Coffin hissed. 'You think I wanted to be in charge? That I wanted to have to pick up the huge fucking debt that Mort left us with? And don't forget, Mort betrayed me, he betrayed you and he betrayed the Slaughterhouse Mob. Now I'm doing my best to pick things up and that's why I took that job with that creep Gosling and his bunch of freaks.' Coffin let go of Shaw and took a step back. 'You want to stay, we're heading on over to the Punchline to get our money back. You want to go, then do it. Do it now, but I'd better never see you again.'

Shaw straightened his shirt out. Looked at Stut.

Stut looked back at Shaw. Waiting for Shaw to make the decision.

'I'm sorry, Joe,' Shaw said.

'Get out,' Coffin snarled.

Shaw and Stut turned and walked away. Coffin watched them until they had left the club.

He stood still for a while, listening to the silence. Something he wasn't used to doing in this place. Apart from two dead bodies, he was the only person here right now.

He picked up the bag full of guns.

Headed for the door.

AN OCTOPUS

Emma woke up shivering and hungry. Her sleep had been fitful, interrupted by nightmares of teeth and blood and sex and bats.

But she was awake now, even if the feelings of terror lingered.

Her legs were curled up, her knees up close to her chest, and she tried stretching them out to ease the ache in her joints. She only got halfway when her feet encountered an obstacle. She was lying on her side, facing the rear of a car seat. Her body stiffened reflexively when she remembered where she was.

Lying on the back seat of Gerry Gilligan's car.

Emma kept very still, worked at slowing her breathing down, at not panicking or showing any signs that she was awake. Gilligan was sitting in the driver's seat, puffing away on a cigarette like it might be the last one he ever smoked.

Last night, the Irishman had dragged her to his car and manhandled her inside. After her experience with Steffanie and Chitrita, Emma had been exhausted and weak. Unable to resist too much.

Besides, the gun he had in his hand kept her from doing anything too rash.

They had driven for several miles until Gilligan had found a place to park. Emma hadn't recognised any place markers in the dark.

Now there was a little daylight, but Emma still had no idea where they were as the windows were all fogged up.

'There's no point pretending to be asleep, young woman,' Gilligan said. 'I can see you're awake, so you might as well sit up now, mightn't you?'

Emma pulled herself up, lowering her legs to the floor. She ran her hand through her tangled hair.

'Where are we?' she said.

'Oh, just somewhere out of the way,' Gilligan said. 'Somewhere to give me a little thinking time, a little planning time, that's all.'

'And what about me? What are you going to do with me?' Emma said. 'Do I feature in your plans?'

'Ah, well now, that is an interesting question, is it not?' Gilligan had his back to her, as though he couldn't acknowledge her presence in his car. He sucked on his cigarette while he thought. 'You know, it seems to me we're both in trouble right now.'

'You're the one in trouble,' Emma said.

Gilligan chuckled. 'You're a feisty one, that you are. You'd have made a man a good wife back in the old country.'

Emma wiped at her side window, the glass cold against her palm, the condensation running down her arm. She could see trees, nothing more.

'Where are we?' she said.

Gilligan didn't reply.

'Where have you taken me?'

'We're in the Clent hills, young lady. I've parked us somewhere out of sight of the road, give us a little privacy.'

Emma pulled at the door handle and pushed at the door, but it stayed shut.

'Child locks,' Gilligan said. 'You wouldn't get far, anyway.'

Emma knew he was right. Last night, after he had bundled her in the car, he had made a point of brandishing his gun in front of her face. As though she hadn't already seen it. Placed it in a recess in the dashboard within easy reach if he needed to use it.

No, she wouldn't get far at all.

Emma watched Gilligan sitting in silence. His head wreathed in a cloud of cigarette smoke. He'd brought her here to kill her, that much was obvious. He knew she was after him for Karl Edward's murder. And that she would never give up, he knew that too.

But why hadn't he done it yet? Why wait until daylight when getting away with murder would be that much more difficult?

Nick would be looking for her, he would have been looking for her all night. What about Joe? Was he even alive still?

But Emma doubted there was much chance of either of them finding her.

'What have you found out then?' Gilligan said, breaking the silence.

She could see his eyes in the rear-view mirror, looking at her. Examining her.

'I don't know what you mean,' Emma said.

'I know you've been digging around, asking questions,' Gilligan said. 'You're a reporter, of course you have. So you've been looking into my background and I'm asking you now, what have you found out?'

'Not much,' Emma said.

'Come on, now,' Gilligan said, still looking at her. 'Don't be so modest. I know what you've been up to, you and your friend Barry.'

Emma's face went cold.

'Now don't you worry your pretty little head, the young lad's got nothing to worry about,' Gilligan said. 'I thought of taking him out, of course I did, but the time's passed for that kind of thing. I'm in too deep for a little killing to make any difference.'

'You're in trouble, aren't you?' Emma said.

'Didn't I just tell you that?' Gilligan said. 'Now come on young lady, I'm curious, what have you found out?'

'That you were born in County Cork in 1975 to a single mother, you moved around Ireland a lot as you grew up and you were always a trouble maker, even as a child.'

'Keep going,' Gilligan said.

'You joined the Real IRA in your mid-twenties, mainly because you thought it would be fun. That's where you met Brendan, not long before he left and moved to Birmingham. That you love playing the game, and you have loyalty to no one, or no cause, but yourself,' Emma said.

Gilligan roared with laughter and smacked the steering wheel. 'Go on, carry on.'

'That you've been cozying up to the Seven Ghosts even while you've been a part of the Slaughterhouse Mob. You've been playing both sides, you're not even loyal to the Real IRA.'

'Well now, you have been a good, investigative little girl now, haven't you?' Gilligan said. 'A right little Nancy Drew, that's what you are.'

'But I'm right, aren't I?'

Gilligan nodded slightly, thoughtful. 'Maybe, maybe. A man's got to look out for himself these days. It's not like the old times when you could count on your friends, on your compadres,' he said, grinning. 'It's every man, and woman, for himself these days.'

'Whose side are you on right now?' Emma said.

'Haven't you been listening to a word I say? I'm on my own side, I'm loyal to me and nobody else.' Gilligan took a drag on his cigarette. Smoke billowed around his head, filling the car. 'You know, I had planned on taking out Craggs and Coffin, getting my hands on the top job. And then that vampire took care of Craggs for me, which just left Joe.'

Gilligan sighed, smoke billowing from his mouth, and then quickly took another drag.

'Why didn't you?' Emma said.

'Those fucking wet girls, Shaw and Stig, were supposed to be with me, helping me take Coffin down. But they backed out, didn't they? Like the fucking spineless weasels they are.' Gilligan shifted in his seat. Wiped his hand over his window and looked outside. 'It's getting late, we need to finish this soon.'

Emma kept her mouth shut. There was no need to ask Gilligan what he meant by that.

'You know, I thought about joining the church at one point?' he said.

'I find that hard to believe,' Emma said.

'It's true. I'd got my mind set on going to theology college and then becoming a priest.' He paused again while he took another drag on his cigarette. 'It's all a long time ago now. I was a young lad back then. I'd been in trouble, done some bad things.' Gilligan looked out of his window, lost in his own thoughts. 'I'd grown sick of it, sick of all the violence and constantly being on the lookout, you know. Like there could be trouble at any moment, and you always had to be ready. And I remember thinking to myself, what's the fucking point? All this hurt, all this violence and anger? Surely there's got to be more to life than that. More meaning, if you know what I'm saying.'

'Why didn't you?' Emma said, softly.

'Well, I started going to church, and I was doing it secretly, you know. If any of my mates had found out about that, I'd have been a laughingstock. And for a while there it were like I were living two lives. There were the one version of me who was doing some bad things, some very bad things during the week. And then there were the other me that went to church on a Sunday, my head still banging with an hangover from the night before. And it just made me feel even worse.'

'You were conflicted,' Emma said.

Gilligan chuckled. 'Now that's some trendy psychobabble, if ever I heard any. But I suppose I was.'

'Do you still believe in God?'

Gilligan was silent for a while, his head bowed while he thought about this. He was quiet for so long that Emma wondered if she should repeat the question. It seemed to her she was on a knife edge here, that the wrong word could set him off. But she had to keep him talking. The longer they sat here, the more likely they were to be discovered.

Eventually, Gilligan stirred. 'I think I do, yes. Seems to me I was right all those years ago, that there must be more to this world than what we have. Pain and suffering and misery.' Gilligan lifted his head and looked at Emma in the mirror. 'I'm a dead man walking, did you know that?'

Emma shook her head.

'The Seven Ghosts, they've got people looking for me. Bad people.'

'You should run, get away from here.'

Gilligan laughed, a short, sharp bark on the edge of hysteria. 'You think there's anywhere I can run to that they won't find me? They're like an octopus, with tentacles everywhere, and they are just growing bigger and bigger and bigger.'

'What do you know about the Jiangchi Corporation?' Emma said.

'Ah, now, you are a clever girl, aren't you?' Gilligan said. 'The Jiangchi Corporation is the legal front for the Seven Ghosts. And the Jiangchi Corporation really does have its fingers, or tentacles you might say, in pies everywhere around the world. Casinos, entertainment, clubs, online channels, everywhere and everything. And all the money they make gets channelled back into their black market dealings, into drugs and illegal investments.'

'But what's the point?' Emma said. 'What are they trying to achieve?'

'What's the point?' Gilligan cackled again. 'Money, power, sex, what do you think? It's always the same old story. The thing is, Nancy Drew, they want a slice of the pie in Birmingham. And although the Slaughterhouse Mob is a shadow of its former glory, the name still carries a certain cache with it, if you see what I mean.'

'Are you saying the Seven Ghosts want to take over the Slaughterhouse Mob?' Emma said.

'If only that were all they wanted,' Gilligan said. 'No, they want to obliterate the Mob. Completely and utterly destroy it, wipe it from the collective memory. And everybody associated with it.'

'But why are they looking for you?'

Gilligan sighed. 'When Shaw and the Stig flounced off, I threw my hand in with the Seven Ghosts. Got myself a contact there, tipped them off where Coffin was likely to be. That big bastard's fucking indestructible. Twice they sent someone to kill him and both times they lost a guy. I tipped them off again, about the robbery on the old bird's place. They sent a fucking army that time, and even then they couldn't kill him.'

Gilligan fell silent.

'I don't understand,' Emma said, finally. 'Why are they after you now?'

'Turns out they've got a man on the inside, someone who's there specifically to kill Joe. No one knew, a case of the left twat not knowing what the right fucker was doing. But now they've got it into their heads that I knew, that I was playing some kind of double bluff, that I was trying to get their inside man killed.' Gilligan put his head in his hands. 'Ah, fuck knows. Whatever those chink bastards think, they're after me now.'

Emma looked out of her window, through the part of the glass she had cleared with her hand. The view was smeared with water, but she could see well enough that the light was growing stronger.

Gilligan had fallen silent. He seemed lost in his own thoughts, morose.

He'd brought her here to kill her, Emma had no doubt about that. But now he seemed to be a little lost within himself, almost as though he had talked himself out of committing murder. Emma couldn't be sure that wouldn't change, though. The man was obviously on a mental and emotional high wire, and when he fell off, it wasn't going to be pretty.

Suddenly, he stirred, shaking himself from his reverie. 'It's getting late. Let's get this done.'

Emma shrank back in her seat. 'No. Whatever you've got planned, whatever you think you want to do to me, it's not too late to back out. You could just leave, now, run as far away as you can.'

'Haven't I already told you? There's nowhere far enough to go. Nowhere.'

'But why kill me? That's what you're planning, isn't it? To murder me?'

'Oh, it's going to be more fun than that,' Gilligan said.

He opened his door and climbed out of the car. He opened the rear door. In his hand, he was holding the gun, and he waved it at Emma, beckoning her out of the car.

'Come on now, or I'll have to shoot you where you are and that's going to make a mess of the car,' he said.

Emma climbed stiffly out. The ground was dirt and gravel. They were surrounded on all sides by woodland, apart from the dirt road leading to the parking area. Emma couldn't see a proper tarmac road, but she had a feeling they weren't far from one. There was one more car in the car park, but it was empty and looked like it had been abandoned some time ago.

'Take the path over there,' Gilligan said, pointing to a narrow path through the woodland.

He slammed the rear door shut, disturbing crows from a tree, sending them flapping upwards and away, cawing as they went.

Emma took the path Gilligan had indicated. It twisted between the trees on an incline sometimes steep enough that steps had been built into the path using thick logs. Every step of the way, she could sense Gilligan right behind her.

With all these trees, Emma wondered if she might have a chance of escaping. If she ran off the path and into the densest part of the wood, Gilligan might have a hard time chasing her and shooting her. But there was also a real risk that she might break an ankle running downhill through the thick undergrowth.

'Take a right here,' Gilligan said as they came to a fork in the path. His voice was startlingly loud in the silence of the wood.

Emma realised it was earlier in the morning than she had hoped. That they were probably the only ones here.

She continued walking, pausing once when a rabbit startled her, dashing from the undergrowth and across the path where it disappeared again.

Gilligan prodded her in the back with his gun. 'Keep moving. It's not far now.'

A thin, white mist still clung to the leaves in some parts of the woodland. The air felt crisp and clean.

The path had grown a little wider, and Emma was aware of a rocky outcrop of sandstone running along the left side.

'Stop here,' Gilligan said.

There was a narrow path to their right. Almost wasn't a path at all.

'Down there,' Gilligan said, gesturing with the gun.

Emma had to push through thin, soft branches and leaves. The woodland was dense with trees here, and the path snaked between roots and tree trunks. They continued walking, their movement and the call of birds above them the only sounds to be heard.

'Stop here, this'll do,' Gilligan said.

They had reached a small clearing. Emma turned to face Gilligan.

He simply stood there and looked at her for a while.

'Take off your clothes,' he said, eventually.

Emma shook her head, jerked it left and right. 'No, no.'

'Take off your clothes or I will shoot you in the foot,' Gilligan said. 'And then if you refuse me again I will shoot you in the other foot, and so on until you do as I say.'

Emma stared at Gilligan, struggling to control her breathing. Her chest seemed to be filling with a heavy weight while her stomach tied itself into a knot of tension.

'Am I making myself clear?' he said.

Emma nodded, another jerk of her head.

She understood.

Still, she couldn't move.

Gilligan pointed the gun at her left foot. 'Start undressing.'

'Why…' Her mouth twisted as she struggled to form the words. 'Why are you doing this to me?'

'Because I hate you, that's why. Because I hate you and I hate your boyfriend too, and when I'm finished here with you, I might just go and pay Mitch a visit, maybe whisper in his ear how you sucked my cock and how much you enjoyed it, and then I'll put a bullet in his head. What do you think?'

'You can't do that,' Emma said. 'You'd never get away with it.'

'Like I said, I'm a dead man walking. I might as well go out with some style. Now get undressed. That's the last time I'm asking you before I put a bullet in your foot.'

Her hands trembling, Emma took hold of her top and pulled it over her head. She dropped it on the ground.

'Now the T-shirt,' Gilligan said.

Emma pulled her T-shirt over her head. It got caught around her neck, under her ears, and she paused for a moment and she wanted to weep. She pulled it free, and she dropped that on the ground too. Her skin goose pimpled in the cool morning air.

She stood there, staring at him. Silently begging him to not do this, to not make her submit to this.

'Take your shoes off, and your trousers.'

Emma kicked her trainers off and then pulled her jeans down and stepped out of them.

The undergrowth was sharp beneath the soles of her feet.

Gilligan's breathing had gone deep and heavy. His eyes hooded, almost like he was about to fall asleep.

'Now your bra,' he said.

Emma reached up her back for the strap.

There was the sound of a twig snapping. Gilligan turned his back on Emma, the gun swinging around with him.

Before she could even think about what she was doing, Emma charged at Gilligan, screaming at the top of her voice. She slammed into his back and he tumbled forward. His head smacked against a tree trunk, bounced off it, and he crashed to the ground. His arms had cartwheeled wildly as he fell, and the gun had flown from his hand, arcing into the air and then disappearing as it dropped into the undergrowth.

Gilligan lay still, his body twisted.

Emma snapped her head around from side to side, but she couldn't see what had made the noise. An animal, maybe. But not a person. Not somebody come to rescue her.

Keeping her attention on Gilligan all the time, Emma backed up to where her clothes lay in a pile on the damp ground. She began picking them up and pulling them on as quickly as she could. Her hands shook and her fingers couldn't seem to work properly.

Gilligan lay still, twisted to one side. There was a purple bruise on his forehead.

Was he dead? Emma couldn't tell.

She had to get out of here, find someone, get help. She had to run.

But if she ran and Gilligan wasn't dead, if he woke up, how far would she get?

What about his car? She could use his car, drive back into the city.

Or his mobile, what about that? If she could find his mobile, she could call Nick.

Emma took a deep, shaky breath and let it out slowly.

Both of those options were good, but both options meant searching Gilligan for a car key or his mobile phone. Or both.

Which meant getting up close to him and going through his pockets.

Emma hoped he was dead.

She got down on her hands and knees beside his body. She reached out to pat his left-hand pocket. There was something in there, felt like maybe a bunch of keys.

Gilligan moaned slightly, his eyelids fluttering.

Emma took her hand away from his pocket. Held her breath.

Gilligan twisted his head, but his eyes were still closed.

She had to do this, do it now, before he came round properly. She shoved her hand in his pocket. Her fingers touched the metal of the keys.

Gilligan's eyes fluttered open and grew wide as he saw her. His hand closed around her wrist. Emma yelped and tried to pull away.

Gilligan dragged her closer. He was fully conscious now.

He rolled over and pulled her right down on to the ground and then, before she could make any move to pull herself away, he crawled on top of her and clamped a hand over her mouth.

'You silly little bitch,' he hissed. 'I told you, we have unfinished business.'

TSUNG TI LEE

C offin pulled over before he got to the Punchline. Shaw was
a fucking idiot, but he had a point. Either Gosling and his
crew were long gone, or they were waiting for Coffin to
turn up and then they could waste him.

Riding up and announcing his presence wasn't going to work.

Coffin parked down a side street in the city centre. It was still
early enough that there weren't many people around, but he had to
work fast. He took the holdall of guns off his back and laid it on the
ground. There was a covered bin against the wall. Coffin lifted the
outer shell and placed it to one side. He placed the holdall of guns
in the bin. He unzipped the holdall and scattered some rubbish over
the top. Then he replaced the outer shell.

He got out his mobile phone and made a call. Explained the
situation. Explained what he wanted.

When he'd finished his call, Coffin left the side street and walked
around the corner and into the Arcadian centre. The Punchline was
one level up on the circular balcony.

Coffin remained in the shelter of a corner, out of sight of the
doorway. He called Gosling on his mobile.

The phone rang five times before he picked up.

'Joe, I've been expecting you,' Gosling said.

'I'll bet you have,' Coffin said. 'We need to talk.'

'That we do,' Gosling replied.

'Meet me in five minutes at the bottom of Needless Alley,' Coffin said. 'Leave the freak show at home.'

'Now Joe, is that any way to tal—'

Coffin disconnected the call.

He returned to Needless Alley and checked on the rubbish bin. After reassuring himself the guns were there still there, he positioned himself on the opposite side of the road, somewhere he could get a good view of Needless Alley without being seen. It wasn't easy when he was that big, but it wasn't impossible either.

Duchess arrived first, wearing men's clothes for once and a hat pulled down over his face. He sauntered past Needless Alley, surreptitiously checking it out. A few minutes later, a car pulled up and Gosling climbed out.

The car drove away.

Didn't the fat bastard walk anywhere?

Coffin wondered who was driving the car. Couldn't be the dwarf, not unless they'd tied blocks to his feet. Had to be the Bananarama wannabe.

Coffin felt the hard end of a gun being poked into his back.

He held out his hands in a show of surrender and turned around.

There was no one behind him.

Then he looked down and saw Stilts.

Stilts nodded towards Gosling.

Coffin got the message.

They walked over to Needless Alley. Gosling broke into a big grin when he saw Coffin.

'Joe, it's great to see you, I would have hated for us to part on bad terms.'

'What the fuck?' Coffin said. 'You killed one of my men.'

Gosling spread his hands. 'Joe, I was defending myself. The Stig turned his gun on me, I had to do something to defend myself. And then with all the shooting downstairs I thought I should get the money somewhere safe.'

'That's bullshit, and you know it.'

'Joe, how about we go back to the Punchline and talk about this?' Gosling said. 'And then we can split the money.'

'No,' Coffin said.

Stilts poked Coffin in the back with the gun.

Gosling grinned. 'Looks like Stilts wants your company at the Punchline, Joe. And Stilts can be very persuasive when he wants to be.'

'We could 'ove a porty!'

Duchess walked around in front of Coffin. He might not have been wearing a dress, but his lips were a bright, glossy red and he had on long, purple eyelashes. He fluttered his lashes at Coffin and then blew him a kiss.

'Right, let's get back inside before we're noticed out here,' Gosling said.

They walked back in to the Punchline, Gosling in front whilst Coffin was urged on by Stilts. Bananarama girl was at the bar fixing herself a cocktail. There were stacks of suitcases by the stage.

'Going on holiday?' Coffin said.

'You know how it is, Joe,' Gosling said. 'Sometimes you just have to get out of town and soak up some sun. Sit down.'

Stilts jabbed Coffin in the back with his gun.

Coffin sat down at the nearest table, placed his hands palm down on the tabletop. He didn't want anyone getting itchy trigger fingers.

'Let's have a drink, Joe,' Gosling said. 'We should be celebrating. Duchess, drinks all round!'

'What then, Gosling?' Coffin said. 'We all have a drink and make up? Or are you planning on putting a bullet in my head?'

Gosling sat down opposite Coffin. 'I thought we could have a chat. You know how it is, there's always that scene where the villain feels the need to explain everything before he kills the hero. Not that I'm a villain, you understand.'

Coffin leaned forward. 'Yeah, and I'm no hero. What the hell are you talking about?'

'I thought you might have questions, Joe,' Gosling said, softly. 'If that's not the case, we can just go straight to the main event.'

Coffin leaned back again. 'No, I'll humour you.'

'I know you've been wondering about me, Joe,' Gosling said. 'Thinking to yourself, where the fuck did this fat bastard come from? And how come I've never heard of him before?'

Gosling lit up a cigarette and offered the packet to Coffin.

Coffin shook his head.

Bananarama arrived with the drinks. A pint of bitter for Gosling and a whisky for Coffin. Stilts stood by the next table, still holding a gun on Coffin.

'Do you think Shorty could put his gun away?' Coffin said. 'He's making me nervous.'

Stilts glanced at Gosling, who nodded.

Stilts put the gun away.

Duchess had clambered up on the stage. He was back in full drag queen dress up mode, sparkly, long flowing dress, sequins, a tiara and a pair of shoes with the tallest heels on them Coffin had seen.

'Ooh, I thort I'd sing us a lickle sung, loighten t'atmosphere a bit,' he said into the mic, his voice echoing around the empty club.

Gosling started clapping.

I'm heading home it's been too long,
I've served my time 'cos I done wrong,

Duchess' voice echoed around the club. He sang the song slowly, mournfully. And, Coffin realised, without any trace of his Black Country dialect.

'Isn't he beautiful?' Gosling said, watching Duchess sing his song. 'Should have been a star, he should. Name up in lights and everything.' He turned back to Coffin and grinned. 'It's a damn shame about that torture and murder conviction of his, because now we'll never, know will we?'

Let's forget the past and look to tomorrow,
I can't stand my heart overflowing with so much sorrow,

'You see, Joe, I'm a man that gets easily bored. I can't stand still. Put me in an office job, I'd top myself before the week was out. So I took to teaching myself a number of skills. Make myself useful, like. This place, it were just a means to an end, really. Get me into Birmingham. The comedy bit was an afterthought. Something new I could do. Thought it might be fun.'

'For you, maybe,' Coffin said. 'Where'd you get your audience?'

'Pay people enough money, call in enough favours, you can get pretty much whatever you want at the end of the day,' Gosling said, and leaned forward. 'Thing is, Joe, I made some enemies along the way. You know how it is in this game, don't you?'

Coffin grunted, picked up his glass and threw his whisky back.

'I owe some money, I've got some silly bastards after me, want it back,' Gosling continued. 'Always the way, isn't it? You and me, turns out we're in the same boat, and that boat's got a dirty great hole in it and we're busy bailing out the water. It's right, isn't it?'

Coffin said nothing. He was sick of talking.

'Like I said before, Joe, you're a man of few words, I like that. Me, I can talk until the cows come home, I can. That's what my mother used to tell me, talk the hind legs off a donkey, she used to say. Anyway, like I were saying, I owe money. And you owe money. And so I thought we'd be a perfect fit for this robbery.' Gosling leaned back in his chair again. It creaked under his weight. 'And I were right! Bloody hell, Joe, but we couldn't have done it without you, that we couldn't.'

'Especially when those bastards turned up on their bikes and strafed us with bullets,' Coffin said.

Gosling nodded, took a swig of his pint, wiped his mouth with the back of his hand. 'Aye, that were a bit unfortunate, weren't it?'

'You knew they were coming, didn't you?' Coffin said.

'Truthfully? No, I didn't.'

'You didn't seem that surprised to see them.'

'Well, there's that, I suppose,' Gosling said. 'It were a bit of a fuck up really, mix up in communications you might say. The left hand not knowing what the right hand were doing, that sort of thing.'

Out of the corner of his eye, Coffin noticed that Stilts had produced his gun again.

Duchess was still on the stage, singing.

Let's get on that plane,

It ain't gonna be no shame,

'They were there to kill you, Joe, nobody else,' Gosling said. 'Thing is, that were the mistake. They shouldn't have been there, not at all. Killing you is my job.' Gosling took a deep pull on his pint of bitter. Wiped his hand over his lips. 'Not that I'm part of the Triads or anything. I'm a killer for hire, that sort of thing.'

Coffin looked at his empty whisky glass. Placed it on the table.

'Why the big charade with the robbery, the comedy act? Why not just shoot me?'

'That would have been boring,' Gosling said. 'Haven't you listened to a word I've said, Joe? Boring's not my way.'

'What now, then?' Coffin said.

'Now I think it's time we got out of town, took the cash, started a new life,' Gosling said, and chuckled. 'When I say we, that doesn't mean you, of course.'

Coffin picked up the empty whisky glass again.

'You want another drink, Joe?' Gosling said. 'I can get you another drink.'

Coffin hurled the whisky glass at Stilts. It smacked him on the forehead, knocking his aim off. The gun fired, the bullet slamming into the floor.

Coffin stood up, lifting the table with him until it was on its side and he had smashed it into Gosling.

Duchess continued singing as though nothing was happening.

Gone five years or more,

I'll soon be back and walking through your door,

Stilts lifted his arm, aiming the gun at Coffin once more. Coffin picked up a chair and smacked the gun out of Stilts' hand. Coffin swung the chair again, lifting it high over his head to bring it down on the dwarf.

Stilts ducked and ran between Coffin's legs. While Coffin was turning to see where Stilts had gone, the little man grabbed his ankle and pulled sharply.

Already off balance, Coffin tumbled to the floor, letting go of the chair as he fell.

Before he could get back up, Stilts was on top of him, throwing punches at his face. Coffin pushed him off. As Coffin climbed to his feet, a shadow loomed over him. Gosling jabbed Coffin in the face, snapping Coffin's head back with the heel of his hand.

For a second or two, Coffin saw stars. Before he could fully regain his balance, Stilts smacked a broken table leg across his shins.

Coffin dropped to the floor like a sack.

Gosling placed a foot on Coffin's chest. When Coffin's vision cleared, he saw that Gosling had a shotgun trained on him.

'Stilts is tougher than he looks,' Gosling said. 'Ain't that right, Stilts?'

Stilts said nothing.

'Here, look after him for me, I need a piss,' Gosling said, handing the shotgun to Stilts.

The little man climbed on Coffin's chest and stood there, holding the muzzle of the gun under Coffin's chin.

Gosling walked over to the bar and unzipped. Coffin heard the spatter of liquid hitting the floor.

'I tell you something Joe, I'm starting to think I need my prostate checked, I'm having to take a bloody piss every five minutes. Then again, I don't fancy having some stranger stick his finger up my arse, so what am I going to do?' Gosling finished and zipped up again. 'Bloody hell, that feels better.'

Duchess stopped singing.

Gosling clapped, and shouted, 'Beautiful, darlin', just like you!'

Coffin stared at Stilts. The shotgun's twin barrels were jammed right up underneath Coffin's jaw. He couldn't speak.

'Right, come on, you two!' Gosling shouted. 'Let's get this place ready.'

Although he couldn't twist his head around, Coffin could move his eyes enough to see Duchess and Bananarama girl with large

jerry cans, splashing what smelled like petrol over all the furniture
and across the floors.

'We're going to have a little bonfire,' Gosling said, looking down
at Coffin.

Coffin gestured at the gun.

'Ease up on him a little,' Gosling said to Stilts. 'I think he wants
to say a few final words.'

Stilts released the pressure on Coffin's jaw.

'I'm going to kill you,' Coffin snarled. 'I'm going to kill you all.'

Gosling tipped his head back and bellowed with laughter. 'You
hear that, Stilts? Joe says he's going to kill us. How about that?'

'Yeah, one thing though before I do that,' Coffin said. 'Tell me
who hired you. Who wants me dead?'

'Oh, there are lots of people out there who would've hired me to
kill you, Joe,' Gosling said, and chuckled. 'You have to be one of the
most unpopular men I've ever met. But as for who actually hired
me, that was Tsung Ti Lee.'

'And who the fuck is he?'

'Tsung Ti Lee is chairman of the Jiangchi Corporation.'

'Yeah? Never heard of them,' Coffin said.

Gosling leaned over Coffin. 'My God, you really are out of the
loop, aren't you? It's probably for the best that you're out of this
mess now, Joe. Because it looks to me like you're in way over your
head.'

Stilts jammed the shotgun under Coffin's jaw again.

'Goodbye, Joe,' Gosling said. 'It's been fun, right? All right,
Stilts, give him both barrels.'

EMMA

Emma wrenched her free hand out from under her back and went for Gilligan's eyes, but he was too fast. He took his hand off her mouth and grabbed her other wrist and they rolled over, tumbling down the slope and getting tangled in the undergrowth. Brambles whipped at Emma's arms and face, drawing tiny beads of blood. They came to a halt against the trunk of a tree, Gilligan on top of her. Scratches criss-crossed his face in a crazy pattern. He stared at her with bulging eyes, his teeth bared in a snarl.

Panting heavily, Gilligan pressed his body on top of hers. He pinned her wrists to the ground above her head.

'You should lie there and be a good girl,' he whispered.

She writhed and bucked beneath him, trying to throw him off, but he was too heavy and strong.

'Lie still!' he snapped. 'If you don't, I'll break your arms. I could do it, you know.'

Emma jerked her leg up, trying to smash her knee into his balls. There wasn't enough room for her to move, and the kick was ineffectual.

'Oh, you silly bitch,' Gilligan whispered.

He rolled Emma over onto her front and yanked her arm up behind her back. Emma cried out in pain, and Gilligan increased the pressure a little more.

He leaned in close, his mouth beside her ear. 'Now what did I say? Be a good girl, or else I'm popping this arm out of its socket.'

Emma nodded, jerkily, bits of twigs and bark scratching against her cheek.

'Good, that's my girl.' He relaxed the pressure on her arm a little.

Emma breathed hard, kicking up shreds of bark and grass in front of her face.

'What the hell am I going to do with you?' Gilligan said. 'You're a feisty one, aren't you?'

'You could let me go,' Emma said between gasps.

'Oh I could, couldn't I? Except you'd be straight down the cop shop telling all the coppers what I did.'

'You said it yourself, you're a dead man anyway,' Emma said.

'Now I did that, didn't I?'

'If you go to the cops, they can offer you protection.'

Gilligan chuckled. 'Ah now, young lady, you've got no idea what life is like on the inside, have you? I'd be dead before the week was out, that I would.'

'What's the alternative?'

Gilligan leaned in close, increasing the pressure on Emma's arm once more. 'The alternative is, we have a little fun out here, and then we go out together. It'll be so romantic, like a suicide pact.'

'Please, my arm!' Emma gasped.

Gilligan leaned back, easing up on the pressure again. 'Oh, I'm sorry, I forget myself sometimes.'

'Isn't, isn't suicide a sin in the church?' Emma said.

Gilligan threw back his head and laughed. 'Oh now, that's a good one. So it is, but do you really think I'm going to be with the good Lord himself anyways, after all the things I've done? I've got a lot of repenting to do if I'm going to make the pearly gates, a lot of repenting.'

'But you don't have to do this!' Emma said. 'You don't have to hurt any more people.'

Gilligan let go of Emma's arm and stood up.

'Turn over,' he said. 'Let me see you properly.'

Emma rolled over on to her back, moving gingerly. Her shoulder felt like it was on fire where Gilligan had wrenched her arm up her back.

'Now you see, we're back to square one,' Gilligan said, standing astride over her, his hands on his hips. She could see the bulge in his trousers.

He began undoing his belt buckle.

Emma closed her eyes.

He was stronger than her. She could fight him, she could kick and scratch and punch and bite him, but he was still stronger. All she could hope to do was hurt him. But that would probably make it worse for her.

She could submit, try to get it over with as quickly as possible. But would that make her feel any better?

Fight or submit? Were those her only two choices?

Either way, she lost.

She could plead with him, beg him to stop, to reconsider. That wouldn't do any good, and even if he listened, even if he did as she asked and walked away, she still lost.

Gilligan had already done the damage. It was as though the violation had already happened. That he had reduced her to this pathetic thing, this despicable piece of shit. Even Gilligan would realise how worthless she was when he had finished with her, because that's when he would discard her.

That was when she would die.

'Open your eyes,' Gilligan said.

Emma opened her eyes. Gilligan had not removed his trousers. He had unlooped his belt and was holding it, coiled in his right hand.

'Stand up,' he said.

Emma climbed stiffly to her feet. Gilligan grabbed her by the arm and hauled her with him to the nearest tree.

'Cross your wrists over that branch,' he said.

Emma lifted her arms up and crossed her wrists over the branch above her head. Gilligan reached up and began looping the belt around her wrists and the branch, pulling it tighter and tighter. His body, up close to hers, gave off heat. And she could smell him, too. The rancid stink of unwashed flesh, of sweat and cigarette smoke.

Gilligan pulled the belt tight until he could buckle it up. Emma's hands had turned purple from the pressure.

Gilligan stuck his face in front of Emma's and grinned. 'Now, don't go anywhere.'

She watched him as he walked away, head down, kicking his feet through the undergrowth.

He was looking for his gun.

Emma yanked hard on her wrists, but the belt hardly budged. It was so tight, already she was losing feeling in her hands. She took a swift look at Gilligan. He still had his head down, searching for his gun, completely oblivious to Emma right now. Bracing herself for the pain, Emma lifted her feet off the ground. The pain was too much, and she had relieve the pressure on her wrists almost instantly by standing up again.

Placing her forehead against the inside of one elbow, Emma bit back a sob.

Something tickled her ankle.

Lifting her head a little, Emma looked at her feet. A white haired cockapoodle was sniffing at her feet. It looked up at her and shook itself.

Emma snapped her head up. The dog's owner had to be somewhere nearby.

And then Emma saw the path. Not the one they had been on, another one. Gilligan had tried to lead Emma somewhere out of the way, somewhere he wouldn't be disturbed, but they weren't that far away from a path of some sort at all.

The dog began wandering away, sniffing at the ground and following a trail of something.

'Hey, no, come back here!' Emma hissed.

If she could keep the dog with her, the owner might well find Emma.

Gilligan had bent over, rifling through the grass and the weeds. It was almost as though he had forgotten Emma.

How much longer would he look for the gun before he gave up?

The dog was sniffing at Emma's feet again.

'Good boy, you stay with me, all right?' Emma whispered.

The dog looked up at her and wagged its tail.

'Oh!'

There she was, the dog's owner. An old lady, but obviously fit and healthy. She had walking boots on her feet and a small rucksack on her back. She was holding a walking stick. Something she used to help her up the steep slopes perhaps, as she certainly didn't look as though she needed its support.

'Please, help me!' Emma hissed. 'But don't make a sound.'

Emma looked over the old lady's shoulder at Gilligan, his back to them.

The old lady saw him. Turned and strode towards Emma.

'Did he do this to you?' she said.

'Yes, but please, you have to be quiet, he's looking for his gun.'

The old lady leaned the walking stick against the tree. She pulled at the belt, trying to work it free.

'Oh dear,' she said. 'This is very tight, and my hands, they aren't as strong as they used to be.'

'Please, hurry!' Emma whispered.

She glanced at Gilligan again. He was further away, Emma could just make him out between the trees and she was sure he had gone past the point where the gun might have landed. If only he would keep his back to them for the next few seconds.

Gilligan turned around.

Locked eyes with Emma, his mouth opening.

'He's seen you,' Emma said. 'Run!'

Gilligan dashed towards them, stumbling through the undergrowth.

The dog began barking.

The old lady picked up her stick. 'I'm too old to run.'

She swung the stick at Gilligan and smacked him in the side. Gilligan grabbed the walking stick and wrenched it out of the old lady's hands. He turned it around and smashed the grip over her head, the impact cracking her skull. Crying out in pain, she fell to the ground. Gilligan smashed the stick into her skull again.

Emma lifted her feet off the ground and kicked out at him.

'Leave her alone!' she screamed.

Gilligan slashed the walking stick at Emma's shins. Emma screamed as her shins exploded in agony. Grabbing her hair and yanking her head back, he then slammed the end of the stick into Emma's abdomen. Emma's instincts were to double over as a sickening pain blossomed through her stomach, but her hands tied above her head prevented her. Instead, she brought her knees up to her chest for a moment and then back down again.

Everything hurt, and she thought she might throw up.

Through the pain, through the nausea, she heard Gilligan delivering blow after blow onto the old lady's skull. The dog was yapping and snarling. Suddenly, its yapping stopped as it let out a yelp and then it was silent.

When Gilligan had finished, he threw the stick away and swung Emma around to face him. Sweat poured from his face. Blood spotted his forehead and his cheeks.

'Now,' he said, panting, 'now you are going to give me what I need.'

Through the pain and the nausea, Emma gathered up all her concentration and spat in Gilligan's face.

He wiped his face with the back of his hand. Licked at it where he had wiped the spit off his face.

Looked at Emma and grinned.

'I'm going to take you there, right where you are,' he said.

Emma shook her head, her tousled hair damp with sweat swinging across her face. 'No, you won't. I will kick you, I will bite you, I'll bite your ears off and your nose and your tongue right out of your mouth if you come near me, I swear.'

Gilligan kept grinning. He unzipped his trousers and put his hand inside. Pulled out his engorged cock.

Emma shook her head again and kicked out, kicked and kicked until he grabbed her by an ankle. Gilligan pulled at her leg, and Emma screamed at the pain coursing through her wrists. Her hands were swollen and numb.

Gilligan let go, and she swung backwards and then forward again.

'Give it to me now!' he growled and grabbed hold of her jeans' waistband and yanked her jeans down around her knees. He pulled at her knickers, his fingers scratching the flesh under her abdomen, and ripped them off.

Emma tipped her head back, stared at the beautiful green leaves, at the patches of blue sky she could see. She felt exposed, powerless.

She sensed Gilligan drawing closer.

Lifting her knees up high, she kicked out, her feet connecting with Gilligan's stomach. With a strangled yelp, he fell and landed on his bottom.

A bird trilled somewhere in the branches high above.

Gilligan stared at Emma. Without taking his eyes off her, he wiped an arm across his face.

He climbed to his feet.

'When I'm done with you, I'm going to enjoy killing you nice and slow,' he said.

'You're pathetic!' Emma hissed. 'Look at you, you can't even get it up.'

Gilligan looked down. He had gone flaccid. He took his penis in his hand and began massaging it.

'Oh, I'll show you how hard I can get,' he said, drawing closer. 'When I stick my cock up your sweet cunt, you'll cry out because it'll be so big, that you will.'

He drew closer still. Emma could feel the heat on him again. His head was by hers as he placed his hands on her buttocks.

Emma twisted her head and clamped her teeth down on Gilligan's ear. Screaming, he tried to pull away, but Emma held on, grinding her teeth together with all the strength she had left. Gilligan tore at her hair, trying to yank her head back.

Still Emma held on, the warm blood spilling into her mouth, the gristle of his ear between her teeth.

Gilligan punched her in the side of the head. His scream had settled into an agonised moan.

He punched her in the head again. Lights flashed in her vision, a grey curtain descended over everything and then lifted again.

Suddenly Gilligan staggered away, free. He had a hand clapped over his ear. Blood spurted from between his fingers.

Emma spat out the piece of ear left in her mouth. Blood dribbled down her chin.

'You bitch!' he shouted. 'You stupid fucking bitch!'

Screwing her eyes shut and then opening them again, Emma worked at staying alert. She felt like she was on the edge of passing out. There was a tremendous roar in her ears, as though a steam train was passing through her head.

Gilligan picked up the old lady's walking stick. The grip end was a mass of matted hair and flesh. He tried snapping the stick in half across his knee, but it wouldn't break. Instead, he leaned it against a tree trunk and stamped on it.

After two attempts, the stick snapped in half.

He picked up one half, the broken end pointed at Emma.

'I'm going to fuck you,' he growled. 'And you're going to let me, or I will gut you with this.'

Gilligan drew close, pressing the sharp end of the broken walking stick against the flesh of her abdomen.

'Now hold still,' he whispered.

Emma was shorter than Gilligan, and the Irishman had to squat to try and get himself in position. He placed one hand against the branch above Emma's head to help steady himself, but still he couldn't get into the right position. Emma had to bite down on her lips as his cock rubbed up and down against her stomach.

Finally, he stepped back, uttering a howl of desperation.

'Fuck it,' he hissed.

He reached up and pulled the belt around Emma's wrists tight. She cried out, but then her wrists were free as the belt untangled and she dropped to the ground. When her numb hands hit the ground, she screamed as white hot pain shot through them and up her arms. Pins and needles began fizzing through her hands as blood was allowed circulation again.

Gilligan pulled his trousers and pants completely off and got down on his knees. Pushing her knees apart, he lay down on top of Emma and placed the tip of the broken walking stick against her neck. His breath was stale and hot on her face.

'Now don't you try anything stupid again, like biting my other ear,' Gilligan whispered. 'You're going to take this like a good little bitch.'

Emma's arms were outstretched behind her, her hands tingling painfully where they lay in the long grass.

She spat blood and saliva in his face. Gilligan flinched and then grinned at her.

He pressed the jagged sliver of wood against Emma's neck.

Emma moaned and arched her head back and to one side so that she didn't have to look in Gilligan's face anymore.

Wait, there in the undergrowth, was that Gilligan's gun? It was right by her hand.

Emma closed her fingers around it, the pins and needles making it difficult to hold. But she had it, and she lifted her arm, holding the gun clumsily. As she brought it around, the gun fired, the loud gunshot in Gilligan's uninjured ear jerking him back upright.

Emma grasped the gun as best she could in both swollen, tingling hands and pointed it at Gilligan, who was now upright and back on his knees.

'Give me that,' Gilligan snarled.

Emma pulled the trigger, and the gun jerked in her hand, the bullet missing Gilligan again.

Gilligan ducked, throwing his arms over his head. He straightened up again, smiling.

'Now, you're a terrible shot young lady, that you are.'

Rage contorting her face, Emma screamed and pulled the trigger once more. Again, the gun bucked in her clumsy grip, but this time Gilligan cried out as he was shoved backwards by an invisible force slamming into him. He hit the ground and reached up for his shoulder.

'Fuck!' he screamed. 'Fuck! Fuck! Fuck!'

A scarlet stain blossomed out from underneath Gilligan's hand where he was gripping his shoulder.

Emma climbed shakily to her feet. Gilligan began to sit up, but Emma pointed the gun two handed at him and he sank back to the ground.

'What, are you going to kill me now?' Gilligan said. 'Go on then, girl, let's see you do it.'

Emma continued holding the gun on Gilligan, her hands trembling almost uncontrollably.

'You can't do it, can you?' Gilligan said. His face was white from the pain, and blood trickled over his hand and down his shirt front.

He struggled back up to a sitting position.

'Stay where you are!' Emma hissed.

'Ah now, if you want me to stay here, you're going to have to use that thing and shoot me, that you are,' Gilligan grunted as he climbed on to his knees.

Screwing her eyes down to tiny slits, Emma squeezed the trigger. The gun bucked in her hands as it fired, and Emma saw a piece of bark exploding on a tree trunk behind Gilligan as the bullet smacked into it.

Gilligan giggled drunkenly. 'You couldn't hit the side of a barn, could you?'

Emma fired the gun.

She missed again.

Gilligan took a step towards her, and another.

'I've decided, young lady,' he said. 'This isn't working now, is it? So, what I'm going to do is kill you first and then fuck you while you're still warm. It'll be a lot less trouble for both of us that way.'

Gilligan cackled.

Emma pulled the trigger again.

The bullet exploded from the muzzle and smacked into Gilligan's abdomen. He screamed and doubled over, his knees buckling.

He collapsed on the bed of leaves and grass on his side, curled up and moaning in pain.

Emma stood over him, up close, the gun pointed at his head.

She pulled the trigger.

This time it clicked on an empty chamber.

Gilligan started wheezing with laughter. 'You've got no bullets left! Oh that is sweet.' He coughed up some blood and spat it out. 'Just give me a second and I'll be with you.'

Emma let the gun drop to the ground.

The feeling was coming back to her hands. She flexed her fingers. The pins and needles were fading away.

Gilligan coughed up more blood. His breathing had taken on a ragged, gurgling quality.

Still, somehow, he was managing to get on to his feet.

He grinned at her, exposing his teeth, stained red.

Emma picked up the broken length of walking stick where Gilligan had dropped it. She held by its broken end and swung the head at Gilligan with all the strength she had left.

The hard, knobbly grip connected with Gilligan's skull with a sharp, wet crunch.

His eyes lost focus and his jaw hung open. Amazingly, he remained standing.

Emma screamed and swung the stick again. The end smacked into Gilligan's skull in the same place, and a spray of blood splattered her in the face.

This time, Gilligan dropped to the ground.

Emma straddled him and swung the stick again, smashing it into his face.

Again and again she pounded the stick at Gilligan's face, pulping his nose into a bloody mush, caving in his teeth and his cheeks, beating him until he was unrecognisable.

Finally she paused, panting, her hair hanging over her blood caked face, her eyes wide and staring.

Then she raised the stick in her hand, holding it high, and lifted her face up to the heavens and screamed.

JOE

'I wouldn't do that if I were you.'

Stilts eased the pressure up on Coffin's jaw as both he and Gosling turned to see who had spoken. Coffin twisted his head to take a look.

'You took your bloody time,' he said.

'We've been here a while, watching the fun.'

Leola had a handgun in each hand, arms outstretched, one pointed at Gosling and one at Stilts. She was standing with her feet planted apart, all in black.

She was smiling.

The Priest appeared from behind Leola. He had a handgun in each hand too, but he looked more casual. He held the guns by his sides.

'Put the shotgun down,' Leola said to Stilts.

Stilts didn't move. Although he had moved back slightly, the shotgun was still trained on Coffin. One pull on the trigger and Coffin's face would be obliterated.

'Joe, who are your friends?' Gosling said.

'Tell the little guy to put the gun down,' Leola said.

'And y'all gone see the good Lord soon if'n you done put down that gasoline,' the Priest said.

Duchess lowered the jerry can to the floor. Put his hands in the air.

Stilts had not moved, the shotgun still pointed at Coffin.

'Looks like we've got ourselves a little stalemate, doesn't it?' Gosling said. 'You see, Stilts has always been a little trigger-happy, isn't that right, Stilts?'

Stilts said nothing, just stared at Leola, blank faced.

'And I'm afraid that if you shoot him, that shotgun of his will probably go off, and then Joe here will lose his head.'

'What do you think about that?' Leola said to Stilts. 'You prepared to die just so's you can shoot Joe Coffin?'

'Ah now, you've never met Stilts before, have you?' Gosling said. 'Thing is, Stilts doesn't say much. You could say he's a little short on conversation.'

'Ohh, look at tha', I've broke a nail,' Duchess said, examining his fingernails. 'I onny painted 'em yisterdey.'

'Don't pay any attention to them,' Coffin said. 'They're just trying to distract you.'

'Tell the little guy to put down the gun,' Leola said to Gosling.

'Well, now you're insulting him,' Gosling said. 'He's not deaf, just mute. You should show a little more respect.'

'Whatever,' Leola said, and pulled the trigger.

The bullet hit Stilts in the shoulder, twisting him around on the spot under its impact and causing him to swing the gun around. The shotgun went off, both barrels narrowly missing Duchess and splintering the bar apart. Duchess screamed and ran, his legs peppered with tiny lacerations from the shot. The petrol soaked bar burst into flames.

Coffin leapt to his feet and yanked the shotgun out of Stilts' hands. Stilts had discharged both barrels, and the gun was empty, but Coffin was able to club Stilts in the face. Stilts' nose crunched under the impact, but he made no noise, no cry of pain. Coffin swung back around to face Gosling.

The big man could move faster than Coffin thought possible.

Gosling threw a punch at Coffin's face, but Coffin stepped out of the way and slammed the shotgun into Gosling's stomach. Gosling doubled over, grunting with the impact.

Another gunshot. Leola, firing at Duchess who was running across the club being chased by a stream of fire.

Gosling, still doubled over, head-butted Coffin in the stomach and wrapped his arms around him. The fat man kept his momentum going and propelled them over and down onto the floor, slick with puddles of petrol.

Coffin hit the floor on his back with Gosling on top. He dropped the shotgun as he fell and it had skittered across the floor, out of reach. The big man had him pinned to the floor. Gosling was panting, and his face was blotchy red and dripping with beads of sweat.

'You look about ready to have a heart attack,' Coffin said.

Gosling grinned. 'Don't worry about me, Joe. Never felt better.'

Suddenly, the air was filled with automatic gunfire. Bullets shredded through furniture and walls.

Duchess was screaming with laughter.

'Duchess, watch where you're aiming that bloody thing!' Gosling shouted. 'You almost took my bloody head off!'

The air was thickening with dirty, oily smoke as the fires spread. Coffin had no idea where Leola or the Priest were.

Coffin used the distraction by Duchess to shove Gosling off. The man was heavy, but Coffin managed to tip him enough that Gosling overbalanced, and Coffin was able to crawl out from under him. He kicked out at Gosling and rolled on his front to stand up.

And came face to face with tongues of fire dancing towards him.

Coffin scrambled onto his feet as the flooring ignited beneath him. He ran to a section of the club untouched by fire, coughing and retching as his lungs filled with black smoke.

All of a sudden, Coffin was aware of his feet growing warmer. He looked down and saw his shoes had caught fire and quickly kicked them off his feet.

The smoke was growing thick enough that visibility was limited. Duchess started firing the automatic again, the bullets slamming into the walls and furnishing.

Coffin got back down on the floor.

Suddenly, the sound of rapid gunfire stopped.

'Duchess?' Gosling roared.

'The man-lady ain't gone fire no gun no more,' the Priest shouted and began cackling.

Where the hell was Leola? Had she been hit? Overcome with smoke? She was a vampire, did she even need to breathe? There was so much about her that Coffin didn't know.

Coffin started coughing again. He had to find a way out before he was overcome with smoke inhalation.

Coffin scrambled along the floor, following a line of skirting board to where he was certain the exit was located.

There was a soft WHOOMPH! and the tinkling of glass as something exploded.

In front of Coffin, a shape began materialising out of the swirling smoke.

Coffin tensed.

It was Stilts, running through the smoke and clutching his injured shoulder. He ran straight past Coffin and disappeared again.

Leola emerged from the smoke too and crawled up to Coffin.

'We can't go that way,' she said. 'It's blocked off.'

'Shit,' Coffin said.

'What happened to your shoes?'

'Had to get rid of them.'

Leola's eyes widened as she looked above and behind Coffin.

Coffin turned around. There was a large, dark shadow emerging from within the dirty, foul smoke.

And it was much bigger than Stilts.

'I'm going to kill you, Joe!' the shadow shouted. 'I'm going to skin you alive and eat your heart!'

Gosling appeared from the cloud of oily smoke. His shirt was ripped and singed in places and his face was slick with sweat running into smudges of black.

In each fist, he was gripping a knuckleduster.

Gosling swung his fist, connecting with Coffin's cheek and opening up the flesh. Coffin managed to block the next punch with his arm and swung around, using his elbow on Gosling's chin. The big man rocked back on his heels and Coffin used the moment to stab him straight handed in the throat.

Gosling began choking. Coffin moved in to deliver a killer punch, to knock the big man on the floor, when he was pulled up short by a yell from Leola and a searing pain in his left calf muscle.

Stilts had his teeth fastened on Coffin's leg. Coffin roared and bent down and grabbed Stilts two-handed. Tried to yank him off.

The little man increased the pressure, sinking his teeth even deeper into Coffin's flesh.

Coffin punched him on the back, right in his lower spine, and Stilts finally let go.

Coffin picked Stilts up with both hands and threw him into the cloud of smoke. Coffin heard a clattering and smashing noise as the little guy landed.

Turning back to face Gosling, Coffin threw his hands up, ready for another attack.

But Gosling had gone.

There was another soft explosion as something else caught fire. A black cloud of smoke began billowing towards Coffin and Leola.

'We need to get out of here,' Coffin said.

With a tearing, ripping sound, a section of the ceiling gave way. It crashed to the floor, sending up clouds of dust and tiny fragments of debris. The smoke was forced outward in waves before swirling back in on itself, but in that moment Coffin saw a path to the exit.

'This way!' Coffin hissed.

Before they could move, Gosling appeared from the black smoke. His clothes, his hair, everything was aflame. He had a burning length of wood, maybe a chair leg, clenched in his fist. His eyes were bulging from his smouldering flesh, his lips had already been burnt away, exposing his teeth.

When he saw Coffin and Leola, he opened his mouth wide and let rip with an inarticulate roar of rage.

Dragging Leola with him, Coffin ran for where he had seen the exit. The route was covered with flaming puddles of petrol. Coffin ran straight for it, his bare feet splashing through the pools of fire.

They both kept their heads down, coughing hard as they inhaled more smoke.

Suddenly, they were tumbling down the stairs. Coffin was the first to pull himself upright. He grabbed hold of Leola and they both staggered outside. Coffin collapsed and Leola pulled off her jacket and used it to wrap around Coffin's smouldering feet.

They could hear Gosling inside, smashing at things, shouting and screaming.

'Come on, let's get out of here,' Coffin said.

'Can you walk?' Leola said.

Coffin grimaced. 'Yeah, just about.'

They both looked up at the Punchline, at the smoke pouring from the windows.

'What about your money?' Leola said.

'That's probably on fire now, like the rest of the place.'

'Wait, the Priest, I can't go without him,' Leola said.

'Why, that's almighty touching, girl,' the Priest said, emerging from seemingly out of nowhere.

Leola helped Coffin up on his feet and the Priest supported him on the other side.

'You okay?' Leola said.

Coffin grunted. 'Yeah, I'm fine.'

The faint sound of sirens carried across the city to them. It was strange, a fire like this, there should have been a crowd, people fleeing the scene.

But the city was deserted. Like a ghost town.

Coffin looked up at the smoke billowing from smashed windows upstairs, and the flickering orange glow.

'Let's get out of here,' he said.

DARKNESS FALLS

Day turned into night and darkness crept over the city and, as it did so, the bats came out of their hiding places. They began filling the skies, turning the evening even darker and filling it with the sibilant rustling of wings beating at the night air. They filled the streets of the city, a black, undulating mass of winged bodies. How could there be so many bats here in Birmingham? Where had they been hiding all this time?

When the first of the bats were seen, anyone outside soon got themselves back inside again. Those that didn't, the curious, the foolhardy, or the ones who lived on the streets and had no place indoors to go to, they soon realised they needed to find protection.

These bats attacked, using their teeth and claws to draw blood.

As the night drew in, more and more of the bats came out of their hiding places.

And with them came the vampires.

BONUS BOOK

As a thank you for buying this book (and I hoped you enjoyed it, unless you skipped to the end to see what this bonus was all about, then I hope you enjoy it when you get around to reading it) I have a bonus ebook for you.

Who is Mr Thursday?

Mr Thursday is my collection of three stories, TOYLAT, The Scarecrow, and Punch. They are separate stories and can be read on their own, but they are all connected by the mysterious Mr Thursday.

And it's yours for free, as a thank you for being a supporter of my work.

Scan the QR code below.

PLEASE LEAVE A REVIEW

Indie authors live or die by their reviews, and so I would really appreciate it if you could leave a review for Joe Coffin.

Thank you for supporting your friendly neighbourhood indie author.

Just scan the QR below to leave your review.

ABOUT THE AUTHOR

Ken Preston lives in the West Midlands on the street where Jack the
Ripper was born, with his wife, two sons, and their cat, Lily.
Besides writing novels, Ken runs creative writing workshops, visits
schools, colleges and universities as a guest author and speaker, and
is a member of the Association of Speakers Clubs.
But mostly he sits in his cellar and writes novels, whilst pretending to
ignore the cat.

PREVIEW JOE COFFIN THE FINAL CHAPTER

Turn the page

LAURA

Laura Mills struggled awake from a fitful sleep. She pulled at the tangled bedclothes, straightening them out. The damp sheet chilled her back. Even the pillowcase felt damp beneath her cheek. Laura didn't want to wake up, she wanted to stay asleep. Even a disturbed sleep full of weird dreams was better than being awake. And her dreams were no stranger than reality these days.

Finally she gave up attempting to slumber and sat up, turning her pillow around so she could lean her back against the dry side. She picked her mobile off the bedside cabinet and woke the screen. She navigated to the BBC news site.

There had been more bat attacks whilst she slept. Last night Laura had sat in her tiny lounge watching the news coverage on the TV as the bats attacked the city. Jacob sat on her lap, sucking his thumb.

Laura knew she shouldn't have been letting Jacob watch this, but he refused to go to bed. She could have turned the television off, or switched channels, but an appalled fascination had stopped her.

It hadn't been just the bats. Vampires had been stalking the streets too, more of them than ever. Most of them seemed to be concentrated near Bearwood, just outside of the city centre. But it wouldn't take long before they spread, infecting the entire city.

Finally, unable to take any more, Laura shut the TV off. But the silence of the room, the blank stare of the dead screen, seemed more terrifying than the news footage of the bat attacks.

Jacob wouldn't go to bed on his own and demanded that he sleep in his mother's bed with her.

As always since the episode in the cellar of that house on Forde Road, she could not refuse him. This was how it went most nights, Jacob sleeping with Laura in the double bed she once shared with her husband.

As always, the routine now just a part of her life, Laura scooped Jacob up in the early hours of the morning and placed him in his own bed as he slept. She wasn't entirely sure why she bothered, except that it seemed important somehow that her boy at least wake up in his bed, even if he had spent most of the night with his mother.

Jacob wasn't going in to school today, Laura would keep him at home. He hadn't been himself lately anyway, and now with all the news about vampires roaming the city, it terrified him to set foot out of the front door.

And who could blame him?

After being kept prisoner in that cellar by Steffanie and her vampire boyfriend, being drained of his blood every day to feed that monster they kept in the house, it was a wonder that Jacob had returned to school at all. But he had, in the end.

He was strong, that boy of hers. Not like his dad, that bastard Tom. He had known about Jacob. Tom might not have been the one to capture Jacob, but the boy was his son and Tom still let them keep him tied up in that cellar and bleed him every day.

Laura wished she'd been there when Joe killed Tom.

She would have watched.

Maybe even helped.

Laura didn't know for a fact that Joe had murdered her husband. Officially, he was still classified as missing. But Laura was sure that Joe killed him and then got rid of the body.

Laura put the mobile face down on the bedside cabinet. Closed her eyes. Why was it she spent her nights wide awake and wishing that sleep would overcome her, and then all day with heavy, drooping lids, barely able to think straight she was so exhausted?

Because vampires roamed the night, that's why.

Laura could hardly believe what she was seeing when the vampires first invaded the city. It couldn't be true. Vampires didn't exist. They were monsters from fiction, from films. Vampires weren't real.

Yet there they were on the news. And really, hadn't she always known? Laura had refused to believe Jacob at first, when he told her that Steffanie had been the one to keep him prisoner in the cellar.

How could that be possible, when Steffanie was dead? Murdered.

Laura had been to her funeral. Watched as they lowered Steffanie into the ground while Joe Coffin, the big hard man of Birmingham, fell to his knees weeping.

Laura had never particularly liked Steffanie. She got on with her all right, made the effort to indulge in small talk with her mostly because she was Joe's wife.

Despite everything, despite Joe cheating on Laura when they were married, and then the divorce, Laura still wished nothing but happiness for Joe.

She still loved him.

Laura wasn't sure if she would ever stop loving him.

She thought about lying down again and trying to get back to sleep. She was tired, but then she was permanently tired. Seemed like she was used to it now, the heavy cloak of exhaustion she carried with her everywhere she went.

Laura knew that there was no possibility of her falling asleep again, and that she would be better off just getting up and getting on with her day. It was early, but already she could see through the window the grey light of dawn. Climbing stiffly out of bed, Laura ran her fingers through her long hair, pushing it back off her face. She needed a shower, but first she would check on Jacob.

Laura padded barefoot out of her bedroom and down the hall

to her son's bedroom. She paused outside his door, open just a crack. The landing light illuminated his bedroom with a soft glow. Jacob no longer slept in the dark. It was like he was a little boy again, scared of the night. Of the monsters lurking unseen in the shadows.

But then, the monsters were real, weren't they?

Laura pushed the door open a little wider and peered into the dim bedroom. Jacob's skinny body lay beneath the tangle of bedclothes, his forehead and hair damp with sweat and his face drawn and pale.

He had no appetite, and Laura had to nag and cajole him to eat, almost force the food down him just to keep him alive. He had little interest in anything, even his computer games. Jacob had never been a lively boy, never been confident. Tom had seen to that with his bullying ways and his lack of interest in his son. But now, what little confidence Jacob once possessed, even that faded away. Snatched away by those vampires in the house and the terrible monstrous things they did to him.

Laura knew she would never get her little boy back again. She knew that his life was changed forever, and for that she felt a semblance of guilt.

If only she had stood up to Tom. If only she had stopped lying to herself, telling herself that everything would be all right, that Tom would change his ways and become a better father and a better husband. She had known in her heart that this would never happen. But she had buried that truth as deep as she could, knowing that if she kicked him out, then Mortimer Craggs would no longer support her or Jacob.

Jacob moaned and twisted in the bed, fighting at the bed sheets. Laura crept inside the bedroom and over to his bed, kneeling down beside him. She placed her hand on his damp forehead and gently whispered to him.

'It's all right, sweetheart.'

Jacob moaned again, fighting at the bedclothes covering him. Laura pushed his damp fringe back and shushed him

The guilt she felt at her part in the destruction of his life rose once more, threatening to consume her. Yes, she was guilty. But she had to shove that guilt away, to bury it deep before it consumed her and stopped her from looking after her son. She needed to be strong, she needed to be here for him.

Laura would never let anything like this happen to him again.

Jacob settled down, growing quieter. Laura climbed to her feet and hovered for a moment, reluctant to leave her boy.

What were they going to do? How could she make this up to him? How could she make his life worth living once more?

Laura left Jacob sleeping and walked down the landing to the bathroom. She switched on the shower and peeled off her damp nightwear. She waited while the spray of water warmed up and then stepped under it.

The hot water hit her face, and she leaned in close, relishing the sting on her skin. She dipped her head and let the water soak her hair and warm her scalp.

The chill from the damp bedclothes faded as the water warmed her through, and Laura's spirits lifted a little.

Today she planned on paying Joe a visit. Since Craggs' death, the monthly support from the Slaughterhouse Mob had stopped. Laura knew that Joe wouldn't have stopped it, that it was just a stupid mistake, but she needed to tell him before she ran out of money.

It would be okay. Joe would always look after her, Laura knew that much.

Her body stiffened at the faint thump, just audible beneath the sound of the shower.

What had that been? Had Jacob fallen out of bed?

Or was it something else?

Laura turned the shower off.

Listened.

The shower head dripped water on the tray.

Laura's skin tingled with the cold.

The house was silent.

Laura reached out to turn on the shower once more, her fingers closing around the tap. She had only thought she heard something, her imagination playing tricks on her as usual.

But still the feeling lingered that something awful was about to happen.

Laura let go of the water control and stepped out of the shower. She wrapped her dressing gown around her wet skin and gave her hair a quick rub with a towel. She stood still and listened once more.

Nothing.

This was stupid. There were no intruders in the house. Jacob and Laura were on their own. She should get back in the shower and wash her hair.

Forget about noises in the house. Forget about intruders and vampires.

And yet…

Laura dropped the towel on the bathroom floor and opened the door. A gentle draft of cool air tickled her wet face.

Where had that come from?

Laura listened again.

A car cruised by outside.

A door slammed shut.

Silence.

Laura padded softly down the landing and looked through the gap between Jacob's door and the frame. Her boy was fast asleep, a rare expression of peace on his face.

That cool breeze again, this time on the back of her neck.

Laura turned.

Someone had opened a window or a door.

Laura and Jacob were no longer alone in the house.

Gathering the folds of her dressing gown around her throat, Laura ran back to her bedroom. She picked up her mobile, the screen glowing bright in the darkened room. She paused, her thumb hovering over the green telephone icon.

Another thump, downstairs.

A crash of something hitting the floor and smashing.

Laura's guts twisted with anxiety.

What to do?

Call the police?

No.

Laura called up her contacts and hit the connect button.

The phone rang out five times before it was picked up.

'Hey. What's wrong?'

'Joe? There's somebody in my house.'

'I'm on my way.'

The disconnected tone blared in Laura's ear. She dropped the mobile on the bed.

Joe, he hadn't sounded himself. There was something wrong.

But he was on his way.

Laura padded over to the bedroom door and peeked out. From where she stood she could see the stairs, the front door, and some of the hall.

She waited, and watched.

Another crash.

A low murmur of voices, more than one voice she was sure, but how many she couldn't tell. Maybe just the two. They were in the kitchen. What were they doing? Raiding her fridge for food?

'Mummy?'

Jacob, standing outside his bedroom door in his pyjamas. He clutched his teddy, nicknamed Bozo, under his chin.

Laura ran softly to him.

'Quick, go back in your bedroom!' she hissed, waving her hands at him, ushering him inside.

Jacob's eyes, half-closed with sleep, widened, and he pulled the soft toy tight to his chest, his fingers almost disappearing into the fur. Laura bundled him through the doorway and closed the door behind her.

She put her finger to her lips. 'We have to be very, very quiet.'

Jacob stared at his mother, his eyes round and wide. 'Is it Steffanie?'

'No, no, of course not.' Laura pulled Jacob close in a hug.

Jacob's question sent a chill down her back. It couldn't be Steffanie.

She was dead.

Laura sat on the bed with Jacob beside her, her arms around him in a protective shield.

More sounds of crashing downstairs. Were they throwing plates and glasses on the kitchen floor?

Laura glanced at the bedroom window, at the curtains still closed. A dirty, grey light peeked around the edges. The intruders downstairs, they couldn't be vampires. Not now during daylight hours.

Laura and Jacob flinched at a high-pitched scream, followed by more crashing noises. Jacob buried his head in his mother's lap. She stroked his hair.

How on earth could she calm him when her own heart was thumping so hard?

Laura swallowed, and her dry throat clicked painfully.

Jacob sat up at the sound of movement outside the bedroom door.

Wide-eyed, tears rolling down his cheeks, he stared up at his mother.

The intruders were climbing the stairs.

Laura clapped her hand over Jacob's mouth before he screamed. 'Stay still, don't make a sound.'

Jacob nodded. Laura took her hand away, her palm damp with the boy's tears.

She glanced around the tiny bedroom, looking for anything she could use as a weapon, something to defend herself with. In the corner below the window sat a dressing-up box. Jacob had loved playing as Indiana Jones, pirates, and superheroes when he was younger. Now the wooden box sat in the corner unused and gathering dust, one of those items that Laura had spent years meaning to sort out but never got around to.

There were a couple of plastic swords in there, a toy gun, a light-sabre, Indy's whip. Nothing they could use, nothing that would cause damage.

Laura cast her eyes around the bedroom again

A Nerf gun, it fired plastic pellets and wouldn't be any use.

A bookshelf full of books.

Boxes of Lego pieces, waiting to be sorted through and organised.

A small pile of cuddly toys.

A laptop on a desk.

'Dammit!' Laura hissed.

The voices outside Jacob's bedroom had drawn much closer. Whoever, whatever, was outside had to be standing on the landing. Right on the other side of the closed door.

Laura stood up. Jacob whimpered. Laura stepped in front of Jacob and clenched her fists. If she could just hold them off Jacob until Joe arrived, that would be enough. He would look after her boy. Joe would protect him.

The door handle moved, began twisting down. Laura watched it, transfixed.

The handle reached the bottom of its movement and the door swung open.

A small boy stood framed in the doorway. Thin and pale, the flesh around his eyes dark and bruised, like he hadn't slept for a week. His hair a greasy tangle, his fingernails long and sharp. His T-shirt, white once with a picture of the Power Rangers emblazoned across the front, now ripped and stained. His jeans were similarly damaged and his feet were bare.

'Michael?' Laura whispered.

The bedroom seemed to tilt. Any moment now she would lose her balance and fall over. But still she remained upright, staring in awful wonder at Joe Coffin's dead little boy standing in her son's bedroom doorway.

Michael stepped through the door.

Cracked, red lips peeled back from elongated, pointed teeth. Dark eyes glittered with anticipation.

Laura took one shaky step forward. 'Get out of here, you monster!'

Michael's fingers twitched, his hands hanging loosely by his sides. Laura couldn't tear her eyes away from those teeth and his lips. Looked like he'd made a clumsy attempt at applying red lipstick and smudged it across his mouth and cheeks.

It was blood, of course.

A shiver ran through the little boy's body, and Laura realised he was tensing, readying himself to leap at her.

If only she had a weapon, anything to defend herself and Jacob with.

Michael pounced.

And now the room did sway and tip as Laura fell onto her back. Michael landed on top of her, knocking the breath from her lungs in a sharp gasp. She threw her arms up to defend herself and Michael slashed at her with his long fingernails, tearing rips in the loose sleeves of the dressing gown.

Laura smacked him under the chin with the heel of her hand, snapping his head back. Spittle flew from his mouth as he howled with pain.

'Michael? What is it? What have you found?'

The little boy jumped off Laura and scurried into a corner of the room, squatting on his haunches.

Laura shoved herself upright, grimacing at the sharp pain across her abdomen from where Michael had landed on her.

Jacob screamed.

Steffanie stood in the bedroom doorway, her mass of red curly hair highlighted by the light from the landing. The light glowed around the edges of the silk chiffon wedding dress she wore. For a second, Laura could only think of eighties' rock songs, female performers back-lit in cheesy music videos while belting out a power ballad about needing a hero.

Steffanie Coffin always knew how to make an entrance. Even death couldn't stop her.

Joe Coffin's dead wife stepped through the doorway. Laura's face tingled as the blood drained away, seemingly retreating from the horror standing in front of her, just as she wanted to. Steffanie stared at Laura with her one remaining eye. And yet the empty eye socket also seemed to have the power of sight. Below the eye socket, Steffanie's once beautiful cheek now had ragged holes in it revealing her broken, pointed teeth.

The right side of her face remained unblemished. The skin was paler than Laura remembered, and her cheekbone more prominent. Her lips had pulled back over her elongated fangs. The wedding dress hung from Steffanie, blood-stained and tattered.

But what hadn't changed, in fact it had grown even more pronounced, was the sense of calculated steeliness.

The cruelty.

Steffanie raised her chin and smiled, those dry, cracked lips peeling back even further. 'Jacob.'

Laura pushed herself to her feet and glanced back at her son. He had scrambled to the head of his bed where he sat with his arms around his knees, still holding tight to Bozo.

Laura whipped her head around to face Steffanie. 'Leave him alone!'

Steffanie crouched and raised her clawed hands, a growl gathering in the back of her throat. That deformed face of hers twisted into a mask of fury as she sprang for Laura.

Jacob screamed and jumped off the bed as Steffanie crashed into Laura. They tumbled to the floor. Laura grabbed Steffanie by the wrists, straining to keep those hands with their sharp fingernails away from her face. Steffanie snapped her jaws at Laura, her red curls cascading over her scarred features.

Twisting her face away, Laura sucked in a breath of air. The vampire stank of death and putrefaction.

Laura's arms trembled beneath Steffanie's strength. How long could she hold her back? Where was Joe? Why wasn't he here yet?

Jacob screamed again, and Steffanie flinched and arched up and back.

'Get off her you bitch!' Jacob stabbed Steffanie in the face with his plastic sword.

The plastic point glanced off her cheekbone. With a snarl, Steffanie wrenched her wrist from Laura's hold, snatched the sword off Jacob and flung it across the bedroom.

Laura, still pinned to the floor by Steffanie, screamed at Jacob, 'Open the curtains!'

Jacob stumbled out of the way as Steffanie made a grab for him. As he turned and fell he grabbed hold of the curtains, pulling the curtain rail down with him and flooding the bedroom with grey, dull daylight.

Hissing in pain as the light fell on her, Steffanie scrambled away and into a shadowed corner of the bedroom. Already, angry purple blotches blossomed on her face and hands. She stared at Laura through her curls of hair hanging over her face.

The two women stared at each other for a long, drawn out moment.

'Joe's on his way,' Laura said, trying to keep the tremble from her voice. 'And when he gets here, he will kill you.'

Steffanie tipped her head back, her red curls falling off her face and over her shoulders, and laughed throatily.

'Poor Joe, he's already tried killing me several times.' She lowered her head and glowered at Laura. 'I'm not giving him another chance.'

Michael crawled across the bedroom, avoiding the square of sunlight on the floor, and sat on Steffanie's lap. He put his thumb in his mouth.

Jacob crawled over to his mother and cuddled up close to her.

The two women stared across Jacob's bed at each other.

CRISPY PANCAKE

Joe Coffin killed the Fat Boy's engine, knocked the kickstand down and climbed off the bike. Across his back he had a shotgun strapped in place, and in his right hand he carried a holdall full of wooden stakes. Laura hadn't said who was in her house, and he wasn't taking any chances.

Coffin strode for the front door, clenching his jaw and grinding his teeth together at the pain in his feet. Leola had applied antiseptic cream and done her best to dress the burnt soles of Coffin's feet, and he had put on two pairs of thick socks before putting on his boots. Still felt as though he was walking across a bed of hot coals.

Pausing at the front door, Coffin glanced up and down the cul-de-sac. The time was still early enough that there was nobody around, but the daylight was strong enough that Coffin doubted there were any vampires at large. Not unless the crispy pancake look was a new trend amongst the undead.

He pulled the shotgun off his back. Planted a hand flat on the door and shoved.

It swung open.

Coffin didn't walk right in. He waited and listened. There, in the kitchen, he could hear movement. What about the living room? Coffin listened some more.

Nothing.

Coffin stepped into the hall and turned to face the kitchen doorway. The window blinds were down. Strips of light ran across the kitchen counters, the table and the floor. Mostly the kitchen was in shadow.

Except for the opposite corner. A pale yellow light glowing from behind an open fridge door. The unit was a floor standing fridge freezer combination, with the fridge stacked on top of the freezer. The open door blocked Coffin's view of whoever was raiding the fridge for a snack, but he could see their legs and bare feet. The trousers were ripped in the left leg from the hem to the hip. Through the rip protruded an old man's hairless, skinny leg. He'd obviously found something tasty as he was making sucking and slurping noises.

Holding the shotgun one-handed, the holdall of stakes in the other, Coffin stepped over the threshold of the kitchen doorway and paused again.

He took a quick look around, just to make sure there were no other vampires lurking in the shadows.

No, he was on his own. Just Coffin and the fridge raider.

Coffin dropped the holdall, the stakes clattering together when they hit the floor.

Coffin gripped the shotgun with both hands.

'Hey.'

The sucking noises stopped.

The vampire's toes curled inward.

Coffin waited.

A hand appeared at the edge of the fridge door. Blood-stained fingers curled around the white plastic.

Coffin's finger tensed against the shotgun trigger.

Waited some more.

Let the vampire close the door, reveal itself. Shoot it in the head. Then stake it through the chest. Drag it outside to bake in the sunlight.

The vampire dropped to the floor on its knees.

Coffin squeezed the trigger. The fridge door exploded. Milk splattered over the kitchen wall.

The vampire scurried under the kitchen table. It was an old man, maybe from the old people's home. It was shirtless, its torso and arms hairless. Wrinkled and leathery, like it had spent its life in the sun before it had been transformed into a night-stalker.

The vampire scrambled across the kitchen floor straight for Coffin.

'Shit.'

Coffin flipped the shotgun around. Cracked the stock over the vampire's bald head. Its face smacked against the kitchen floor and left a blood smear on the scratched, faded linoleum. The vampire grabbed Coffin's ankle and sank its teeth into his boot.

Coffin swung the shotgun like a golf club and smashed it into the vampire's face.

Its head jerked back, and it rolled over. Broken teeth spewed out of its mouth and scattered across the floor.

Coffin smashed the shotgun's stock into its face.

He grabbed the holdall and unzipped it. Pulled out a stake and a lump-hammer.

Straddling the vampire, Coffin pounded the stake into its scrawny chest.

Cold blood spurted over his hand as the vampire squirmed and squealed.

Finally, it lay still.

Coffin stood up. Reloaded the shotgun.

Standing over the vampire's body, feet planted either side of its torso, he paused.

Listened.

Movement from upstairs.

More of the bastards?

Coffin stepped over the vampire's body and out of the kitchen, leaving bloody footprints across the linoleum floor.

'Joe!'

Coffin whipped around, raising the shotgun.

Laura ran down the stairs, Jacob right behind her.

Coffin lowered the shotgun as Laura flung her arms around him. Jacob stopped at the bottom step, gazing at Coffin with wide eyes.

Laura pulled away and wiped a ripped dressing gown sleeve across her tear-stained face.

Coffin looked past Jacob, up the stairway. 'Are there any more of the bastards upstairs?'

Laura shook her head. 'They've all gone.'

'Steffanie was here.' Jacob's voice was small and timid.

'And Michael,' Laura said.

'What the hell were they doing here?'

'I don't know, they seemed scared almost, like they didn't know what to do.'

'I don't want to go back in the cellar,' Jacob said.

Coffin looked at the little boy. He seemed even smaller than Coffin remembered, when he had carried him out of that cellar where he had been kept prisoner and drained of his blood.

'You won't, you're staying with me.' Coffin turned to Laura. 'You should both come back to the club, I can look after you there.'

Laura nodded. 'Yes, yes I'd like that.'

Coffin looked through the open doorway. Had he seen movement in the bushes? There couldn't be vampires outside now, not in this light. Their skin would pop and sizzle like a slice of chicken on a griddle.

'Pack some clothes, whatever you need,' Coffin said. 'We're leaving now.'

Coffin dragged the vampire outside. Left it lying on the driveway to fry in the sunlight. He walked around behind the hedge where he thought he had seen movement, but there was nothing. He scanned the street to his left. Curtains twitched at a window. He turned and looked in the opposite direction. A car reversed off a drive. Coffin watched as it turned right out of the cul-de-sac.

He turned his attention back to the curtain twitcher across the road. More movement. The front door had been left slightly open. Whoever lived there had probably been leaving for work when they saw Coffin and his shotgun, and took the obvious decision to step back inside the house. They were probably on the phone to the cops right now. Suspicious-looking characters holding shotguns had that effect on most people.

Coffin wondered how long he had before they turned up. The police had been overwhelmed with the bat attacks last night. But with the daylight, the bats had gone.

Coffin turned his back on the curtain twitcher and headed inside. 'Laura, we need to get out of here before the cops arrive.'

'Almost ready!' Laura called down the stairs.

Jacob appeared from the kitchen. 'You killed a vampire.'

'Yeah,' Coffin said.

Jacob gazed up at Coffin with round, wide eyes. 'Will it come back?'

'C'mere,' Coffin said, placing a massive hand on the boy's skinny shoulder and guiding him outside.

Together they watched as the vampire's flesh sizzled and popped in the sunlight. Its eyes were two bubbling pools of blood. Most of the flesh had sloughed off the skull. Its chest cavity bubbled with a thick, brownish goo and smoke poured off the body.

'There's no way that fucker's coming back,' Coffin growled.

Jacob nodded. 'Good.'

Coffin gave the boy's shoulder a gentle squeeze.

Laura walked out the house carrying a small, battered suitcase. She stifled a scream when she saw the sizzling body on the drive.

'It's all right Mum, it's dead. There's no way that fucker's coming back to life now.'

Laura dropped the suitcases and pulled Jacob close.

Coffin noticed the movement of curtains across the street. That same window. And that door, still open.

He crouched by the holdall and unzipped it. He pulled out a single wooden stake.

'What's wrong?' Laura said.

'Stay here, both of you.'

Coffin crossed the street. Kept his eyes on the window, on the closed curtains. He walked up the drive, past the parked car. Placed the flat of his hand against the door and pushed it open wide. The interior was cool and dark. He stepped across the threshold. The house's interior layout looked identical to Laura's house.

At the foot of the stairs lay the crumpled body of a young man. His white shirt was drenched with splashes of red blood. His throat had been ripped wide open. Coffin doubted the man had time to realise what was happening to him before he was dead.

Gripping the stake tight, Coffin walked past the body and stepped into the living room. He waited by the living room door, watching for movement in the gloom, waiting for his eyes to adjust from the sunshine outside. Once he was sure Steffanie wasn't lurking in a corner, waiting to spring on him, Coffin strode across the thick carpet and swept the curtains back.

Bloody hand prints on the windowsill confirmed that Steffanie had been the one twitching the curtains. Michael too, from the look of the smaller hand prints.

Were they still inside the house? Possibly. They would want to keep out of the sunshine. But they would know he was here now, that he was looking for them. Coffin stepped back into the hallway and then into the kitchen. No vampire in here raiding the fridge.

Coffin left the kitchen and craned his head back to look up the stairs. There, on the wall above the top step, a single small, bloody hand print.

Coffin stepped over the corpse and took the stairs two at a time. At the top, he paused. Another hand print on the landing wall, by the door to the bathroom. Two more doors, leading to bedrooms no doubt, both open a little.

Coffin waited, head cocked as he listened. He heard birds singing, the slam of a car door further down the street, the engine starting up.

He felt the touch of a cool breeze on his cheek.

Was there a window open up here?

Coffin stepped through the doorway of the nearest bedroom. The closed curtains rustled in the breeze. Both Steffanie and Michael stood in front of the curtains, their eyes fixed on Coffin.

Steffanie wasted no time in her usual small talk. She turned her back on Coffin, whipped the curtains apart and leapt through the open window. With a snarl at Coffin, Michael followed his mother.

Coffin sprinted across the bedroom and pulled up short at the window. Watched his vampire wife and son scurry across the lawn and scramble over the garden fence.

Coffin was too large to fit easily through the open window. He charged out of the bedroom and back down the stairs. Outside he ran down the side of the house, between the garage and next door's brick wall. He was met by a six-foot high garden gate. Coffin leapt at it and scrambled over the top.

He landed heavily on the patio and the soles of his burnt feet erupted with pain. Grinding his teeth together and ignoring the pain, Coffin scrambled over the fence where he had last seen Steffanie and Michael. In next door's garden his boots sank into the soft flower bed, crushing the plants. The expanse of lawn was empty, but Coffin could see smeared bloody hand prints on the opposite fence.

'Get out of my garden!'

Coffin ignored the thin, quavering voice yelling at him from the upstairs window. He ran across the lawn and launched himself at the next fence. The wooden fencing splintered and collapsed beneath his weight. As he crashed through it and rolled onto the lawn, he heard a high-pitched scream. He jumped to his feet. Saw Steffanie and Michael running through open patio doors and into the house. The woman who had screamed shrank back against her garden fence, clutching her dressing gown closed tight at her throat with one hand and a mug of coffee in the other.

Coffin had lost his wooden stake. He picked up a length of fence panelling and snapped it in half. Carrying both pointed sections with him, one in each hand, Coffin approached the patio doors.

'Run,' Coffin growled at the woman.

She dropped the coffee mug, and it smashed on the patio. 'My children…'

Coffin shook his head. 'Shit.'

He stepped inside. A trail of blood spatters across the carpet led to the opposite door. Coffin squatted to take a closer look. No, not just blood, but scraps of flesh too. Steffanie and Michael were burning up in the sunshine. They had invaded this house to escape from the sun's power, because they knew if they stayed outside much longer they would burn up and die.

Coffin straightened up at the piercing sound of a child's scream. He followed the trail of blood and flesh out to the hallway and up the stairs.

Michael squatted on the top step. His eyes were red and weeping. Boils had erupted on his face, leaking blood and yellow pus. Patches of his burnt scalp showed through his hair. But still he stared at his father with an expression of utter hatred.

Coffin bit back the urge to speak to his son, to try and reason with him. Attempt to find him, to locate whatever might be left of Michael within this monstrous thing squatting on the landing. But Coffin knew it would be useless, that he was past trying to save his son. Michael had been murdered by Abel Mortenson. This thing in front of Coffin? It was nothing more than a shell, housing an evil monstrosity that needed to die.

Coffin lunged at the vampire, thrusting the two improvised stakes at it.

Michael, spitting thick gobbets of saliva, leapt away.

Steffanie appeared behind her son.

Clutched tight to her chest, a toddler squirmed and kicked. The little girl was trying to scream, but Steffanie had a bloody hand clamped across her mouth. The toddler's eyes were wide and round and brimming with tears.

Steffanie looked to be in a worse condition than Michael. Strips of flesh had peeled from her face and her hands, and hung in bloody ribbons. The once white wedding dress was now stained red, with bloody patches seeping through the chiffon. Steffanie's one remaining eye had turned dark with burst blood vessels.

'Leave now!' she hissed. 'Or I will rip this child to pieces and drink its blood in front of the mother.'

'You'll do that anyway.' Coffin glanced at Michael, then back to Steffanie again. 'You won't be able to help yourself.'

Coffin took one step forward.

Michael growled.

From inside the bedroom came the wailing and sobbing of another child.

Steffanie flung the toddler at Coffin. Dropping the two lengths of fence panel, he managed to catch the screaming child as she slammed into his chest. Coffin wrapped his arms around her as she kicked and hit him. Holding onto her was like wrestling an octopus. A tiny hand smacked at his face and then grabbed his ear, twisting and yanking at it.

Coffin got down on his knees and placed the girl on the carpet, but kept hold of her. He looked up.

Steffanie and Michael were gone.

'Get off my daughter!'

Just as Coffin heard the mother screaming at him his skull exploded in a shower of stars. He dropped onto the carpet and rolled onto his back. The mother stood over him, clutching a broad, heavy frying pan. She swung the pan at him again, but Coffin grabbed it and twisted it from her hand.

He threw it to one side. 'I was trying to save your children.'

He sat up. Paused a moment, waiting for his surroundings to stop swaying. His skull throbbed where she had hit him.

The toddler had run to her mother and wrapped her arms around her leg. The woman bent down and picked her up. She didn't take her eyes off Coffin.

From inside the bedroom, the other child wailed and called out for his mother.

Coffin clambered to his feet. 'Go and see to your children. The vampires have gone, you're safe now.'

The woman eyed Coffin uneasily. 'I've called the police.'

'Yeah, I'm sure you have.'

He stepped around her and down the stairs. Outside, he crossed the road and walked over to Laura's house. Laura and Jacob were standing on the drive, waiting.

'Joe?' Laura placed a hand on Coffin's shoulder. 'Is everything all right?'

'Let's go,' Coffin said.

He climbed on the Fat Boy, put the key in the ignition.

Laura opened her car door and threw the suitcase in the back.
'Joe?'

Coffin twisted on his saddle and looked at Jacob.

'Can I come with you? On the bike?'

Coffin switched his attention to Laura. 'It's okay. He can sit in
front of me. He'll be fine.'

Laura nodded. Didn't say a word.

Coffin thought maybe she was holding back the tears.

He picked Jacob up and placed him on the Fat Boy.

'Put your feet here, your hands there. Hold on.'

Coffin gunned the engine into life, the deep, throaty roar a
familiar, welcome sound.

They pulled off the drive and Coffin opened up the throttle.

Jacob looked up at Coffin and grinned.

BACK AT THE CLUB, Archer and Choudhry were waiting for Coffin.
Neither of them looked like they had slept all night. Archer's jacket
and trousers were creased and tired looking. Not his usual sharp,
professional appearance.

The club looked like a tornado had torn through it. And in a
sense it had. A tornado named Shanks Longworth.

Leola was preening herself in front of a full-length mirror. A
crack zigzagged down the glass, refracting her image into shattered
pieces. Leola didn't seem to mind. She had changed into a short
summer dress which revealed more than it hid, and the thin fabric
clung to her like a second skin. The tattoos crawled over her brown
flesh like insects.

Choudhry couldn't take his eyes off her.

Coffin dropped the bag of wooden stakes on a table. They
rattled together. Leola turned at the sound. She slid her hands over
her hips and down her thighs.

'You're a bloody hard man to find, Coffin,' Archer said. He
glanced briefly at Laura and Jacob.

'You look like shit,' Coffin said.

Archer ran a hand through his tousled hair. 'Feel like it too.'

Coffin turned as he heard a small gasp. Laura had pulled Jacob close. Jacob stared wide-eyed at Leola, who was looking at him and smiling.

Those teeth of hers were a dead giveaway.

Coffin turned them away and leaned in close.

'It's okay,' he whispered.

'But she's a vampire!' Jacob hissed.

'She's on our side.'

'Really?' Laura said. 'How can you be sure?'

'Believe me, I'm sure.'

Laura didn't look convinced.

Coffin wondered if he had done the right thing, bringing Jacob back here. Angels was no place for a kid, but Coffin couldn't think of anywhere else they would be safe. Steffanie had been outside in the daylight, which meant she was desperate. And breaking into Laura's house had been deliberate, not simply a matter of survival, or coincidence. Steffanie knew what she was doing. Choosing Laura's house had been a way of hurting Coffin. If Laura hadn't called him, Steffanie would have ripped Laura and Jacob to pieces.

She was out there somewhere with Michael, hiding from the sun. Waiting for the night. And what about the other one, Chitrita? Was she with her?

'Coffin.'

Coffin turned back to Archer. 'Yeah.'

'Have you seen Emma since last night?'

'No.' Coffin's chest tightened a little at the mention of Emma's name.

'We can't find her.' Archer scrubbed his hands over his face. 'If you know where she is, you need to tell us.'

'I have no idea.' Coffin held Archer's stare. 'Last time I saw her, I left her with you.'

'What about Gilligan? You seen him recently?'

Gerry Gilligan. With everything that had happened in the last twelve hours or so, Coffin had forgotten all about Gilligan.

'No.'

'You sure about that?'

'What the hell does Gilligan have to do with Emma?'

Archer scrubbed at his face again. 'I don't know, but both of them have disappeared. And Gilligan kicked the shit out of Emma's boyfriend, Mitch, put the poor bastard in hospital. You know anything about that, Coffin?'

'You think I sent him round to do that?'

'I don't know what the hell to think right now.' Archer glanced around the club, at the broken mirrors, the smashed tables and chairs. 'That must have been some party you had last night.'

'I was at the old people's home with you, remember?'

'Yeah, I remember.' Archer turned to Choudhry. 'Let's get out of here.'

'Huh?' Choudhry tore his gaze away from Leola.

Archer sighed. 'Put your eyes back in their sockets, or I'm telling Parvin.'

Leola stuck her pointed tongue out and ran it across her top lip.

Archer shook his head and walked off.

'If you hear from Emma, let me know,' he called back as he left the club.

Choudhry took one more lingering look at Leola and then left too.

Coffin glowered at Leola. 'You going to stop acting like a tart now?'

She grinned, showing off those pointed teeth again. 'It was fun. He could hardly control himself.'

Coffin sat down next to Laura and Jacob. 'I know this isn't the greatest place to be right now, but you'll both be safe here. Take Jacob upstairs, you can use one of the rooms.'

'Craggs' old room?' Laura said.

'No, one of the others.' The Stig had been murdered in Craggs' office. Stut and Shaw had taken the body down to the cellar, but a massive blood stain dominated the carpet.

Laura raised an eyebrow, inclined her head towards Jacob.

Of course. The other rooms were the 'Fuck Rooms' as Craggs had named them. Water beds, sex toys, porn hanging on the walls.

'I'll clear one out for you.' Coffin place a hand on Jacob's shoulder. 'Hey, you want a drink? A Coke?'

Jacob looked up at Coffin. The thrill of riding on Coffin's bike had initially brightened him and brought him back to life a little. But after seeing Leola, Jacob had retreated into himself again. His dark, hollow eyes darted back and forth between Coffin and Leola and Laura.

'I'll get some drinks,' Laura said and stood up.

'Be careful of broken glass. We had an incident.'

'I can see that. What do you want to drink?'

'Coffee, black.' Coffin twisted on the seat, looked over at the bar. 'There's a machine, I'm not sure how it works.'

'I'll be fine.'

Coffin watched Laura walk away. Turned back to Jacob.

'You okay?'

Jacob nodded, but said nothing.

'I'm going to look after you. You're safe now.'

Jacob leaned into Coffin, rested his head on his chest.

Coffin saw the scar on Jacob's arm where Steffanie had repeatedly bled him.

Coffin thought, *I'm going to kill her.*

READ NOW

ACKNOWLEDGMENTS

As usual I must thank Carrie Rowlands for her initial critique of the first draft, and her questions about where the story was headed.

Also deserving my thanks are Jamie Few, Blanche Padgett, Julian White and Philip Daniel Angel.

Thanks also due to Kerry Hadley-Pryce for her translation of Duchess' dialogue into deepest Black Country dialect.

And also a big thank you to you, the reader, for your continued love affair with Joe Coffin.

Printed in Great Britain
by Amazon

78572353R00219